Rendered Flesh

A LitRPG Zombie Horror

by David Cartwright

GW00671536

Copyright © David Cartwright 2021

The moral rights of the author have been asserted.

All rights reserved. No part of this publication may be reproduced, stored in or introduced into a retrieval system or transmitted in any form or by any means, electronic, mechanical, photocopying, recording or otherwise without prior written permission from the publisher.

This novel is entirely a work of fiction. Names, characters, places and incidents are either the product of the author's imagination or are used fictitiously, and any resemblance to any person or persons, living or dead, is entirely coincidental. No affiliation is implied or intended to any organisation or recognisable body mentioned within.

Published by Level Up in the United Kingdom in 2021

Cover illustration by Sippakorn Upama
Cover by Claire Wood

ISBN: 978-1-83919-136-7

www.levelup.pub

This book is dedicated to you if ever felt chewed-up and spat out by the daily struggle to be seen or accepted for who you are in the face of conservativism, fascism, racism or common-or-garden ignorance.

Closer to home, it's dedicated to my fantastic beta readers among the LGBTQ+ community who helped a simple cis white writer make these diverse characters' experiences authentic, and my partner, who stalwartly read through every revision and guided me on non-binary and trans representation. Could not have done this without you, my social-activist firebrand.

Chapter 1

I was dying.

I'd always been dying, day by day, hour by hour. The old adage that your body is renewed every seven years is a fantasy. In truth, your body is just fighting a losing battle against the ravenous consumption of time. Even as you're born, you start to die, but we'd made it all so much worse for ourselves. Pollution and rampant corruption poisoning our planet and our societies with moral and ethical repugnancies. I'd realised this, and I wasn't alone.

A few others around me realised the truth, that we were infected, every single one of us. We'd all contracted the disease, been introduced to the contagion as surely as if we lived in a petri dish. Most people ignored it, a standard response based on fear or ignorance. They shuffled around, letting the virus rot their brains until they had nothing left but to shamble and consume. Some of us fought back, trying to build up our immunity to the virulent plague, challenging its carriers and hoping to sterilise the paths of infection.

But body and mind were just the start; the virus had been eating away at everything for far too long; morality, society, the environment, all of it consumed by the virus infecting humanity.

Greed, privilege, entitlement, it has many names, but the effects are all the same.

Companies and corporations consume our lives, sacrificed in the name of profit. Governments gnawing away at our liberties, offering our soft bellies up to the gnashing teeth of corporate culture. Those who try to stand in the way of the disease are showered with the catalyst agent, money, until their own infection becomes terminal, or, if they resist even that, then they are infected with a form of social Ebola until no-one will listen to them.

The people wander through the intellectual apocalypse, drip fed what they need to know, but their rations are padded out with more toxic additives than sour candies. Hatred, intolerance, fascism and tribalism all slither through the words and images on the latest hi-spec phones, not so hidden under the veneer of 'nationalist pride'.

They learn to hate what they fear, fear what they don't understand, and they don't understand because they refuse to learn. The powers that be have turned them away from the pursuit of knowledge, made the 'experts' the enemy to be hounded and devoured in a tide of down-votes and flame wars by the trolls. Ghouls who live in the shadows, who have given themselves fully over to the virus, though they are reduced to scavenging scraps.

The carriers, the 'patient zero's, sit atop their mountains of economic effluence, bloated by wealth and moral turpitude, riding high on the stolen years of countless employees, but their profits cannot buy them immortality. They too are dying, and in their fear they scrabble for every token of 'wealth' and badge of 'success' they can claw from the ether, to convince themselves their time wasn't a waste. In their frantic spasms the tentacles of the Cthulian Corporations' gouge the land and spoil the air. They leave in their wake scorched earth and the empty shells of human beings, void of empathy and filled with a ravenous hunger for profit and success.

The landscape is polarised. The Boomers gorged at the festering teat of Capitalism in a time when your paycheck denoted your worth. The words 'success' and 'career' were embraced as the new religion. The Millennial activists try to fight the social injustice they see, but their hands are tied as they try to claw some actual influence back from the concrete foundations of the regimes of the wealthy. GenX watch and laugh, their ingrained nihilist cynicism colouring their outlook varying shades of black. They discovered the rot, railed against it, but didn't have the tools, didn't have the technology of social media to allow them to organise spontaneously and enmasse.

This is what we are all born into, this state of decay where you get onboard with the machine before you're left for dead, clinging to the dying light of social activism.

My parents argued endlessly, not so much *with* each other as *at* each other. They didn't sit on opposite sides of the divide, but the virus knows how to defend itself. They'd argue over what was more important, regenerating the environment or social reform, rooting out corrupt politicians or challenging the capitalist demagogues who funded them. The arguments would go around and around, devouring their own entrails in their futility.

When I was old enough to understand, I dove into this miasma, joined the social justice groups and socialist websites. I endorsed the principles of equality, tolerance and basic human compassion. I might as well have disembowelled myself and jumped into shark-infested waters.

Trolls flocked to shut me down, each one stripping a little of my will to fight. Others like me supported me, but the flame wars burned me all the same.

I took to the streets with my ideals. Many of us marched for our beliefs, even as the establishment ignored us. The callously thrown words (among other things) of the infected, our institutionalised detractors, wore on us and worried at our wills like feral dogs at a starving man.

I couldn't work out how the figureheads of the cause had the will to go on. Their resolve seemed to me to be made of iron, or granite. And here I was, simply one voice among the many, the hate and vitriol that got spat at me bringing me to the edge.

How did *they* cope?

Some days it felt like they were all tearing at my guts. The socialists, liberals, conservatives, and fascists, the neo-luddites, transhumanists, the bigots and the non-sectarians all reaching in to grasp a bloody handful of my being and gulp it down raw.

A couple of years of watching the world burn while trying to find my way through the labyrinth of modern politics and morality, and I was all but burnt out, all that time sucking down the venom of those who stubbornly supported the machine.

Stress, depression, and anxiety were my 'reward', doctor's appointments and antidepressants my 'answer'. I spent days at a time, my only comfort the dark satisfaction that the mindless cadavers, those who held up the pillars of the ever-hungering capitalist regime, would one day be ground to pulp between its broken, rotting teeth. It was just a shame others like me would be caught up alongside them.

Then I found it, my catharsis, something to lift me away from the grasping hands of the ravenous throng.

It was a zombie game called '*Z-vival*'. Just a simple thing, an independently developed app, a free-download I happened on by chance, but

3

it opened the door and let me, for a time, barricade myself against the world outside.

The idea that here was an enemy, as mindless and vicious as those I faced every day, that I could oppose and overcome without guilt. That I could do so without second-guessing their motives was a resuscitating breath in the rank-stink of my festering world. Every bigot, every fascist, every troll I encountered online populated the pixelated hordes I waded into, ending their pustulant existence with bullet or blade.

Pretty soon, I had a carefully selected library of games with titles like 'Risen', 'Anti-Death' and 'Waking Rot' that I'd use to breathe some semblance of life back into my otherwise bleak existence. Night after night, I'd spend long hours online, building outposts and communities held together by the simplest of goals, survival against the moaning, clamouring, shambling hordes. Whenever I looked outside I realised, more and more, that I wanted *this* to be my reality, not endlessly trying to wrestle through the tangle of entrails that was morality and social activism, but simply to be, to survive, in the simplest sense.

I stepped off the bus a few streets from my house, hood up, head down, my phone screen a shield against unsolicited social interactions. I turned onto my street and looked up just long enough to wave to my across-the-street neighbour, Mr Nadkarni, and to catch sight of a small pack of young white men. I knew them, the proto alt-right with their hand-me-down hostility, views and attitudes but only a passing grasp of the politics, and they knew me. My gender-non-conformity fell far outside of their self-limited comprehension. To their toxic braggadocio I was 'just another lesbian who needed to be fixed'.

If I went straight to my door they would no-doubt spot me, leading to an encounter that would send me into a downward spiral for a few days at least. I hated them, hated that their bigoted outlook made me feel guilty for existing. Rather than risk a confrontation, I slipped into the alleyway a few doors down and waited for them to move on, trying to ignore how I was shaking slightly.

My messenger app chimed, Indi had come online.

My best friend *Indéfin1*. The tag was French for 'Undefined', a statement about his trans-masc status and the division between assigned gender vs. actual identity. His social media profiles proclaimed proudly that

4

"Nobody can define me, but me." To me, he was Indi, using the French masc style as he preferred, far more socially active than me, and openly trans despite the hate it engendered. He was a student from Toulouse and since we'd become regular gaming buddies we spoke often, via the medium of instant messages. We supported each other when the trolls and bigots started to wear us down, when dysphoria threatened to overwhelm us. On the days when my small chest and undefined hips, my general 'boyish' build wasn't good enough for my femme side, or my shoulders too narrow, my features too soft and androgyne for my masc side, Indi was there for me and vice versa. The trials and tribulations of being genderfluid.

If I sound flippant it's because I have to be. It's the way I can fight the rot inside me, that flows through me. The depression started when I was at school, I was noticed to be 'other', to be 'different'. Someone learned that I liked boys *and girls*. Despite the ground gained by the LGBT community, lots of parents instil hetero-norms on their kids without even realising it. Media and TV do it as a matter of course. While exploring who I wanted to be, I wore short hair and skirts, baggy t-shirts and jeans with earrings, other kids jeered "are you supposed to be a boy or a girl?" but no one ever hung around to hear the answer. So I was bullied, relentlessly, until I found others, people who got it, who had been through the same; an online community who supported me and helped me. I decided that I wouldn't let those bullies win, that I would fight back, and I'd been fighting ever since.

That group was where I'd 'met' Indi and, although we'd never met face to face, we'd supported each other through some pretty emotional shit in the intervening years.

Indi, what's up? I typed, firing the message off almost reflexively.

Same old, same old my friend. Indi messaged back. *My folks insist on swallowing the establishment's Nationalist 'anti-Islam' message. I swear my father is *this* close to joining Nouvelle Droite.*

The cursor blinked. I could feel my friend's frustration.

I'm sorry Indi, I typed. *I'm here for you.*

Thanks, came the response. *I'm telling you Lez, they might accept me and not dead name me but...*

The sentence sat, unfinished.

Whoever said 'blood is thicker than water' was talking shit. Autocratic loyalty to inherited genetic material is an outdated fallacy. Found family is

5

more relevant, more valid these days, and I'm so glad I found you. So, how's Jack?

I winced, I'd broken up with my erstwhile boyfriend a couple days before but we'd agreed not to make a big deal of it on social media, hence I hadn't told Indi.

I'm sure he's fine, I typed hesitantly, *wherever he is, whoever he's with.*

You broke up and you didn't tell me? I could feel the accusation behind the words.

It was amicable, though largely influenced by his parents, I added to myself. *I didn't really want to talk about it yet.* I typed quickly. *We both felt it was time to move on and explore other options and hey, I get the satisfaction of having dragged a fence-sitting conservative to the left with my debauched liberal sexual wiles.* I tried to stifle a brief pang in my chest as I added a 'wink' emoji.

Hah! Indi shot back. *That boy was so vanilla, can you imagine if you'd told him you were game for a threesome? His head would've exploded!!*

Wouldn't have been my first. I hit the 'devil' emoji. *And he wasn't 'vanilla' so much as 'repressed by societal conditioning'; he'd never had a chance to let his freak flag fly. At least now he's a little older, a little wiser, a lot less a tool of the establishment, and a whole lot more sex-positive.* I smiled sadly as I typed before adding, *Also a threesome's a *little* hard to organise when you still live with your parents.*

The cursor blinked at me for a moment.

So, any potential candidates for a replacement? Come on, boy or girl, both, neither? For some reason Indi couldn't resist poking into my private life.

I really don't know, I smirked. *I'll see who comes along.*

Well, I'm always here if you get desperate. Indi tagged on a wink emoji of his own.

I'll bear that in mind next time I'm passing through Toulouse. I chuckled.

The cursor blinked at me for a few moments.

Hey, LeZion. Have you seen this?

My gamertag, *LeZion.* It delighted my cynical side when I came up with it, the interplay of the phonetics between 'legion' and 'lesion'.

There was a link attached to the message.

What's this you're sending me? I replied, my cursor hovering over the embedded hyperlink.

New game! I've been following a breadcrumb trail on the horror game and activist boards for weeks and now I found it!

6

Again, I hesitated. The web address ended '.onion'.

Indi, is this a Darkweb site? I could feel my anxiety spiking but my curiosity was also piqued.

Maaaaaybe, was all the answer I got.

Come on Indi, spill! I prompted, frustrated and slightly anxious all at once.

Okay, yes it's Darkweb. I could almost feel my friend's reluctance to give the game away, but he knew me well enough to know what he was doing to me.

But it's not a pirate; it's an old game that's been reworked. The company folded years ago and now this hacker group has shared their reworked, updated version. It's full immersion!

That caught me. I'd gotten a VR rig when I built my PC, but hadn't yet found a proper zombie game to try on it.

And it's safe? I queried, daring to hope.

I downloaded it a couple of days ago and so far, nothing strange. No viruses, no security alerts, not even junkmail! I wanted to get you and @JoaKingKong into it before I really play.

I flexed my fingers hesitantly. *Okay Indi, you get Jay on board and I'll play.*

JoaKingKong, or Joakim, was another of our gamer group, and particularly knowledgeable about the risks of bootleg games. He worked IT from his home in Sweden, and if he signed off on this find then I had nothing to worry about.

I'll PM him now, go check out the site, you don't have to download anything right away! Indi urged.

I mean, it wasn't like I hadn't gone into the dark web before. I was a member of two liberal activist boards on there already, the very fringe of my political activities. Still, this felt somehow different so, making it back into my room and up to my PC, with a flutter of tension in my gut, I clicked the link.

Rendered Flesh

The screen was black save for the title, written as if in dripping blood but slightly pixelated. I dimly recalled some comments about this game from one of the horror game boards. The posters had discussed the title in the sense of a nostalgia trip for zombie fans, much like the reworks of

Wolfenstein was for the FPS crowd or *GTA*. Way back, when it had been something of a cult arcade hit, but that was before the current rise of Zombie popularity, and the company behind it had dwindled and died. Why it was back now was anyone's guess.

Seeing no other option, I passed the cursor over the text and clicked. The title resolved into high-def, smooth lines and more subtle colours before fading, replaced with another line of blood red text.

> *"To live is to Suffer. To survive is to find some meaning in the*
> *Suffering."*
> — Friedrich Nietzsche

A little highbrow, if still kinda cheesy, I thought to myself before the screen brightened and displayed a sepia-toned landscape. In my headphones I could hear the whisper of wind in trees. The screen showed some dilapidated industrial buildings and hillside fields, but apart from a toolbar with a 'download' button, that was it.

What was I meant to see? I mean, the site graphics were nice and all, but it wasn't exactly selling me the game now, was it?

I stretched and glanced around my room, trying to spot my coffee cup when I heard panting and whimpering coming through the phones.

From behind the PoV, a human figure, dragging a bloodied leg emerged and held on to the 'camera'.

"Help me!" they begged.

The detail was incredible, the voice acting sounded almost real. I watched as the eyes widened and a bead of sweat rolled down the character's temple.

"They're coming, oh God they're coming!" the character lurched away from the screen and hobbled maybe half a dozen steps before they fell. More figures passed by the 'camera' and threw themselves at the prone character.

These weren't human, at least not anymore. Their clothes were ripped and bloodied; limbs were bent and dragged unnaturally. Their shambling gait and hissed, rasping breathing announced them for what they were; *zombies*.

The dead fell upon the living character who started to scream, a shrill cry of animal pain and fear as the zombies tore into the avatar, a brutal frenzy of tooth and nail.

I watched, equal parts repelled and fascinated by the 4k depiction of gore, the hi-def details of glistening, pulsing organs being dragged into display on my screen. The zombies clustered around, gradually hiding the corpse from view as the screaming took on a choked saw-edge and then stopped. The show, it appeared, was over.

Leaning back in my chair, I blew out the breath I'd been holding.

'Damn,' I thought, 'If those are in-game graphics, this is going to be a ride.'

Chapter 2

I spent the next day in a distracted haze. My shift at work, meal with my family and even my limited gaming was all filling time as I waited for Joakim to come online and give me the 'go' on *Rendered Flesh*.

Hey LeZion. The message box popped up on my screen and I could barely contain my excitement.

J, what did you find?

So much for niceties. Whether it was rueful or a little hurt I couldn't tell, text content only equates to seven percent of communication. My other online interactions had taught me as much.

Sorry J, I'm just a little excited, I typed in contrition. *How are you?*

Ah, you know, he typed. *Keeping tabs on backroom deals in the industry, scanning for insider reports that the next gen of high capacity network is going to fry our brains, or our balls, or both. My usual nouveau-anarchist shtick.*

For a moment I thought I might lose Jay into one of his reveries; *'Did I tell you I spent the latter half of the 90's undermining Microsoft from the inside by distributing free Office licenses to my friends and family with small businesses? No? Well I did now.'*

But, for once my friend-slash-mentor stayed on track.

Anyway, screw that noise, I've got the goods to dish on this new game. Hold on, I'm going to ping 1ndéfin1.

I waited, my finger itching, for Indi to join the conversation.

Bonjour, Indi responded, finally, as he entered the group chat.

So, I didn't find much for definite, Joakim admitted, *but I've got some tasty rumours for you.*

I was urging him to type faster, spill the goods and end my tormented anticipation.

First, I checked over the programme itself and, from what I can see the download is just a server access portal. It's pretty chunky but I can't see any actual game files or graphics in it. It looks safe enough, no data-mining protocols. That was a less than promising start.

Next, I tapped a few 'professional' contacts. That was 'J-speak' for his hacker network. As an independent IT security analyst, Joakim had contacts on both sides of the black and white hat network.

And what I could find is that whoever wrote this is supposedly some kind of next level genius.

What do you mean? I urged impatiently.

Well, I know you two have top spec machines, since I supplied the build specs and parts.

It was true. After Jay found us in the gamer community and had taken us under his wings as protégés, he'd insisted we have top grade gear. He'd paid for and shipped most of it to us himself, and talked us through the installation and setup process.

And merci beaucoup for that! Indi cut in before I could.

What else am I going to do with all this dirty corporate money I've earned? Jay joked. He knew our politics and, though not hugely political himself, he strongly disapproved of anything he saw as corporate malfeasance or profiteering. While he'd stung a few big companies for their transgressions (at least in an online sense) he would still tease us from time to time over our 'socialist agenda'.

Anyway, the point is you don't really need it. All you need is the capability to run VR.

What are you talking about? I typed, perplexed.

Apparently the game has a kind of subsurface graphic signal, like subliminal marketing or hypnotic suggestion, it encourages your mind to fill in the blanks, so whether you're running at top spec or 8-bit, you 'think' you're getting the same 4k experience.

That sounds a little shady, I typed hesitantly.

It's probably all bullshit in any case. They've probably just found a way to 'appropriate' any nearby processing and graphics capabilities on the local area network (which is no less impressive). Supposedly they've hooked into some high-level corporate servers to run on, but it's not the first time I've heard that rumour.

What else? Indi chimed in.

This one has a little more credibility. Supposedly there's a two-hundred and fifty thousand dollar prize for 'winning' the game.

That's bullshit, it's a sales ploy! I'd barely thought it before I'd typed and sent it.

It's more plausible than subliminally augmented game play, Jay argued, and I couldn't fault him.

But how do you 'win' a zombie survival game? And where do indie game developers or hacker collectives get that kind of money? I challenged. I couldn't believe it, my imagination leapt on the figure, images of owning a house and cars flashing to my forebrain. I fought down the little demon of avarice consciously steering my thoughts to the good I could do with that much cash.

You'd be surprised but, just as likely, you wouldn't want to know, Jay replied cagily.

So, are we going to do this? Indi was probably impatient, given the messages from the day before.

I'm game, I want to see if the rumours are true, especially the one about the prize money. Jay tagged a 'wink' emoji, he was a hardcore gamer, always looking for the next tech advance. The money was just an aside to him, the rumours about the supplemented graphics alone would have brought him aboard.

Yeah, I'm in, I typed, only a little hesitantly. *When?*

This time tomorrow? Indi prompted.

Sure you can wait that long? Jay teased again.

Fuck you J, Indi typed. *Cya tomorrow.* And logged out.

I stared at the screen for a little while.

You still there Lex? Joakim used my 'real' name (or the shortened version I'd supplied him). It always seemed odd seeing it on-screen instead of my tag.

Only I can feel you worrying from here.

Maybe a little, I admitted, finally.

Don't worry, I've got your back, he typed reassuringly. *If anything goes wrong I can scrub any trace of this off your drives and we can restore from back-up. If anything goes really wrong-*

The type-cursor blinked on the screen tantalisingly a couple of times.

It's only a game.

I spent another day dragging my feet through a mundane routine, champing at the opportunity to explore a new world.

I'd set the download going after I'd signed off with Joakim, and just as Indi had said, it didn't take that long, so all I had to do was wait.

I spent some time glancing over the latest proposed self-serving abortion of policy from the incumbent party. A socio-political back-step orchestrated by the dissociated Eton and Oxford ass-hats in Parliament. Another stealthy tug-on-the-rug upon which rested the support network for the most vulnerable members of our so-called 'civilised' society.

I spent an hour going through the motions with my local activist group, discussing protest opportunities, sharing and reblogging the pieces about the 'Polite and Quiet Genocide' being enacted under the establishment.

I didn't read the comments that came back at me, I was too tired. My piecemeal protests stirred the venom that gnawed guiltily at my guts. I knew I couldn't do more without breaking myself, but that didn't stop me wanting to.

The clock ticked away. I thought about going for a walk instead of sitting and waiting, but the late spring sunlight had washed all colour, all the life out of the world. I wondered briefly if I'd remembered to take my antidepressants today. Another bitter pill, the necessary evil of passing funds to profit-centric pharma companies, just so I could struggle through another day fighting for the moral values they ought to be championing.

I took a moment to just breathe and still the disquiet within.

My messenger chimed.

Ready? It was Indi. If anyone was going to be more eager to start, it was him.

Just waiting on J, I sent back.

Then wait no more. Another chime from my messenger and Jay added, *Let's Pwn some n00bz.*

Wait, wait, wait I typed, sighing in mock exasperation.

Lolz, from Indi as I typed my next line.

We don't 'Pwn n00bz'. I don't spend my days fighting bigotry and toxic culture just to add to it online, and neither does Indi. We game for healthy catharsis and you know that Jay. We make the world better, whether it's real or virtual.

No pwning n00bz? :sad: Came his reply, dripping playful sarcasm.

No pwning noobs. Bad Jay, no biscuit I typed back, smiling wryly to myself.

You know I'm just playing, Jay sent a winking emoji and the last second of my patience in waiting was passed.

Let's do this! I typed excitedly, as if I hadn't been sitting in front of the pre-game screen for the last hour.

A couple of clicks and I jumped out of my chair, strapped my handhelds over my wrists and pulled my headset from its suspension rig and into place.

"You guys hear me?" I checked through the mic.

"Got you." Joakim's deep voice came clear and crisp.

"*Allez,* what are we waiting for?" Indi, likewise, sounded like he was standing in the room with me.

I'd filled in the profile details; username and password was all that had been asked for, so I was ready to click and go.

Tingling with excitement, all my anxiety over the dubious source of the game forgotten, I raised my hand over the start icon, pressed the button and the screen went black.

Rendered Flesh

The title screen text oozed like fresh blood. Kinda cheesy but weirdly nostalgic.

> *"The passion for destruction is also a creative passion."*
> – Mikhail Bakunin

The dissonant nihilism of the quote brought a sly grin to my lips before the screen flashed to life. Suddenly I was bombarded with strobing images and my brain fired and flared at the sudden rush of input. Thoughts, feelings and memories flooded my head. Fear, loss and isolation, running, screaming and confusion. I yelped and raised my hands to tear the headset off, but as quickly as it had begun it finished, leaving me panting and disoriented.

"Thanks for the epilepsy trigger warning," I growled breathlessly, my vision flashing with spots and my heart pounding.

No one replied.

"Jay, Indi?" I asked aloud, but my startled eyes had started feeding me input again and I could scarcely believe it. My open eyes had opened again.

A soft wind blew through the green canvas. I looked around hurriedly, taking stock of my immediate surroundings. I was in some kind of military tent, laying on a medical gurney. The other beds looked to have been shoved around and some were bloodstained, old brown stains on the rumpled sheets. The floor was littered with scattered medical equipment.

So, no opening cinematic, I thought to myself. I sat up and swung my legs off the bed and waited a moment, nothing happened. Apparently there was no tutorial walkthrough, character selection or skill point assignment either and, since I was clearly alone, no party allocation.

I couldn't guarantee that my friends were in the immediate vicinity or even if they were on this server. They might have been bumped onto regional servers in their own countries. I was half-tempted to back out and check on them, but the reality of the game held me captivated. Dust motes drifted past in the pale light from the covered plastic windows. The frame of the tent creaked slightly and I could smell the canvas.

It was amazing. I could feel the bed beneath me, even though I was sure I was standing in my room. I could feel it as a slight breeze brushed my legs under the hospital gown I was wearing (well, no points for originality there). The whole rumour about subliminal sensory feedback was apparently true. My movement hadn't been consciously triggered by my hand-helds, and it was too well timed to my impulse to stand to be any kind of cut scene; I'd felt the motion.

I held my hands up in front of my eyes. They didn't look like mine. As I turned them over I noticed a stat display illuminate on my forearm. Maybe there *was* a tutorial of sorts.

STM	███████████		

HLT	█████████████	

STR	████				

I wasn't sure about the last one, it could be Strength but I'd figure it out later.

Along with the stats was a short list of skills.

First Aid: 2	Auto: 2	Combat: 1		

I had two vacant slots alongside my current skills, so that could come in handy later.

Below that was a list of 'Traits';

Athletic	Educated	Driver

So, I wasn't one-hundred percent, but I had at least some idea of what I could do. I looked down at my 'body'. The avatar was presenting femme, curves here and there (a novelty to me, my own frame spare and androgynous) but athletic. That was another thing to explore more closely later.

On the table beside the bed was a scrawled note on a piece of crumpled paper.

"There is no cure, don't even try. There is no treatment, only mercy. There is no living, just survival."

That was kinda creepy, but it made me suspicious. The outright statement that there 'was no cure' struck me as an immediate double-bluff.

A quick search around the bed turned up a rucksack and some clothes. Whoever had programmed this had either ignored the industry standard of highlighting interactables, or everything was interactive. At least, as my hand hovered over it, the clothing came up with a faint *'Wear'* option in a little see-through box that hung in the air. I selected it; nothing happened. That was odd. I held my hand over the clothes again and, out of habit, my fingers grasped the material. I could feel it in my hands as I lifted the shirt from the pile. I recalled Carroll's 'Alice in Wonderland'. "I guess it's a kind of Drink Me thing," I said under my breath. The boxes wouldn't activate an object, I had to do that myself.

I dressed. Every time I'd encountered custom dress on avatars there was a level of supposed 'decency'. Nudity in games meant incurring age restrictions that Rendered Flesh as an underground indie release gave no shits about; my current wardrobe options went right down to smalls and a bra. The underwire bra was something I usually disdained out in the world. Society would have me believe that 'I wasn't blessed' in that particular area, so to my mind society and its obnoxious underwear could go fuck itself. Absently, I bagged the bra, a habit I'd derived alongside collecting bottle caps, mountain flowers and any other in-game interactable, and turned to the rest. Thick, practical cotton cargo pants, a band t-shirt, a really 'inconspicuous' bright orange hoodie and low top sneakers (that

I'd have to change at some point, I'd seen too many movies where characters got bitten on the ankles). I pocketed the note and checked the rucksack, holding my hand over the item for a second as I had with the clothes. This time I got an inventory window. It had six available slots for inventory. My pockets each indicated another slot. Some of the slots were already filled. I also had a tab for 'Documents' with one entry marked already. There were two Energy drinks, I assumed they were for stamina, stacked into the same inventory slot and I smiled to myself. Good to know I could make the most of my limited inventory that way. A couple of bottles of prescription-looking painkillers, for health, also stacked. I wouldn't know if they were a short term boost or fully restorative without trying them, and a packet of cigarettes; distasteful, but an apocalypse trope to be sure. Perhaps a trade item?

What I didn't have was any kind of weapon. I quickly and quietly scavenged around the tent. I found a first aid pack, but when I opened it there was only a roll of gauze and some highlighted spaces. One of them read 'painkillers', so I took one of the bottles from my pack and held it over the slot. It slipped in, and the pack briefly registered as fifty percent full. So, I guessed the pills were temporary and I needed to find tape and alcohol wipes, as the vacant slots were labelled, to complete the kit for a full health restore.

Still, I needed a weapon and there was nothing in here besides a broken assault rifle. It might have been good for parts, but I had no way to break it down, I either needed a workbench or a specific skill.

The breeze came through the tent again, carrying a pungent smell of putrefying meat.

I paused.

I was alone, unarmed and, while the smell might just be ambient, I wasn't just going to assume that. I listened at the tent-flap for any sound, before I, ever so gently, pulled the canvas aside.

Early morning sunlight flooded in and I had to give my eyes a moment to adjust. The bright sun lent a washed out-sepia tone to the colours around me, in a colour-restored, *Night of the Living Dead* kinda way. Directly in front of me, maybe ten feet away was another tent, presumably just like this one, but the canvas front bore bloody handprints and flapped ominously. I glanced left and right, starting to pick up details of my surroundings. There were buildings beyond the tent in front and to my right and a chain-link fence beyond the rows to my left. It reminded me of my

17

old high school, at least if the schoolyard was being used as an emergency military medical station. I looked down to the asphalt to see if the old tennis court lines were still painted there, and saw my first in-game corpse.

The background smell of putrefaction, that I'd been slowly getting used to, hit me full in the face. The soldier, judging by the camo and helmet, wasn't likely to be getting up. He lay in a huge patch of dark, dried blood. His head was lolling on a tenuous connection of ripped flesh, and his abdomen had been torn wide open exposing what was left of his entrails. More were scattered in pieces around the body. My vision greyed out before I could process any more details.

My gorge rose in my throat and I backed into the tent trying not to be sick, clinging to the canvas to keep from falling to my knees. I flashed back to a memory when, driving with a friend, we'd stopped on a country road one night to check on a deer that had been lying by the road. When we got closer, we saw how the impact had split the animal open, and all the memories of the smell, shock and revulsion came back to me. The simulated corpse was so real with the smell and the small but identifiable pieces scattered around, but the worst part was the wide eyes and rictus scream on the ravaged face.

My forearm started to throb gently and, as I turned it over to look, the STR bar rose a measure.

So it wasn't Strength, maybe it was *Stress*.

I ducked back inside the tent, gripping the rough canvas tightly. I had to get a hold on myself, I was a veteran zombie-horror gamer, and it was embarrassing that I'd lose my cool over one corpse, no matter how many pieces it was in.

I'd heard about a game based on an old alien movie where they'd used a *paranoia* bar to measure emotional stress, so maybe this was something similar, maybe the game was artificially stimulating my reaction. I tried to cling to the mechanics to stop from heaving.

My hands shaking, I went into my bag. If there were stabilisers for health and stamina, there must be something for stress.

My hand pulsed weakly as it passed over something, so I pulled it out holding, the cigarettes!? Really? Hardly believing what I was doing I slumped to the floor against the canvas, drew one of the cancer-sticks out of the packet and patted down my pants pockets for a lighter.

Chapter 3

I tried as best I could to stifle the coughing, the dry tang taste of the cigarette still made me want to hurl but at least my hands had stopped shaking. Not that I'd never *tried* smoking before, but I'd never liked it. Jesus, what was the betting that, later down the line the game writers had added alcohol, weed or some harder drugs for dealing with more serious mental trauma? I pulled myself to my feet, opened the tent-flap again and stepped outside.

The buildings around did indeed resemble my old school, probably another effect of the subliminal graphic enhancement, and the yard seemed to be deserted. I wondered for a moment about searching the other tents in the yard for supplies, or to try to get a better idea of where I was. Just because I was alone out here, didn't mean there weren't zombies in the buildings. Maybe this immediate area was some kind of safe zone, and the minute I moved out of it I'd find trouble. Or, perhaps there was a pack of zombies moving this way and I wasn't safe at all.

"*J'excuse!*"

I started at the sound of another voice, thankfully one I recognised.

"Indi?" I held my hand to my brow, shading my eyes from the sepia sun.

"LeZion!" my friend came jogging toward me and gathered me up in a thick-armed hug. Indi's avatar was maybe six-two, pretty hench with a dark beard and strong jaw. The plaid and denim jeans completed the 'lumberjack' aesthetic.

With some difficulty, I pulled out of the hug and held him at arms' length, inspecting his new identity critically. 'Goddamn it,' I thought, 'Why couldn't I have gotten one of those?"

"That's a good look on you," I smiled eventually.

"Ah, if only real life were as simple, *non?*"

19

"Where did you come in?" I asked. If Indi was here then there was a chance Joakim was around somewhere too.

"There was a house, just up the road. I followed signs for the military aid point. I thought there might be something useful here, you?"

I jerked my thumb back over my shoulder. "In there. I haven't got far," I admitted sheepishly, and waved a hand toward the corpse.

"*Merde,*" Indi gasped, raising a hand to his face. "That is messed up."

"Not as messed up as these stats," I showed my arm. "I had to have a cigarette to stabilise my stress bar."

"Urgh!" Indi grimaced. "So that's what that bar is?"

"How come it's not affecting you?"

My friend flashed me his wrist.

"*Iron Constitution,* huh?" I observed wryly.

"*Oui.* Now come on, we have to find Jay and some weapons."

"And then figure out what we're going to do," I paused thoughtfully. "I think this is a school. Maybe there's some sports equipment somewhere."

"What good will that do us?"

"We might find bats or hockey sticks, maybe javelins?"

"There might still be some guns around here, on the soldiers' bodies."

"You want to go rummaging in *his* pockets?" I waved towards the disembowelled, dismembered corpse and my stomach lurched unsteadily. "Be my guest."

"Maybe we can find another one? One that's less, gooey?"

"Absolutely," I agreed, in earnest.

We made a quick sweep of the schoolyard. There wasn't much to find. I let Indi check the more ruined tents. I didn't want to risk my stress bar and having to suck on another cigarette, but besides another bottle of pills, we didn't find anything useful. The only things we found vaguely resembling weapons were scalpels and forceps, and I pointed out that I didn't want to get *that* close to this game's zombies until we'd figured out the combat system.

Our search led us closer to the buildings themselves. The ground-floor windows were protected by more chain-link and the rooms inside were dark, but I thought I saw some motion inside. I edged around the fence to get closer and, shielding my eyes with my hands, peered in through the dirty glass. In the gloom, I thought I could make out pillar drills and the silhouettes of tools on a white-painted shadow board.

"Hey Indi!" I tried to call as quietly as I could. Since our group chat programme was disabled, it made sense that the game was feeding my voice to my friend, and anything else close enough to 'hear'.

"This looks like a tech room!"

I turned back and nearly jumped out of my skin as a pale hand thumped on the glass from the other side. I jerked back into the fence and it rustled metallically.

My heart was hammering in my chest and again I felt sick. I thought I'd gotten used to jump-scares, but, damn. Either the game was messing with my head or I wasn't as hardened as I'd thought.

The zombie shambled out of the darkness and leaned its forehead against the dirty window, face rolling to and fro as the milky eyes searched for me. Its face was bloodied and sunken, its lips curled back from broken teeth in a rotting grimace. Patches of its scalp were missing and congealed blood stained its exposed skull. The collar on its filthy shirt was ripped wide and a mouth-sized chunk had been bitten out of its chest at the collarbone.

It struck the glass again and I flinched. Still it rolled its head left and right against the glass, apparently unaware of me, until I took a step along the fence.

One sideways step, one subtle motion, and the pale, dead eyes suddenly locked on me. The hands started a slow, rhythmic pounding on the glass.

"What did you do?" Indi hissed from the other side of the fence.

"I was just looking, I didn't see it right away," the window rattled again and I flinched.

"We should get out of here, before it draws anymore."

Even as Indi said that, two more shadowy figures were shuffling unsteadily toward the window from the dark depths of the room.

"Come on!" I urged, "If we can get in there we can take these things, it's just a game." My words sounded much more certain than I was.

I scurried out from behind the fence and we headed toward the corner where the two buildings converged. There was a covered walkway between the structures, a sign for the gym, and more signs pointing to the cafeteria, office and library.

We skirted the tech block. The building was U-shaped. You could've fit a car through the covered walkway, or a good sized zombie-horde.

21

We turned right into a quadrangle. Now we were flanked on either side with the main building looming behind us and only the double door to the tech block ahead. The hairs on the back of my neck prickled, the situation was feeling more and more like a trap.

I approached the door and gave it a push. It gave just a little before stopping with a 'clunk'. I glanced at Indi who was watching our six. My friend made an urgent gesture toward the door and I knelt to examine the lock.

A text box wavered into being in front of my eyes.

Security Skill Required

I rose to my feet shaking my head.

"We can't get in. Let's head to the gym." I pointed toward a sign at the corner of the quad.

"Maybe we'll find Jay or something useful. We might be able to get some height and check out the area."

We skirted the tech block, watching the shadowy windows closely for signs of movement.

The gymnasium loomed ahead of us, the sun shining from beyond it. The lowest level was concrete block-work, but became drab, brown-painted corrugated panels just above the lone blue door with its dark, slit window.

"I don't see any windows," Indi stated bluntly.

"I don't see any other doors either," I had a bad feeling about the looming gymnasium. "This might not be such a good idea."

I skirted the ugly, squat building looking for another way in. Around the nearside, through a break in the hedge line, I could see a narrow section of the sports field rolling away and, beyond that, fences, trees and houses. I could also see a scattering of motionless, standing forms clearly enough to tell, even at a distance, that they weren't adults.

I knew it was a game, I knew intellectually that this. Was. A. Game. And it wouldn't be the first time I'd encountered child-zombies in books, films, T.V. or in games but...

This was all *so* real.

I could feel the sun on my cheek, smell the scent of grass, spoiled meat and blood on the wind and feel the tremor of anxiety in my chest. Given my response to the adult zombie, I just wasn't ready to get any closer to the pre-teen undead this early.

"We should go," I returned to Indi, keen to get gone but unwilling to tell my co-op partner why. "We don't have any lights and it looks really dark in there. We shouldn't risk it."

"Then where do we go?" Indi's accent thickened the way it always did when he was frustrated.

I heard a sound behind us, one that had become familiar to me from a hundred movies and games, and I turned. Half a dozen zombies were lumbering toward us from the yard, wheezing and moaning, some dragging their feet, some dragging their trailing guts.

"Anywhere but here," I insisted, and we took off down the side of the main school building. The red-brick schoolhouse was set lower than the tech building, and we hurried down the cement slab stairs and dog-legged, following the wall toward what I assumed was the front of the school. High hedges obscured the view to the East so, on we went, effectively blind to anything except what was directly ahead of us. Some of the windows to our left were broken, some showed bloody handprints. Besides that, a couple of ravaged bodies in camo lay on the tarmac ahead.

It took a few steps for me to realise Indi had stopped.

"Come on, let's go!" I urged.

"Wait a minute," he held up a hand and rummaged through a dead soldier's camo-trouser pockets. "The game appears hyper-realistic, so I thought, perhaps the designers paid really close attention to detail and..." he pulled a wad of paper out of the pocket. "I was right."

"What have you got?"

Indi rifled the papers quickly before standing and striding past me, beckoning me to follow.

"Orders, check sheets and," he waved one sheet triumphantly, "a map! Soldiers on urban deployment carry maps. This will give us the immediate location at least."

We rounded the corner of the building and stopped.

The front of the school was a litter of burnt-out vehicles. A military cloth-back truck had skewed; it looked like a civilian car had hit it. Two burnt out school buses offered their blackened skeletons to the sky, along with those of their passengers. Lines of sandbags and crowd-line fencing had been disrupted and displaced where the vehicles had run into and over them, and some mashed bodies lay trapped along the length. One started to moan and flail its arms as we caught its attention. A banner, denoting the school's status as a 'Medical Aid Centre' had been partially burned and hung limp, trailing to the ground from its remaining fixtures. More bodies, blackened, rent and desecrated, littered the floor and the brassy shine of scattered and spent bullet casings glimmered here and there. The details of the scene were so stark, so clear, that it brought me to a skidding halt.

Once again the immediate sight lines were obstructed. Low, red-brick buildings with high roofs and clay tiles crowded around the front of the school, trees and topiary sprouting here and there. It all looked strangely familiar, like the old market town I'd grown up in.

Shaking off my hesitation, I looked around. To my left was a limited view of a line of houses and a road cutting down the far side of the school. Ahead, slightly to the right was a narrow road past a couple of bollards and lined with old houses. The spire of an old church sprouted from beyond the trees ahead.

"Which way?" I shuffled from foot to foot nervously as Indi tried hurriedly to orient the map.

"It would help if I knew where we were going!" came the terse reply.

"We need somewhere safe to come up with a plan to find J." My mind was spinning. Between the unbelievable realism and the stress of being unarmed, I was struggling to make decisions.

"And we can't do that here."

"Or now!" Indi snapped.

Looking to my left I saw shamblers rounding the far corner of the school. Added to the ones coming from behind, our choice was being made for us.

"Let's go this way," I waved frantically, and we scrambled toward the road ahead that ran parallel to the churchyard. It sloped steeply downward, snaking left then right, quickly blocking our line-of-sight beyond the S-bend with the church yard's high, flint wall on one side, and a row of aged terraced houses on the other.

"I hope there aren't more waiting for us down there," Indi commented darkly.

"Don't jinx us, come on." I picked up the pace. I noticed in this avatar that running caused me some physical discomfort; I was starting to regret dismissing the bra out-of-hand...

As we rounded the bend the road ahead bottomed out. It branched from a sharp turn that went to our left from a short, steep hill straight ahead of us.

"Left!" I ordered abruptly. A scattered pack of milling figures turned at the sound of my voice, and more lying on the ground started to heave themselves unsteadily to their feet.

We ran on, past a car park. Some of the vehicles might have been driveable, but I caught glimpses of blood and scorched bodywork that made me uncertain and in situations like this, Jay would cheerfully say, uncertainty got you killed.

"There's an alleyway ahead," I barked, but Indi was lagging so I slowed down.

"Stamina?" I asked urgently. Indi nodded breathlessly. Despite being down to half, I was still running pretty easily, but Indi was puffing and struggling. I wondered idly if the game took a standard template of stat values and applied bonuses in line with the assigned skills, my Athletic skill making my stamina last longer say, or if a pool of 'points' was randomised between the stat values and they dictated the skills. I leaned toward the first. The second option could produce some truly terrible builds and the kind of publicity *that* would breed would be bad for any game, Darkweb release or not.

I pulled up by the fence that led into the alley. It was gated and a food truck sat beyond by a roller shutter door. Removing my pack, I pulled out the energy drink and handed it to my friend.

"Thanks," Indi nodded and cracked the ring pull.

Looking around, I noticed the walkway on the back of the first floor and the laundry lines strung up.

"Come on," I urged. "I have an idea."

I half-dragged Indi's hulking avatar down the alley and cautiously approached the far end.

The mouth of the alley opened onto a main street. I got low and edged closer in the shadow of the alley walls, scanning left to right. As far as I could see, zombies stood motionless, staring skyward and swaying, gently moaning and rasping. More than twenty to my rough count.

I crept back to Indi.

"It looks," I began quietly, "like there are shops on the other side of this wall, but there are apartments upstairs. There should be a door to the stairs on this end. If we can get in, we can block it behind us and give ourselves a chance to breathe."

"What if it's locked, what if it's not there?" worry coloured my friend's voice.

"It's better than sitting in this alley," I countered. "So let's go."

Without waiting for more objections, I headed out onto the main street. The door, a green farmhouse style affair with old, flaking paint, was right where I expected it to be.

"Shit!" I swore quietly.

"What?" Indi loomed over me, jostling me as he tried to peek over my shoulder.

"It's just a latch, we can't lock it except... grab one of those chairs."

Despite our hushed voices, the zombies closest started to turn toward us.

"What good are they?"

The chairs, standard cheap restaurant chairs, lay scattered on the pavement outside the cafe occupying the unit next to the stairwell.

"Just get them!" I insisted and swung the door inward. The hinges groaned noisily.

"Shit!" Indi swore, snatching up a chair as directed and we hustled inside.

Swinging the old door shut behind us, I took the chair and laid it on its back, placed all four legs against the door and jammed the backrest down to wedge it against the bottom stair.

I watched the door, waiting for the 'thump' of a zombie against it, feeling the rise and fall of my chest. The short run from the school had me panting and again I took a moment to wonder at the way the game fed me the sensation of slight breathlessness. Checking my wrist I'd dropped two bars of Stamina in a run of maybe five-hundred yards. I thought about using the other energy drink, but dismissed the thought. I had few resources. I had to conserve them for now.

"As long as we don't make too much noise and the z's hold to canon, they ought to lose interest before enough show up to force the door," I explained quickly. "Now come on, let's make sure these flats are unoccupied."

Chapter 4

We climbed the dark steps and emerged onto a balcony that ran along the flats, overlooking the alley we'd just vacated. Taking a quick look down that way, I was reassured to find a dividing wall separating a block of three flats. At the end of that was a set of concrete stairs leading down to the small, chain-link fenced yard below. Luckily, the gate was shut and, to a cursory glance at least, clear of zombies.

"We need to clear these flats," Indi murmured quietly.

"Without weapons?"

"It has to be done. Look, they're small and between us? We can muscle any goons we find off the balconies out front. We clear, then we properly secure, okay?"

I took a deep breath and nodded. "Okay."

The first door was ajar, luckily for us.

"I'll make for the balcony door, you watch for trouble," Indi directed, and pushed into the flat. The door opened into a cramped kitchen with another door opposite leading to the lounge. I watched from the kitchen as he hurried to the balcony door then cased the two bedrooms and bathroom.

"All clear," he called quietly. "Next?"

I pulled back onto the balcony and nodded.

The next door was also slightly ajar but resisted as, my confidence growing, I pushed against it.

"Give me a hand here?" I gestured for Indi to lend his weight.

The door gradually eased open with a waft of mortuary air and I stepped through, and over, the body that had fallen against it. Not a good sign. The layout was exactly the same, but I hesitated in the kitchen, waiting for Indi to slip through the door. We stood over the fetid corpse, its stomach distended with gas.

"What do you think?" I whispered. "Spent avatar, set dressing, or is he going to go all uncle Rege and try to jump-scare us?"

"I think I'll feel better once we throw his dead ass over the balcony, get his feet."

It was as we tried to lift the body between us that it started to shudder and convulse.

"It's waking up, get up here and get his other arm!" Indi commanded.

The dead weight and clammy feel of the thing was repulsive. Feeling the cold flesh tense and twitch in my hands banished my earlier bravado entirely. Between us we dragged it, snarling and snapping, toward the balcony door.

"Open it, open it!" Indi tried to control the monster's head by grabbing a handful of rank hair, but the flesh of its scalp started to peel away.

"Hurry, hurry!"

I held the struggling corpse under one of its arms and tried to pry the latch open with my other hand. Finally, the sliding door came open and we bundled through, pushing the zombie ahead as it got its feet beneath itself. It hit the rail and came back at us, arms stretched out and hands clawing at us.

"Kick it, kick it!" I urged, standing behind the larger avatar for protection.

With a grunt, Indi planted a big boot in the thing's chest, and heaved it over the edge. Stiffly the zombie pitched over backward, legs spasming in the air as it went.

A wet 'thump' sounded its impact, and a chorus of low moans marked the roused attention of some of the zombies below.

Panting, we grinned sickly at each other. Neither of us wanted to look down in case the bloated body had split.

"One more?" I asked weakly.

"Only if you promise not to try and feed me to anymore zombies," Indi replied critically, heading for the front door.

As we stepped into the kitchen, the bathroom door burst open and a snarling, reaching zombie piled into him. He crashed against the kitchen table, which collapsed under the combined weight.

"Get it off, get it off!" Indi cried in panic, fighting for purchase to hold off the snapping, cadaverous woman.

I reached out to grab the thing's shoulders, but the skin was slick with blood and grime under the spaghetti straps of a floral summer dress.

"Kill it, kill it!"

I looked around desperately for a weapon. The first thing that caught my eye was one of the ruptured tables' legs. I snatched the thick piece of wood up, raised it grasped in both hands, and froze.

"It's only a game, it's only a game," I whispered under my breath, but the experience so far, the detail and realism, worked against me. Before, I'd had the luxury of detachment. All I had to do was press a button on my controller, but now?

Indi howled, "Kill this fucker!" and I snapped out of my hesitation and swung the improvised club downward.

The impact made a grotesque squelching crunch, and the shock of the impact ran up my hands, through my wrists and elbows. My stomach lurched as a wave of nausea rode over me.

"Again!" Indi commanded, pushing the weakly flailing body up. Trying not to be sick, I bludgeoned the zombie again. Blood and skin and other things I didn't want to see splattered the wall as the zombie's skull gave an audible, wet 'crack', and the head rocked from the blow. Indi used the opportunity to roll the thing over and off him. Grasping the dead woman firmly around the throat with both hands he lifted the slight body into the air as it pawed feebly at his avatar's strong arms.

Hauling the drunkenly twitching zombie through the living room and out onto the balcony, Indi tossed it bodily into the street below.

I stood, shaking and clutching my dripping weapon as adrenaline coursed through my veins.

My hands and wrists throbbed with the aftershocks of the trauma I'd inflicted, and my guts squirmed in revulsion. The pulsing at my wrist was strangely rhythmic, and I managed to look down at it. Over the black blood that now stained my hands, my stat display flickered.

STR		

Even as I watched, another mark appeared. In a panicked haze, I staggered into the living room and rummaged in an old side dresser cabinet. The cupboard yielded a bottle, some kind of spirit and, acting on instinct, I fumbled the cap off and drank deep. With my back to the wall I sank to the floor.

"*Merde*, are you sure you should be doing that?" Indi came back in, wiping his hands on his jeans.

29

I simply held out my arm as an explanation. As much as I knew I wasn't actually drinking the liquor it still burned my throat.

"Let's hope you build up some more emotional resilience before too long, eh?"

I waved the bottle toward the blood-stained kitchen. "If it's a 'rinse and repeat' to build up XP type game, they can keep it."

"You know that improving a skill in most of these games means using it. We'll just have to find a way to build yours gradually."

"Yup, great. Looking forward to it," I sulked.

"Come on, one more flat to clear, then we can make sure the place is secure." Indi held a hand out to me. After a brief moment I gripped it, and let my friend haul me back to my feet.

"I don't know how much more of this I can take Indi, it's all too real," I admitted, shakily.

"We can't leave until we find Joakim," Indi replied, firmly.

"What if Jay already logged out when he couldn't find us?" I toyed with the bottle anxiously.

"He might have done but we've not even been in an hour, so I doubt it," if Indi was trying to reassure me it wasn't working.

"So, one more?" he winked wryly.

I took another slug from the bottle and grimaced. "One more," I agreed.

The last flat was locked, much to my relief, and we didn't want to make more noise breaking in so we retreated to the first to take stock.

"So, what do we know?" Indi prompted.

"Just give me a second." I winced and picked up my backpack. What with the running and fighting, my avatar's chest was getting too sore for comfort. I slipped into the flat's bedroom to make the requisite, resentful addition to my wardrobe.

Indi was turning out cupboards when I re-entered the living room.

"No tutorial," I mused aloud. "But everything seems to be intuitive anyway. Like, unbelievably intuitive,"

Indi picked up a paperback from the carpeted floor. "Pretty much everything seems interactive too and I've never seen this level of detail before."

"What is it?" I asked idly.

"*Nausea*, by Jean-Paul Sartre," he read from the cover.

"I can't believe they programmed a whole book into the game," I scoffed.

Indi flicked the pages and shrugged. "Looks like they did."

"May I?" I held out a hand for the book. Indi passed it and I blinked in surprise.

"This isn't Sartre," I said, confused, "it's Rogers, *A Way of Being*."

"It was Sartre when I passed it to you." Indi shuffled closer, brow furrowed. "Still is, as far as I can see."

"Wait, wait." I held up the book. "I did psych in college and we read Rogers. Did you ever read *Nausea*?"

"I was going through an existential phase," he replied sheepishly.

"Joakim said there were rumours that the game stimulated the subconscious to fill in the details," I began thoughtfully. "Here, look at this."

I handed Indi the note I'd found back when I arrived in-game.

"No cure, no treatment, just survival," he muttered softly. "Your French has gotten better I see."

"But when I read it, it's in English," I clarified eagerly, feeling certain that I was on to something.

"Maybe the programmed documents are the same, but the set dressing ones just trigger memories of books we've read."

"Okay, that's something. What else do we have?"

"Well so far, all we've seen are '*Romeros*'," I replied, indicating the classic shambling dead seen in the iconic director's movies. "No variations or mutations so far."

"No sign of any NPC's offering tasks or quests either," Indi added. "And, although there have been signs of guns, I haven't seen one yet."

"The whole setting reminds me so much of the town I grew up in, it's uncanny," I began, "but it also means we're in the UK, which means guns are going to be pretty rare."

"Apart from the books and signs I was just thinking that this doesn't seem much like France," Indi supplied. "You think they've gone to the trouble of setting up a dedicated UK server? That's a stretch."

"Wait a minute, wait a minute. So, we're not getting exactly the same experience?" I pondered.

Getting to my feet I beckoned Indi to follow. Out on the balcony, I gestured across the street.

"What do you see?" I pointed at each of the shop fronts across from us.

"Cafe, chemist, hardware store," Indi shrugged, bemused.

"Yeah but, what are they called?" I demanded. "If we get separated or find radios and decide to split up, there's no point in me telling you to meet me outside Boots Chemist if you see something else."

"Never split the party," Indi stated sternly, "but I get what you're saying. What about the street names?" he pulled the map from his pocket and held it up.

I pointed at three roads in turn.

"Greenway, Rowdowns and Kingsmead," I read aloud.

"Those at least tally up, English or *en Francais*." Indi sighed, relieved.

"So we can navigate, alright. Now, how do we find Jay?" I sucked my teeth and tried to come up with a plan.

"Well, we made enough noise throwing those two out," he flicked a thumb toward the balcony and the zombies we'd evicted from the flat. "If he didn't hear that, then he's not that close."

I shuddered in recollection. "Are they still there?" I asked tentatively.

"*Oui,* flopping around like fish, but not really dead yet."

I gagged. I'd hoped we'd killed them and the bodies would despawn after a time, but no such luck.

"And they've got friends now."

I didn't need to look, the wheezing and rasping of the crowd below us was plenty loud to hear.

"Great, so even if he was around I doubt he'd want to come near a large group of Z's. So what do we do?"

"We can sneak out the back and go looking for him, or we can make more noise and try to bring him to us."

"Neither of which is a 'good' option," I grunted. "If we go looking we're more likely to miss him, but if we try to draw him to us, well, I doubt that door downstairs will hold up to much punishment."

"Maybe we ought to search this place properly and see what we have to work with?" Indi suggested.

"You take next door," I insisted.

"*Non.* We talked about building up your mental fortitude, this is as good an opportunity as any."

"What happened to 'not splitting the party?" I whined.

Indi stared at me. "You're going," he stated flatly, "next. Door."

My shoulders slumped but I could see the logic. "Alright. Hey, maybe take a look at the map and pick out some likely spots Jay might head for, okay?"

"Okay," Indi agreed.

I dragged myself up and went out to the walkway, table leg in hand. I hovered outside the door before slowly pushing it wide. The pool of blood on the floor was brown, but the scent of iron still hung in the doorway. Stepping inside, the smell coming from the now open bathroom made me gag. I went to the kitchen sink and tried the tap. A trickle of water came out, and I gulped some and splashed a little on my face.

"Okay," I murmured to myself, "here goes."

I decided to leave the bathroom until last, and headed toward the bedrooms.

The main bedroom yielded nothing but clothes and cosmetics, not even a pair of decent boots to replace my sneakers. I mean, what was I expecting? A machete, a shotgun, a tricked out AR-15 and a couple of spare mags?

I had a little more luck in the second room. The posters and console marked it as decked out for an adolescent. I managed to upgrade my table leg to a field hockey stick, and found a couple of shin guards that I could about fit over my forearms. A message in my HUD discretely informed me that I'd achieved a mere five percent armour rating, but I reasoned it was better than nothing. I turned the stick around, trying to see if it had any values in the same way as the medkit had prompted me. But, if it *did* have any attributes, like *Damage* or *Durability*, nothing flashed up. Great.

The living room offered me a couple of small bottles of spirits, a gas lighter (one of the ones that look like a little jet engine when alight) and more cigarettes. Given my stress situation I slipped the lighter and cigarettes into my pocket, noting for a moment how they became a combined item. I likewise bagged the water and spirits.

Inventory Full

"Shit!" I hissed quietly. I needed to find a bigger bag.

The kitchen offered up some non-perishable food items that I stacked on the counter, vowing to find a carrier bag or something, and a selection of crappy knives, not one of which I was eager to bet my life on. I didn't find any first aid supplies in the kitchen so that left... the bathroom.

33

As I pushed the door wide, the stench got worse, even through the dish-cloth I held over my mouth and nose. There was a story here, and it wasn't a pleasant one. The floor was awash with foulness, and the shower curtain hung torn and bloodied from the last few rings and draped over the side of the bath. It was dark so I tried the pull switch. The bulb stuttered to life and illuminated the rest. A mangled and chewed corpse lay in the tub. I stared in horror, my unbidden imagination putting together the story of a mother turning, attacking her child in the bathroom and the father locking them both in, an act of anguished desperation. The 'corpse' gurgled wetly and weakly flailed an arm toward me, but all the muscles were savaged, all the tendons torn. It couldn't really do anything but lay there and rasp.

I felt dizzy, my stomach turned flips and my chest heaved with the need to puke as I turned my back on the scene. My eyes burned with unshed tears. I wanted to search the mirrored cabinet over the sink, but the damp sounds of the corpse in the bath brought new waves of nausea every time I tried to turn around, and my wrist started to throb a warning as my stress metre started to rise.

Whoever programmed this game was going to hell, or to the next convenient parallel dimension.

Chapter 5

I stepped out onto the walkway that linked the two flats, thinking wretchedly about the empty slots in my first aid kit. The items I needed could be just feet away, yet I couldn't bring myself to go back into the bathroom to open the stupid cabinet.

I looked out over the small loading yard. I'd been thinking we could retrace our steps from the back gate and maybe slip through the zombies on the hill, but the sound of rustling chain-link drew my eyes down and I swore quietly. In the time we'd been in the flat, the walkers from the school had made their way into the alley. There must have been thirty or more, and they were strung out along the alley, blocking our exit. Even as I watched one saw me and began to beat on the fence. Others looked dully about and then started pressing on the fence themselves. The weak barrier began to flex under their attack.

I went back to Indi to break the bad news.

"We're surrounded; we need to come up with a plan, quick."

"*Merde*," he swore. "Well, I have some options," he pointed on the map. "Over here, about half a mile away is a police station, our best bet for guns."

I shook my head. "There's no guarantee, especially if this game is modelled after a British setting. We'd need an army camp or something, Jay knows that."

Indi shrugged. "Okay, if we go the other way there's a supermarket, and further off a hospital."

"Meds and supplies," I stroked my chin thoughtfully. "It might be a better bet, there might even be a vehicle we can use to get out of town."

"So, how do we get out of here and get there?" Indi asked.

"Maybe we should try to restore our bars to max first?" I suggested.

"Do we have time?"

"I'm not sure," I admitted. "I haven't looked at the door downstairs, but it's been quiet. Once we start moving around again, there's no telling how long that'll last, and the fence doesn't look so strong either."

"Can we distract the pack? Draw them away somehow?"

I pulled up my bag and reached into it for one of the bottles of liquor. "Maybe."

"What's the plan?" Indi frowned.

"In most games and movies, zombies are drawn to movement and sound, so," I looked around and saw a discarded t-shirt. I toyed with the idea of trying to tear the material, but wasn't about to embarrass myself if I failed. Not that Indi would judge.

"Did you find any scissors?" I asked.

"Here," he passed me a combat knife. "Took it from one of the dead soldiers on my way into the schoolyard," he explained.

I took the knife and cut a thick strip from the shirt and shoved it into the open neck of the bottle.

"Molotov cocktail," I announced proudly.

Indi rolled his avatar's eyes. "Give it here, you've obviously never done this before."

I watched carefully as my friend took the bottle and, with deft moves, refined my crude incendiary. A small line of translucent text appeared in the air beside the item.

Learned craft item, Molotov Cocktail

Offering it back to me Indi asked. "So, what now?"

"Okay, we throw this down the street, the zommers outside will follow it and draw the alley crew with them. Then we'll hop across the balconies to the next set of apartments and go out the far door to the street."

"What if the other apartments are 'occupied'?"

I thought for a moment. "We could get up on the roof pretty easily, go to the last flat and minimise the risk?"

"Okay," Indi nodded firmly. "Let's go."

We stood and I hefted the bottle. It was only a smaller, hip-type bottle; it probably wouldn't burn for long. Out on the balcony I looked down. The zombies there milled around. 'Dad' had managed to get back up but 'Mum's' legs were broken, bones sticking out awkwardly as she flapped around on the concrete. I turned my attention back to what I was doing with a shudder.

Taking out the lighter I'd found, I applied the flame to the rag wick. It caught readily and started to burn. Leaning out over the rail a little, I threw the bottle as hard as I could. It arced out over to the other side of the street a little ways away and smashed on the ground with a soft 'whumph' of ignition. The zombies' heads whipped around at the sound, and they started to shuffle away.

"Let's go," I said in a hushed voice.

Indi came out with the packs and the 'weapons' I'd found. I slung my pack.

I indicated the roof lip, "Gimme a leg up?"

There was only a slight overhang to the roof, but with Indi's help I made it up easily, dragging myself onto the flat, gritty shingles. I spun around on my belly and offered out a hand. Taking it, Indi climbed onto the railing and, with a jump and a grunt (and a little help from me) came up to the rooftop beside me.

I chanced a glance over the edge as we hurried to the far end. Between the zombies in the street and the schoolyard group that joined them there must have been around thirty clustered around the fire from the Molotov. Some of the first to reach the spot had been shoved forward by the zombies behind and their greasy clothes had caught fire.

"What do you get when you set zombies on fire?" Indi took my hands and lowered me to the balcony below.

"I know, I know, flaming zombies," I replied. It was a running joke between us. Fire wasn't a reliable way to kill a zombie, even in games. A lit zombie could shamble or run for a significant time span before it finally 'died'. Not having to worry about fluid loss or pain, they'd shamble until the fire completely dried out their muscle tissue or boiled their brain.

"But they'll distract themselves now," I offered.

"At least they're downwind." Indi handed down our stuff and lowered himself to stand beside me. "You get the hockey stick. It'll give you some reach, and don't forget you can hook and trip too."

I took the offered weapon. "Did you actually play field hockey?" I asked.

"Of course, that's where I learned to hook and trip."

I grinned. "Let's get out of here and find Jay." I opened the sliding door and slipped into the flat with Indi behind me. The living room was clear and the bedroom doors were closed, so we stayed quiet. In the kitchen, Indi reached for the front door handle.

"Wait!" I mouthed the word urgently and turned to the bathroom.

Opening the door, I crept inside and made straight for the medicine cabinet. Besides the toothpaste and perfume bottles in there, I found a roll of medical tape and a packet of alcohol wipes. I slipped them into the pack as quickly as possible.

> First Aid kit assembled, restores up to fifty percent
> health relative to skill rank

A message box over the finished kit told me of its effects.

"Thank you," I whispered to the programming gods.

I might try to fool myself that there was always an easier way, but I doubted that, not in this pre-programmed apocalypse. Just because I got away with it this time didn't mean that there'd always be an easy way or, in fact, ever be an easy way.

Back in the kitchen I gave Indi the nod.

The door opened with the barest of creaks, and we lit out and down the stairs toward the street. The block's front door had been held ajar by a traffic cone.

I didn't need to ask 'which way', we'd made sure to throw the Molotov away from the direction we wanted to go, so away from our 'fan-club' was all the direction I needed right now.

The noise of the mob was drawing in a few stragglers from ahead of us, but they were scattered across the wide street and we slipped through them easily.

"Go left," Indi instructed quietly and I crossed the street and flattened myself against a shop front wall, edging toward the corner.

Indi's large hand grabbed my shirt and jerked me back.

"What are you doing?" he hissed urgently. "This isn't an FPS!"

"Right, right," I nodded, gasping slightly from the shock of being grabbed.

In a tactical First-Person Shooter you hugged cover and cornered cautiously and tightly in case of incoming fire. That was a mistake in zombie games, you might bump into a lurker and then it was curtains for you. We cornered wide and fast in our games, so anything skulking around the corner couldn't reach us, and if it looked like there were too many enemies, we could just go straight across before we were even noticed.

"Maybe I should take point?" Indi suggested with a quick backward glance.

I smiled weakly. "No, no. I got it,"

Taking a few steps back I stepped away from the wall, following a wider arc around the corner. There were a couple of zombies in the road, and a line of parked cars against the curb. I dropped down behind the nearest car and beckoned Indi to follow.

"Down the end and to the right, the store is directly across the road."

"Which end is the loading bay?" I asked quickly.

"It's a block on a map, Lex," Indi replied, "I have no idea."

With a grimace I started to jog, doubled over, along the line of cars toward the junction. Even if my chest was no longer trying to move independently of the rest of my body, skulking doubled-over behind a row of parked cars was pressing the underwire into my sternum unpleasantly. That in itself was a new sensation for me, but a stiff breeze carried a scent that stopped me dead. Above us clouds were sweeping the sky and the scent of rain came heavy on the air.

"Do you smell that?" I gasped astonished once more.

"I do, it's incredible, but we have to keep moving."

Shaking my head in wonder, I forged on. At the end of the road I stopped.

"Okay, store's on the right of us but your guess is as good as mine as to what's front and what's back," I murmured.

I really wanted to go in via the loading dock. Most people would head to the front of the store out of sheer habit, but that was a mistake. The front was likely to be awash with shamblers, like the mall from *Dawn of the Dead*. It was a familiar place, where unprepared, clueless Joe-Public would rush to panic-buy or loot supplies. The loading bay shutters at the rear, unless the whole store had been shut during the outbreak, should be open and the yard should be secure.

I knew that was a lot of 'shoulds' but I'd done my stint in a good-sized supermarket before becoming a barista, so this was familiar ground for me.

Indi pointed to the zombies behind us. "We need to put some distance between us and them."

"Okay," I agreed, "we go right." And, with some reluctance, I took off at a jog.

The building across the road was a large flat red-brick affair, just like everything else in this fucking town. The side facing us was almost devoid of features past the ground level ornamental bushes and the large letters high on the side identifying the chain.

We got a dozen steps toward it before I stopped. "Wait," I pointed. "Smoke."

Beyond the cars strewn on the road ahead, beyond the huge store building, a thin column of smoke was rising.

"Could be anything," Indi grunted and ran on.

It was a good seventy yard stretch to get to that end of the building, but I made it with only a slight pulse from my wrist. We pulled up short of the corner.

"How are you doing?" I asked quietly.

Indi, panting hard, shot me a wink. "I'm okay," he reassured me.

"Hold up," I took off my rucksack and pulled out the last of the energy drinks I'd found back in the med tent. "Drink this."

Indi eyed the can with distaste. "Urgh, I hate this fucking poison," he grimaced, but cracked the ring pull and slurped it down anyway.

"Better?" I asked.

"For a given value," he replied sourly.

I punched him lightly on the arm and offered him a wry smile. "Okay, let's go."

We crept forward slowly until we could get a look at what lay ahead.

"Shit," I hissed urgently, "not this way."

"Yup, let's go back," Indi agreed.

We'd mistakenly approached the front of the store. The car park ahead of us was a mess of burnt and burning cars, and burnt and burning zombies milling around aimlessly. Even as we watched, one blackened rotter collapsed with a weak sigh.

I gave a sickly grin. "See, it does work."

"Eventually," Indi growled. "Come on, let's go around the back."

We retraced our steps and hurried to the far end of the building. We followed the wall until it dropped to a slatted wooden fence. Peering through the gaps, I grinned.

"Yes, jackpot!"

Beyond the fence was the delivery yard. The actual gate was a few metres ahead of us.

"Over the fence?" Indi asked.

I took another look and shook my head. "Under the gate," I gestured. The gap under the big iron gate was more than high enough for us to scoot under.

"I don't get it," Indi rubbed at the stubble on his chin, "no barbed wire, easy entry. Besides the fence, where's the security?"

I pointed up to either side, "Cameras, plenty of security for a place like this. If a robber got caught or injured on barbed wire there'd be a lawsuit. Between that and a little lost inventory, the big chain stores will take the loss over the bad publicity. C'mon."

"Can't the Z's follow us?" Indi asked.

"Not if they can't see us so let's get inside!" I urged.

I took off my bag and tossed it under the gate before going belly down and sliding under.

As Indi crouched to lay flat on the ground, there was the sound of tearing cloth.

"Did I just rip my pants?" he asked in slow surprise.

I took a quick look. "Yes," I nodded, kinda surprised myself.

"*La vache*," he spat and dragged himself out from under the gate.

"I guess they applied durability to clothes in this game, huh," I offered playfully.

"*Ta gueule*," Indi growled irritably, "Shut up!"

I chuckled. "Nice underwear by the way,"

He waved a stern finger under my nose. "*Vate faire enculer!*" he snapped.

"Don't mind me, just gonna walk back here for a minute," I winked.

"Like we don't have other things to worry about than my torn fucking trousers," Indi grumbled.

I laughed quietly. "I'm sure we can find some more inside, as long as we can get into the cage."

Indi stopped. "Cage?"

"Yuh," I nodded. "It's where they keep all the higher value non-perishables like clothes, DVD's, toys and things," I explained.

There was no trailer at the loading bay, but the big shutter was up, point for us. I vaulted the four feet up onto the concrete and cast a wary eye around. Roller cages and plastic boxes were stacked or shunted off to the far end of the bay. The doors into the rear storerooms proper were closed. The wall across from us was one big caged area full of boxes and rollers.

"This way," I beckoned as Indi heaved himself up the lip, accompanied by a further ripping sound.

"Don't say a word," he growled as I smirked.

I hefted my hockey stick, "Alright, game face on." I approached the doors which swept back automatically.

"Power?" Indi mouthed to me.

"Generator for the freezers," I whispered and stepped into the supermarket's warehouse.

Chapter 6

The lights flickered erratically. Between bursts I could see where the pallets of goods had been ripped open. It could have been done while the store was operating normally, except that some of the foodstuffs and groceries were strewn on the floor.

I moved forward cautiously. The door to the shop floor was jammed shut with one of the powered trucks the staff would use to haul pallets to the floor for restock. The motors whined as the door tried to open against the blockage.

To one side was a narrow corridor which I assumed led to the cage and stairs to the offices and staff areas. I turned away from it toward the walkway between the fresh goods chiller and the in-store butchers. The chiller hummed and the heavy plastic curtains to the butchers flapped and slapped gently. There were more stores beyond but, before that, another door to the shop floor. Creeping forward, I peeked around the corner, trying to see if there were any zombies.

Nothing.

I tried to peer through the door's windows, keeping back in case they opened automatically. The plastic panels were scratched and scuffed so I shuffled a foot forward, stepping closer.

"I wouldn't do that if I were you," a soft voice issued from my right. "Those doors still open and there are a lot of geeks out there."

I pulled back and looked quickly around.

"Jay?" I called quietly.

"Lex?" the voice replied, astonished.

I near sobbed with relief. "Holy shit, we've been looking for you since we dropped!"

"It's good to see you." Jay stepped out from behind a pallet. I'd seen his profile pics and we'd video chatted occasionally, but the dour-faced

43

adolescent avatar standing before me looked nothing like the beaming, cheerful, thirty-something friend I knew.

"They put you in a teenager?" I blurted and it was true. Jay's new 'body' was slight and spare, all up and down, 'gangly' was probably the right word. If he turned sideways you could easily miss him and his features spoke of Asian heritage, possibly Korean. He was styled and dressed like an emo, slick hair, black metal t-shirt, board shorts and a sullen expression. I hesitated; not sullen exactly. Much to my surprise, I realised that Jay looked nervous, which in turn made me nervous.

Jay waved toward my companion. "Who's this?"

"What, you don't recognise Indi?" I spoke lightly. Jay's eyes darted toward the unbarred doors with alarming frequency, but my words seemed to catch his attention.

"This big bear is Indi?" he blurted.

Indi smiled broadly, white teeth showing from the dark beard. "Makes a change from being the smallest twink in the room, don't you think?"

"Okay, well. Follow me, we should see what we're working with and maybe lay down a plan before we log out." He stepped past us toward the end of the warehouse we'd come from. "The offices and staff areas are clear, so we'll be safest there."

I followed and watched Jay's furtive, hesitant movements. Something was deeply wrong here.

We passed the cage I'd told Indi about earlier, the padlock firmly in place, and past a lift, metal doors stained with bloody handprints. A few steps beyond that and we ascended the stairs, stained with brown footprints. More blood, old and dried on the concrete floor and pale cream walls, a mass of smeared and scuffed foot and handprints. All of them heading down and away from what I could tell.

"There are a couple of bodies in the changing rooms," Jay explained.

"Dangerous?" Indi grunted.

Jay shook his head, "No, not enough of them left."

He led us to the canteen. Chairs lay scattered and at least one vending machine was broken open.

"I'm guessing the first one turned here," Jay offered. "The staff ran, but some of them went into the changing rooms and the Z followed. All the footprints come out of there."

"You've had plenty of time to put together the narrative," Indi sounded a little suspicious. Maybe he was picking up the same 'rabbit in the headlights' vibe I was getting.

"I've been trying to find the key to the pharmaceuticals." Jay pulled a chair up to a table and sat. "I woke up in the first aid room, I haven't been outside yet."

"You didn't even come looking for us?" I was a little surprised, this game seemed like a perfect opportunity for Jay to strut his gaming stuff, put all the theory into practice. "I thought you'd have killed a hundred zombies by now," I joked.

Jay didn't laugh.

"Show me your arms," he stated bluntly.

Indi and I shared a look. Something was up, but I held out my arm and my stats display flickered to life. Indi did likewise.

Indi had:

Combat: 2	Craft: 2	Survival: 1		

Iron Constitution	Strong	Hardy

Jay looked over our skills and traits thoughtfully.

"Educated? Do you know how it works?"

"Not really," I admitted. "I mean, I had a half-empty med kit which showed me what was missing, but that might tie-in with the first aid skill. I tried to make a Molotov from what I learned in the movies, Indi had to finish it but the game did tell me I'd learned a new construction blueprint just from that."

"Suggesting you're a fast learner in this game. So, you're the brains and Indi's the brawn," he mused thoughtfully.

"Then what are you?" Indi asked pointedly.

Jay looked hesitant.

"C'mon man," I tried to lighten my tone despite the atmosphere. "We showed you ours."

Jay took a deep breath and offered out his arm.

Electronics: 2	Communications: 2	Stealth: 1		

| Observant | Creative | Squeamish |

"You are kidding me?" I eyed him, open-mouthed. "Squeamish?"
He nodded, clearly embarrassed. "Yeah," he admitted quietly.
"That can't be right," Indi chimed in.
"It can't be," I agreed.
"Well it is," he put his head in his hands. "I can't even go in the changing rooms to scavenge because I get faint at the sight of the bodies and my stress meter goes through the roof. I'm no good, I should just crap out and regen."

"Now hold on," I held up my hands. "Indi and I went through a lot to get here, and this subliminal feedback system doesn't take any prisoners, am I right?" I looked over to Indi for support.

"It's true, I wrestled one of the deadheads and I nearly shit myself just from the smell," he supplied.

"Yeah, no-one expects the smell," Jay mused sarcastically. "They think 'rotten meat' but don't account for the bowel and bladder relaxing at the moment of death. Shit and piss together with rotten meat? That's a winning combination."

"Which doesn't bode well for character death," I concluded. "So let's not go there yet."

"But I'm no good to you as I am," Jay mumbled.

"Like hell you're not," I insisted. "You're our Yoda, our Ripley, our Max fucking Rockatansky. You know more about the zombie genre than Romero himself!"

"Wait, wait, wait," Indi chimed in. "Ripley? I don't know Lex, the survival rate for her co-cast isn't great."

"Yeah well, the pool of 'Female Mentor Figures in Action Movies' isn't exactly deep," I shot back.

"Galadriel?" he suggested.

I shrugged. "Maybe, but the mentor thing falls mostly on Gandalf in that series."

Jay raised his head from his hands. "More than Romero?"

"Yes Jay, more than Romero," I spoke with certainty.

"Then what's our plan?" Indi cut in.

Jay tapped the table for a moment. "Figure out how to win the prize money I suppose."

"Are we sure that this cake is not a lie?" Indi chuckled softly.

I snickered. "Please, that meme is older than you,"

"No, it isn't," he protested, primly.

"It's not far off," I winked and fished around in my pocket. "I found this, it might be something." I pulled out the 'No Cure' note that had been on my bedside in the medical tent.

"How do you know it's anything?" Jay asked.

"There was a book," Indi offered, "but it was different for both of us, maybe based on past experience. This says the same for both of us."

"Except that for Indi it's in French," I supplied.

"*Ett språk är aldrig nog,* I was wondering when either of you had learned Swedish," he replied wryly.

"So, what do you think?" I pressed.

He rubbed his smooth chin thoughtfully. Jay had rough stubble in most of the pictures I'd seen of him. This fresh-faced version was weird. "It *might* be something,"

"I mean, such an outright declaration so early on? It's like the Cow Level, classic reverse psychology. What else have we got?"

Indi had moved to scan out the canteen windows but he hurried back, rummaging in his pocket. "I lifted a bunch of papers from a dead soldier. I was looking for a map but I kept the rest just in case."

"Good move, they should lead us to the regional HQ. We can probably find some more info there once we're done here."

"Why, what are we doing here?" I asked.

Jay, sitting on an orange plastic chair, pulled one leg up to his chest, wrapping his arms around it and resting his chin on his knee. "We're going to knuckle down and learn how to survive this game. I think it's clear we can't just dive in and try to learn from our mistakes here. I mean, it took you nearly two hours to find me, and even then it was more luck than judgment. If any of us die and respawn? There's no telling where we'll end up."

"So, are we holing up?" Indi asked carefully.

"For now, and let's keep it low-key, we don't want to draw any unwanted attention or hangers on yet."

"Fine chance of that," Indi scoffed. "We haven't seen any other players yet."

"No players?" Jay seemed surprised, "Any NPC's?"

"Not yet," I replied.

"That's odd, but I'm not willing to bet that we have the server to ourselves just yet."

"We have power." Indi grunted from his vantage by the window, "We could shut the back doors, barricade the interior door to the shop floor and use the security cameras for surveillance."

"If they work," Jay grumbled, "this isn't *Five Nights* you know."

"After what we've seen, I wouldn't be surprised," Indi shot back. "Oh I forgot to ask, how many did you two kill on the way in?"

I glanced down guiltily at Indi's bloodied club lying on the table.

"None," I said quietly.

"What?" Jay prompted.

"None," I admitted. "We fought a couple but we didn't kill them,"

Jay sighed heavily. "Well, look at us. Badasses of the zompocalypse."

We sat for a minute in silence.

"Look, if this is too much-" Jay let the statement hang in the air.

Indi spoke up. "We're only just starting out, and none of us expected this level of realism."

I pushed back my chair and went to the broken vending machine. "It's certainly a far cry from just mashing X." Reaching carefully past the shattered glass I pulled out a few snack bars and bottles before returning my haul to the table. "C'mon, let's refill our stam and then lock down before we log out.

"I still need some new jeans," Indi declared indignantly.

"I thought we'd just leave you, y'know, swinging free," I chuckled as he snorted in affront.

"Alright, alright I'll check the manager's office for spare keys," Jay offered. "Other than that, we either have to track down the duty manager or try to force the lock."

"But that might need the security skill," I cut in. "We tried a locked door on our way here, the game straight up told us that we needed the security skill," I explained.

"Hmm," Jay rubbed his beardless chin thoughtfully. "We really need those keys. Okay, let's make sure we're secure first," he said seriously. "Indi, can you blockade the far door to the shop floor? Lex, drop the loading bay shutters, and I'll see if I can find the manager's keys and some radios okay?"

We reconvened in the cafeteria a few minutes later.

"How did it go?" Jay asked.

"I managed to block the doors, made a little noise and the dead got a little riled, but no problems," Indi reported. "I'm a little worried about the doors to the bakery and the butchers, but you have to pull them from the other side and I doubt the geeks can work that out."

"Okay, Lex?"

I sighed, frustrated.

"I closed the shutter and checked the yard. There are a few zombies at the gate, I'm hoping they move on and don't draw any more attention to us but for now? There's nothing I could do about them. You?"

"The office was locked, so if we want the keys we'll have to find the manager. I did find some radios though and," he reached down beside his chair and lifted a carrier bag onto the table. "I did get into the supply cupboard. There's some trousers in there for you Indi, there's also boots and gloves should we need them."

"Thanks Jay," Indi smiled, relieved.

"Zombies at the gate huh?" He leaned back, sucking on his teeth. "That gives me an idea." He leaned in again, all serious.

"We need to see just what it takes to kill these things, so I suggest we get into the yard and drag one under the gate for practice."

"Can't we do that next time?" Indi moaned.

"There's no guarantee they'll still be there next time," Jay replied evenly. "We have an opportunity now. All we need to do is get one in the yard and then come back inside before we log out."

"You don't want to secure it, like tie it up first?" I asked.

"I don't think we'll need to," Jay shook his head. "The pedestrian door is concealed behind the trash compactor. As long as we get back inside before the thing gets back to its feet we'll be fine."

Indi looked thoughtful. "Do you have a plan for how this goes, Jay?"

"I do, Lex and I get the pack's attention, then you grab one by the ankles and pull it under the gate. Simple."

I rolled my eyes. "What could possibly go wrong?"

"Don't say that," Indi wailed, "you know the rules, Lex."

"Sorry," I shrugged sheepishly.

Indi sighed, absently wiping his hands on his jeans. "You said there were gloves?"

We headed down the stairs and out the back door.

"Shit, there's more there now," I grumbled as we laid eyes on the back gate.

"How many were there?" Jay asked quietly.

"Five when I left."

There were eight now, ragged arms reached through the bars of the gate as we walked into view and the dry voices rose into moans.

"I don't get it, why don't they crawl under like we did?" Indi asked of the air.

"They react in the most basic way to a given stimulus," Jay shrugged. "Unless they're on the ground already they stay upright. They're not exactly problem solvers."

"It'd be a whole different game if they were," I said in reply.

"Alright. Indi, go stand to one side, try and get out of sight," Jay ordered.

Indi chuckled, gesturing to his broad frame. "Pretty hard to keep all this 'out of sight' Jay."

"Just do your best. Lex, with me."

With Indi hunkered in position to one side, Jay and I simply stood a few feet from the gate until the zombies noticed us. We didn't have to jump around, wave or shout to get their attention. Eight sets of milky-white, cataract-coated eyes gradually locked onto us with unerring precision.

"Slowly step right," Jay murmured. "Indi, get low and grab the last one as it walks past."

We stepped and the zombies came slowly with us. Indi, down on his belly by the gate, clamped a gloved hand around a passing ankle and the zombie teetered, then fell face first into the asphalt and laid still.

"Congrats, you killed it," I grunted.

"*Non*," Indi protested. "They're tougher than this, probably it's just stunned."

"How do you stun a zombie?" I shot back.

"Argue later," Jay hissed. "Indi, drag it under and let's get back inside. There's more coming,"

Indi dragged our test subject under the gate and we hurried back into the loading bay.

"Alright, upstairs and let's wrap it up for today," Jay instructed.

"How do we even log out?" I asked as we headed back up the stairs.

Jay stopped on the steps, looking down at me and answered simply. "It's the second screen on your wrist menu, you didn't know that?"

"We didn't exactly have time to investigate," I grumbled. "I didn't even know there was a second screen."

"Swipe right my friend," he winked, a little of his true character shining through. "Just swipe right."

Chapter 7

"So we can just exit?" I asked incredulously.

Jay tilted his head, speaking slowly as if talking to a child. "Well yeah, why wouldn't we?"

"I don't know, I haven't had much time to think about it, I'd probably just take my rig off and figure it out from there," I replied.

Jay nodded knowingly. "Try it," he said simply.

Confused, I raised my hands to my head, thinking that, in the real world I'd be taking my VR headpiece off. Nothing happened.

"I can't feel the rig," I said aloud. "Or my remotes for that matter."

"It's amazing isn't it?" Jay enthused. "Total immersion, minimal input from our external bodies. I have no idea how it's achieved but, as soon as I log out I'm going to figure it out!"

"When we log out," I held up a hand, stilling Jay's building excitement, "what happens to our avatars?"

"Good point," Indi chimed in. "I don't want to lose this one. I like it a lot." He flexed to illustrate his point.

Jay nodded soberly. "Yeah, one of us should stay behind for a minute or two, see what happens. If we despawn then great. If not, well. We'll want to be secure."

"I'll do it," I said, softly.

Indi frowned, doubtful. "Really?"

"Yeah," I gave my most reassuring smile, it probably looked like I was going to hurl. "You two just sit down away from the door out of sight and log out. I'll be along in a bit."

"Okay, if the avatars stay, secure the door and come on out."

"Don't wait up for me Jay, it's late IRL. I might go straight to bed."

"Just let us know you got out okay, promise?" Indi insisted, concern softening his words.

"I will," I assured them both.

"Same time tomorrow?" Indi asked eagerly.

"Maybe a little earlier," Jay suggested and grinned.

I nodded my assent more hesitantly.

That settled, my friends sat down in a corner away from the door. They brought up their menus and held their fingers over the options.

"See you on the other side," Indi winked.

"Go on," I chuckled and, with a quick press, their eyes closed and they slumped together, leaving me alone.

I flexed 'my' hands. The blood from before had dried and was flaking off, but I could feel it as I clenched my fists. I wasn't quite ready to leave yet, so I went out into the corridor to the changing room and, through that, to the staff toilets. Just as Jay had said, there was a blood trail leading out of the men's. I listened at the door and slowly opened it. The smell was awful. The strip bulb flickered on, casting dim, brown light through the gore-splattered sheathing, but there were no lurking zombies, just the eviscerated and dismembered remnants of their victims. I let the door swing shut, and, bypassing the disabled (because even in the apocalypse there are some things you just don't do) pushed open the door to the ladies'.

Inside the light was clean, and only the faint smell of bleach assailed my senses. I stepped over to the sinks and checked out my avatar properly for the first time. Long dark hair tied back in a ponytail, I'd probably cut that short at first opportunity, and olive skin smudged with dried blood. Unfamiliar hazel brown eyes stared back at me from strong, Mediterranean features.

My hoodie was spattered with blood, so, taking the shin pads off my forearms, I slipped it over my head. I turned the tap and, with only a slight rattle from the pipes, the sink began to fill with water. I washed my hands and face, tried to get the worst of the blood off my skin and clothes, wondering the whole time at the feel of the water. The game kept surprising me with sensations. Smells that I could taste in the back of my mouth, textures that I could feel against my skin. No other game experience even began to compare, but that just made me more anxious about the inevitable violence we faced.

To take my mind off it, I stepped back from the sink to get a better look at my avatar. Many modern games offered me at least a little freedom to choose what or who I wanted to be, and this arbitrary allocation was jarring to say the least. Catching glimpses of the stranger in my reflection

53

had me flinching and I could do without the extra jump-scares. I needed to get used to 'me', and while I was getting some idea of what this body was capable of I still had to think about my actions. I needed my responses to be as fluid as they would be in the real world, I needed to be as familiar with this body as I was my own. With a frown and a huffed breath, I made a decision. Holding my hands over my boots, the words '*Undress*' appeared in the air and, with a thought, I selected it.

I untied the new boots and kicked them off under the sink. I unbelted the cargo pants and shimmied out of them, then stripped off the t-shirt and chucked it down on the pile. My own body was sitting in my computer chair at home, but here was this new body, lithe and athletic, just as the trait on my character profile said. Now free of any limits imposed by seams and cloth I stretched and squatted to assess how limber and responsive this avatar was.

Before I'd actually realized it, I fell into my Zumba routine, there in the bathroom in the avatar's underwear. I went through the whole set twice, eyes locked ahead, losing myself in the feeling of the heat of effort, the rise and prick of sweat on my skin and listening to the tunes I played in my head.

I didn't want to go back, the exercise routine was easier, I was fitter here. I wanted to do the workout again, push on to get a better sense of my new stamina, but the wire of the bra had been rubbing uncomfortably throughout the exercise so I stopped and smoothed a hand along the sore skin. Glancing aside I froze, there was a stranger in the mirror.

There were always days when there was a stranger in the mirror. Days when the world got dark, when the cat-calls, jeers or the endless, thoughtless misgendering carved through my armour. Usually the image resolved into the familiar, slightly underwhelming androgynous figure that was me. But not here, not today. The stranger remained a stranger, watching me intently.

I had a fantasy that I indulged sometimes in moments of privacy. I would be in a gym or a swimming pool changing room and someone, some stranger would be watching me, checking me out. I was there now; it wasn't me in the mirror, it was the stranger from my fantasy. At that moment I wasn't alone in the bathroom, I looked at her and she looked at me with growing intensity.

We locked eyes and she drew her hand across the skin under her breast, I stood there just feeling the soothing sensation of her touch on my skin. It was so strange, so dreamlike, watching the woman in front of me running her hand slowly across her stomach but feeling the caress myself. She stepped toward me, shoulders squared, bold, strong and athletic. I watched the sweat glistening on her skin as the hand moved to cup her breast, finger and thumb brushing at the nipple and I felt that too. My breathing came slow and deep, but not so much with exertion any more. I could feel the touches as I/she explored our body and, in the warm afterglow of physical effort, I liked it.

The sensations were familiar, it wasn't as if I'd never touched myself before, but I hadn't yet identified the face in the mirror as 'me'. The thought was peripheral, those weren't my eyes, that wasn't my face, or hair, or skin. I was in one of those rare moments when someone looked at me as I wished they'd look at me. It gave me affirmation.

Her hand wandered down her body and I felt it trailing through the sweat on my stomach, down to the waistband of her/my underwear. The briefest touch brought my breath out in a gasp and...

My wrist pulsed. Not like before, this was like a warm breath on my skin. I turned my hand over to look.

> **Stamina Lvl 2 achieved, bonus will be applied after rest period**

I let my hand drop to my side and looked back at the reflection in the mirror. It suddenly struck me that I was standing, nearly naked in a simulated public restroom, touching myself, and I flushed with embarrassment.

Just as quickly I wondered 'why?'

This wasn't the real world. In this apocalyptic setting, the rules of so-called 'civilization' didn't matter.

This avatar wasn't my body. The novelty of a new face, a new form, had briefly disassociated me from the societally imposed and internalised guilt and shame that weighed on me like an anchor in real life. I'd been momentarily free of that ever-present influence that had been enforced upon me daily, and able to revel in that novelty without judging myself.

My own body, all straight up and downs, with neither curves nor muscle mass to recommend it, wasn't one that satisfied me when I looked in the mirror, but this avatar? It responded to my commands with a level of coordination and competency I didn't have 'out there'. It possessed those feminine attributes I occasionally aspired to, as well as being quick and strong. Maybe not the raw muscle power of Indi's avatar, but strong enough for me. Sure my avatar was hot but, more than that, it was powerful, it was like I was Lucy Lawless in *Xena* or Ming-Na Wen and maybe, if I could let go some of my hang ups in here, I could eventually let them go out there.

When I logged in, the game had stirred up my anxiety and fear, heightening my emotions for what came next. I had been relieved to see Indi but, underneath that relief had been a glimmer of doubt that it was actually them. On the run from the school and the flats, fear had underpinned everything and, even with my senses alert to danger, I'd still hesitated when it came to a fight. I'd have to work on that but, through it all, I hadn't once thought about the cluster-fuck of the outside world, just the moment to moment choices in the game.

Not to mention the relationship of sex to death, and the urge to reaffirm life when faced with near-death situations.

Maybe I had just fallen into some kind of dissociative trance and been seducing myself like the opening of a porno, I certainly wasn't about to start self-shaming my sexual urges. But this wasn't the time or place to get into the impacts of social stigma relating to sexuality, although I did need time to think about the experience.

I moved quickly to the sink and used fresh water to clean myself up. I dressed as hastily as the game mechanics would allow and fled the restroom.

Back in the cafeteria, I dragged a table over in front of the door and set a chair on top to block the little window. With that done, I went over to sit in the corner with my friends and logged out.

I took the VR headset off and breathed a deep sigh.

The hum of the tower died as I powered it down and picked my phone up from the desk. I fired off a quick message to Jay and Indi to let them know I was out and our avatars were safe.

It was dark outside. We'd been in-game for about three hours, so I took myself downstairs for a drink and then headed to the bathroom to wash up before heading to bed.

I threw a little cold water over my face, and as I brushed my teeth, took a good look at the real me.

My face was wider, paler than in-game me. I was a little less broad in the shoulders too. For a minute I felt a sense of disorientation. I'd not seen my in-game face for more than a few minutes, but it was all still so vivid. The outside world, the real world, seemed pale and dull in comparison, and, by association, so was I.

I took my glass of water, went to my room, swallowed down my depression meds and went to bed.

In my dreams, I walked naked among the horde in a press of cloying, clammy flesh until my game-self emerged from the crowd and embraced me. Her hands ran over my skin and her lips felt mine. In her tightening arms and the increased pressure of the cold crowd, the sounds of our passion were drowned by the moans of the dead.

All too soon the alarm on my phone went off and I awoke, confused and feeling out of place.

I'd been asleep for seven hours. I had to get ready for work.

Downstairs, my parents were talking in the kitchen.

"Morning kid, you were quiet last night." My dad's smile carried a weight I was used to. Long, unsociable hours spent dealing with people at their worst or lowest moments, with no apparent prospect of advancement despite his efforts, had done that to him. My dad was a social worker, grinding away against the results of decades of social inequality.

I went to the kettle to pour some tea. "New game," I explained simply.

My mum sighed. "Take the joy you can, Alex, there's precious little of it left. Have you seen the news?"

"No, Mum," I replied wearily. "I haven't looked at my phone yet,"

"Do yourself a favour, don't." She bit down on the words.

I lifted my mug to my lips, inhaling the steam and the scent. "The rise of modern fascism?"

"The rise and further rise," my dad shook his head sadly. "Sorry Lex, we didn't want to kick off your day with our worries."

"Seems to be the only way these days, and your worries are my worries. Or will be soon." I tried to make light of it but couldn't raise a smile.

"Roll on the apocalypse," Mum mumbled as she buttered her toast.

"I've got to go. If I'm lucky and work hard, I'll be able to afford a deposit and a mortgage by the time I'm fifty." Again, I tried to joke but it just sounded sad.

My mum stood up, came around the table and put her hands on my shoulders. "You're bright, motivated, capable, and you got great grades. What are you doing serving coffee?" she asked rhetorically.

"Same thing as a lot of the factory workers, shelf stackers and street sweepers my age." I leaned into her, my cup still under my nose. "We're overqualified and under-experienced. The top spots aren't being vacated because the rich live forever, so there aren't the opportunities for advancement there once were, if there ever were," I huffed cynically. "Hell, even if I had an idea for new businesses, getting a start-up loan is a non-starter. Sometimes I think that the only opportunity left to us is to play the lottery of who's the next big social-media influencer."

Mum nodded sadly. "The rich get richer,"

"And fuck everyone else," Dad finished with cynical cheerfulness.

"Language, you!" Mum chastised. "Alright Lex, off you go," she smiled and kissed my forehead.

I ghosted through another day, distracted. Not by the anticipation of a new game, I'd gone beyond that. This time I tried to decide whether I *wanted* to go back.

The air of the real world was clean of the rotten meat and smoke smell of *Rendered Flesh*, but part of me missed that. The burnt rubber and diesel stink of my bus was a poor substitute. The faces of customers staring blankly at their phones or grimacing at whatever news stories they were reading as they waited in line reminded me of the expressionless faces of the computer-generated dead.

There was an election coming up, and the campaigns were bringing out the worst in people. Division, derision, separatism, racism and bigotry were on show for all to see. Every time I saw a slogan about 'the last chance to save democracy' I couldn't help but think darkly that we'd already missed that chance. That they weren't just flogging a dead horse, but had saddled it and were parading its bloated corpse around in the same tired old dog and pony show.

In the game, I didn't have to think about it. It was just me and my friends versus the game, it was so simple, and there was a beguiling, siren call in that simplicity. I thought back to the moment I'd hit the zombie as it tried to gorge itself on Indi's flesh. The nauseating shock of the impact, but then, then the exhilaration once we pitched it over the balcony, the relief at being alive.

I wanted that again, that pure feeling of triumph, of survival.

Sure, it had been a slow, stomach-churning start, but like any game, we'd get better. The temptation of the prize was a good reason to go back too.

I finished the morning shift and bid my co-workers goodbye for the day. The sun was still warm but there were clouds on the horizon. I walked to the bus stop to get my ride home, watching the people I passed with a low-key anxiety, unwilling to draw attention, trying to discourage interaction through my posture and body language. I listened to music on my earbuds as I rode the bus, willing people away from the open seat beside me.

I haven't always been so afraid, but my interactions online in the political landscape had coloured my view of people at large. I wanted to believe in the common decency of humanity, but time and time again, all I'd been exposed to was hate and ignorance.

Arriving home, I opened the door to my parents' empty house; they wouldn't be home for hours yet. I spared the lounge TV the briefest of glances before heading upstairs. There was nothing on the Right-Wing dominated media I felt I could stomach watching.

I thought about the quotes *Rendered Flesh* had displayed on its homepage and title screens. Nihilist philosophy wasn't exactly my strong suit, but a lyric from a half remembered song lurked tantalizingly in my memory. Something about the beautiful, terrible creature that was humanity, the limitless scope of our compassion, our unfathomable capacity for cruelty.

Eventually I caved and Googled it. *Sophia* by the Crüxshadows.

As far as I could see the 'unfathomable cruelty' of a few was stirring and feeding the 'petty everyday cruelty' of a much greater number of people.

I was starting to spiral, but for once I recognised the signs. Usually at this point I'd go online, try to make some small difference via social media and get hassled, shouted down and abused for my troubles. That would exacerbate the cycle and I'd end up lethargic and depressed, crying myself to sleep for the afternoon until my parents came home.

I didn't want to do that, not today. I still had a while before logging back into *Flesh* so I took up my phone and threw up a tweet.

Won't be around as much for a bit, new game eating up my life. And chucked a zombie emoji on the end.

It was as good an excuse as any, and, much as I could call out my mental health, I didn't feel like receiving a slew of well-meaning messages of support when I didn't feel I warranted or deserved them.

I tagged it *'#Gamerlife'* and *'#WWOWD'* as an afterthought for my supposed self-indulgence, and put my phone down on my desk. I tapped my fingers on my teeth thoughtfully, what *would* Oscar Wilde do? 'Probably go on an opium-bender' I thought to myself. Well, I couldn't get any opium, but there was still reliable-old-dopamine. I went and rummaged in my wardrobe. Pulling out some old sweats, a vest and some worn but comfy trainers I changed my clothes, picked up my phone, earbuds and keys, and went down to the kitchen to fill a bottle of water before going out for a run around my block.

Chapter 8

The run didn't make me feel better, but it did stop me feeling worse. I managed about five-hundred yards before giving in and dragging my sweaty body home. I gave my Zumba routine a go and struggled through most of a set thinking longingly back to the conditioning my avatar enjoyed.

I threw myself into the shower afterward, and that, combined with the exercise, helped some. I wasn't about to stop taking my meds, but, if I could keep up the effort, it *might* help quiet the black dog for a little while, if I could keep it up. In the meantime I had to go and learn how to kill zombies without the comfortable distance of a control pad or keyboard between me and them.

I wanted to talk to someone about my dissociative episode in the supermarket bathroom, but I wasn't really sure who to go to. My first thought was to talk to Indi, but I was still embarrassed about being embarrassed about it. The clock was running and it was time to log in.

"Freedom is what you do with what's been done to you."
– Jean-Paul Sartre

The words passed in front of my eyes before the fierce glare of flashing lights induced my pulse to pound and my anxiety to peak, which dragged an adrenaline rush in its wake.

Squinting through spots, I glanced around the room.

Indi was just coming to, but Jay was already up and stood by a window overlooking the delivery yard.

"Is our playmate still out there?" I asked muzzily, still a little disoriented.

"Just standing there," Jay reported. *"Tja* Lex, you okay?"

I groaned as I pulled myself to my feet. "Yeah, I'm good."

"Indi, you with us?"

"*Vouloir, c'est pouvoir.* I'm coming, I'm coming."

"Okay," Jay announced, "priorities. Go." He pointed at me.

"Give me a break, Jay, I feel like I just woke up," I complained.

"Well, it looks like someone woke up on the wrong side of the binary," Indi grinned smugly, stretching.

"Bite me," I grumbled.

Indi winked at me, waggling bushy eyebrows comically. "Happily."

"In a way you just did," Jay's voice cut through our banter. "But you need to learn to work under pressure." He turned and thrust a finger at me dramatically. "Lex, priorities."

"Sustenance, security, situation," I repeated one of our basic mantras carefully. "We make sure we're full HP, safe and secure, and then plan our next move."

"*Good*, so how are your bars?"

I checked my wrist, and a message flashed up on my display.

> Stamina Lvl 2 bonus applied. Stm increased by
> 12%, Stm drain decreased by 5%

"Stamina's full, health is down a bit and stress is low. I'm guessing we have to 'eat' at regular intervals regardless of any damage taken, and maybe the log in blast is to simulate nightmares? This 'game' plays more like a sim the more I think about it."

"The audience demands realism." Jay turned away from the window. "There are a few geeks hanging around the gates and scattered around from what I can see, there's not much we can do about that right now."

"So," Indi managed around a mouthful of chocolate bar that he waved as he spoke. "Once we've checked that we're still secure, what then?"

"We go down to the yard and figure out the best way to 'kill' a zombie," Jay replied simply.

"With a table leg and a hockey stick?" I queried doubtfully.

"We'll see what we can find. In the meantime, we grab a few things to supplement our supplies but don't go crazy. We don't want anyone who does get in to suspect that there are other players here."

"A little paranoid there, Jay?" Indi cut in.

Jay regarded him sternly. "You know enough about the gaming world to know you can't count on everyone playing nice. You got lucky with your avatar Indi, Lex not so much. Didn't Gamergate teach you anything?"

"That you can't escape bigotry and sexism, even in a fantasy world?" Indi replied dryly.

"Yeah, there are some pretty nasty players out there."

"Fight the dead, fear the living?"

Jay nodded. "Words to play by."

"Come on, that's not everybody," I objected, adding to myself, 'just most of them'.

The conversation was cut short as strains of piano music came from outside.

"What the hell is that?" I wondered and went to the window.

Jay joined me. "Schubert?"

All I could see was a stereo sat in the road a little ways from our back gate, couldn't have been much more than thirty to forty yards away from where we were standing, watching.

The nearby zombies shuffled urgently toward the sound.

"Chopin, one of the Nocturnes," Indi commented as the piano rose to a tinkling crescendo.

"But why?" Jay's question echoed my own confusion.

The music played on and the two dozen or so scattered dweebs in the area shuffled relentlessly toward it. They formed a milling crowd, the press of them muffling the stereo before a loud, mechanical cough echoed off the surrounding buildings. It had hardly faded before another sounded and was followed by a high buzzing whine.

"Who's this asshole?" I asked as someone, who I assumed to be another player, stepped out of the shadow of a low apartment block up the street. I assumed it was a player because I couldn't imagine the programmers, who'd put all the effort we'd experienced into this game, would ever outfit an NPC with a welder's mask, high-top boots, white boxer-briefs... and a chainsaw.

"Will you look at this dumbass?" Jay breathed quietly as the figure revved the saw a couple of times, the burble of the engine building to a high roar. The crowd of deadheads turned and lurched in the direction of the awful cacophony.

Raising the howling saw above his head, the mostly naked figure (and I shuddered at the possibilities for injury from the saw, let alone the added zombies) started a slow run toward the zombie 'pack'.

Indi scanned from side to side, obviously searching for the players' comrades or support. "Can that guy even see through that welder's mask?"

"Do we go and help?" I asked.

"Another *Battle Royale* player, all instant gratification, no patience. Just watch," Jay replied.

The figure reached the first zombie and swung the chainsaw, the engine howling at top revs. The saw took the zombie's head clean off in a brief splatter of dark gore. The weight pulled the player slightly off balance, but he recovered well, sidestepping the reaching, headless body as it lurched past, falling to the pavement.

"Lucky, lucky," Jay breathed.

The player heaved the saw around in a back swing and caught the next corpse in the midriff. More brown blood sprayed, coating them in the foul effluence. The engine note, starting at that familiar ear-splitting roar, suddenly dropped to a dull grumble.

"It's jammed?" Indi asked, open-mouthed in disbelief.

"The clothing," Jay stated grimly, "all that goo and cloth. Chainsaw is a stupid weapon."

I felt a tightness in my chest and my arms trembled with the need to do something, "Should we help, what can we do?"

Jay fixed me with an empty gaze. "There's nothing we can do, the idiot brought it on himself."

The engine growled and grumbled as the unknown player tried to rev it into motion. We were close enough to see the saw bucking, as the little motion the blade did achieve jerked the zombie closer still. The player bellowed in sudden frustration and fear as rigoured hands grasped bare shoulders, and the engine finally stuttered and died. The player's shouts rose to screams as the zombie leaned in for the bite and bright red blood gushed from the wound.

More zombies flanked the screaming player. Trapped by his death grip on the saw and the pressure of the crowding zombies, the screams took on a shrill, desperate note rising beyond panic and pain as the dead started to bite and rend.

"Why doesn't he log out?!" Indi demanded.

"I don't think he can," Jay's voice was flat and hard. "He can't reach his wrist." He turned away from the sight.

I couldn't look away, much as I wanted to, much as the pulse of my wrist demanded I do. Even as I watched, a zombie freed one of the player's arms and started to savage the inside of the elbow, biting again and again, all the while pulling and tugging until the limb severed, it's ragged end dripping more bright blood.

The ravening horde was pulling ribbons of dripping flesh and jelly-like strands of organs from the howling player. Red hands raised the pieces high before bringing them down between gnashing teeth. Arterial spray pulsed over the crowding corpses a couple of times, painting the feeding cadavers red.

It was a relief when the avatar stopped screaming and dropped out of sight into the clamouring zombies. My gorge rose but I fought it and kept it down.

"*Enculer!*" Indi breathed in disgust and finally ripped his gaze from the scene.

"There's got to be a cut-out." I rounded on Jay. "The devs can't be letting players experience being eaten alive, right?"

"Your guess is as good as mine, but it's a good incentive not to get eaten," he shrugged.

"No shit, Sherlock," Indi shivered, making revolted noises.

"You're being awfully cold about this Jay," I said accusingly.

"You can't tell me that that idiot didn't bring it on himself," Jay replied disarmingly. "They're probably live-streaming the whole thing too, just a cheap gimmick for hits."

"Yeah, but—" I started.

"No 'buts', we've got our own shit to do. Let's make sure we're secure and then we'll see what the situation is out back."

We made sure none of the shop floor shamblers had wandered in through the bakery or butcher's area, and checked the fire exits were still locked before meeting up in the loading bay.

"What's going on outside?" Indi asked.

"The pack's still distracted, our 'guest' is trying it's best to get out to the buffet."

"Jeez Jay," I felt a little sick at his nonchalance, "nice turn of phrase."

"It's the zompocalypse out there Lex. Get used to it."

"So, what do we do now?" Indi pressed.

"Well, we have two blunt weapons and a small selection of blades. Lex, you'll put those to use, Indi you stand by just in case."

I lifted one of the short, stout blades. "What are you going to do?" I asked.

"Supervise," Jay replied. "I've got to overcome this little squeamishness issue, but you've got no such excuse. Besides, I have literally no combat skills, we need to know how effective yours are and then we start working on mine. I want to be sure that either of you can save my ass *before* it gets chewed off in training."

"And I thought games were supposed to be fun," I muttered darkly.

"It's an experience, isn't it? Something you'd never get to do in real life. What's 'fun' about horror games?"

I picked up the hockey stick. "I can't believe I'm fucking doing this," I sighed.

"You can log out anytime, but don't you want to win the quarter mil'?"

I couldn't really argue. As morally bankrupt as capitalism had become, a quarter million pounds, or dollars, wasn't to be sniffed at. I nodded slowly.

"Good!" Jay smiled, "Now, get out there and kill a zombie."

The three of us traipsed outside into the yard. The ever-present scent of smoke and spoiled meat carried hints of petrol and blood in it now.

The sun was bright and the breeze was soft, and I had to kill a zombie.

Our subject was standing at the gate, reaching through and trying to get to the group still eating the player's spent avatar.

I let out a deep breath and turned to Jay who was holding off a few yards away.

"So, what do I do?"

"Get its attention; we need to figure out their reaction times, how good their hearing is, or smell if it comes to it."

"And then what, brain it?" I asked incredulously.

It was Jay's turn to sigh. "You're not getting arrested for assault here. The repercussions for your actions are purely psychological, a predilection to violence isn't unnatural, it's uncivilized. In this environment you need to overcome your societal conditioning just as you would if you were an MMA fighter or other violent sports participant. And remember, the subject isn't even a zombie, it's a bot. It is not, or indeed ever was a human, try to keep that in mind."

Indi let out a wry chuckle, "Way to break it down, man."

"Okay, go to it," Jay urged.

I took a breath, handed the table-leg club to Indi and hefted the hockey stick. Taking a couple of steps toward the zombie at the gates, I blew out a low whistle.

No response.

I whistled again, louder.

The zombie's head twitched so I whistled again.

The bedraggled thing turned slowly. I took a moment to look it over. The clothes were dishevelled and stained, the face pallid, eyes sunken and the lips drawn back from browned teeth. It snarled breathily and continued its jerking turn to face me. The stomach showed, bloated and purple from just under the torn shirt and it took a faltering step toward me, arms outstretched.

I shot a look over my shoulder to Indi, standing poised to intervene, and Jay who just waved his hands to urge me on.

I took a firm grip on the stick, blew out a harsh breath through my teeth and took a swing.

It connected at the bottom of the ribcage, the impact less jarring as it connected with the soft flesh of the gut. The zombie twitched a little but kept coming.

"Higher, harder!" Jay called quietly. "It's dead, no pain response."

I took a step back from the thing and held up my weapon.

Grimacing I swung again. The blow glanced from the thing's shoulder and connected with its lower jaw. I heard the teeth crack and my stomach lurched.

"Again!" Jay urged.

Fighting down a scream of disgust, I raised the stick high and brought it straight down on the crown of the zombie's head.

The blow jarred my wrists, the skin of its scalp splitting and tearing as it stumbled, but it refused to fall.

Jay let out a sound of pure frustration. "The skull is one of the toughest bone structures in the body. Hit the temple."

I could feel the sting of tears in my eyes and a sob threatened to come from my throat.

My breathing was ragged, but not from exertion. "I can't even see how much damage I'm doing!" I protested.

"Then focus on technique, go for the crit!" Jay called back encouragingly.

"I can't do this, Jay!" I wailed.

"It's not real," Jay reminded me.

I gritted my teeth, fighting the tears. "It feels bloody real!" I snapped back.

"Push yourself, c'mon. This is part of why we game, exercise your catharsis or whatever."

I skipped back and side-stepped a slow lunge before swinging again.

The stick took the zombie in the side of the head. There was a sickening crunch and, when the staggering zombie righted itself and turned back to me, its eye was hanging out onto its cheek.

My stomach heaved. "That's it, I'm out!" I announced, trying not to hurl.

Jay rubbed a hand wearily across his brow. "Indi, you're up," he instructed.

"About time," Indi grunted.

He had set the other weapons we'd collected on a waist-high stack of pallets and selected a short, stout-spined kitchen knife, not like the paper-thin blades we'd seen back in the apartments. Holding it in a reverse grip, Indi strode confidently up to our test subject, reached out a long arm and clamped thick fingers around the zombie's throat. Without any of the hesitation I'd shown, Indi jammed the blade fully into the recently vacated eye-socket.

Drawing the blade back he shoved the zombie away. It collapsed gracelessly onto the concrete.

"*Voila!*" he announced with a triumphant flourish of the knife.

"Well done." Jay's congratulations were perfunctory. "See, Lex? It's not so hard. Target the eye sockets, temples, the soft palate or the occipital region where the skull sits on the spine."

"Easy for *you* to say, sat back there watching us."

He rocked as if I'd hit him and his words came out withdrawn, sullen. "I'd be doing this with you if I could, if I had any ranks in combat at all; in the meantime, all I can do is share the benefits of my experience." He visibly shook himself, discarding the morose moment. "Let's get another and try again."

"Same drill as last time?" Indi seemed more than eager.

"Throw number one over the fence on the other side first, and let's not get overconfident already, eh?"

While Indi dragged the corpse away, Jay and I approached the gate to lure another target in.

"Are you okay with this?" Jay asked quietly.

"I don't know," I admitted glumly, "it's all too real,"

"Like I said, quit any time," he said reassuringly.

I replied with a weak smile. "I'll be fine, I'll get on top of it,"

"Good, you're up again after we get another one under the gate."

"Great." I didn't sound awfully enthusiastic because I wasn't.

Chapter 9

We practiced for nearly an hour, stopping for breaks and discussing strategy. The whole point was to bring the target down as quickly as possible and be safe to move on to the next one. We dragged six zombie 'dance partners' under the gate, and out of those I didn't kill one.

I went at the first few with my hockey stick, but just couldn't deliver the required catastrophic cranial trauma quickly enough. Indi invariably stepped in and finished them off. Then I tried a short blade just like Indi's first attempt, but that resulted in my friend's larger avatar having to drag the stinking thing off of me before I got bitten for my troubles.

It didn't seem to matter what I tried. I just couldn't seem to do it.

It was on number six that we learned something very important.

Number six was bigger than the others, nearly as big as Indi's avatar, but Jay insisted I keep at it.

"Maybe if we can level you up, you'll have more success," he commented as I stepped up to the plate once more.

I tried to keep my head up but his reassurances didn't really help. "I should be so lucky, I don't even know if I'm getting any XP for damage,"

"Try a different approach," Indi suggested. "Instead of going for the kill, try a dodge, hook his leg and when he's on the ground go for the kill, eh?"

I shrugged. "Alright."

I let the big lug shamble forward, and when he lunged for me I stepped aside and under his reaching arms. As he staggered past, I hooked the zombie by the ankle with my stick and pulled, but the smooth wood slipped. I'd misjudged it.

The damn deadhead stumbled into an unprepared Indi, who nevertheless managed to get his short knife up.

We all heard, over the ragged rasping of the Z, the sharp, metallic 'ping' as the blade snapped.

I let out a panicked cry, "Shit!" as the zombie bore Indi to the ground.

"Help him!" Jay called and I took a couple of quick steps to the struggling pair, bringing my stick down hard on the back of the zombie's skull. With a sharp 'crack!' the shaft broke.

I was left looking at a pointed stake gripped in my two hands.

Jay stood on the stack of pallets and shouted "Do something!" as Indi grunted and swore, the zombie's teeth clacking mere inches from his face.

"With what?" I demanded.

Jay waved at the stake of wood in my hands, "Stab it!"

So I did. Even broken to a point, it took some effort and all my weight to drive the stick into the zombie's rotting flesh, and the smell as foul liquids gushed out was nauseating.

"Not there!" Jay called urgently, "The occipital bone!"

"What?" I cried frantically.

"The base of the skull!" he pointed urgently at the top of his own neck.

Indi was straining to keep the zombie's champing teeth away from his face, as I pulled the stake out from between its shoulder blades with a horrible sucking noise. My wrist throbbed, but that was an afterthought to the adrenaline coursing through me.

I tried hard not to think as I grabbed the nasty's matted, greasy hair, yanking its teeth away from Indi, and drove the stake in as instructed. There was a spurt of dark, stinking mush from the Z's mouth before it slumped and went still. Indi heaved it off from on top of himself.

Did I say I didn't kill one zombie? I killed *one* zombie.

Indi rose to his feet like an angry bear. "Why the fuck do I always have to be the one under the zombie?" Spitting and wiping at his chin and lips he retched and gagged. "Urgh, I think I got some in my mouth."

Jay hopped down from his perch, snatching up the broken end of my hockey stick and inspecting it critically. "Didn't you get any warning that the weapon was about to fail?"

"*Non*, I thought it was fine but it just broke," Indi was still spitting unhappily.

"I haven't been able to find the weapon qualities at all, have you?" I asked him.

Indi finally stopped gagging and straightened up. "I can see them on the weapon I'm holding."

Jay sighed and rubbed at his forehead. "Lex, we have to use our wrist menu to look at the properties of whatever we're holding, I assumed you knew that already."

"Yeah? Well assumption makes an ass out of 'U' and 'umption'. The only thing I got a prompt from so far was my medkit and—" I concentrated briefly. "If I focus I can 'see' both your health bars."

In fact, Indi's health bar was pulsing, like they do in some games before you actually take damage. Even as I watched, it settled into stable transparency and faded from my view.

"Aha!" Jay cried triumphantly. "We have learned."

Indi rounded on him angrily. "What the fuck did we learn, Jay?"

"Well, I think we learned that at level two in a skill you can 'see' the properties of a relevant item without going to your wrist menu," he stated happily. "For Lex, that's medicines and things, and I would assume, regardless—" he shot me an amused look, "of 'umption', that Auto means cars and vehicles. Indi, you have combat, so weapons, and craft. Your account of the Molotov might fall under either."

"That's good to know," I nodded.

"Yes, unfortunately I think we also learned that, besides durability loss, there's a random chance for weapons to break in combat."

Indi grunted, finally tossing away the broken knife handle. "That's not so good."

"Agreed. Let's go back inside," Jay gestured toward the door. "That little episode has riled up our fan club over there."

True enough the geeks in the street had come to the gate and were working themselves up into a slow, erratic frenzy.

"And do what?" I asked.

"Start preparing to leave. If we're going to track down a cure and 'win', we ought to start with the papers Indi pulled from the soldier's pocket. If we can track back to their regional base, we might find some good intel on where to go next."

"And if we can't?"

Jay smiled evilly. "Then we go back to the schoolyard and find better information."

"Oh good, I'm looking forward to that. So. Much," I shot back sarcastically.

"I thought you might," Jay grinned. "How's your stress level?"

I looked at my wrist menu and my eyebrows twitched in surprise.

"Not as high as I would've expected."

"Good, your emotional fortitude is increasing."

"He means you're becoming a sociopath." Indi winked. His humour seemed to be returning at least.

"My guess is the game provides a buffer between you and traumatic input," Jay supplied. "It explains why Indi's so resistant from the off, while you respond 'normally' and I'm such a wuss."

"Hey," Indi stepped in, "you're not a wuss. The game is just skill-balancing. If this was really you, you'd be out there like Conan the fucking Barbarian ending these dead-heads. It's just a random negative effect, we'll work around it until you adapt and overcome."

We gathered our remaining weapons, such as they were, and went back inside, pulling the door shut behind us.

"I'll go upstairs and start looking at the paperwork. You two see if you can't get some idea of where those manager's keys might be." Jay headed from the loading dock toward the stairs leaving me with Indi.

"And how do we do that?" I asked the world in general.

"Well," Indi mused, "we have the radios, what was the situation with the security cameras?"

"There's one monitor in the back corner of the main office, there's maybe six cameras, but wouldn't you know it, only four work, one of which covers the loading bay." I spread my arms and twirled to indicate the large, keyless space, "and one of the others fritzes from time to time."

"So, only two dependable cameras on the shop floor?"

I gave Indi a mockingly cheerful thumbs-up, "Yup."

"Well, let's see what we can see, *si amigo*?"

"I didn't know you were trilingual, Indi," I smiled.

He chuckled playfully. "*Mais oui*, I am a very cunning-linguist."

"Oh jeez," I groaned and clapped a hand over my face. "Sex-jokes? That avatar's getting to you."

Indi grinned smugly. "Walk a mile my friend, walk a mile. Let's go."

The view from the cameras wasn't good, and that was without the black frames on the screen.

I was growing anxious, chewing my avatar's fingernails. "There are a lot of shoppers down there," I mumbled.

On the low-res screen, I could make out the swaying zombies in the aisles.

73

"But the placement for the cams is pretty good," Indi mused over my shoulder. "I can direct you pretty well I think."

"Wait, you direct *me*?" I blurted.

"You think it would be better for me to club my way through them?" Indi countered. "*Non*, you can sneak more effectively than I can in this beefcake."

"Maybe we should send Jay," I suggested but without any real intent.

With a quick wave Indi dismissed my concerns. "Worst comes to the worst, you can climb the shelves. Look, there." He pointed to the screen.

One of the cameras was set to close-cover the customer service desk. As I watched, one of the zombies turned slowly to reveal a ring of shining keys.

"The manager," I stated flatly. "That's all the way down at the front of the shop."

"So, it won't be easy. You can do it."

"You've got a plan?"

"I do," Indi pointed to the monitors as he explained, "you sneak out through the bakery."

"In the back opposite corner?"

"Yes, out through the bakery." His finger traced over the aisles on-screen. "Go to the tinned goods aisle and roll a couple down there. You ought to draw some of the bots away from the front of the store, then you sneak over to clothing and use that as cover to get to the front desk."

The floors of the aisles were strewn with packets and tins that had been knocked from the shelves by the uncoordinated zombies. Any careless missteps might see me trip on a can or pop a packet. If that happened, things would get interesting pretty quickly.

"So, I just have to navigate the fucking scenic route, and then lift the keys from the belt of a zombie who can see me coming."

"Be sneaky, maybe he *won't* see you."

"Maybe?" I prodded his broad chest with a stern finger, "let's not rely on 'maybe's' too much huh? Especially when it's my arse on the line."

He clicked his tongue against his teeth and grinned. "Mmm, and *what* an ass."

I gave a mock groan and his grin softened into an earnest smile. "Have a little faith, I'll see you through. Where are the radios?"

"Over there." I flipped a thumb toward the charge stand. Half a dozen sockets held a mere three radios.

"Oh," Indi sighed from the desk.

"What?" I asked, still watching the swaying zombies on the screen.

He winced like he didn't want to give the bad news. "No headsets," he explained.

"The minute you talk to me it'll be like ringing the dinner bell," I gasped in exasperation.

"Maybe not," Indi said thoughtfully, and turned two of the units on. Switching them to the same channel he depressed the 'call' button on one and the other unit chirruped briefly.

"If you turn the volume down I can press once for 'stop' and twice for 'go'. It shouldn't alert the geeks, unless they're right on top of you anyway."

I was already thinking of everything that could go wrong. "And what if you need to tell me anything else?" I asked.

Indi stayed firm. "Then we'll just have to risk it."

"You mean I'll have to risk it," I countered, annoyed.

"You say 'tomato'," he quipped glibly.

Not missing a beat I responded, "and I say 'fuck you'."

"Enough talk," he handed me a radio, "get out there, killer."

"I refer you to my previous statement," I growled but took the radio.

The radio was followed by one of our remaining knives. "And this, just in case."

"Yeah, sure." I took the offered weapon gingerly. After the events of the yard I wasn't all that confident in the blade. I headed for the stairs.

Lots of horror properties have used the dark to scare the audience, but sometimes what you can see can scare you more, and what you *expect* to see can be even worse.

The security footage was grainy, but alongside the scattered merchandise, there had been bloodstains and bits of viscera. I mean like blood loss you don't recover from, and viscera as far as it applies to stripped skeletons, separated limbs and discarded shoes with the nubs of severed feet poking out of them.

I got a waft of spoiled meat from the butchers and an old milk reek from the cold chiller as I passed, a sharper tang in the general fug that hung constantly in the air. As I quietly pushed open the bakery door, it occurred to me how similar the smell of soured dough was, that same acid stink. Maybe it was the bacteria or something.

I moved through and towards the counter, the lights clicking and flickering overhead, and hunkered down. My heartbeat was already climbing, so I took a shaking breath to calm my nerves and raised my head to peer through the glass display window.

The zombies I could see stood, swaying slightly in the aisles, staring at the shelves. Without actual stimulus, that seemed to be the whole remit of their behaviour routine.

The canned goods aisle was near the middle, maybe twenty feet away, but, as luck would have it, the store seemed to have been running a special. There was a display just to the left in front of the bakery stocked with tinned soups at 'discount prices'. Like the store's own brands were any different, all that set them apart was a brand name and a butt-load of sugar.

Sure, here I was about to creep through a zombie-infested supermarket, and what was I thinking about? How we pay for brand labels instead of products. Yay me. I stopped to listen and it was in the relative quiet of the shop floor that I realised how virtually silent the zombies were.

Zombie shows and games only ever briefly spent time with 'dormant' zombies. Without stimulus they stood as silent, macabre statues to the inevitability of mortality. Slowly rotting, never caring or fearing their ultimate end. Given stimulus, there came motion and noise. The zombies wheezed, moaned, susurrated, some even chattered their teeth as they sought to gorge on terrified, unwilling flesh. But here, in this quiet tomb of consumerism, they made almost no sound at all. That was worrying; you could turn a corner in an abandoned building and walk right into one's fetid, clawing embrace.

I rose and stepped quietly over the low gate, not wanting to risk a squeaking hinge giving me away, and out into the aisles. I tip-toed quickly to the special offers shelf and carefully picked up a can. There were a few z's loitering further over, but they had their backs to me. I skipped a few aisles along, trying for as much distance between the customer help desk and the noise I was about to make as possible. Glancing down the aisle next to me, I made sure nothing was looking my way and then tossed the tin underarm.

It hit the floor with an unnaturally loud, metallic 'thump' and the z's came to 'life'. They started to move, before they even tried to orient on the sound. Those facing away lurched in shambling, wide turns into the aisles, snarling and growling, clearing my path to the clothing section on the far side of the store.

I listened for any chirps from the radio, but none came as I walked quickly, the noise of the zombies' own steps smothering mine. I stopped at the last aisle. From here, the shelves reoriented and the walkway was wider. Another quick glance showed me a couple of stragglers still headed toward my little diversion, more accurately now, following the noise of their fellows. I was interested to know just how long they could distract themselves for, but I didn't have time. I scooted across the avenue into the shelves and hurried to the end. Now I was in the back corner parallel to the desk, I just had to make it the length of the store, lift the keys from the manager and make my way back.

Easy.

I hunkered down and crouch-ran toward the front of the store and the side of the customer service desk, pulling up just as the racks of clothes made way for magazines and newspapers. The radio chirruped.

"Lex," Indi hissed over the open line.

I stopped, scrambling back to cover, away from the storefront and hunkered down, fumbling the radio from my belt and up to my lips.

"What?" I hissed.

"The Z's are spreading out again, the ones in the aisles are making noises and they're just wandering now. Get the keys, but listen for my signals on the way back. Do not, repeat, do not go back the way you came."

"Got it," I signalled, and put the walkie back on my belt.

I crept back toward the desk. One side was a low gate, just like the bakery, but it was topped with a scratched and stained plexi window to dissuade customers from trying to gain access. No point trying to force that. I could see the manager staring out across the floor. In 'life' he'd been tall and broad with maybe a hint of middle-age sag coming in, his belt buckle appearing just above the counter. Zombie-dom hadn't changed that, but the signs of comfortable-living about his physique had all become that much softer with rot. His shirt was stained with the fluids of early stage decomposition and his muscle tone was loose and sagging. He obviously wanted to follow the rest of the zombies who milled though the shop, but the counter cubicle rendered him unable to do so. He was reaching, leaning forward, but every time he threatened to fall over the counter he leaned back, staggering to right himself. That was my opportunity.

I scooted forward again, lower and more carefully, right up to the windowed gate of the desk. Sitting on the floor I shuffled around to the front of the counter. As I looked around to make sure it was just me and the manager, I saw the door.

The glass in the outer doors was spider-webbed with cracks, and the frame looked like it had bulged and ruptured, not quite like being hit by a vehicle, and painted with gore. The inner doors seemed jammed closed but had cracked too. Maybe a dozen zombies were shuffling their feet through the shredded remains of, what I assumed were more zombies that had been crushed against and then torn apart by the outer doors and the weight of zombies behind them. Those ones were pawing at the cracked glass, obviously trying to follow the others, the movement their stimulus. Then they caught sight of me. My heart started to race and I watched, entranced as pawing turned to pounding.

That broke my trance and I remembered why I was there, I looked up to see the cadaverous grin of the manager looming over me.

He didn't have to pull his lips back to snarl, he didn't have any lips left, just ragged edges where they'd been torn from his flesh. I'd planned this; I knew what I was going to do, so I did it.

As he leaned forward he started to overbalance and tried to right himself just as before, so I grabbed his tie and, with a tug, helped him along.

Chapter 10

Just my luck, it was only a clip-on, but even though it came away in my hand, it was all the help he needed.

I'd thought it was a good idea; it had seemed like one about thirty seconds ago when I came up with it. But, as the big zombie pitched over the counter, legs straight and body stiff, he hit the floor and fell onto his back beside me. His stomach, distended with gas, split. Noxious fluid from his belly came bursting out with a stench I wasn't ready for. As I gagged, he started to flail for me and, in rising panic, I did my best to fend the clawing fingers off with the hand holding my knife, while grabbing for the keys with the other. The practice we'd done in the yard had no relevance here. I wasn't facing a standing target; the damned thing had all but fallen on top of me. Writhing and struggling, I wrestled for my virtual life as the zombie-manager did his best to end it.

My wrist was throbbing as my stress meter peaked, my movements frantic and uncoordinated as I reached toward the shining ring of keys on the zombie's belt. Then my fingers passed through it.

Ice cold terror shot through me and I froze. The zombie took the opportunity to latch onto my wrist with both hands, dragging my arm to its mouth to bite.

It was just fortunate I'd looted the shin guards.

The teeth skated on the plastic padding and brought me out of my terror. I snatched the knife with my free hand and leaned over the stinking, seeping, struggling zombie and plunged it downward into its eye.

The zombie shuddered beneath me and went still.

I pushed myself back away from the body, shoes sliding in the muck on the floor. My breath came in ragged gasps, my pulse thundering in my ears hard enough to dull the pounding from the zombies at the door. The stress indicator in my wrist throbbed urgently.

79

A sharp sound broke through, and I glanced across to see the cracks in the glass spreading with each impact of dead fists.

I hurried back to the body on hands and knees, eyes stinging with tears and a lump in my throat making it hard to breathe. My hands, shaking, hovered over the corpse.

Loot?

The prompt between my palms startled me and I flinched away reflexively.

The manager's inventory slots sprang up in front of me as I forced myself to acknowledge.

The keys were all he carried, so I shifted them to myself and they appeared in my hands.

A sound to my right snatched my attention that way and I saw zombies emerging from the aisles, drawn by the pounding on the glass.

I fled, back up the wide aisle toward the back of the shop, my feet slipping under me as the effluence from the manager's corpse hampered my traction. The radio chirruped and I almost ignored it before my panicked brain overtook my 'fight or flight' reflex. I came to a sliding halt on my knees at the break in the rows halfway up the store.

There on my knees, trying to stifle my panting, trying not to cry or retch I heard, rather than saw the zombies shuffling across the break in the aisle over from me. But I *did* see the ones that came around the corner way ahead of me.

In their shop assistants' uniforms they looked vaguely comical, like a scene from *Shaun of the Dead* and I had to stifle a hysterical laugh. Then the radio chirruped twice and I dragged myself to my feet and stumbled around the corner.

I made it nearly halfway, almost right to the centre of the shop before the radio signalled me again.

I stopped and looked around. Zombies, in every direction.

Some ahead, some behind, to left and right.

The aisle to the back of the store had maybe three in it so I took a chance and dashed that way, ducking and scrambling madly past them.

The bakery counter was too far, more zombies there, but the low gate into the butcher's station was close, and blocked by a single zombie.

I flexed my fingers and then realised I'd left my knife in the manager's eye-socket.

My mind raced, panic rising again. I'd played many games where you could 'mantle' a zombie, and in my frantic state that was the thought I clung to. I rushed the thing and leapt, but whether it was the stress, or the fact that the very idea of vaulting over a zombie was dumb and the developers had written it out, my leap didn't put me in a position to bypass the zommer and I cannoned into it.

We went down, over the gate, hard. I tried to struggle loose but the thing had its clawed hands in my hoodie and my wrist pulsed in warning. I tried to roll, to get some leverage. Don't ask me how, but I pulled us both to our feet and we spun around the room as the sensation in my wrist built in intensity. The zombie lost purchase with one hand, so I used the opening to lever it away, grabbing the greasy hair as we collided with a cutting table. I desperately slammed its head down onto a blocky industrial unit bolted to the table itself; a ham slicer.

I held it as it struggled and wheezed, my wrist burning as the zombie flailed. Unthinking, I flipped the first switch that came to hand and the machine let out a metallic whine as the blade spun up.

Still holding the head down, I grabbed the block at the end. I whimpered as my shaking hands pushed both block and head forward.

The first cut of the zombie's face on the blade sprayed black blood all over and, sobbing, I worked the slicer again and again, the pain in my hand becoming almost unbearable.

> Psychological Trauma Imminent, seek assistance

The blade protested as it bit into the bones of the skull, a shrill whine and smell of burned bone filling my ears and nose before, eventually, the spinning blade jammed and the motor gave out.

I stepped away, dripping and gasping as the zombie continued to flail, its face gone and its brutalised skull jammed in the machine.

I wiped foul juices and tears from my face and ran for the door.

> **Combat Lvl 2 achieved, bonus will be applied after rest period**

I barely registered the message. I was so messed up that I tried to push through the door, it took Indi to open it from the other side, hauling me through to relative safety.

"Jeez, Lex," he gasped. "You're a mess."

Strong hands took hold of my arm, and for a second I fought blindly against the grasp.

"Cut it out!" Indi commanded using strong arms to still my struggles as he clamped his hands over mine and turned my wrist over.

My stamina was drained, but my stress bar was nearly full and flashing urgently.

"Jay, pass me the liquor. Here drink this," Indi ordered as a bottle was thrust into my hand.

I took a shaking sip which became a long slug of the fiery liquor until the trembling subsided.

"Thanks guys," I breathed, finally.

Jay's voice came from behind Indi, full of concern. "How do you feel?"

I took a minute, trying to blink gunk out of my eyes. Despite the fear and the horror of what had just happened, I felt exhilarated. I called the keys into my hand and held them out, grinning triumphantly.

"Never better," I panted. "Although I'm questioning the message of alcoholism as a coping strategy for trauma, and I could do with a wash."

Jay twitched his head in the direction of the stairs. "Indi, go with them, and Lex; well done."

I handed the ring to Jay. "I just hope they're the right keys."

Upstairs in the washroom I eased painfully out of my hoodie as Indi lounged against the wall. Fighting is a painful business and I was sore.

"Isn't it a little voyeuristic, you watching me like that?" I asked.

"Maybe," Indi shrugged, "but, am I really watching 'you'? In a very real sense, 'you' are back in your room, just like I am. These are just avatars. I mean, I'll go if you want, consent still matters, even in the digital world."

I gave it a moment's thought, but I'd been thinking along those lines myself since the last time I was in here. Looking Indi square in the eye I pulled my shirt over my head.

"Stay," I replied. "The truth is I've been meaning to talk to you, and you smell a little funky yourself."

"*Touché*," Indi smirked, stepping forward and drawing water in the sink beside me.

"At least with the keys, we can get some fresh clothes. I didn't want to loot the uniform locker for a change, that polyester shit makes my skin itch."

"*Oui.* So, what did you want to talk about?"

I took a double handful of water and splashed it on my face, leaning over the sink before replying.

"When you two logged out before I sort of, hung around," I admitted, staring into the now discoloured water.

"Uh-huh," Indi grunted, taking off his own shirt. Sniffing it, he made a 'yuk' face and tossed the flannel away. Beneath a white vest the avatar's chest was broad and a little hairy.

"Nice tattoos," I commented on the designs inked across his back and upper arms. "I kinda wanted to get 'acquainted' with my avatar."

Indi ran a hand through the short, dark beard on his chin. "How 'acquainted'?"

I hesitated a moment. "Like, third base 'acquainted'," I admitted finally.

Indi looked at me and smirked. "Nice!" He drew out the word lecherously.

I snorted, feigning disgust. "I don't know what happened, I was looking in the mirror and it just sort of started happening."

"I can understand," Indi nodded, "it's not 'your' face, you had a dissociative episode brought on because you don't associate that face or body with your own."

"I thought you might understand," I smiled, relieved.

"Don't get me wrong," he rubbed his hands together in the water, "dissociation and dysphoria aren't the same thing, you know that as well as I do, but I have an idea where you're coming from." He threw water in his own face, huffing through it and splashing me into the bargain. "Hell, given a chance I'd go to third with your avatar," he winked playfully.

I clucked reprovingly but my words came out low, breathy. "That's really inappropriate."

We stood quietly for a moment, the only sound the trickle of water from the taps.

"So, have you…?" I began suddenly, turning back to the sink and trying to shake away my burgeoning impulse to throw myself into my friend's arms, lock my lips on his and find out what the 'French' in French-kissing *really* meant.

"What?" Indi asked, teasing.

"You know," I gestured like it was obvious what I meant. "Looked in your pants?" I blurted.

I'd meant to derail that line of conversation; obviously my subconscious wasn't onboard with the plan.

"Ah Lex, Lex, Lex." Indi shook his head. "Why do you think it took me so long to find you when we first got here?" he winked.

I thought about that for a while.

"That good?" I asked.

Indi smiled broadly. "*C'est magnifique.*"

"How far do you think the game would let us go?" I asked slowly.

"I 'think' you just went through a life-threatening experience, simulated or *non,* and you're reaching for a life-affirming one to counter it," Indi replied, all the playfulness dropping away as he regarded me seriously.

"But I feel good," I protested.

He shook his head, "Hmm, euphoric even? It won't last, Lex, and I wouldn't want you to look back on a choice you made now and regret it. Don't get me wrong, I'm as curious as you are, but this is not the time."

"Okay, okay," I agreed finally. "Why don't you go get us some clothes from the cage? Jay should have it open by now, and try to find me a sports bra? This underwire is killing me."

"*Oui,*" Indi nodded. "What size?"

I was forced to remember my IRL lack of curvature for a moment. "You'd know better than me."

Indi sized me up for a moment, maybe just a little longer than was necessary. I didn't mind.

"Okay, it might not be the solution you think it will, but okay. And no, how you say, 'having a sly wank' while I'm gone. Or, at least, do it in the stalls and try to be finished before I get back."

"No promises," this time I winked. "If you hurry back you can help me finish."

Indi left with a startled, uncertain grin painted across his face. Once he'd gone I looked at 'myself' in the mirror, a little startled to realise I had only been half-joking. Had I really just propositioned Indi for sex? In a *game*? I mean, we'd shared erotic fanfic before, and more than a few fantasies, but this? I mean, cyber-sex was one thing, but this was like proper next-level transhumanism; virtual sex with virtual identities and *real* sensations. If my own initial experience was any indication, it was possible. Whether that was exciting or frightening I couldn't really say. Humanity had put greater technologies to far darker purposes before.

That thought hit me like a cold shower and I was immediately thankful for Indi's words about holding off. As horrifying as this world was, there were some horrors that only people could bring into it with them.

Cleaned up and changed up, we decided to log out after the session's excitement and leave cataloguing the contents of the secure cage until next time. Jay had hinted at plans, and that left me eager to ghost the IRL and get back.

It was past midnight when I emerged into the 'real' world. As the screen on my computer blanked, I caught sight of a reflection, cast by my bedside light in the glass. For a minute I was confused before I realised it was me. Great, rather than having two identities, online and offline, now I didn't even have one. I shook my head and rubbed at my eyes. I was just tired.

I went to the window and looked outside. The street lamps cast orange light and deep shadows. A taxi rumbled past, and I could see the light of a TV through the blinds of a window across the road.

Despite the late hour, despite my tiredness, I felt elated. Getting the keys like that was something I'd never have dared in real life, but then, the game was as real an experience as I'd ever had. I'd seen accidents sure, had near misses when my heart raced with adrenaline. But I'd never felt in control in those situations, those had happened *to* me. It might have been decided that I would be the one to go for the keys, but I could have refused. In some small way, by accepting the job I'd chosen to go, and everything I'd done after that had been me.

I popped down to the kitchen for a drink to find mum at the table, laptop open.

Opening a cupboard I reached for a glass. "Working late?" I commented.

Mum stretched and sighed. "Just some research, an odd case got bumped up to Neurology today."

"Uh-huh." I wasn't really listening but I could tell when mum needed a sounding board.

"Young adult male, admitted to the A and E suffering a seizure of some kind. The fit subsided but the doctors could find no cause, and the patient has yet to regain consciousness."

"Drugs?" I suggested, not that I had any knowledge of the subject.

"Nothing in the blood, the roommate said he was on his computer a few minutes before."

I felt a twinge of alarm but quickly dismissed it; it was just a coincidence, right?

"Well, I'm headed to bed, good luck figuring it out Doctor Mum."

"Goodnight sweetheart," Mum mumbled, and I went back to my room.

I drank my water and watched the night time street through my window.

Maybe I was still feeling euphoria after the shop floor experience or maybe I was lightheaded from fatigue, but I felt somehow stronger, surer.

I stepped away from the window and switched the computer back on. While I had this energy I would use it. I hit the boards and groups. Over the course of an hour or so, I did more online than I'd done in a month. By the time I hit 'send' on the last post I was truly exhausted, mentally and emotionally.

Mum's coma case was still nagging at me, it had to be a coincidence but I just couldn't shake the suspicion that there was more. Despite my fatigue I scrolled some game boards and forums, looking for any signs that might provide a link.

I didn't even recall crawling into bed but, finding nothing to confirm my suspicions; I must have at some point.

The morning brought a buzzing alarm clock and a slew of notifications on my phone.

I checked a few, and despite the brief rise with each message of support, every venomous response or callous comment in reply to my good intentions washed a little more colour out of my view of the world. A part of me was a little surprised. Usually I'd feel sad or defeated, but right here, right now in my room, all I felt was a cold and heavy hardness gripping my heart.

I pressed the button to send my phone screen black, set my jaw and headed downstairs to breakfast.

Chapter 11

Jay, why are people so hateful? I'd arrived home, had something to eat and stared at my computer screen for fully fifteen minutes before turning it on. Having seen Joakim marked as 'active' on my messenger, I'd pinged him.

Bad day huh? He replied.

You could say that.

What's up Lex?

I sighed and flexed my fingers.

I know you don't get into politics like me and Indi, but you see it too, right? In gamechats? All the players sending awful messages to each other?

I waited, watching the cursor blink while Jay typed his response.

I do, I suppose it's like any sport. The players are amped up, the focus is winning and they don't like to lose. More than anything it's the anonymity of cyberspace. Aside from any punitive action from mods, there's little in the way of repercussions, so they can say and do what they like.

Watch out, you're showing your age. No one says 'cyberspace' anymore. I typed back, a sly smile on my face.

Well, in the opinion of one of my advancing years, I chuckled as the words wrote themselves on the screen, *it's not *the* problem itself, just a symptom of a much wider loss of empathy for our fellow human beings.*

"Don't I fucking know it?" I said under my breath but my fingers danced on the keys. *What, you mean like that dickhead with the chainsaw? If it were to turn out that they'd been hurt, like really hurt by that little gag even I'd have trouble feeling sorry for them, it'd be their own fault.*

Really? Jay typed. *That sounds more like me than you.*

So what if it does? I stabbed at the keys angrily.

Oh don't get me wrong, I like to indulge in more than my fair share of misanthropy but that's why I have you and Indi around. To balance me out, remind me that there's good in people. And I need that because sometimes we all have to pull together or the corporate scumbags will walk all over us. I don't want to sound like a conspiracist, but the people in charge (and I don't mean the Governments) don't want 'unity', they want a number of factions they can play off each other while they sit at the top and reap the rewards, he typed.

I sighed, running my hands through my hair in exasperation.

All I try and do is encourage people to see that the world would be better if we worked together!

I know, Jay typed back, *and I sympathize, but the people in charge have made 'social reform' and 'Socialism' synonymous with 'Communism', and they spent decades demonizing Communism in the Western world.*

But, Communism *was* bad, wasn't it?

I never said it wasn't complicated Jay typed back. *But everything that's wrong is the culmination of many, many bad things at once, and the papers, under direction from on high, render it down into a 'he said, she said' situation, faced in exactly the opposite direction from the real problems. Why should the average American be concerned about vote manipulation when they're more worried about the rise in violent crime in ethnic communities? They're so afraid that the black guy down the street is gonna steal their TV that they can't see that it's the white guy with a bad wig and awful fake tan that's bagging up and selling off their Constitutional privileges and freedoms. They're afraid of Russia or ISIS blowing them up, when they should be afraid of Amazon or Coca Cola destroying their rights and liberties as workers.*

It's like this new global network set to replace 4G in a few days. Suppressed reports suggest it has the potential to increase levels of aggression and anxiety and impede empathetic impulses in the majority of test subjects. But the company behind it has donated millions in political donations across the developed world, and employs a number of senators and MP's on their board of directors. The refurbishment of the existing infrastructure was contracted without tender.

Without tender? I typed. *You mean there was no competition for the contract?*

None at all, Jay supplied. *The company behind it was allowed to name their price, no counter offers, no negotiations. Simply put, a handful of very influential, old-monied white men across the northern hemisphere are earning billions off of this project at the expense of taxpayers across the developed world.*

I had always found it hard to process the concept of 'greed' at an intellectual level. To me the ability to live, clothe and feed yourself and your family, to afford the odd holiday and have something put by for emergencies seemed enough. Yes, I have my luxuries and they have their own cost, but to have so much personal wealth? To have an amount of money that really means nothing to the average person? I just couldn't comprehend the concept of being personally 'worth' more than a small country, and then to sit on that wealth, accruing interest while that same country starved, or burned, or drowned in blood.

If this was happening in one of the so-called 'People's Democratic Republics', Jay went on, *it would be reported as bribery and corruption on a grand scale, but because it's the capitalist west, it's just business as usual.*

So, you're telling me the people at the top are like ultimate tier trolls? I couldn't really type cynicism, but I was trying.

Why not? They're selfish, uncaring of the effect they have on others, and generally turn to stone when the light of day hits them.

That raised a small smirk from me.

The problem is that they've got a lot of other people thinking just like they do, but on a much smaller scale. Look, do you want to talk about this more in-game?

I shook my head as I typed. *No, we've got shit to do and, really, I'd rather focus on that for a bit.*

You see why I stay out of politics? I could almost see a wry smile on his lips.

No, you'd be really good at it.

Please, I'd be lobbying for genocide by the end of a week. You logging in now?

Give me an hour, I want to shower first. Not to mention try to clear my head of the fug of righteous indignation and complete disappointment I felt for humanity at large.

Alright, see you in an hour.

I stretched in my computer chair. I'd often identified the most vocal of the right-wing idiots I'd encountered online as 'mindless zombies of the increasingly fascist state' but now? Now I was wondering if that wasn't cruel.

To the zombies.

"I believe that we are all, openly or secretly, struggling against one or another kind of nihilism."
– Ellen Willis

Combat Lvl 2 bonus applied:
Dmg increased by 12.5%, stamina drain reduced by 5%, Crit chance increase 6.25%

"So," I asked, the transition into game was getting easier, a brief stretch and I felt ready to go. "What's on the agenda today?"

Jay looked up from his seat at one of the cafeteria tables as I walked toward him.

"Come here," he beckoned me to stand beside Indi who was already looking over his shoulder. I'd seen photos of Indi, posted in his social media pages, of a day trip to Calais he'd taken. It was getting less and less incongruous to identify the hulking man-form of his game self with the slight figure in those pictures.

"I've been going over the military documents," he spread his hands over the papers on the table, "they're of some use, no doubt, but they don't have any details on the higher level of command. We can't go anywhere until we know where we're going."

I picked up a bottle of water from the table. "You still think the military is our avenue to trace the cure?" I queried, taking a swig.

"I think so and here's why." Jay held up a document and pointed to a name at the bottom. "This is just a timetable for guard rotation, but look at the duty officer's name."

"Pisarev?" I shrugged. "So they're Polish, so what?"

"Russian," Jay corrected. "Dmitry Pisarev was a Russian writer and philosopher, his works influenced the revolutionary generation that included the likes of Lenin. One of his famous quotes states: *'What can be broken should be broken'.*"

"Sounds a bit nihilistic to me," I said thoughtfully.

"Exactly!" Jay beamed. "Haven't you noticed? Every time you log in there's a philosophical quote from the school of…" he let the statement hang.

I ventured an answer. "Nihilism?"

Indi was smiling too. "Bread crumbs, Lex, just like the ones that led us to this game." He leaned forward eagerly, scanning for more clues in the pages. "This is good, maybe the goal isn't the cure, and maybe it is, but we've got a possible route and maybe a means to guide ourselves by."

"We look for references to nihilism?"

"Yes! I mean," Jay shrugged, "it's a zombie game, yes? Isn't that what the genre is known for?"

"So what's the plan?"

Jay's voice lost a little of its enthusiasm. "You and Indi need to go back to the school." I noticed he excluded himself, perhaps that was why he sounded less than excited. "What we have shows that there's a room overlooking the yard. A room that was repurposed for the command of the emergency evac station, a music room I think. There should be something detailing the location of the next step in the command chain there."

"Okay," I nodded slowly. "Any other goals?"

"We could use a car or some kind of transport. I'm not kidding myself that this will be walking distance."

"I just can't believe we're leaving all these supplies behind," Indi grunted. "We basically spawned on top of the mother lode."

"It's a honey trap, Indi," Jay spoke levelly. "It's meant to tempt us to stay. You know what happens to characters who stay in shopping malls in zombie films?"

"How big a vehicle, how much are we taking with us?" I cut into the conversation, *I* knew what happened to those characters.

"Four by four, high ride and long wheelbase," Jay specified. "We could try to bring it into the yard, but that risks drawing attention from other players."

Indi scoffed loudly. "What other players? We haven't seen another player since 'Chainsaw Buffet' outside the back gate."

"Really?" I chided. "You're not going with 'Captain Underpants'?" Despite my joke I flashed back to the coma case, the possibility, at least in my mind, that they might be one and the same player. I considered mentioning it, but I had no proof, just unfounded suspicion.

"Or 'Player IQ Unknown'?" Jay grinned, derailing that train of thought.

"We can load more if the car's in the yard," Indi insisted.

"We don't *know* that we have the key for the padlock," I ventured. "And why not just get a car from out front?"

"The front car park is a mess," Indi shook his head, "and any keys will still be in the customers' pockets. Jay's right, we're better off looking in the residential area near the school."

"So we go to the school, get any intel' documents we can from the command post, and bring a car to the back gate." I was just getting everything straight in my head.

"That's the plan," Indi confirmed.

"Why don't you come with us, Jay?" I urged. "You're never going to level your stats sitting around here."

"I'll just slow you down." Jay's voice carried just a hint of disappointment, or maybe it was shame.

"You need to get out there sooner or later, and we can't be carrying your low-level ass if it's 'later'." Indi winked.

"Come on, we'll look out for you," I encouraged.

He sighed, finally relenting. "Okay." But I could hear his reluctance even then.

We snuck out under the back gate. The air was colder now. The skies overhead had turned grey with clouds and the threat of rain. The washed out sepia that I'd kind of stopped noticing was now almost a monochrome of greys and faded colours. We'd checked from the cafeteria windows that the way was clear; well, as clear as it could be. A few zombies stood staring blankly up at the sky from the road where a stripped corpse lay next to a bloody chainsaw and welder's mask.

We edged along the back of the supermarket toward the road and the wrecked cars that Indi and I had used as cover on the way in.

"Pay attention to the shops on the way," Jay had said. "There might be something useful."

We each carried a knife, a radio and rucksack. Personally, I was pretty desperate to find better weapons, but the programmers seemed to have put all the convenient gun shops elsewhere. Down the road to the main street was nothing but hairdressers, a cafe, bridal shop and a funeral parlour.

I wondered for a moment if that counted as 'irony'.

A few more of the dead wandered aimlessly in the main street. Looking around, there wasn't much here either, not even a hardware store. Coffee chains, a bookshop, a mobile phone store and a couple of banks. Nothing screamed 'apocalypse survivors' supplies' to me.

We moved swiftly and stealthily down the street, quickly coming to the little grocery store and apartments Indi and I had taken shelter in before. On the pavement, a familiar body raised its head and hissed at us. Maybe the zombie had some dim memory of us throwing it off the balcony, but I doubted it. It wasn't as if it had fallen that far, but it had obviously landed awkwardly, legs splayed at unnatural angles, broken bones jutting through putrid flesh. There was no way it could get up and come after us. I felt oddly sad, leaving it there to flail impotently, but I wasn't about to expend any of my little knife's durability on the zombie.

Looking at the map, we had decided to avoid the alley on our way to the school. The route was longer, but the roads were wider and held more possibilities to avoid the dead should we come across them.

The turn we were looking for was maybe a hundred yards further on, and even as we approached, I spotted a couple of charred corpses sprawled in the road. Given the lack of any other players so far, I made the leap that these were some of the pack I'd 'distracted' with my improvised Molotov. They'd got some way before the heat had done enough damage to bring them down. Indi had been right; flaming zombies.

The old houses here had small front gardens, encompassed by low stone walls. A couple of mooks watched us from the windows, pawing at the glass. We moved on before they got too riled and, passing the church, came to the front of the school.

"Go around or go through?" Indi spoke in a hushed voice.

Jay, a little breathless replied, "Here, this way."

We retraced the steps Indi and I had taken when we fled the school toward the brooding bulk of the gym.

I risked a glance up to the first-floor windows of the main school and saw several pale faces watching us from the gloomy interior. Much as I had gained a little confidence in dealing with adult zombies, I still did not want to face any zombie kids.

We skirted around to the covered avenue between the two buildings, with the gym behind us and the yard in front.

Sheaves of paper in hand, Jay looked up at the tech block. "If I'm right, the command point is in this building on the second floor," Jay informed us.

"But it's locked, we couldn't get in before, we didn't have the skills," I objected.

"Maybe we can force the door, or go in a window, I'm sure we can find a work around," he countered optimistically.

"There's a tech room on the ground floor, last time we were here there were a few Z's inside," Indi filled in. "We could get some better weapons there."

Jay seemed a little nervous. "I'd say let's be quick and quiet, but at this point? Let's just do what we need to." If it weren't for his damned trait he'd be taking the lead, but instead he hung back as Indi and I crossed the sheltered yard to the door.

I held up a hand, bringing Indi to a sharp stop. Reaching cautiously forward I placed a hand in the double door and pushed. Just as I'd suspected when I saw them hanging just out of line with each other, the doors swung easily open.

"Has someone been here?" Indi asked.

"Maybe, maybe it's just a programming inconsistency," Jay opined from behind us.

"Let's be careful," I grunted and led the way into the darkened building.

School had never been my favourite place, in much the way of many people. There had been run-ins with bullies and occasionally teachers, and attacks of adolescent and social awkwardness and embarrassment, memories that still came back to me late at night for no other reason than to cement my adult insecurities. The game stimulating memories to 'fill in the blanks' had sounded cool, but I hadn't expected at that point for it to take me back to school. At least when I was at school, there hadn't been gutted corpses strewn about.

The double doors gave way to an open space. Lockers lined the walls, and stairs led to a mezzanine ahead and onward to the second floor. Pin boards on the walls advertised that this building was dedicated to drama, music and tech; kind of an odd combination. Discarded shoulder bags, body bags and bloody footprints filled out more of the story.

Doors to our right and ahead led to the workrooms. I'd already had a glimpse into the room that ran alongside us, and I followed as Indi headed that way, combat knife in hand.

The door opened with a faint squeaking of hinges. The air was musty and smelled of wood and metal. Over by the window, three zombies stood between big lathes and stared out of the glass into the schoolyard. They'd have a tough time coming for us, as half the room was occupied by two long, high tables. Indi, Jay and I stepped quietly into the room.

The feet of a cheap school stool scraped noisily on the floor as one of the others, I don't know who, blundered into the thing, dragging its feet against the laminate floor.

The zombies turned, snarling and lurching out from between the big pieces of classroom machinery. I took a few steps forward, keeping the tables between myself and the Z's, trying to split one from the group. A set of dull-eyes tracked me as the zombie shambled obligingly my way.

Indi strode confidently forward, grabbing the nearest goon by its white lab-coat, kicked one of its legs out from beneath it and struck its head violently against the cast-steel casing of a lathe as it fell. The next zombie seemed to have caught its sleeve on a sharp edge of one of the machines and it jerked repeatedly, trying to wrench itself free, snapping its blackened teeth in my direction.

My own zombie pulled itself around the end of the table, hand-over-hand on the surface like it was stalking me before shuffling my way. I raised my knife hesitantly, the stress indicator on my wrist pulsing like a second heartbeat, and then decided against the frontal attack. One of the high classroom chairs lay on its side on the floor, so I kicked it toward the approaching zed. The chair squealed against the tile floor for a second before it tangled my playmate's legs, and the thing went down hard.

The head of Indi's zombie rang repeatedly against the lathe with dull, wet thumps, but I hurried forward and pressed the point of my knife into the base of my zombie's skull and, one hand over the other, pressed the blade into the opening. My pulse spiked at the sound and sensation, but I wasn't panicking, not like before. I checked my bar.

| STR | ████████████ | | |

The sound of ripping material announced our third 'friend' pulling itself free and it came lurching desperately toward me. Leaving the knife where it was, I looked to the tool board and quickly snatched at the first handle to present itself from a rack. I swung the object, heedless of the light weight, the zombie's head flinched to the side in a fine spray of gory bits. I took a moment to look at the 'weapon'. The ghost of tech classes past came back to tell me I was holding a 'bastard file' or 'coarse rasp' and I dropped the bloodied thing, which had more in common with a cheese

95

grater than a weapon, to the floor. The zombie turned back to me, the flesh of its cheek ripped and ragged as, taking a little more time to be selective, I lifted a claw hammer from where it hung.

Indi dropped the dead weight of zombie number one and, stepping quickly, looped his arms under the last zed's in a smooth full-nelson. I raised the hammer high as Indi struggled to hold the zed in place, and swung downward at the thing's skull.

There was a sharp, cracking pop and a brief shower of black blood as the hammer went in.

The zombie sagged and went still. Indi spat some of the spattered gore and blew out a long breath. Jay puked. I gave the hammer a quick tug, but it had lodged itself in. As I felt the skull crack a little more, I had to struggle not to be sick myself.

Chapter 12

We stood for a moment before Jay started to chuckle, then Indi and then, finally, I couldn't help but join them. There was an edge to our mirth, but still we indulged it for a moment until a creak from the ceiling above and a brief fall of dust sent us all into silence.

"Someone upstairs?" I mouthed pointing upward.

"Zombies?" Indi mouthed back.

Jay held out a hand and we fell silent, listening.

I left my spot by the tables and crept quietly back to the tool rack on the wall, gently lifting another hammer from its spot.

Another soft creak and another fall of dust.

Indi ripped the hammer I'd left behind out of the zombie's skull with a wet sucking sound, and once more I struggled not to retch. Jay looked positively green, but managed to keep it together. One hand to his mouth, he pointed up, motioning us to go.

I reclaimed my knife and took another hammer from the board on my way to the door. Indi swung by to add another hammer to his arsenal.

Outside we stepped quietly to the foot of the stairs and looked upward. Nothing waited for us on the upper mezzanine, so we crept quietly up the stairs. I looked up, tracking for further signs of disturbance. A door closing softly on its sprung hinges caught my eye. Something had come out of the room, something with enough brains to pull from the inside.

With a finger to his lips, Jay motioned us upward. The next flight led up right beside the point where the first left off. The brief squeal of a rubber sole on the floor caused the three of us to freeze.

"Someone's up there," Indi murmured.

"We go together," Jay urged and we started up the stairs again.

Jay silently pointed out the room that was our objective. In my mind, if we were lucky, whoever was up here would be in one of the others and then they could slip past us and get away without any fuss, but if they were in there, then what?

Indi barged into the room in a rush, hammer held high, and I followed closely. This classroom must have been a music room. A number of instruments, amplifiers and a drum kit were piled in a corner. Around the walls, maps and charts obscured parts of posters depicting composers and musical scales. The tables that hadn't been pushed up against the walls and loaded with radio gear were arranged in the middle of the room, a larger map spread over them. Beyond that, a young black woman wearing faded denims and tight cornrows struggled to keep two camouflage-wearing zombies at bay with a chair.

"Well?" She called to us in frustrated desperation. "Help me!"

Indi strode ahead, deposited the hammers on a table in passing and pulled the combat knife. I swung around the other side of the table, a little unsure. The zombie soldiers were wearing helmets, so the hammer was a bad option, but their attention was completely focussed on the intruder, so we had an edge.

Using his avatar's height, Indi reached over the first zombie's head, grabbed the lip of the helmet and dragged the head back, jamming the knife up through the lower jaw and into the skull from below. I didn't have the height or strength advantage, so I grabbed the thing's tactical vest, kicked out its legs, and plunged my knife under the lip of the helmet and into its temple as it fell to its knees.

'Wow', I thought to myself, 'I'm getting good at this.'

Pulling my blade out still caused my stomach to flip, it was the awful sucking sensation, but I'd be damned if I was going to blow chunks in front of a stranger, so I swallowed it down.

The young woman, or the avatar of a young woman, still held the chair defensively and was alternating between holding it at Indi and myself. I realised that, not only was I still holding the knife, but I was standing as if I was about to use it. With a conscious effort, I relaxed.

As we watched each other nervously, a brief gust of wind stirred the papers that had scattered around the room. At some point one of the windows had been shattered, and a soldier's corpse was snagged in the large pane. Probably held there by shards of broken glass in its back, I thought with a shudder.

"Who are you?" the stranger demanded.

"*Un moment*," Indi spoke tersely. "There are three of us so you will answer our questions, *oui*?"

"Okay," they replied grudgingly.

"Who are you?" I asked.

"My tag is NegKDTwenty-Ten, but my online friends call me Ned." The voice seemed to match the avatar. The game hadn't altered any of our voices (Indi's light French lilt coming from the lumberjack for example) so it seemed that the player might in fact be a young woman, but I wasn't going to assume, and right now didn't seem the time to ask.

"Are you alone?"

The answer came without hesitation. "Yes." So either the player had thought this through or was telling the truth. A slight tightening at the eyes told me Ned hadn't meant to answer us so readily, or honestly.

"What are you doing here?" Jay asked from the back of the room.

"What? You think girls can't game, 'dude'?" Ned snapped, accusingly. "Come over here and I'll shove this chair up your ass to prove it!"

"No, no," Jay held out his hands. "Gaming's about skills, you either got 'em or not. What I meant was, what are you doing 'here'?" and he indicated the room around us.

Ned scowled at Jay but answered. "The same as you I'd imagine, scavenging weapons and med supplies." She glared defiantly, daring us to question her motives.

"Where have you been or where did you come from?" I asked.

"I've been moving around the outlying villages, trying to level before I started going into bigger towns. This was my first time into a town like this." Having answered the first questions seemingly honestly I guessed Ned was sticking with that formula.

"Where are you holed up?" Indi demanded.

Ned shook her head. "I'm not answering that." Well, refusing to answer wasn't lying at least. "And I'm not telling you where I live IRL or my real name and I definitely won't 'send noods'." She spoke around her tongue, the words thick and mocking.

"Well, if you won't I'm not gonna." Indi bristled and Jay laid a hand on his arm.

I stepped between them, "You can't blame her for that, Indi. We all have a right to some confidentiality. Alright," I turned to Ned, "you've answered our questions, now I'll tell you all I'm prepared to, about us." I placed a hand against Indi's avatar's chest, ignoring Jay's sullen scowl.

"I'm LeZion, or Lex, this is Indéfini also known as Indi, and Joakim, or Jay if you prefer. Yes, we're here scavenging like you, but I'm sure there's enough to go around," I offered. "We're here in town; like you, I'd rather not say where, but-" I pulled my radio off my belt and stepped slowly forward, motioning Indi to pull back. "If you're on your own and get in trouble you can call us on this on the channel it's set to. We log on around this time every day."

Ned didn't drop the chair but let it hang at her side while she took the radio from my outstretched hand.

"Thank you." The gratitude was stilted and hesitant, but it was there.

"Well, we'll let you go about your way then." Jay cut in stiffly, "There's not much in the way of weapons up here, maybe try the gym?" Jay was encouraging Ned to go, I could tell and I wondered if Ned could too.

"Don't go to the gym," she offered. "That's where they put the bodies, I mean, before the place got overrun. It's full of Z's."

"Nice to know," I smiled in what I hoped was a disarming way.

"Well, I'll be on my way then." Ned put the chair down and walked cautiously between us and out of the room, obviously still wary and more than a little suspicious.

"Alright," Jay said quietly after a minute. "Let's find what we came here for." He moved to the main table and began sifting the papers that had fallen from the desks to litter the floor.

With Ned gone the tension in the room eased.

Rolling my shoulders I tugged at the biting elastic under my shirt. "I don't know how you cope!" I shot sullenly toward Indi.

With both hands and a grunt he pulled the soldier's corpse from the frame, setting it down beside the other two while snatching glances out the window. Shrugging he set to rifling the pockets.

"I don't," he drawled, still rummaging through the corpse's fatigue pockets. "I bind."

While poring over the big map with Jay, I voiced a thought I hoped we were sharing.

"What did you think of Ned, Jay?"

"I think maybe letting her go wasn't such a good idea," he replied darkly.

"What, you think we should've ganked her?" Indi sounded more than a little shocked, I know I was. "Then why let me give her the radio? You're not usually that way inclined Jay, are you okay?"

"Just second guessing, thinking of the practicalities," he murmured, still shuffling paper on the floor.

"Maybe, if this were a normal RPG I'd agree with you," I said hesitantly, "but it's not. And, as much as we're getting used to killing the zombies, I'd like to wait until we absolutely can't avoid it to kill an actual PC, I'm sure there'll be repercussions."

"They die, they respawn somewhere else. If we're gone by the time they get back, how're they going to track us?" Jay's tone dismissed the chance of any great threat to us.

"I'm not talking about the repercussions from them," I stated bluntly. "I'm talking about what it might do to us. Killing a human being is about the most traumatic thing you can do."

"But it's not a human being; it's a game character, an avatar," Jay protested.

"You know that and I know that, but do you think the game will let us keep thinking that?" I found Jay's stubborn pragmatism immensely frustrating given his flawed skill set. If he couldn't kill a zombie how could he expect us to kill PCs in cold blood?

"*Non*," Indi cut in, "we don't PVP unless we have to. Not even griefers, not until we know a little more, understood?"

Griefers, a particular subspecies of troll, I wasn't sure if I wouldn't enjoy a good beat down on one of those. Their addiction to endless drama and attention seeking had cost me many hours of my life I could never get back. It was just another mode of toxic existence I couldn't understand and wouldn't mind burning out of existence. I could dream.

"Fine," Jay huffed petulantly, "not even the griefers. We'll file that alongside our 'shared loot' and 'no kill-stealing' rules shall we?

We went back to searching in silence for a while and I gave some thought to Jay's words. With all I knew about the zombie horror genre and gamers in general, it was almost a given that we'd come into conflict with other players but, with all we'd learned about this game already (and the unresolved question of the coma patient still lurking at the back of my thoughts), I was starting to hope that the fiction was actually at odds with the 'reality'. People helped each other in disaster situations back in the real world (alright, *some* took advantage in the very worst ways) and this game was close enough to 'real' that I had to believe the same would be true here. It was certainly something to think about, but I couldn't bring myself to identify with Jay's cold pragmatism on this one.

From the floor, he rustled some papers. "The PvP argument aside, if she truly is on her own, maybe we might consider recruiting her. But first I want to be sure we aren't getting played, and I'd like to know what skills she has," Jay continued, clearly grimacing at his own weak skill set. "But it'll have to wait for now, I don't want to be out here and longer than necessary."

That was Jay all over. As a clan-leader I knew he'd orchestrated some really ballsy raids and actually pulled them off, but that was it, he'd planned them, laid out the sequence of events, time-frame and run the numbers. Going off-mission, getting distracted, it wasn't Jay's style. A new objective, like recruiting Ned, was something to be thought through.

Working from the big map, and a couple of pages I found strewn on the floor, I managed to piece together what I thought was a promising lead.

"Come and look at this," I beckoned to the others. "So, it looks like the military was co-ordinating out of a base here," I pointed on the map. "From what I can piece together, we're over here, about twenty miles away."

Jay looked over my evidence.

"I think you're right," he mumbled thoughtfully.

"There are a couple of big towns between here and there,"

"And who knows what else?" I muttered darkly.

"But," Indi continued, ignoring me. "We can bypass them if we stick to the main roads." He traced routes on the map to illustrate.

"Alright," Jay nodded before indicating the corpses. "What did you find on the bodies?" he asked.

"Couple of empty pistols, combat knives, a wad of orders and protocols and…" Indi flourished a small white object, "this."

"What is it?" I asked.

"A key card maybe?" Jay mused, taking the plastic swipe card with photo ID on the front from Indi's thick fingers. "Where'd you find it?"

Indi thumbed over his shoulder. "The body in the window is sporting captain's pips, I thought this might be useful."

"What's the name on it?"

Indi beamed. "Pisarev."

"Score!" Jay smiled and straightened up, glancing around. "Let's take the map and anything else that looks authoritative. We'll swing through the yard and see if there are any more medical supplies, part kits and such, and then we'll go car shopping."

I realised as we were leaving that some of the classrooms actually had first aid kits mounted conveniently just inside the doors. We already had the one I'd put together, so we grabbed a couple more, and then I filled out the blanks by salvaging what I could on the way through.

It was as easy as popping my head in the door and grabbing the kit from the wall, any zombies inside barely had time to look around before I'd ducked back out.

I left the thought in my head unspoken, that there *must* be some kind of armoury or ammo store around here somewhere, but the sky was darkening and the school buildings seemed to be crowding in around me. I didn't want to hang around or go rummaging any deeper into the building's guts.

We decided to head roughly north. It meant venturing further away from the supermarket, but since Indi had come from that direction and a mob of Z's had followed him, it kinda made sense that there wouldn't be so many around (I mean, they *might* respawn, I didn't know.)

There was a graveyard to our right. In my mind I heard the mocking words '*they're coming to get you, Barbara!*' and was about to chuckle when I spotted a couple of figures making unsteady progress through the headstones. Shit, they really were.

Further down, we reached a left turn junction into a series of low bungalows and more two-story houses. The biggest problem I could see, was that I *could* see. The houses were spaced out and the hill rolled down and then rose again to peak maybe two-hundred yards away. What laughably passed for 'walls' around the properties were no more than two feet high, and any kinds of fencing topped out at maybe four.

On another offshoot road maybe fifty yards away and off to our right, I could make out a short parade of local shops, but as I looked around, I observed the scattered zombie stragglers the herd had left behind.

"Alright, cars in driveways. Quick and quiet, let's go!" Jay hissed and we started forward down the road. We had plenty to choose from, hatchbacks, saloons, a few people carriers here and there. I disregarded anything that was stopped in the road, I didn't expect there would be fuel, or even keys left in them. Maybe if I saw something that really suited our purposes I'd look, but I wasn't hopeful.

The roll of the landscape dropped and the buildings reduced visual range as we walked. We wouldn't see a horde shambling up ahead until we crested the next rise, and if that happened we'd be that much closer to it before we saw it.

It was eerily quiet, at any moment I expected the dramatic score of a climax event to kick in. All I got was a few bird calls and the occasional sussurence of the rain or the wind or from the throats of the few zombies we crept silently past. I realised then how much I'd relied on music to distance myself from the horror in games and movies. Real life didn't have a soundtrack, but neither did *Rendered Flesh* it seemed.

Chapter 13

"Over there," Indi stopped short, and pointed.

Further ahead, sitting on a short drive, in front of a small two-story was a large, silver truck. I could make out four doors, and the back was covered with one of those solid but removable roofs you sometimes got. I wasn't sure of the make, but it looked to be exactly what we were looking for.

I could also clearly see a dozen or more zombies between us and it.

We hunkered down behind an abandoned car.

Jay turned to us, speaking quietly. "Okay, here's what we do. Lex, you take Indi through the gardens, get into the house from the back and find the keys. I'll backtrack a little way and try to create a diversion on one of these side roads, then loop around and meet you back here."

"Why don't I go cause the diversion?" I asked.

"Because you have the Auto skill and Driver trait. Until we get a little more time to experiment, I don't want to mess around with that."

His reply didn't make me any happier. "But I don't drive."

"Maybe not IRL, but here that doesn't matter. You'll be fine," he reassured me.

Indi tossed his chin toward Jay. "Why don't I go with you?"

Jay shook his head. "If things go wrong, I'd rather you were with Lex. Anyway, it's time I started pulling my weight around here."

"What kind of distraction do you have planned?" I asked, relenting on the point of who should go where.

"I'll try and set off a car-alarm or, failing that, I'll put something through one of those store-fronts and hope they have alarms," he replied evenly. "Then I'll cut through the gardens myself to get back to the road."

"I'm not sure," I said, uncertainly.

"Well I am," Jay insisted, indicating his radio, "Let me know when you find the keys and I'll bring the noise."

With that he hurried off. A heavy hand landed on my shoulder.

"Let's go," Indi instructed, and with a sharp nod I followed.

We darted down the side of the nearest house, through a flimsy side gate that hung conveniently open, and into a back garden. Plastic play furniture littered the small lawn, and the wooden panel fence across from us hung, as if someone had already forced their way, or been forced through it.

I clambered through the gap and glanced left and right. Not far from the broken fence, a trail of blood led through an open slide-door into the house. I edged forward. Despite trying not to look into the darkened living room, I caught a glimpse of a figure crouched over a corpse. The shoulders jerked rhythmically as the thing ate. I eased the sliding door shut as carefully as I could.

> **You have unlocked the Stealthy skill. Select now
> and it will be added after a rest period.**
> Yes/No

I pulled back against the wall, out of sight. If I dismissed the message, would I get the chance to select the skill later? I made a snap decision, indicated '*Yes*' and dismissed the message.

"Everything okay?" Indi asked.

"Yeah, just unlocked a new trait," I replied. "Let's go."

The next fence was intact so I hurried across the lawn and, trusting to my stats, vaulted into the next garden.

I hit the grass and rolled forward, clearing the way for Indi.

My friend, after some huffing and muttered complaints, dropped heavily onto the grass behind me.

"Graceful," I commented wryly.

He came awkwardly to his feet. "Screw you."

"You wish."

"Oh, we're back to that, huh?" he winked.

"Later," I replied. "Two more gardens."

We managed it without Indi bringing down any fences or making too much noise and, finally, we stood in the back garden of the house we wanted. I checked the windows, seeing a kitchen and living room, but nothing moving inside.

I tried the backdoor. It opened into the kitchen. I could smell corruption in the room, but nothing seemed out of place.

Indi followed me in and I raised a finger to my lips. I listened intently for any sounds of movement in the house. I didn't hear anything.

I held out a hand to Indi. "Give me the radio."

Clicking the 'call' button I spoke softly. "Jay, we're in the house. Just need to find the keys."

"Ready to go on your word," Jay replied in a whisper.

"Where do we look?" Indi asked.

"I'll look, you make sure nothing jumps me."

The kitchen door led to a small hallway, with the stairs to the first floor. Coats hung on hooks beside the front door. My wrist pulsed softly.

I checked the front windowsill first, looking for a bowl for keys. Finding nothing, I started searching the coat pockets.

A floorboard creaked upstairs and I froze. Indi caught my eye and tilted his head to indicate upstairs. I nodded and went back to the coats, while he slowly climbed the stairs.

Letting my friend go into danger while I rifled pockets didn't seem right. It nagged at my concentration, but I pushed on. Indi, or at least his avatar, was big enough to handle himself.

The pockets turned up empty, so I reluctantly went into the living room that ran from the front to the back of the house. The room was turned over. 'Signs of a struggle', they called it in police dramas. I let my eyes wander among the overturned furniture, the pictures and ornaments strewn on the carpet.

I heard muffled impacts coming from upstairs, heavy footfalls and impacts of bodies against furniture. Indi *was* in danger.

Should I go up? Lend a hand?

Just then, my eyes alighted on an overturned bowl, coins and other pocket debris scattered on the carpet beside it, and, in among them, a ring of keys and a car key fob. I let my hand hover over it just a second, and my patience was rewarded with a little identifier tag:

Car Keys

I gave a quiet cry of victory and snatched them up before heading to the foot of the stairs. From the floor above I heard a loud splintering of wood and a vocal curse from Indi.

I ran up the stairs and into the main bedroom just as Indi, half in the broken doors of a fitted wardrobe, heaved a dead zombie off of himself.

"You okay?" I asked anxiously.

"Yeah," Indi huffed. "I levelled."

I offered a hand and dragged him from the debris before holding up the keys.

"Are those the right ones?" Indi asked.

"Let's see," I replied, and headed to the front window.

I pressed the button on the fob and the lights of the truck flashed.

I smiled at Indi. "Jay, we're good to go," I said into the radio.

"Alright, see you at the rendezvous," Jay's voice came back, crackling with static.

We headed back down the stairs, although too far away to hear the crash of glass, the shrill sound of the shop alarm carried over the houses, signalling that Jay had done his part. The zombies in the street came alive and lurched away toward the noise.

I reached for the door handle. Indi laid down his massive paw over my hand.

"Wait," he said, eyes locked on the shambling figures.

I tugged at the door but Indi's hand wouldn't budge. "C'mon, the longer we leave it the more risk to Jay."

"We don't want them coming back on us either," he said coolly.

Indi held the door closed for another, eternity-spanning moment before withdrawing his hand. Finally he nodded. "Okay, go."

I yanked the door open and made for the car. Twilight was well on its way by now, the first time I'd seen it in-game, and I momentarily wondered what time it was in the real world. Dismissing the thought I hopped into the driver's seat:

> **Driver Trait, vehicle durability and handling increased 12.5%**

I was slightly surprised by the message and accompanying green bar that sprang into being over the steering wheel, the durability bar I assumed? But I shook it off as the words faded out and shoved the key in the ignition.

Much as I was anxious to get back to Jay, I didn't want to undo his good work. Tentatively I held the key. Although I didn't consciously command it, one foot fully depressed the left pedal, I near panicked, expecting the engine to race. My right foot applied a little pressure to the outermost pedal and my hand automatically turned the key. The engine rumbled quietly to life, rev's low and I let out a relieved breath. Without understanding fully how I was doing it, I pulled the truck gently out of the drive, engine purring softly, and eased it up the road. It was a strange experience. Most of the games I played, if they had a driving feature, you mashed the accelerator button and just steered or braked as required. This was a whole other game. I was clutching and shifting, not fully understanding what I was doing, but at least at this low speed, I was doing it on instinct or, more likely, the game was 'filling in' for my lack of practical knowledge.

I pulled up to the car where we were supposed to meet Jay.

"He's not here," Indi said, glancing around.

"So," I asked, kinda redundantly, "where is he?"

Indi pointed ahead. "Over there!" At first I thought a zombie had just pitched over one of the low walls but, as the figure pulled itself unsteadily to its feet, I recognized Jay's lanky avatar.

"It's Jay," Indi said.

"And he's hurt," I gasped and pulled the truck around the car, racing the engine just a little to get to our friend.

Jay stumbled, and I could see blood on his shirt as I drew up. Indi got out and threw an arm around Jay, dragging him into the back seat. Ahead of us, a couple of zombies fell over the same wall Jay had just crossed.

"Go, go!" Indi urged and I drove as fast as I dared away from the houses and their ex-occupants.

As I turned onto the school road, Jay grunted. "Slow down, we don't want... the attention."

"He's bleeding," Indi snapped and I risked a glance over my shoulder.

"Penetrating abdominal wound," I said aloud without thinking.

"So what do I do?"

"Apply pressure, I'll look when we get back to the supermarket," I instructed in clipped, precise words. "What happened?" I asked over my shoulder.

"Zombie, hit me with a plank," Jay winced.

"What? Did it have nails in it?" I asked in disbelief.

"Yes."

In short order I pulled the truck around behind our current base, avoiding the car park entirely. I jumped out of the car and opened the door for Indi. As he helped Jay out from the back, I secured the vehicle.

"Lay him down by the gate," I ordered. As Indi lay Jay down, I looked at his wrist.

HLT			

The third bar was flashing, and failing.

I scooted under the gate and, taking charge of Jay's head and shoulders, dragged him under. He let out a shout of pain as we dragged him, but Indi crawled under behind him and we picked Jay up off the floor.

"Let's get upstairs," I commanded.

Jay fumbled weakly in his pocket. "Keys."

I unlocked the door and Indi carried Jay up into the cafeteria.

"Lay him on the pool table," I directed Indi, pulling my medkit from my hip.

Jay was down to one flashing bar.

Working quickly and, like the driving, not fully understanding everything I was doing, I cleaned, stitched and bound the seeping puncture wounds in Jay's abdomen. I topped my ministrations off by tipping a few tablets from the bottle of pills into him.

> **Health restored +10% for skill level**

I checked Jay's wrist again, two lousy bars. At level two, with a full (now mostly depleted) medkit, I could heal two lousy bars. So, the kit on its own was only a ten percent heal which meant I'd need level four (if the percent boost for skill was standard) to be able to restore to even half in similar situations in future. I'd need to factor in a boost to level nine if the game stuck to the ten percent per level template to get a player back to full, and that was assuming the game allowed skills to level that high at all.

"Good job, Lex." Indi laid a bloodstained hand on my shoulder as I ran the numbers in my head.

"Was it?" I grunted.

"Think about it. If it were me, it'd probably only stabilise him," he shrugged.

I shook my head. "The kit itself is a ten percent heal. Hey Jay, how do you feel?" I asked.

"Hurts like hell," he winced. "Seriously, even after what we've experienced, part of me didn't believe it, but it really hurts."

"And you didn't get bit?" I asked.

"No, no. Just this," Jay gestured to his midriff. "If it's okay by you guys, I'm going to log off while the avatar heals up."

"Sure," I nodded, "and Jay? Good job."

"Thanks." He gave me a less than genuine grin, and, with a motion of his hand on his wrist, lay back as if sleeping.

"What about you, Lex? Are you logging out?" Indi asked.

I gave it some thought.

"Not just yet," I replied quietly. "Come on, let's get you cleaned up."

In the bathroom, I ran a sink of warm water. I'd already looted a couple of towels and some shower gel. A gentle noise from Indi as he took off his shirt caught my attention.

"Are you hurt?" I asked.

"Just a little sore. I went through a wardrobe unless you hadn't noticed," he said playfully.

"I had." I laid my hands on Indi's avatar's broad shoulders, and turned them this way and that. I took the bottom of his undershirt and lifted that over his head too.

I trailed my hands over his skin. "A few cuts and scrapes, nothing to worry about," I reassured him.

Indi leaned over the sink with a sigh and I took a cloth and cleaned the scrapes.

"Is that okay?" I asked, my voice low.

"It's amazing," Indi breathed. "You wouldn't know it's a game."

I tossed the cloth into the sink and stepped in close behind him. "Speaking of games," I murmured, letting my hands wander around to caress the skin of Indi's chest. The short coarse hairs tickled my palms.

> **Notice, you are initiating sexual activity. Both players must be consenting.**
> **Continue Yes/No?**

I quickly indicated yes and waited a moment until Indi did the same.

Indi's back stiffened briefly as I ran a fingertip around a nipple. I let out a gentle breath across the nape of his neck.

"What are we doing?" Indi sighed huskily.

"Oh, you didn't know?" I teased and let my hands fall lower, tugging at the belt and buttons on my friend's jeans.

"Are you sure?" Indi's voice came out in a breathy rush.

"I checked 'yes' didn't I? And how often do you get a chance like this?" I replied and thrust both hands into Indi's shorts. "Oh!" I started.

"What did I say?" Indi chuckled. "*C'est magnifique,*"

I let my hands linger a moment, feeling Indi's shuddering breaths through my own chest.

After a moment, Indi pushed gently away from the sinks and turned around. Letting me keep one hand in the front of his pants, he took my other and held it to his chest, slipping his other hand around to the base of my spine.

"Just, once more, for me. Tell me why?"

"Why not?" I smirked. "We're friends, we're in a game, and we've got this once in a life-time opportunity. No strings and no regrets."

"Just because we're not really here, doesn't mean we're not really here, *n'est ce pas?*"

"What do you mean?"

"I mean, whether or not this is 'just a game', the part of us that really counts *is* in here with us."

"Is that a 'no'?" I asked, letting my hand tense a moment.

Indi stiffened and let out an unsteady breath.

"*Non*, but, just because I only just got one of these, doesn't mean I'm going to let it do all my thinking for me."

I leaned into Indi's chest as I spoke.

"I know what I'm doing, and I know what I'm asking. The only question is, what's your answer?"

With barely a grunt of effort, Indi wrapped strong arms around my avatar and lifted me, turning as he did, to sit me on the counter.

"You want an answer?" he drawled, pouring his accent over the words like syrup.

With a deft motion and a dramatic flourish, Indi whipped my slacks and shoes off my legs.

"*Et voilà!*"

Chapter 14

Any joy I'd felt about the night before faded with the coming of the morning after.

In the kitchen, the news was showing election coverage, and the smug, self-satisfied smirk on the face of the interviewee for the incumbent party made me want to vomit. The impassioned statements of the opposition rep were met with pompous derision and the interviewer's feeble jokes. I mean, it wasn't even as if it mattered. The election would be rigged, the corporate agenda would dictate the result, and the morally devoid puppets who sold their souls would take the helm as they were directed. They didn't even take pains to hide it from us anymore.

I kept my head down as I hurried, late, to work.

I passed windows with posters urging people to vote for the nationalist, isolationist, racist parties and worse, the established capitalist elite. I heard snippets of conversation reciting the lies and false promises that had been rolled out again and again. In the face of the evidence, I wondered how people could so willingly swallow such flagrant deception, and the abuse of power it actually promised. Anger boiled in my stomach and quickened my steps.

When I finally hurried through the door into the shop my boss was waiting.

"You're late," she announced without malice.

"Sorry." I offered no explanation or excuse.

Looking up from the till screen she frowned, concerned. "Are you okay? You look tired."

I hung my coat in the staff room calling back. "Stuff at home."

"Well," she offered me a brief, sheepish smile, "I'm here if you need to talk but try to be on time, okay?"

I made a noncommittal noise and dropped my apron over my head.

Throughout my shift, I watched the people who took down the newspapers from the rack near the counter. I watched for those who picked the establishment press, headlines victimising and demonising immigrants, socialists and people on welfare. Watching them consume the lies like so much rotten carrion. The hate, the bias, the racism and intolerance spread like a virus from those cheap, flimsy pages, and it galled me that the chain kept them. Of course, it was a business; people expected papers, and head office probably got a nice incentive from the presses themselves.

I tried to maintain my 'service face', but the mask was cracked and slipping.

My shift ended and my manager stopped me in the backroom as I collected my things.

"You're not yourself today, what's up? "she rested on the doorframe, folding her arms casually.

I snorted a breath through my nose. "You really want to know?"

She thought for a moment. "If you want to tell me," she replied eventually.

"I'm tired of being taken advantage of," I stated bluntly.

To her credit, my boss stayed calm. "You think we take advantage of you here?"

I shook my head. "Only in so much as society encourages it. No, I'm tired of the system, the patriarchal, capitalist hegemony. Those born into money stay there, and play the rest of us against each other. Even here, I can feel customers judging me for being 'just' a barista. For one, if I wanted to be a barista, what's wrong with that, and what right have they to judge? For two, I have a degree for chrissake, and I can't get work in my field because I'm 'overqualified' for entry level positions and don't have the 'experience' for roles I'm qualified for. I'm going nowhere, and the one percent are steering the world down darker and darker paths to hide the extremes they're going to as they leech more and more so-called wealth," I finished hotly.

Taking a deep, thoughtful breath, my boss gave me an appraising look.

"Okay, you've got tomorrow off anyway. Take Friday and Saturday too. I'll work the rota, maybe get you a couple of make-up shifts next week."

I started to object but she held up a hand.

114

"Look, you're a smart kid. Take the time and work it out. Throw out a few applications or whatever, exercise some self-care, it's both big and clever. I don't want to see you spiral because of stress."

"Thank you," I muttered softly.

"Go home, I'll see you Sunday."

Kid? I thought as I walked out. My manager was five years older than me at most.

When I hopped off the bus, there was a police car and ambulance outside a house down the street. One of my neighbours, a middle aged lady I knew as Ezzy was standing at her door, cup of tea in hand.

"What happened?" I asked, stopping to stand beside her.

"Mr Nadkarni and his family, a couple of thugs forced the door and beat him. It sounded awful."

"What?" I said, taken aback. "Mr Nadkarni who runs the chippie?" I asked in disbelief, "Why?" The man was well known and liked around this part of town as far as I knew.

"Like I told the police when I called them," Ezzy sighed sadly, "they knocked on the door, two of them. White lads, those ones who keep hassling you, I saw that much. They shoved it in when he opened it, then there was a lot of crashing and shouting. They ran away while I was on the phone to the Bill, doesn't look like they took anything."

"What were they shouting?" I asked, almost not wanting to hear it.

Ezzy took a deep breath.

"They were calling him a 'Paki' and a 'black bastard', they told him to 'go home'." Ezzy was still staring across the road as the paramedics wheeled a stretcher out, and I heard the faint crack in her voice when she next spoke. "He was born in Basildon, Lex. He's lived in this street longer than I have."

I just watched the dark square of the open door across the road. For a moment, I thought I saw sallow skin, sunken eyes and a yawning maw, but it resolved into another police officer coming out. I watched and felt the turn of the world stutter under my feet, felt the change in the air as an act of mindless hate tainted my street, my home.

I gritted my teeth as angry bile rose in my throat, and went to my door, my room, to distance myself from its stain.

"Everybody thinks of changing humanity, and nobody thinks of changing himself."
— Mikhail Bakunin

Stealth Lvl 1 applied

"I want you to kill me," Jay stated simply.

I didn't even try to hide the shock in my voice. "You what?"

"I don't want to be a burden anymore. If you kill me I can respawn with a new build. Maybe I'll get lucky."

"You've been lucky enough to land in this town. On this server!" I railed, "You might not get so lucky again."

"It's a risk, I'll grant you, but *'den som väntar på något gott, väntar alltid för länge'.*"

"And what does that mean?" I demanded.

"If you wait for something good, you always wait too long," Jay shrugged. "We can figure out how I make my way back between sessions."

"So, what? We're supposed to cave your dumb head in with a hammer? Or maybe we should smother you after you log out?"

"Oh no," Jay protested. "I want to be logged in for it. It'll be an educational experience for us all to know what it's like to die."

I sighed, frustrated. "Indi, will you talk some sense into this idiot?"

"And say what?" Indi shrugged. "On the one hand, he wants a new build and there's no 'start new character' option, so this seems the only way. On the other, there's no telling where he'll end up *if* we go through with it. Also there's the question of whether it's a group call or is it Jay's decision alone to make?"

"Bollocks to this!" I snapped and, snatching up my hammer, I headed to the door.

"Where are you going?" Jay asked.

I spun, angrily brandishing the repurposed tool at him. "I need to blow off steam, and we *still* need some better weapons." I shook the hammer at Indi, "Don't let him do anything stupid while I'm gone."

"Never go alone, that's the rule," Indi protested.

"I can't just sit here listening to this!" I snarled savagely and gestured toward Jay. "Besides, I need the practice."

"Just be careful," Indi warned.

116

I hit the yard. The sky was still grey and the concrete wet. I vaulted the gate and took a look around. Apart from the remains of our friend with the chainsaw, I was seemingly alone. Unlike the movies, where stricken corpses lay intact and slowly bleaching in the sun, this one was broken and scattered, like the kills in documentaries of wild dogs or big cats on the savannah. I shuddered as the ghosts of cold fingers tugged at my chest, and set off at a jog around our truck and away down the road. I was sick of this town, these streets, these *people*.

No, not people, *zombies*. But zombies I could deal with. You could change a zombie's mind with a quick blow to the head. Admittedly you changed it from 'on' to 'off', but that was the idea anyway. People were a whole other level of complexity.

I'd thought I could escape the rampant stupidity of the real world, but no. Jay wanted a respawn and wanted us to, to *euthanize* him to achieve it.

Rather than head to the main street, I took a wider back road that ran parallel. On my right, a big, industrial looking complex loomed, and on the left was parking and the backs of the pubs and shops from the main drag.

I didn't bother to hide, and the dead that I dodged past started the slow shamble behind me.

I needed a hardware store or a sports shop at the least. Knives and hammers were short and weapons of last resort. I wanted something longer, heavier or, at the outside, a projectile weapon, a bow or crossbow.

I was angry and frustrated, but I wasn't going to let that turn me stupid. Ahead I saw a sign for hardware. It was something at least, but by the time I drew parallel, I realised I'd already passed the car park entry fifty yards back. The pack I was drawing along behind me was already there, but the wall was low and, negotiating the ornamental bushes, I hopped it and approached the back of the shop.

A zombie was standing among the cars ahead of me. Steeling myself, I took a couple of quick steps and shoved the thing. It sprawled over the bonnet of a car, and I took the hammer vigorously to the back of its skull.

As the body slipped off the car, I glanced behind to see the group following me coming into the parking area. Ahead of me, another zombie stumbled through the jammed automatic door, clawing and snarling.

I ran forward, reaching out to grasp the newcomer by the collar, keeping it at arm's reach as I delivered a downward blow with my weapon. I heard the skull crack, but the zombie didn't even flinch. Shifting my feet to keep steady as its fingernails caught on my clothes, I turned the hammer in my hand to present the claw side and swung that down. The metal bit deep and, letting go of the collar I let the thing lurch forward, dragging it down with the hammer. It stumbled and fell, the handle hit the tarmac and jerked the head back awkwardly. A quick stamp of my foot finished breaking the thing's neck.

I checked my wrist.

STM	████████████████████

HLT	██████████████████████

STR	███

The top bar of my health indicator was flashing, I needed to eat, but only one bar of stress. Maybe the anger was helping me cope.

I slipped quickly into the shop. It wasn't large, and I could look right out onto the main street, though admittedly I only got a limited view of it. The shelves were thrown over. A quick check showed me that batteries, torches, and anything first aid related was already gone. I kicked through scattered boxes of screws and fixings and, under the clutter of boxes, I scored.

I picked up the axe that had been concealed by the mess. It wasn't too heavy, not like I'd expected, as I hefted it for a moment. I'd left the hammer in the zombie in the car park. That was a habit I was going to have to kick… so I scanned for a back-up.

Hanging among the gardening tools I found a short-handled blade that curved to an angle at the end, maybe a foot long. It said it was a 'brush hook', but it looked like a weapon to me, and one that might help account for my inability to deliver a clean kill-shot, so I took it and stuck it through my belt. I'd brought my backpack with a couple of bottles of water. My medpack was on my belt and my jet lighter and cigarettes in my pocket, just in case. The pack had six slots, so I liberated a replacement hammer and a longish crowbar that I found, securing them so they wouldn't rattle about too much.

As I stowed the gear, my mind was spinning. People in authority had been blaming games, movies and music cultures for breeding violence for decades, all the while fostering division among nationalities, cultures, economic classes and sexual orientations and identities as a means to retain power.

Killing the zombies, the bots in the game, didn't *make* me want to hurt the men who'd attacked Mr Nadkarni. Their own actions, their ignorance and bigotry, their callous disregard for an innocent who worked hard to provide for his family made me want to hurt them. I wanted to grab them and shake them and teach them that their enemy wasn't people with different coloured skin or beliefs or ways, it was the people who weighed human life in pounds and pence, dollars and cents. The game didn't make me violent; it offered me an outlet for those fleeting impulses.

Mindful of the zombies coming up behind me, I slipped the pack back on and headed to the front of the store. The door glass was shattered and crunched underfoot as I edged closer. The main street was surprisingly clear, but down by the little grocery shop, I spotted movement.

I hesitated.

A slight figure in a hooded jacket came out the now broken front door, skirted the shop fronts and crept into the alley; Ned.

I paused a second longer and then set out quickly across the street and into the alley.

Making an effort to keep my own footsteps light I hurried along, listening for the sound of retreating footfalls.

At the far end I slowed and moved forward cautiously, sweeping my eyes from left to right until I caught a slight movement. Ned was hurrying up the hill toward the church. The road was wide and clear, not a lot of cover beyond a few cars, so I took a chance and sprinted for the vehicles.

I couldn't really explain why, aside from morbid curiosity, I was following our 'neighbour', but it kept me away from Jay's momentary madness, so I indulged.

At the top of the hill, Ned crossed the road into a narrow street lined with tight-packed, terraced houses.

I didn't like it, not one bit. The road was quite narrow, no gardens and not much in the way of alleys to duck into. Really the only way in or out of the street was from either end, or through one of the houses themselves. If it was an ambush, or if the dead closed off either end, I was probably done for, but some part of me wanted to see if Ned was on the up and up. If I could bring another player into our group, maybe Jay would have second thoughts about respawning. But first I needed a better idea of who Ned was.

Chapter 15

I couldn't stay out in the open for long. I'd dropped a bar on my health score and stupidly hadn't brought any food items with me. There was also the risk of drawing unwanted attention, so I decided to play the 'scavenger' angle, checking the houses on the opposite side of the road from Ned's hole-up, and see if I could draw her out. I considered trying the radio to tell Indi and Jay what I was doing, but decided against making any more noise than I had to on this quiet, empty street. Plus, Ned had one of our radios. My ploy would never work if I told Ned herself what I was up to.

I went door to door, gently trying the handles. I certainly wasn't going to try forcing any locked doors on my own, but I could see at least one door up ahead that was open, and then I'd have no excuse to stay out in the street.

By the time I reached it, there was still no sign of Ned, but I started to notice troubling details. The door hadn't simply been left open. It had been broken open, the deadbolt ripped from the jamb. I went carefully into the house, stepping over two double-dead zombies in the hall. I listened for any sounds of habitation, living or otherwise, and crept stealthily forward to glance into the living room. The lower floor was trashed, all the doors open and furniture and belongings cast about as if there'd been a big fight. But there were other, more troubling details. Another pair of ravaged, gutted and mostly masticated bodies lay on the living room floor but these corpses gave me pause.

By each one lay a pack and a weapon. Survivors then, or, more accurately, players' avatars. Laid out with their gear in easy reach, but why? Leaving the morbid scene, I went into the kitchen. The back door was still locked, but the signs of the struggle and accompanying bloodstains continued into the room. From the look of it at least one of the players' remains had been dragged from the kitchen to the living room. I had an uneasy feeling, like I was in a graveyard or tomb, a place of remembrance. I had to give myself a shake to remind myself why I was here. Looking around I checked my options. The fridge was right out; no way was I opening that, so instead I started a gentle rummage of the cupboards. I easily located a tin of baked beans. The pantry cupboard was nearly fully stocked. I took the tin and a can opener from the kitchen side and stood, facing the open door as I worked the mechanism. I ate straight from the tin with a fork taken from a drawer. The fact I could taste the beans was still something of a wonder to me, and, having finished my snack, I set about assembling any other canned foods on the side.

"What are you doing here?"

Ned's stealth skill must be higher than mine because I hadn't detected her approach even though I'd been half listening for it.

I turned, careful not to seem too surprised by her appearance. "Foraging," I answered carefully.

"Well don't," she stepped into the kitchen, squaring up some of the tins on the side. "This is my patch."

"Oh, I'm sorry. I didn't realise," I lied. My axe was on the counter, but Ned hadn't given me any reason to think I was in danger, yet.

"Well, now you do."

"I'll be off then," I stated casually, and, leaving the food items, reached carefully for the axe.

Ned watched me closely, mirroring my movement around the room, keeping the kitchen table between us.

"Not a strong position if you ask me," I commented absently. "Limited fields of vision, restricted access in or out. Doesn't seem like a spot an experienced gamer would hole-up."

Ned's eyes narrowed. "Good thing I didn't ask you then."

She was certainly being more careful with her answers but then, I was in her house, figuratively speaking.

"Oh come on, Ned," I smiled disarmingly, trying to ease the tension. "You wouldn't be in this game if you didn't know what you were doing, so why stay in this death-trap?"

"I don't stay here, I'm across the road," she snapped and then flinched as she realised she'd said more than she'd meant to.

"Well, why don't you come with me?" I replied quickly, glossing over her slip.

"I... I can't," she admitted finally.

122

Trying not to seem too eager I pressed her. "Why not?"

She folded her arms, closing herself off from me with the gesture. "I'm waiting for some friends, alright; happy now?"

Something in the way she said it didn't sound right, there was almost a fearful note in the words.

"Ned," I said quietly. "Are you alright?"

She turned her head, fixing me with her dark, penetrating eyes. Ned watched me, more intently now than when I'd picked up the axe. "Why should you care?"

"If I'm going to leave you around here, I just want to be sure you're gonna be okay," I stated, matter-of-factly. "I mean, at least tell me what happened. Where are your friends, when are they coming back?"

Ned's mask of bravado slipped momentarily and she hugged herself as her chin dipped to her chest.

Her reply was little more than a whisper. "I don't know,"

"Ned, what happened?" I asked, more insistently.

She drew in on herself until, with a frustrated toss of her head the barriers came down and the words poured out in a tide. "We'd been playing a couple of days, it was all so amazing. The full immersion, right? And we came here to scavenge. We were going to make a base here in town, stop messing about in the villages, but we got trapped in this street by mobs, then we got trapped in this house, and then they got Richie and he just screamed and screamed, so I..."

"You what, Ned?" I prompted gently.

"I ran upstairs and hid, okay?" Tears of defiance were in her eyes now, daring me to judge her. "I hid in a wardrobe while they ate Stephan too."

"Okay," I nodded, not making a move. "What happened next?"

"I... I logged out, thought I'd catch them on face-time and say sorry and we'd start again but..." the words tailed off into rough silence.

"But what?"

"But I haven't seen them online since." She admitted in a breathy, scared whisper. "I thought maybe they were ghosting me because I ran away, but I've messaged and called and watched their Facebook, their Twitter, Instagram, nothing. They haven't come up since, so I come back in, at the same time as we gamed to see if they come back for their stuff."

A sick feeling started a cold crawl through my stomach. "When were you attacked?" I asked.

She let out a shuddering breath. "Three... three days ago," she said softly, turning her back to me.

There was no reason for me to believe that the mob that attacked Ned and her crew had anything to do with the mob that had followed Indi and myself down from the school when we first started. They might have already killed Richie and Stephan by then, and spotted Indi heading for the school as a result. But, for some reason I couldn't help but feel guilty and more than a little sick. It just made me want to leave the town even more. It also made me think again of mum's coma case and I made a mental note to dig deeper.

"Look, Ned," I said gently, "you've got the radio, you can call my group if you get in trouble, but maybe you should take some time out. Y'know?"

She shook her head. "I can't, we started playing to win. I've got to win, for them."

So, Ned and her friends had known about the 'prize' too.

"Well, you won't win if you stay here and, if you get caught on your own..." I let that hang.

The look she gave me was still tinged with suspicion as her eyes glistened with burgeoning tears. "You want me to join you?" Ned replied eventually.

"I want you to think about it," I said evenly. "Now, I've got to get back to my friends before they get worried."

Ned stood aside from the door.

"Go, I'll think about it," she assured me as I left.

I slipped under the gate and made my way back into the supermarket. Upstairs I heard voices coming from the manager's office and headed that way.

"What's going on?" I asked as I stepped inside and shrugged off my pack.

Indi shot a relieved glance my way, "Jay's trying to hack the game," he stated bluntly. Absently I held out the axe to him.

"For me?" he grinned, raising a hand to his chest in a gesture of coquettish surprise. "You shouldn't have. *Merci-beaucoup.*"

But I wasn't paying Indi's theatrics any attention as I leaned in to take a look over Jay's hunched shoulders. The office computers were a non-starter, but he'd rigged a keyboard to a smart-phone and was tapping away industriously.

"Why are you trying to hack the game, Jay? And shouldn't you be outside to look at the code?"

Eyes glued to the screen, paying me the barest of attention, he pushed non-existent glasses up his nose, a carry-over tic from his real body.

"Firstly, because I'm interested. I want to know how they're achieving total immersion and sensory feedback. Secondly, since I struck out with the actual gateway programme IRL, I figured I might be able to access the programmer's console from within, like the drop down in other games."

"So, you're looking at the internet?"

"Not 'inter', 'intra'. The game's own internal intranet."

I sighed, an exaggerated and exhausted sound. "Trying to IDDQD your way to a better build? You know we don't cheat, Jay."

"IDDQD wasn't a cheat; it was a programmer's shortcut," Jay sniffed. "And no, I'm exercising the IRL skills I have to get a better idea of what's going on. Call it 'professional curiosity'. What have you been doing?"

"Well, I ran into Ned," I stated. "In that I spotted her and followed her to her base camp."

"That's cool, what'd you learn?" Jay asked distractedly.

"That she started playing with two friends a little before we did, and that a couple of days ago her group was attacked. Her friends got ganked by Z's, and she hasn't seen them since."

"Maybe they got shunted to another server?" Indi noted pointedly, laying a hand firmly on Jay's shoulder and giving it a shake. "Aren't you glad we didn't agree to kill you now, Jay?"

I bit my lip anxiously, "It's not just that, she hasn't seen them at all. In game or out."

Jay stopped typing and turned slowly in his chair to face me, Indi too.

"You're not suggesting..." Jay started slowly.

"That the game, what? Killed them?" Indi joked in evident disbelief.

I had a flash recollection of my mum poring over the case file in the kitchen the previous night.

"I don't know, maybe?" I shrugged. "I mean, at the least they're suffering mentally from the trauma. Maybe they'll come back in another day or two, I don't know. I just think we really ought to be sure this prize-money is worth the possible risks."

On the table the radio squawked to life.

"Let me in, someone let me in!"

It was Ned, and the anxiousness on her voice bordered on fear.

The three of us shared a look before we hurried down the stairs to the loading dock. Indi unlocked the outer door and tried to ease it a crack but Ned, despite the difference in size, barged inside, slamming the door behind her and leaning on it.

"We've got to go! We've got to go now!"

"What the hell?" Indi challenged, the axe, held loosely in hand, coming up to ready.

"How did you find us?" I demanded.

Ned waved frantically for us to move. "I followed you, alright? You followed me so I followed you, now come on!"

"What's this all about?" Jay said a note of uncertainty in his voice. Surreptitiously he slipped the phone into his pocket.

"Geeks, Z's, whatever you want to call them, hundreds of them headed this way!" Ned's breathing was ragged and the cricket bat she held trembled visibly in her hand, she was pumped full of adrenaline.

Jay's face paled as he looked up at Indi and me. The three of us, Ned in tow, hurried to the cafeteria since its windows had the best view of the approaching roads.

"I can't see anything," Indi stated as Ned stood behind us, obviously agitated, but then, "*Merde!*"

We could see three approaches to the back of our supermarket base, the hill road where our chainsaw-wielding friend had met his grisly fate, the road that ran parallel to the high street where I'd gone for my little recon, and the little road leading to the shopping precinct which we'd traversed on our first day. All of them joined at a little junction and all of them were full of zombies headed slowly our way.

"Get the maps, get the bug-out bags and get the weapons." Indi's voice carried not a hint of a tremor. "We're leaving."

My breath caught in my throat.

"Maybe we can ride it out?" Jay suggested anxiously.

"Not a chance, we have to go!" Ned pleaded.

I could feel my wrist throbbing again as my stress bar rose but I couldn't tear my eyes from the rolling tide of flesh. "But they're coming in from the east, we need to go east."

"We'll backtrack west and find a way around. We're going, end of discussion." Indi's hard tone brooked no opposition.

I knew he was right, if the Z's got into the front car park in those numbers they'd flood in through the shattered doors and fill this place to capacity. No door would hold them out under such pressure. Indi was right, but I didn't want to be out there either.

"I'll take Ned and get the bags," I said, trying to sound decisive, but it just came out scared.

Indi's voice sounded unnaturally calm given the situation. "Meet us in the loading bay," he instructed, turning to our map-table to gather up the more important documents.

I beckoned Ned, "Come with me." I took the keys from Jay's unresisting hand and led the way to the stairs.

"What've you got on you?" I asked curtly, still trying to stay calm.

"Food and water. Med supplies have been a bit thin on the ground," Ned grimaced.

I hurried to the secure storage cage and unlocked it. We'd managed to put together two bags each, one to wear and one to carry. Each one had a selection of water, food, med-supplies, liquor, cigarettes or a secondary weapon inside, almost maxing out their six slots each.

"Here." I handed Ned a bundle of loose meds, dropping some as my hands shook. I hoped Ned would think I'd dropped them in my haste. "We'll put you together a proper kit later, for now we take the bags to the back door."

It took precious minutes for us to make the trips, but Jay and Indi were waiting for us as we took the last bags to the back door. Indi grim faced, Jay looking pale.

"Once we go out there, we're locked in until we reach a safe house, okay?" Jay seemed to be holding it together but I noticed that his hands had started to tremble, much like my own.

We all nodded silent agreement.

"Keys." Indi held out the truck keys to me. I guess I was designated, having the Driver trait.

He opened the door and, bags in hand, we hurried out into the yard.

"Oh fuck," Jay breathed and slowed.

The zombies had already reached the truck. There weren't enough to block the gate yet, but there were enough to be dangerous. I fumbled the keys and pressed a button.

The truck's alarm howled and the lights flashed.

"Shit, shit, shit!" I wailed.

"Turn it off!" Ned urged frantically.

I thumbed the other button on the fob and the alarm died, but already I could hear the breathy sounds of hundreds of zombies shuffling closer.

"I'll go left, Ned goes right. We use the nearside doors and get in as quick as we can," Indi commanded.

I took a step, but realized Jay wasn't moving. He was wide-eyed and shaking.

"Jay!" I shouted, reaching back but, fumbling the axe and the rucksack into one arm, Indi grabbed Jay by the shoulder and dragged him toward the gate.

We scrambled under, pushing the bags ahead and trying to regain our feet as quickly as possible. A roar from Indi told me my friend was already fighting. He jabbed a zombie with the head of the axe, and as it staggered back, brought the blade down on the crown of its head. Blood spattered the paintwork and windscreen of the truck as the axe made a ruin of the zombie's skull. The smell of stale blood and rot filled my nose. I'd seen the same gimmick in movies, but, without the dislocation of the screen, the sight and smell made me want to gag. I looked quickly away, pulled open the car doors and threw the loose bags inside.

A quick look the other way showed me Ned as she smashed a zombie's knee with her bat, then cracked it's skull against the gate on the backswing as it stumbled.

I dragged Jay to his feet, shoving him into the back seat and climbed across to the driver's side.

"Get in, get in!" I shouted as cold, dead hands started to hammer on the windows.

Indi sat heavily in the passenger seat beside me and I watched in the rear-view as Ned fell into the car, struggling with a clawing Z.

Jay squeezed himself away from the rotten thing as Indi, half turned in the seat, took a firm hold of Ned.

"Drive!" he roared and, engine howling, I shifted into gear and stomped the accelerator. The 'door open' chime rang softly over the grunting and swearing of the struggle to keep Ned in and get the zombie out.

Lurching forward, the truck bounced zombies off the bumper and leapt as two disappeared under the big tyres.

"Help me!" Indi snapped and I half turned, grabbing Ned's jacket. Indi shoved at the zombie fighting to get its teeth into Ned, Ned kicking it loose until the asphalt dragged it away, nearly losing her grip until Indi grasped her out-flung hand.

I ploughed through the fore-runners of the horde and took the left turn at the corner of the store, taking us west, away from the zombies and away from our intended objective.

Breathing hard, Ned pulled herself fully into the truck and the door closed.

I slewed through discarded vehicles, desperate to get distance on the wave of dead crashing over our erstwhile refuge, my chest heaving.

"Which way?" I managed finally.

"Keep going west. We'll find somewhere to stop and get our bearings but for now, keep going," Indi panted.

I was more than happy to comply.

Chapter 16

We left the town and found a convenient bypass to turn back on. Green fields rolled under the grey sky as, with Indi giving directions, I drove the truck on.

I pulled to a stop atop a rise overlooking the town.

"Jesus Christ," I breathed. I could see most of the streets and the hills beyond. Zombies had flooded in from the far hills and were flowing through the streets like a stinking, shambling river.

Indi grunted and went back to studying the map.

"How is everyone?" I asked. "Anyone hurt or bitten?"

"No, I think we got away with it," Ned replied.

"How's Jay?" I turned in my seat to look.

Jay was rocking gently back and forth in his seat.

"Shit. Ned, go into one of the bags and get him a drink would you?"

For my own jangled nerves, I reached into my pocket and pulled out the packet of cigarettes I had there.

I managed to light the thing with shaking hands before taking a drag, grimacing at the taste. "We have to find a better solution to the stress mechanic than this," I grumbled.

"For now, I'll settle for you rolling the window down," Indi mumbled.

For a moment I fumbled the packet, lighter, cigarette and steering wheel, trying to free up a finger for the window button. "Crap, sorry," I replied, the window rolling down with that quiet electric hum.

I could hear Ned talking quietly to Jay and the slosh and glug of a bottle.

The road ahead was a broad dual carriageway, littered with abandoned or burnt cars. It wasn't the complete gridlock that I'd seen in other zombie franchise movies, but there was enough that I'd have to weave a bit here and there. I'd never live it down if I crashed the car and killed us all...

"Listen, I'm sorry about the alarm," I said softly.

"Don't be, the situation was fucked anyway," Indi reassured me with a smile that was just short of believable. "But try not to do it again, alright?"

I took another stomach-churning drag, flicked the bulk of the rancid tab out of the window and started us moving again. "Oh believe me, I'll do my best."

We sat in silence for a while, Indi glancing out the windows then back at the map as I eased us through the tangles of abandoned or crashed vehicles.

"What does the route look like?" I asked, just to make conversation.

"Eh, not good," Indi muttered. "The base is surrounded by what looks like residential and commercial estates. We'll have to be careful."

"It might be worth us just looking for a place to hole up on the way then?" I suggested.

He flipped out another panel on the map. "Maybe, there are a few isolated farms before we get there. We could park up, shore up and log out for a while. But let's get some real distance on that horde, huh?"

"No argument there," I replied. "So, Ned, I'm thinking you didn't get much chance to consider my offer?"

"Uh, not really," Ned said from the backseat. "I mean, I just wanted to know where you were based, for my own security, y'know? But it seemed every road behind me was suddenly full of geeks, so I had to make a decision. Seeing you guys work though, I'd like to take you up on it. I can't go back, and sitting on my hands by my friends' dead avatars wasn't getting me any closer to the win anyhow, but I'm not going to get far on my own so… here I am."

"So," Jay spoke hesitantly. "You know about the money then?"

"And you're still chasing it after all you've been through?" I added.

"I'm not sure I can really explain it," Ned shrugged. "The prize, yes I know and yes it would kinda make up for what's happened already, but that's not it. I'm not sure I really understand it myself, but I want to keep playing."

"Not so much helping us out of the goodness of your heart then?" Jay asked wryly. He seemed to be coming back to himself.

Ned smiled wryly, the first expression I'd seen other than fear or suspicion, it was a definite improvement. "I did mention the money, didn't I?" she replied dryly.

"And I guess you want a share if we win?" Jay chuckled anxiously.

"I don't know if 'shares' come into it." Her smile widened, became just a little smug, "I heard it was a quarter mil' apiece to the winners." That was new, something we hadn't known before, and quite welcome under the circumstances. "Whatever. I'll tell you what. I'll tag along with you then, if my team shows up again, I can go with them or we can all work together. Whatever works at the time, deal?"

I looked at my friends' faces in the rear-view. Indi seemed indifferent, Jay still looked pensive. Seemed it was up to me.

"Looks like," I offered, with near enough genuine enthusiasm.

"What's that up ahead?" I wondered quietly, almost to myself.

Indi emerged from behind the map with a rustle of paper. "What?"

At first glance, all I'd seen were the backs of cars but, looking past them I could see a couple of big, canvas-backed trucks flanking the road, reducing it to single file traffic.

"Looks like a roadblock." I sucked my teeth thoughtfully and tried to see past the stationary vehicles for a way through.

"We could take the bank," Indi suggested.

I pulled up behind the last car, shifted into neutral and set the hand-brake. "Yeah, but I don't want us getting stuck if things go bad. I think we better check it out on foot," I suggested reluctantly.

"There's no telling how many zombies might be around here," Jay chimed in from the back.

Indi craned his head, scanning around, "I don't see any."

Jay chuckled darkly. "Rule number six, 'you might not see any, but they're always there'."

I clucked my tongue against my teeth. "I could honk the horn."

"I wouldn't," Indi shook his head doubtfully.

I tapped my thumbs against the steering wheel. "Screw it," I declared at last, killing the ignition. The tank was near full but there was no use wasting what fuel we had. "Ned, you come with me. Indi, stay here with Jay and be ready to get us out of here fast."

I opened the door, getting out before anyone could lodge a complaint, and stood in the road. A slight drizzle was falling and the wind was mournful in the trees that lined the road. To the left, the bank Indi had suggested we drive along rose sharply to a thick hedge of tall, coarse ever-greens. To my right, the central barrier blocked any vehicular escape. Ahead was a queue of about forty cars, most with doors open, some marred by bloody handprints.

I took the brush hook from where I'd set it beside the driver's seat and closed the door.

Ned appeared around the back end of the truck, cricket bat in hand.

Parked cars in large numbers were always a risk in films or games, too many angles and hiding places. "We'll take the bank," I gestured with my weapon, the grass beneath the dense trees was clear of anything but partial corpses, "see if we can squeeze through the roadblock," I said.

Ned nodded.

Without any immediate threat in sight, we walked along the line of cars, just out of reach or grasping hands and far enough from the trees to run if there was trouble. It soon became apparent that the trucks had been parked behind a couple of Land Rovers which, in turn, were behind a pinch-point constructed of sandbags. At a guess, the game's narrative had had soldiers checking anyone headed this way, letting only one vehicle approach at a time. There was a good thirty feet between the start of the queue and the checkpoint; easy to traverse in our truck but, between the sandbag walls, blocking the checkpoint, was a family estate car.

As I approached another scene of horror unfolded itself. The rear and front passenger doors were open, bodies lay at each one. Ducking a little to look inside I could see the windscreen, stitched with bullet holes, the glass spider-webbed crazily around each one and, in the driver's seat, a shadowed figure.

I crept closer to the car. We would have to move it before we could get through. I glanced down at the bodies on the ground. The first was no threat; most of its head was already gone. I edged forward and nudged the second with my boot from as far back as I could manage. Nothing.

I leaned down to the open door to get a better look at the driver, who turned and rasped at me, leaning to reach my way and stopped only by the seat belt.

"Shit," I hissed as the car rocked softly.

I looked at Ned.

"Keep its attention, will you? I'll go around the other side, cut the seatbelt and, when it crawls out, you brain it."

Ned nodded and tightened her grip on her bat.

I walked around the back of the car, climbing into the passenger seat behind the driver. Taking my hook blade, I grasped the seatbelt, pulling it tight and pinning the straining zombie before slashing the nylon belt. With a groan the Z slumped across the front seats, headed for Ned. I eased myself out of the rear, a greyed out and shut off part of my mind vaguely wondering about the blood and toys in the backseat.

'What happened to the kid?'

Almost as I thought it, I felt the grasp of small hands around my ankle and pitched over forward, twisting as I went. I landed on my side with a brief cry of surprise and glanced down my body to my ankle and the little zombie, covered in blood and grease and dirt, hidden under the car seat where some snag of clothing had held it despite its post-mortem pre-teen efforts. I yelped and tried to pull away, but all I achieved was to drag the child-zombie with me. It started to pull itself toward my flesh, cold hands dragging at my clothes, dead eyes intent and teeth gnashing behind foam-flecked lips.

In pure desperation, I kicked. My foot glanced off the dirty forehead, ripping the skin. God help me, I kicked again.

I kicked it in the head and felt the nauseating, jarring sensation in my leg as the little skull hit the car's frame behind it. It took two more awful blows before the bones cracked and the meat and blood spattered against the metal. The wide-eyed little nightmare sagged and released me from its grip.

I scrabbled back, jumped to my feet and hugged myself, shivering in revulsion at the act I'd just committed.

A smack of willow on bone and squelch of displaced organic matter snatched me from my little world of personal trauma. My stress meter blinked at three bars. If I could avoid any further negative stimuli it ought to settle on its own, but my own reaction, beyond the game's mechanics, was a personal nightmare that my brain would store away for those dark moments later on.

Ned straightened up, bloodied bat dripping, and looked at me, confused.

"You okay?" she said quietly.

With a final, full-body shiver I took hold of myself.

"Fine," I replied curtly.

I walked briskly up to the roadblock and saw that the road beyond was mostly clear.

"We need to move this car." I turned back to Ned. "Keep an eye out." Luckily there was a blanket on the back seat, beside the abandoned toys I did my best not to see. I took it and tossed it over the mess the driver had left behind before climbing into the driver's seat. Even with the doors open, I could smell the corruption of the recent occupant.

The car sputtered and grumbled, but started with a decidedly unhealthy rattle, so I carefully eased the protesting vehicle out of the way. The engine must have taken a bullet or two and I was glad we didn't have to rely on this squealing, stinking hunk of junk.

We hurried back to our truck and I took the wheel as Indi scooted over, mounted the bank and drove up to the checkpoint.

Just as I navigated between the army trucks Indi commanded, "Stop."

"What?" I asked, but pulled up as directed.

"We should check the vehicles and bodies for weapons and supplies," he replied, opening the door and stepping out, just as I had done not so long before.

I followed, Ned and Jay getting out behind me.

"We need to get to shelter," I called as loudly as I dared but Indi ignored me.

"Spread out," I grumbled. "Let's get this over with."

We quickly turned up a couple more knives, a rifle with half a dozen rounds and a box of ammunition for the two empty pistols we'd found at the school. But it was Indi who hit the mother lode.

One of the canvasbacks held a wrapped pallet of forty-eight-hour ration boxes.

"Wow," I stated dryly, "how are we supposed to get *that* in the truck?"

"One box at a time *mon ami*, one box at a time," Indi grinned.

"You know that'll take too long," I protested.

His grin became just a little less friendly. "Not if we get on with it," he shot back.

I gave in, brought our truck closer and we formed a chain, stacking as many boxes as we could in the covered back of our vehicle.

"Good, done. Can we go now?" I asked my guts churning. The cloud was giving way to dusk and the sunlight breaking through was casting the world in straw yellow. Whenever I saw it outside the game I called it 'Land of the Living Dead-Light', but here, within the game, it seemed like an omen of bad things to come.

"Relax, Lex," Indi jumped down from the cargo bed of the big lorry. "There's a farmhouse, secluded, not five miles from here. We'll be there in minutes."

My Drive trait levelled before we found the track and then we were off the wider black asphalt and onto a single-track back road.

True enough, there was a turn off just a few miles down the new road. We turned off onto a dirt track, wet and muddy with rain, that ran under a thick cover of trees.

"How far?" I asked, eyes searching for anything unusual.

"Maybe three miles," Indi grunted.

We rolled forward slowly, the yellowing light occasionally breaking through the shadows under the trees. We passed a couple of secluded cottages, the subtle signs of violence quite apparent to the watchful eye. A wrecked car had pulled off into a ditch. The road ended at a large double gate, reinforced with six-foot sheets of corrugated steel and topped with barbed wire. Brick walls stretched into trees on either side.

Even as I formed the words, "it looks like someone lives here," an avatar, average height, dressed in hunter's camouflage gear stepped out of the bushes. Pushing back their hood they revealed a leathery, wind-tanned face with a scraggly red beard and cropped hair, with a double-barrel shotgun hanging easily in the crook of an arm. He stood motionless, making no move to raise the gun or threaten us any more than he was already.

"Let's just pull back, nice and easy," Jay suggested quietly from the back.

"No argument here," I replied softly.

I shifted into reverse and checked my wing mirrors just in time to see two more figures, players I assumed, stepping out of the undergrowth to either side of the track. Like the avatar ahead of us, they were dressed in hunter's camo, not army.

One of them stared into the back window, frowned and shouted to his friend.

The two behind us raised assault rifles, probably scavenged from the road-block, but the figure ahead raised a hand and strolled confidently up to my window.

I froze, unwilling to do anything that might make our situation worse.

The barrel of the shotgun tapped lightly on the glass and, reluctantly, I pressed the switch to roll down the window.

The player gave me a smug smile, apparently confident that we presented no immediate threat.

"Evening," the voice was deep, clearly adult and full of syrupy good humour, drawling the words in a manner just short of 'patronizing'. "What brings you down our way?"

I consciously kept both hands in sight on the wheel and my voice low and even as I replied. "We're just passing through, looking for a place to hole-up and log off,"

"Well, usually that wouldn't be a problem." Syrup turned to full-on smarm, the player obviously enjoying the pantomime. "My group would be happy to put you up or let you go about your merry way, your choice,"

"So, what *is* the problem?" I asked. He was baiting the question, but right now I could play along if it kept the conversation going.

"The problem," he replied, his voice hardening with every word, "is that's *our* fucking food you've got stowed in the back of your truck."

Chapter 17

"Bullshit!"

I usually really enjoyed hearing Indi swear. His accent made the experience something that made me smile. But it was hard to enjoy when I was staring down the barrel of a gun.

"I did not see your name on it!" he added hotly.

"Indi," I muttered in warning, hoping to calm the situation.

The man at my window smiled again but it didn't reach his eyes. They stayed hard and cold.

"I tell you what, drive it inside and we can work this out with the boss."

He gave a quick, shrill whistle and, after a moment's pause, the gates opened smoothly.

Indi laid a hand on my arm. "Don't do it, Lex," he warned quietly.

I met his gaze. "We don't have a choice," I said softly as I put the truck in gear and drove it into the farmyard.

I'd been picking up the smell of livestock all the while we sat outside the gate, but in the yard the sharp smell of animals was stronger. It almost made me long for the smell of spoiled meat again after the fresh air of the road.

The yard was muddied by the rain and flanked on three sides by buildings. A vehicle shed, barn and the farmhouse itself were set at the back. The guards flanked us as we rolled in slowly and stopped in the middle of the yard. I could see a dozen other avatars either stationed on make-shift towers or crossing the yard with armfuls of supplies, each one with a holstered pistol or fire-arm of some kind. Striding purposefully toward us was a tall femme avatar with handsome features, striking silver/grey hair and piercing blue eyes, carrying 'herself' with a confidence that was, frankly, intimidating.

"What have you got, Kay?" the new avatar called in a deep masculine voice.

"Looters," the man with the shotgun, identified as 'Kay' called back. "They're loaded with the ration packs from the checkpoint."

"Alright, you head back out. I'll deal with this."

Kay seemed reluctant to leave, but turned and exited the gate with his team.

The new player came up to the car and smiled apologetically.

"Sorry about that, Kay's a little intense, but he's not so bad once you get to know him. Would you all step out of the vehicle please?"

I shared a worried glance with my passengers. Indi gave a surreptitious glance to our liberated assault rifle but I shook my head, opened my door and stepped out into the mud.

"What's your name?" they asked as I stood before them, steely eyes looking down from a clear head taller than me.

"Maybe you could tell me yours first?" I asked, adding hesitantly. "And your preferred pronoun?" I wanted to gauge their reaction, get a better feel of the person I was talking to.

The tall avatar favoured me with a thoughtful half-smile for a moment.

"Well, my given name is Tariqe and it's 'he'. Some people call me 'Rick' IRL but, in-game it's CaliphEighty-Four or 'Cal'. And you?"

"LeZion," I supplied, "or Lex."

Cal/Tariqe waited to see if I might supply a real name, shrugging when none was forthcoming.

"And your team?"

I indicated each one as I gave their callsigns. "Indi, Jay and Ned."

"Okay Lex," Cal nodded, apparently satisfied for now. "The problem Kay has, or Killer-dot-exe to give him his gamertag." He favoured me with an amused sparkle in his eyes and lowered his voice. "His real name is George but don't tell him I told you." Cal's bright smile was encouraging and I felt my own lips tweak in return.

"Kay's objection is that we've been scavenging the check-point and had those rations earmarked for a later pick-up."

I shook my head. "I don't see where that's *our* problem." I wasn't really trying to be argumentative but, as they say 'first come, first served'.

Cal winced theatrically. "Well, you say that, but each of those packs is two days of food for each of my people. And that's important, having it nearby meant we could let it drop down the priority list. It meant we could dedicate scavenging runs into the towns, runs that put my group at risk, to looking for more essential supplies."

"Still doesn't make it our problem," Jay chimed in.

Cal took a breath through the nose in frustration but retained the bright smile.

"*Your* problem is that we have plans, a timetable and a lot of that hinges on that food. I can't just let you leave with it, so what can we do?"

"What do you mean?" I asked, pitching my voice carefully.

"Well, obviously we don't want to kill you all and take it. Violent confrontation in a survival situation is a good way to get dead. What services or goods can we supply in barter?"

Ned cut in before I could. "Bed and board would be a good start, we've been in-game for hours."

"With an assurance of hospitality and safety," Jay clarified quickly.

"I'll tell you what," Cal held up his avatar's hands. "We'll get you bedded down and work something out later. Just pull the truck into the vehicle shed and I promise you, no-one will touch it."

"Just give us a minute?" Jay asked politely as we huddled up. "Can we trust them?" he asked.

"How can we possibly know at this stage?" Indi shrugged. "We'll only really know if we log back in and find ourselves in new avatars."

"I tell you what." I held up a hand. "I've got a few days off work and, God knows I'd rather game than deal with real-life right now, so I'll hang around a bit, see what I can learn. Then, tomorrow, I'll log back in early in the morning and, if we have all been murdered in our sleep, I'll let you know."

"That seems about all we can do," Jay nodded thoughtfully. "Thanks Lex." He smiled and we turned back and waved Cal over.

"Alright, we'll stay, for now," I declared on behalf of the group.

"Great." He smiled and waved over another player. "Go with Khali and she'll see you bedded in."

"Mind if I hang on a moment, Cal?" I asked.

"Sure, I'll even give you a tour if you like," he shrugged.

With my friends following the guide toward the large farmhouse, I let Cal direct me as I parked the truck, and then tried to look casual as I walked to his side, swinging my hands idly. I took in the rough, shanty-town walls that had been added to the fences around the farmyard. More

140

corrugated steel and pallets, reinforced with scaffold poles and other things.

"So…" I started.

Cal grinned knowingly. "You want to know what our shtick is, right?"

I gave the tall avatar a sideward glance. "I'm that easy to read?"

"I'd want to know," he answered openly.

"Okay, alright," I nodded. "We're brought in at gunpoint, and then you say you *don't* want to take our stuff by force or kill us. What's the deal?"

He winced. "Like I said, Kay can be a bit intense, but the deal is this, eventually I'd like to convince you to stay."

"Come again?"

"My crew came into this game with a plan. We're going to survive, rebuild. First we built this outpost, we recruited passing players and, soon, we'll have the numbers to start clearing a town. Once we fortify one town we can look to clear another, and another. We're going to build secure, stable communities that will endure. We're going to win."

'Win', I thought. Someone else in it for the money.

"How many players in your clan already?" I asked.

He replied without hesitation. "Right now we're running three shifts of fifteen or so players each."

"And you're going to clear and fortify a town?" I asked doubtfully.

"Eventually, go big or go home, right?" he shrugged.

I thought on that for a few steps. "Is Kay one of your original group?" I asked finally.

"Why do you ask?"

"Oh, I dunno. I get a kind of 'gaming's for dudes', bro-gamer vibe. Like, he was entirely on the wrong side of Gamergate."

"I see we've found a sticking point." Cal nodded to himself. "Kay's competitive. He competes in FPS leagues and is a little more obsessed with his KD spread than is healthy, but that's kind of why I drafted him. But, I'm slowly weaning him away from calling people 'noobs', and he only tea-bags one in five these days." He smirked.

"That's a good way to get your balls bitten off in this game," I joked. "So, you brought him in?" I asked, honestly curious.

"I found *Rendered Flesh*, convinced some friends to play, although Kay's more of an 'acquaintance'. Some are here, others are… elsewhere." He finished distantly.

"Where?" I pressed.

"I honestly couldn't tell you," Cal shrugged. "Only four of us spawned in together. We've built the group from there."

"So it's a commune?"

"A collective," Cal corrected, "we all contribute. We want to beat the game, to survive."

I thought about that.

"I know it sounds like a sales pitch, and frankly it is, but give it some thought." He stopped, turning to face me. "If I might ask, what brought you here?"

I considered not telling him. Information was as good a currency as anything else, but decided against it, for now.

"We spawned in a town a few miles down the road," I started. "We holed up in a supermarket to get a feel for the game. We were there a couple of days, and then this huge herd wandered in and we had to leave."

"No shit? How big a herd?" I couldn't tell if he was impressed or surprised but his interest in the zombies was genuine.

"It didn't look so bad coming in over the fields, but once it hit the town they were filling the streets. You ever seen footage of ants on the move?" I shuddered at the memory.

He nodded sombrely. "Yeah."

"Like that. You were lucky it passed you by, this place would never have survived."

He looked thoughtful for a second. "We'll have to take measures," he said finally.

"Can I ask you something, Cal?" I ventured.

"Go ahead."

"How have you kept this place together? Gotten all these gamers on board like this?"

He grinned. "Well, my skill set helps." He flashed me his wrist. In among his traits I picked out a word: Leadership.

"What does that do?" I asked.

"As far as I can tell, the avatars around me don't suffer stress build-up as quickly. I'm like a group buffer for horror. I mean, in-game I can only be as persuasive and charismatic as I am, but this helps."

I gave a rueful chuckle. "Wow, luck of the draw right?" I thought about Jay's build. Maybe Cal could help reduce the effects of his Squeamish trait, enough to let him be as useful as he desperately wanted to be.

"Anyway," he took a deep breath of the fecund air. "I'll let the next shift know you're here when I do hand-over, and let them know the deal. When your group logs back in we'll talk more. There's a room in back at the top of the farmhouse, we put new arrivals in there until we get them settled in a watch. Your friends will be there."

I gave him my thanks and walked toward the farmhouse, my mind turning.

Cal had mentioned 'winning' but did he know about the prize?

If I was generous I might say he didn't. His group's goal of 'winning' sounded like a lot of hard work and gaming hours. Ours seemed to me to be a more likely proposition, achievable by a small group after a quarter mil' cash prize but really, who knew if there even was a prize?

I was still mulling it over when I got to the room, locked the door behind me for a semblance of security, and logged out.

Back in my room I stretched and yawned. The room was illuminated by my home-screen and the orange of the streetlights. I checked the time. 2AM. I stood to go to the light switch.

The sound of a skittering bottle in the street startled me and I turned, pressing my back against the wall on reflex.

After a moment I heard someone cursing drunkenly and I managed to slow my breathing.

I left the light off and headed downstairs, dark thoughts swarming my brain.

The world was dying. Society was rotting. Well, no, 'society' had always been rotten. The illness was running just as rampantly as it ever had. We were just better informed these days, or maybe just more vocal about it.

Mum was up late again.

"What's up?" I asked, rummaging in the cupboard and taking down a can of soup.

She smiled, her eyes shadowed and weary. "It's nothing, really."

"You wouldn't be up this late over nothing." I pulled the top off the tin, ring pull cans are so convenient, and got a spoon from the draining board.

"You're eating that cold?" she asked.

It actually hadn't occurred to me to warm it up. In-game I'd been eating cold soups and beans and snack-bars. I guess I was forming a habit.

"It's fine," I replied round a mouthful of vegetable chunks. "Come on, what's up?"

Mum sighed and ran her hands through her hair. "More cases like the one I told you about have turned up. The Department of Health wants a briefing."

"Why?"

"Because my patient is now on a ventilator, and seizures resulting in a persistent vegetative state don't usually manifest without any history or an underlying cause." She flexed her hands in frustration and I could hear the pain in her words.

I prodded into the can with my spoon. "The world's getting darker, people are looking for relief."

Elbows on the table she let her head drop into her hands and massaged her temples. "What has that got to do with it?"

I wondered for a moment about bringing up welding-mask guy, or even Ned's disappearing friends. I was sure there was a link but, without proof, how could I convince even my mother?

"I dunno, it's late." I shrugged eventually, "You should get to bed. Nothing worse than a tired and cranky neurologist, you should know that."

She shivered, despite the absence of a chill in the room. "You should get to bed too, you've been gaming all night. You know your reactions get slower, decision making takes longer, your KD spread suffers."

"Alright, alright." I spread my hands—as far as tin and spoon would allow—in surrender. "I just want to take a shower first, okay?"

"Okay, but get to bed," she insisted.

"You too." I finished the soup and headed back upstairs.

In the shower I let the water run over me for a little while. I needed something to lift me, something to distract me. I closed my eyes under the spray and thought about Indi and our little 'experiment' in the super-market bathroom. The press of that looming body, the warmth of his breath on my neck, the sensation of strong hands on my skin and supple flesh under mine. But, as I tried to make the most of the memory, the hands turned cold, the eyes dead. Even under the hot water they clawed and dragged at me, and I had to open my eyes to shake myself free of their grip.

I finished up, frustrated and kinda tetchy. In order to feel like I'd achieved something, I dried off and went back to my room, picked up my phone and tapped out a quick account of everything Cal had said before I logged off and addressed it to Jay. I left out my thoughts about Cal's Leadership trait. We could have that discussion in real time. After a moment's thought, I CC'd Indi in too. I would have added Ned but I didn't have an email address, and I didn't have the energy to cyber-stalk her tonight to get it.

I lay back in my bed, listening to the world outside my window. If Cal's collective was as he'd described it, maybe there was something in this world worth saving. As I drifted to sleep, my mind wandered back to the thought of warm hands on my skin but, as I began to dream, the hands once more turned cold, only to be followed by rancid breath and gnashing teeth.

Chapter 18

The mob prowled the dark streets and I was deep within it, a part of the cloying, scrabbling, dead-eyed masses, the press of cold flesh enfolding me in its clammy embrace. Through dark streets we hunted, overrunning and consuming those who were 'different', those that didn't 'conform' or 'obey'. People of different religions, ethnicities, orientations or identities ran before us; unionists, activists, conservationists. The mob moaned their crimes, announced their 'otherness' as they were pulled down and pulled apart, screaming and begging in front of me. Their blood spattered my face and clothes, and the stench of the slaughter filled my nostrils.

The whole time, all I could do was pray that the horde didn't discover that I was 'other'; that I didn't share their ideals or consume the same propaganda they did. That I wasn't truly one of them. It was inevitable but, soon those shambling alongside me started to glance side-long at me. Then they stared, eyes milky-white but clearly hostile, before they reached for me with rasping cries of 'Liberal', 'Socialist' and other pronouncements about my gender and sexual orientation that sent stabbing pains through my heart. They piled into me, hands reaching as I tried, feebly, to fend them off. They bore me down, fetid breath and spittle in my face and clawing fingers pulling at my clothes and flesh. They tore open my stomach and started pulling out ribbons of entrails as I screamed and, finally, awoke.

I was tangled in the sheets and drenched in cold sweat. Panting, I lay there and thought about the dream and the message underlying the whole zombie-horror presentation.

I let out a long breath and hauled myself upright. "Fuck those dev's and the goddamn rabble-rousing right-wing press, seriously." I groaned, cursing the makers of *Rendered Flesh* for successfully creeping me the hell out and the tabloids for the creeping dread I felt every day. Rubbing sleep from my eyes and headed downstairs.

I hadn't even overslept, not really. The front door opened as I hit the foot of the stairs, dad was coming in from night-shift.

"No-one mention policing, please," he groaned as he dropped his bag in the hallway.

Mum appeared, steaming cup of tea in hand. It wasn't long before she'd have to leave for the hospital.

"Rough night?" she asked, concern evident in her voice.

"Got into it with a client, a substance abuser. I thought they were in recovery but," he sighed deeply. "I don't know, they relapsed. Whatever they were taking it was more like fighting an animal than a person. I had to call the cops in for help," he added with a grimace.

I stopped, shocked; it must have been bad for dad to call in the police.

"Are you alright?" Mum asked earnestly, tugging at him, checking for bites. Not bites, injuries I reminded myself.

"I'm fine." He winced, gently taking her hands. "It's not like he was armed, but I could murder some toast."

Mum frowned and went back to the kitchen as Dad collapsed heavily into one of the living room chairs. I stayed by the door, leaning against the door frame.

He laid his head back, eyes closed, and asked the world in general. "What happened to 'helping people'?"

"You know I wanted to be a copper once?" he stated, squinting over at me before his head lolled back against the cushions. "Glad I didn't. It was bad enough that the government started treating them like a private security force, but then they actually got their own private security; bunch of jack-booted thugs. I thought going into social care, I could act as an intermediary, help both sides, but they treat us the same! It's not even that they see me as a cop but as an 'authority'. I swear, the public don't see police officers anymore, they just see…"

"The faceless, baton-wielding storm-troopers of the neo-fascist establishment?" I suggested as Mum passed me a cup of tea which I relayed into the grateful hands of my father.

"Well, yes," dad harrumphed. "I mean, I don't want to agree with the ACAB rhetoric, but it's hard to argue with evidence. The service is stripped to the bone dealing with social and mental health issues they have no place going into. The officers are pushed to the limit and drowned in paperwork. It's no wonder the few good officers snap or escalate just to get an arrest on the books and have it done. The bad ones? The ones who

147

joined up for the authority, the power? They don't even give it a second thought. And don't even start me on arrest quotas. It shouldn't ever be about arrests, it should be about the *right* arrests, but no, that straw-haired, fridge-hiding muppet plops another private-school prick in as Minister for Crime and Policing, and demands they cut the budget. Never mind the safety and well-being of the populace and the officers themselves. I mean, do they hand out *1984* at Eton and Oxford like it's a fucking how-to guide? Take it from me kid, steer clear of cops, at least in London."

I kept silent as he took a sip from his tea.

"So, what's going on here?"

I shrugged and smiled sadly. "Not a lot. Mum's coma case has gotten worse, a gamer friend's worried about some missing friends..." I didn't want to trouble dad, not now, but the words just slipped out, luckily;

"Right, I'm off!" Mum called from the hallway.

Dad and I chorused, "have a good day!"

The door clicked shut and I heard the keys in the lock.

"Missing?" Dad asked, tilting his head intently.

"They've gone quiet on social media, disappeared from the game they were playing." I shrugged. As much as I felt that there must be a link it still felt a little absurd to say it out loud.

Dad yawned. "They're probably just ghosting your friend for some over-inflated reason. I swear, just talk about your problems, there's no need for drama."

I smiled. "You get to bed, Dad, I'll keep it down, try not to disturb you."

He yawned again. "Thanks kid. I swear, I never wanted this to be the world we made for you, all the fear and hate. I hope your generation can salvage something."

I couldn't think of anything to say to reassure him so, with a sheepish smile, he took his tea and headed upstairs.

'Maybe my generation could build a better world, it just won't be in this one' I thought to myself and headed up to my own room.

I logged in, and discovered with relief that our avatars were just as we'd left them. I took a look out of the window and, seeing no-one I could recognise under the dim, night-time lighting of the yard, logged out.

Jay, are you online? I messaged, and watched the indicator in the message window.

'Joakim is typing a message…' It informed me shortly before…

Yeah Lex, everything okay?

I logged in, everything seems to be okay I informed him.

Good, I've got something to try out.

Yeah, me too. I chewed my lip as I waited for his reply, wondering if he'd pick up the thread.

Okay, I'll bite. What's yours?

I took a deep breath. *I really wanted to F2F this with you, but don't know if we'll get time. Cal has a trait called Leadership. He says it reduces stress in allied players. It might help us reduce the effect of your Squeamish trait until you can get on top of it.*

The message box stayed frozen for a while, the only motion the blinking icon in my 'reply' bar.

It's at least worth thinking about, he finally replied. *Also I've been chatting with Ned, she knows what Educated does.*

I thought it was just learning stuff faster, I typed. I hadn't really thought about it but since Jay had brought it up it must be good.

It *does* that, but it's also a skill emulator. Apparently you can use certain skills being demonstrated by other PC's in close proximity.

Damn that's broken, I typed. *Cool no doubt, but still broken.*

The revelation about the skill brought a broad smile to my lips. It must have been a rare and lucky roll to get such a useful skill.

So? I replied after a moment. *What's yours?*

I've been working on a little something the past few days between sessions.

'Oh God,' I thought. *What are you up to Jay?* I typed.

I want to know how they're generating full immersion through standard hardware. These programmers have the next generation of immersive entertainment software and, according to my sources, they've not patented it or licensed it, neither have they released it but, instead they're using it on a shareware game. I don't know about you but that makes me curious, doesn't it make you curious?

Well… I thought about it. *I mean, yeah. But you checked the gateway installation and looked for the in-game console and got nowhere.*

That's what I've been working on. Jay's reply came back almost instantly.

It's a tether programme I can carry into the game that'll hold the connection and let me get to the core programme for a look around.

I thought about that for a moment. The prospect made me very uneasy.

You're not considering stealing their programme, are you? I asked.

No, let's just call it professional curiosity, Jay replied.

You know what you're doing better than I do. When are we going back in?

I've got some things to finish off but should be ready about 2, your time. Drop a message to Indi and let him know, yeah?

Alright.

> "*Everything is born without reason, prolongs itself out of weakness and dies by chance.*"
> – Jean-Paul Sartre

I opened my eyes. I'd been restless and unable to wait so I found myself, once again, in the room with the recumbent avatars of my friends.

I couldn't explain it. Objectively we hadn't accomplished that much, we'd barely come twenty miles, but during our time in-game it felt like so much more. Other games had more in the way of constant action, but also that sense of detachment. The immersion and looming dread made *Rendered Flesh* compelling, especially when you factored in the ability to act, to resist. Compared to the real world, the desire to stay logged in was pretty hard to resist.

I checked my bars:

STM		

HLT		

STR					

I hadn't eaten before I'd logged out. From what I was seeing, Stamina might be linked to Health, and I knew health faded if you didn't eat. We'd left our bags and supplies in the truck, damn...

The bright morning sunlight pierced the patina of grime on the window, bleaching out the room's colours. I looked around the small simple back bedroom. The walls bore the same wallpaper it might have had since the seventies, drab and faded green with a simple floral pattern, water stained in places and marred in one particular spot by a dark brown handprint. The sparse furniture was as dated as the wallpaper. A bed, wardrobe, chest of drawers and dressing table looked like they were part of the existing decor. The worn carpet smelled musty with a hint of unwashed bodies and bore tell-tale stains too, dark brown blobs peeked out from beneath a couple of more recent additions, two modern camp cots that had been set up for 'guests'.

I heard the creak of floorboards and voices from downstairs, and felt that anxiety that comes when you stay over in a house full of people for the first time, but you only know one of them and you're not sure they're there. The feeling of being an intruder in someone's home.

Jay stirred and sat up, blinking in the light. A beat later Indi came awake too.

We exchanged glances.

Indi swung long legs off the bed and stood, stretching. "So, what's the plan?" He yawned.

Jay, sitting with his arms wrapped around his knees, answered.

"We need to negotiate our release and get back on the road. I appreciate Cal's intentions, but we've got our own goals and, the longer we stay, the more comfortable we'll get."

Nodding my head toward the still 'sleeping' avatar on the last cot I asked, "what about Ned?"

"Won't be logging in for an hour at least," Jay supplied.

Still stretching out Indi grunted. "What do we do in the meantime?"

"We should probably wait for Cal," I suggested, "which shouldn't be too long if they run a three-shift watch like he said they do."

"Okay," Jay paused thoughtfully. "Skill check, how are we doing?"

Indi shrugged. "I've levelled in Combat, like twice, and Stamina, but haven't really used the others, and I'll be damned if I can figure out how to boost my other traits."

"I've increased my Stamina, Combat and Drive," I offered. "I've also unlocked Stealth but, likewise, I haven't used the others enough."

"That's good," Jay hesitated. "I suppose it's no surprise that I haven't managed much, beyond a level each in Stamina and Observant."

"It's okay, Jay," I replied reassuringly. "We'll get you on track." He smiled bashfully.

"What about Ned?" I finished, deflecting the focus away from his insecurities around his build.

"I asked last night," he replied, perking up slightly. "Combat at two, Stealth at three and Scavenge at two."

"Any traits we should know about?" Indi chimed in.

"Ned has Athletic, Awareness and Security."

I thought about that then commented. "Sounds like a thief build."

Jay gave me a wry grin. "It certainly explains how she spotted you following her."

"Alright," Indi announced loudly, "I say we head down. Try to get some food." I frowned, this was completely at odds with my earlier advice.

"It would help us get a better picture of this group," Jay agreed.

I wondered briefly at the changes in our group dynamic. With Jay, so long our 'leader', having been handicapped was Indi trying to step into Jay's role? I wouldn't have considered it before but, maybe the avatar's physical superiority was going to his head. And just days before Jay would have argued such a blatant challenge to our established plan.

My hesitation brought them both to stare at me expectantly.

"Alright," I gave in. "But let's stay together, okay?"

Downstairs we entered the kitchen and I knocked on the doorframe to announce us.

The player at the sink turned and frowned at us for a moment.

"You must be the new ones," they said in dawning realisation. "Food's outside, see Carrie."

And that was all the instruction they gave us.

Out in the yard, blinking in the light, we spotted a gazebo with a table set up underneath. A large pan sat on a gas stove with bowls and spoons beside it.

A broad-set male avatar spotted us and waved us over.

The player shook hands with each of us in turn. "Lex, Indi and Jay, right?" The voice was youngish and not unfriendly.

"That's us," Jay confirmed.

"Nice to meet you, I'm Carnivale but everyone calls me 'Carrie',

Carrie turned away to the heated urns then, some internal decision seemingly reached turned back to us, expression set. "And it's they, them," they pronounced.

I must've gone wide-eyed in shock because Carrie thrust out their chin defiantly.

Shaking off my momentary surprise I indicated Indi and Jay, "He, him," then myself, "They, them."

Carrie blew out a deep breath, visibly relaxing.

"Fuck it's good to able to say that," they smiled, full and genuine.

"I hadn't even," I began, "you mean you're-?"

"There's quite a few of us in the co-op, seemingly throughout the game," Carrie chattered happily, spooning porridge into bowls. "I'm the shift cook and admin. I've got instructions to see you get fed and point you to the shower block."

"Why the shower block?" Indi replied brusquely.

Carrie eyed the big broad avatar warily. "Your health and stamina drop when you're hungry. If you're hungry and dirty, the effect starts to speed up."

Fed and refreshed, our new guide led us over to our vehicle to get to our bags and a change of clothes. As assured, it seemed everything was just as we'd left it.

"I'll get the clothes you're wearing laundered," their warm manner reassuring to me at least, but Indi rounded on them as if to argue.

Taking a step back Carrie offered a hurried explanation, "it seems to renew the item's durability."

I felt for the younger player; (younger, they might have been my age!) Indi's sudden aggression was quite out-of-character for my usually personable friend.

Jay stepped in letting his gaze roam around the farm yard. "This is quite an impressive setup," he commented, maybe trying to ease the tension. "Have you been here long?"

I picked up the soft, manipulative tone and the sly look on his face, so not easing the tension, giving the appearance of easing the tension while pumping our guide for info. I knew Jay well enough to spot it, Carrie didn't.

"A couple of weeks," they confirmed blithely, though still shooting wary looks at Indi. "Which is about as long as we've been here, I joined the group a couple of villages over. I started this game alone, and my build wasn't helping me any. I mean, what kind of skill is 'catering' to a lone player? I was glad to find a clan."

Jay, sensing an easy mark pressed the questions. "What have you seen while you've been here?"

"Co-operation, largely. A dozen of us found the place, cleared it and set about fortifying. We scavenged nearby for essential items, met other

groups moving through or just wandering around. Some joined, some…
didn't."

I didn't miss the meaningful pause but Carrie wasn't about to fill in the blanks.

I'm sure Jay caught it too, also Carrie's brief flinch as they said it but, rather than pursue the subject Jay switched focus. "And the plan is to what? Expand?" We knew that was the play, Cal had told us, but Jay asked the question as if speculating, trying to catch an inconsistency in the story.

"That's right," Carrie beamed. "Build our numbers, take back a town and build a proper community. It's kind of an experiment. I mean, if we can do it here, why not outside?"

"I suppose the zombies are a step of difficulty below the establishment," I mused. "You don't have to second-guess their motives."

"The zombies, *non*. Although I wonder why you all put up with that Kay asshole," Indi grumbled.

Carrie frowned, lips pursing like they'd just swallowed something sour.

"Believe me, a lot of us have asked the same question," Carrie sighed. "He's capable, I'll give him that, but it doesn't excuse him from being toxic. I think he's Cal's pet-project. If Kay can be taught a little basic human decency, maybe anybody can."

"Hmmm, Cal might be setting goals that are beyond even *his* reach. Still, 'shoot for the stars', as they say," Indi chuckled.

"Exactly," Carrie nodded. "Well, here we are." They waved up at the large, corrugated steel barn.

It struck me that, although Indi had picked up the trail of the game on a left-leaning political forum, and while most of the players we'd met seemed to have liberal leanings, Kay was proof-positive that the dev's weren't gate-keeping the game. How could they? There'd been no registration, no signup, not even a character generator. If there were assholes in here, either we brought them in with us or they'd somehow found their own way.

"The showers are to the left, leave your clothes on the benches and I'll get them taken care of. Shift change isn't far off, so as long as you stay out from underfoot you'll be fine. Cal will be with you soon."

I smiled and meant it. "Thanks Carrie."

The barn was huge and split into rough sections by tarp walls. The showers were just off to one side.

"Wonder what else is in here?" I mused as we undressed.

Jay looked up. The tarp walls hid us from sight but the cavernous ceiling space stretched out over us. "Stores," he suggested. "Maybe it's a barracks for the inactive avatars," he shrugged.

"That sounds kind of creepy." I shivered at the thought of all those inactive bodies, just on the other side of the tarp walls.

The showers turned out to be a rough but serviceable affair. A slightly raised platform covered in lino kept our feet out of the mud, and plastic sheeting separated each 'cubicle'. A large water tank hung above us with pipes, taps and shower heads spreading out like white plastic and chrome tentacles. Towels hung on nails, which was a bonus as we didn't have any ourselves. Turning the tap a rather limp, gravity drawn shower of water, cold enough to make me yelp, splashed my shoulders.

Indi chuckled until I grabbed him, wrapping him in the cold plastic curtain.

"Cut it out you two," Jay chided us with mock weariness.

Standing under the chilly water, soaping my avatar's hair, I gave voice to the thoughts I'd been turning over since the night before.

"Would it be so bad to stay?" I asked tentatively.

"Come on Lex," Jay scoffed. "That's not the game we agreed on."

Indi's voice was muffled as he rubbed soap on his face with both hands, "At best this is an optional fallback point, a safe house maybe."

I tried to keep the sulk out of my voice. "So we're intent on moving on?" But they were right, this wasn't what we were playing for. Maybe Cal's leadership trait had another effect he hadn't told me about.

"Yes," Jay said firmly. "But we might be able to gain some benefits while we're here. We'll see what they can offer us for the food."

"Let's not push too hard," I cautioned. "Cal said that they don't want to kill us over it. He didn't say that they wouldn't."

Chapter 19

"All washed and fed?" Cal asked brightly as we emerged.

I answered him with a genuine smile. "Yes, thank you."

True to Carrie's explanation, my stamina and health bars had topped out after hot food and a shower.

"Alright, let's get to it then." Cal rubbed his hands together gleefully. "I spoke to the other community leaders and we outlined what we're prepared to offer you in exchange for the food supplies."

Jay folded his arms, closed body language so as not to seem too eager. "Okay," was the only reply he offered.

Cal paused, looking Jay up and down, assessing him carefully. "Well, the first thing I can offer you is a safe place to train some of your skills."

Jay nodded. "That's a good start, but we're going to need something more material as well."

Cal rolled his eyes, but in a way that suggested he knew that was coming.

"Well, should you still want to leave, we can offer a couple of days' worth of tinned supplies."

"And?" despite his measured tone I knew Jay was enjoying himself. Inwardly I worried that he'd push too hard but I made an effort to keep that worry from my face.

"And we do have a slight surplus of weapons." Cal sighed theatrically. "I'm empowered to offer you a place to improve what you have, or give you a reasonable pick of what we've got put aside."

With Jay on one side, playing cagey customer, and Cal on the other, embodying the beleaguered vendor I started to wonder just how long this might go on for.

"Do you have ammunition?" Indi asked suddenly.

Jay's eyes tightened, a flash of annoyance at the intrusion. Cal though, latched onto this new avenue of negotiation.

"A limited supply but I'm sure we can work something out," he sniffed nonchalantly. "How many guns do you have?"

"We picked up two pistols and a rifle," I said quickly. Jay shot me an aggrieved frown, but I could see him stringing this out and, as he'd reminded me, we had plans and places to be.

Cal stroked his chin thoughtfully. "Alright, well. We might even be able to offer you another gun and we can definitely set you up with holsters."

"Is that important?" I asked.

He smiled, letting his negotiation facade fall away. "The standard player loadout is, as I'm sure you've noticed, a little stingy on inventory slots. A pistol holster is a bolt-on slot, it's dedicated to your sidearm, but it means it doesn't take up one of your more versatile standard slots."

Figuratively (and literally) elbowing his way back into the conversation Jay nudged me aside. "Let me talk to my associates for a moment." He gave Cal a tight smile, his expression betraying little as Cal took a few steps away.

He glared at us both, lodging his disapproval of our interruptions before. "Well, what do you think?" he asked finally.

"I think we should take it," I answered immediately.

"I don't know, I think we could maybe get more?" Indi stated firmly. I'd noticed changes in his demeanour since we first dropped into *Rendered Flesh*. Indi had always been a more competitive gamer than me, but never at the expense of his compassion. My fear was that he was becoming hardened, less empathetic.

"I don't know," Jay rubbed a hand along his jaw. "We shouldn't undervalue the chance to gain some levels here."

"And, Cal might be able to help you along Jay," I threw in.

"Alright," Jay conceded. "We'll take it."

Indi grunted unhappily but didn't raise any firmer protest.

I waved Cal back.

"Do we have a deal?" he asked, optimistically.

"We have a deal," Jay confirmed and they shook hands.

"Good, I'm glad we could help each other." Cal smiled broadly. "So, let's get the food, get your vehicle set and ready and then we can figure out who needs to go where for skill training."

Being split up was a bit weird, but once we'd unloaded the ration boxes from our truck, Indi went to the workshop and Jay was told that the community was in the process of trying to set up a radio room. Despite my urging to see Cal and explore the possibilities of the Leadership trait Jay insisted on seeing the co-op's communications setup, so he went there. Maybe he suspected that the gear there would help him unlock the game-code, maybe he was scared that Cal couldn't help him. I hoped it was the former.

I stayed in the vehicle shed. I wanted to explore the bounds of my Auto skill, so I popped the bonnet of our truck and let the skill direct me from there. It turned out to be very much like when I'd found the med kit all those days ago. The engine sat there before me, a cold grey lump and, as I passed my hands over it, indicators hovered over the parts. I checked the oil and fluid levels, pulled the spark plugs and ran through what might be considered casual maintenance.

I wasn't exactly left to my own devices. A couple of other players were working nearby but I didn't engage them, content to do my own thing until Cal swung past an hour or so later.

"Lex, I've got a favour to ask," he announced.

Wiping my hands on a piece of rag, I let the bonnet close.

Auto increased to Lvl 3, bonus to be applied after a rest period

---

I swiped the notice away. I'd seen a couple of the co-op players swiping at nothing, what I now realised was their own level up notices. I still felt a little self-conscious, waving my hands through text boxes no-one else could see, but Cal took it in stride. "What do you need?" I asked.

"The military vehicles up at the roadblock, our community could really do with them going ahead, but they need refuelling to bring them back. You're your group's driver and mechanic, yes?"

"And medic," I supplied.

"Really?" Cal smirked. "I didn't have you pegged as the type."

I stiffened reflexively, ready for a fight. "What type?" I demanded. "I swear to God, you use the term 'healer girlfriend' and I'll deck you right here!"

Cal held his hands up defensively. "No, no, you just seem a lot friendlier than most gamer healers. They're usually pretty salty, jaded even. You seem, like I said, pretty okay."

I relaxed. "Well, new people, I'm on my best behaviour. Spend an afternoon with me," I winked, "you'll see how salty I can be."

"Well alright then, we should do that," he smiled. "Getting back to it, what rank in Drive do you have, if I may ask?"

"You can ask, you just did." I waggled my eyebrows and offered a playful grin; he placed his hands on his hips in mock exasperation, grinning and shaking his head at my sorry attempt at a joke. I was coming to like Cal. "My Drive trait is level two," I offered finally.

"Good," he nodded. "You need drive two at least for the fixed body trucks. I think you need three for artic's."

"What about tanks?" I half-joked.

"Maybe four, probably five," Cal replied seriously. "Anyway, I wondered if you might go with a few of my people and bring those vehicles back?"

"What's the catch?" I asked, still joking.

Cal suddenly seemed hesitant. "Yeah, about that..."

"You mean, there is a catch?" I was surprised, I'd honestly been joking. He had the good grace to look a little sheepish.

"You'll be going on foot," he told me evenly. "Four drivers carrying two jerry cans of diesel each, and two more along for security."

I had a bad feeling about this. "Who?"

"Rudi, for one. She's good people and a very capable fighter and..." he hesitated so I finished for him.

"Kay?"

"Yeah," he confirmed. "He won't start any trouble," he added quickly.

"If he does, I'll kick his ass," I growled.

"Be my guest." Cal's shoulders sagged in relief. "He could do with it sometimes. I swear, if I could spare anyone else..." he wrung his hands together, avoiding my gaze. "So, you'll go?"

I folded my arms, made a big show of looking personally aggrieved then shrugged. "Yeah, I'll go."

"Great and, by the way," he gestured at his cheek, "you've got a little something..."

I dabbed at my face with the cloth.

"Better?"

He chuckled and shook his head. "Worse, much worse."

A few minutes later I had reclaimed my medkit and my hook blade. Cal had given me some bullets and a holster for one of the pistols we'd salvaged from the school. Not that I was keen to use it. Zombies were drawn by noise, and the important thing to remember about guns is that they are very, very noisy.

I was standing in front of the gate with five others. Four drivers waiting for our 'escort', two cans of red diesel apiece, and a shared feeling of low grade nervousness, plus two replacement sentries who stood apart from our little group talking to each other.

The sheet metal rang as someone knocked from the other side.

The gate opened with a soft creak of protest and there stood Kay and Rudi.

I hadn't really noticed, but as the sentries moved out, the drivers had gravitated into a sort of line. Kay strode up to us with the proprietary manner of a B-movie parade ground sergeant, looking each of us up and down until he got to me.

"Ready for a little walk in the woods, sweetheart?" he smiled greasily, obviously amusing himself as he let his eyes wander up and down my avatar.

Something about my waist caused him to frown and he gestured to my gun. "Here, you know how to use that?"

"I've got Combat," I stated bluntly.

"Doesn't mean a thing," Kay grinned smugly. "If you don't have Firearms you can only use a pistol or a shotgun, you have to use both hands and you've got a twenty-five percent chance of missing even then, and the percentage chance increases with range."

"How did you figure all this out?" I sighed, already tired of his superior manner.

"I'm a *serious* gamer," he said, leaning in toward me. His eyes dipped down toward my avatar's chest. I gave him a rough shove and he staggered, eyes flashing with anger.

"Leer at me again," I said quietly, "and I'll shove your shotgun up your ass and brush your teeth with the trigger."

He blinked in surprise, but then the smile just widened.

"Oh, this is gonna be fun," he chuckled.

Great.

"Alright, noobs, listen up!" he raised his voice to address us all, and again there was a dissonance. Kay's avatar put me in mind of a wiry, forty-something poacher or game warden. Skin like tanned leather and red hair shot through with grey, but the voice was much, much younger.

"It's five miles to the roadblock and our objective. We'll stick to the road rather than cut through the fields, more mobs but easier terrain. Rudi will scout ahead while I run security on your candy asses. No unnecessary talking and no-one fires a weapon or instigates combat unless I tell them to. We'll run this just like any raid, clear?"

'Remind me never to raid with you', I thought to myself.

A couple of the others muttered 'Yes Kay.'

He raised a hand theatrically to his ear. "What? I didn't hear you?"

"Yes Kay," the others declared clearly, if not loudly. I kept my mouth closed. Kay did not miss that. He favoured me with an undisguised look of contempt but said nothing.

"Move out," he ordered, and we started the walk.

Aside from the weight of the fuel cans, it started out like a simple walk down a wooded lane. Rudi was on point some fifty yards ahead and the rest of us, Kay included, kept up a brisk pace behind. The persistent drizzle of the last couple of sessions had let up, and now the weather engine had given us overcast with some sunshine.

Kay walked alongside us, head up, turning this way and that, but he wasn't looking exactly. At one point he stopped, slung his shotgun over his shoulder and, pulling out a wicked looking machete, gestured for us to keep moving as he stepped off the path.

He reappeared just a couple of minutes later, cleaning dark blood off the blade with a piece of rag. He was good, I'd give him that. I hadn't heard a thing before or during the kill.

We made good time, the sloshing of our fuel cans and our footfalls the only accompaniment to our progress. After the lane we turned up the short road toward the main carriageway. I hadn't noticed the strange desolation of the cottages on either side of the road when I'd first driven my team through. The houses were older, thatched in places, with black stained timber bracing, a stark contrast to the almost uniform white of the walls. Leaded windows with dark interiors glared like baleful eyes, and I imagined packs of zombies behind each darkened pane. Here and there the windows were open and, in one particular window, the white net curtain had blown out and flapped gently in the wind, its edges stained with old, dried blood.

Up ahead, Rudi had taken down a wandering lone zombie and possibly spotted another. The curve of the road, hedges and buildings took her out of sight as she hurried forward.

"Dammit!" Kay hissed and gave a brief sharp whistle.

I'd guessed that they had an agreement for Rudi to stay in sight, and the whistle was supposed to call her back, but she didn't reappear.

"Faster," Kay commanded tersely and upped the pace to a jog.

As we rounded the bend, Kay cursed and took off at a sprint. Rudi was struggling with a Z while backed up to a hedgerow, and, even from here, I could see pale hands reaching through the brush to grab her.

"Wait here!" I ordered the others and dropped my cans to follow Kay.

He hit the Z Rudi was tussling with and bowled it to the ground.

I unlimbered my blade, and, as I reached Rudi, dragged her as far from the hedge as I could and struck downward, severing a hand that grasped her jacket.

The hedge gate opened with a rusty whine and two more of the dead stumbled out.

I hacked off another hand that was restraining Rudi, my pulse like a drum in my ears, and spared a glance toward Kay. He sat astride his zombie, viciously smashing its head against the rutted rural pavement.

"Heads up!" I snapped, finally freeing Rudi from the hedge of hands.

Kay spared a quick look and scrambled to his feet, his gun had fallen away so he drew his machete.

"We've got to keep them in the garden," he ordered, and delivered a quick coup-de-gras to his fallen target.

I brushed past Rudi, who had drawn her own back-up weapon, some kind of pick or rock hammer, and brought my blade down across the crown of an emerging zombie's skull. I dropped the cadaver in the gateway and the others, coming up behind and dragging their feet as they were, stumbled and fell over the thing.

Given space to move, Kay easily finished the zombies who'd escaped the garden, and Rudi and I made short work of the others as they fell over each other. There were about ten in all.

When it was done, Kay picked up his gun.

"You bit?" he asked hotly.

"No," Rudi replied. "I'm sorry Kay, I got distracted by the hands in the hedge," she offered weakly.

Kay picked up Rudi's rifle and thrust it at her.

"Don't break line of sight again," he hissed and, with me behind, we headed back to the group.

"So, you game?" he asked, his voice still angry.

"I'm here, aren't I?" Maybe not the most considered of replies but, while I could admire his skill, I still didn't like the guy.

He ground his teeth, "Well, good work back there," the praise was as reluctantly offered as it was grudgingly accepted. "But," he rounded on me with his finger raised warningly, "don't break formation again!"

"Alright," I answered, adding just for myself "dickhead." I went back for the cans of gas I'd left with the others.

The check-point was pretty much how we'd left it. A couple of drifters had wandered in and now stood aimlessly on the tarmac but, at the edge of the road I spotted something that I hadn't noticed before. It looked like a digital camera, fixed to a short rod, stuck in the ground.

"What's that?" I asked quietly.

"That's how they stream those promo-videos on the main site," Kay grunted brusquely.

That meant that the 'video' I'd watched had been a live stream and... I shut down the chain of thought as Kay carried on.

"Alright, shut up and listen up," He ordered tersely. It probably sounded better in his head.

"One can each for the Landies, three-apiece for the lorries. No-one shoots unless I do. Newbie, take the lead Landie, got it?" he stared at me as he finished the instructions.

"Got it." I was getting fed-up of being singled out. As soon as Jay was up to speed, I'd push for our group to move on and leave this asshole behind, but still I hurried over to him as the group broke apart.

"I thought I was driving one of the trucks?" I asked, keeping my voice firm.

Kay stopped, turned.

"Your precious 'Drive level two'?" he dropped the air quotes mockingly. "Cal might rate it, might want to keep you around because of it, but not me. You drive what I say you drive and, if you're lucky, you'll level again, eventually," he sneered as I fumed silently.

Rudi and Kay went forward to deal with the new arrivals, and then I and the other drivers scurried forward to do our part. I dropped off a can by one of the oh-so-valuable trucks and hurried on to fill the furthest Land Rover. The sooner the job was done, the sooner I could get Kay off my back. That happy thought occupied me as I quietly poured the fuel into the vehicle's tank.

As I finished, one of the others put a can down just a little too hard, the hollow metallic sound catching me by surprise. I started upright, spilling a little of the precious fuel and stopped. There was a rustle in the trees on the bank. The thick evergreens trembled as if stirred by a strong breeze where there was none.

I popped the cap back into place and, glancing around to see if anyone else had heard the sound, put the empty can gently into the bed of the Rover and crept toward the trees that lined the roadside. The bank was steep, the trees started a little ways up, and I couldn't see through or beyond them. I was approaching the edge of the tarmac when, a little to my left, a zombie slid from under the trees, face down, and rolled onto the road. Another followed it, then another, off to my right, the rustling getting more intense as I backed away.

The others were starting to look up at the noise, but couldn't see the source around the bulky military vehicles. I had to warn them, and I didn't have time for anything fancy. There was only one word for what was coming through the trees toward us.

"Horde!" I called frantically and dived for my Land Rover.

I climbed in the passenger side, shifted over to the driver's door, punched the lock down and began to wind the crank to close the window as more zombies fell through the trees.

Kay, the dumbass that he was, appeared at the passenger door, probably to remonstrate me for 'breaking noise discipline' before he actually saw the tide of bodies dragging themselves unsteadily to their feet. He clamped his mouth shut and scrambled into the car.

"Where's the key?" I demanded and he pointed to the sunshade.

I tugged it down and a key ring dropped into my lap. As soon as I had it in I twisted it and leaned on the horn.

"What are you doing?" Kay demanded, desperately as I drew the attention of the horde to our vehicle.

Firing the ignition and pumping the gas hard I brought the engine grumbling to life, "Whatever I can!" I snarled back.

Chapter 20

It was only a short while later that our little convoy pulled up to the gates of Cal's co-op. Kay climbed out and rapped his knuckles on the sheet-metal gates. When they swung open, I drove my vehicle into the farmyard for the second time. The two trucks followed behind me and the gates were pushed closed.

I stopped the engine, killed the ignition and let out a deep breath. I still had the packet of cigarettes in my trouser pocket so, with unsteady hands I pulled one out and lit it with the jet-lighter. I sucked in a breath, puffing out a stream of harsh smoke as I watched my STR bar drop.

I could see Cal hurrying up through the mess of spider-web cracks and spattered blood on the windscreen.

"What happened?" he demanded, and I noticed just then that, femme and aging as his avatar was, it was still taller than Kay, and looked down at him almost imperiously.

Kay avoided Cal's eyes.

"A horde, just off the road. We lost Aben and Rudi, their car got swarmed, nothing we could do about it."

"Nothing?" Cal demanded, his voice came hoarse and harsh but there was no accusation there.

Kay lifted his head to meet those storm-grey eyes.

"If Lex hadn't warned us, none of us would've gotten away."

Cal shifted, uneasily. "I'll check in on them after log-out, for the meantime let's look over the vehicles you did save."

"If you don't mind, I'm going to take a minute." Kay shouldered his rifle and headed off toward the canteen tent, Cal just staring after him.

I opened my door and stepped out and away from the vehicle into the fading light of the afternoon. I hunched down to check for any 'passengers' I might have dragged along with us but, aside from blood and bits, there was nothing intact enough to cause any trouble.

"What happened?" Cal asked as I straightened up.

"More or less as Kay said," I shrugged. "A horde came out of the trees just as we finished filling up. The trucks and I got rolling, but the other Landie must have flooded. By the time we got ahead of the pack and turned around to go back and see what we could do, it was too late. The Z's had already crossed onto the other carriageway, so we had to plough through. Someone'll have to check that." I flipped a thumb at the Land Rover. "It should be okay, but it was rattling on the way back."

Cal saw right through my sanitized report. "How bad was it?" he asked flatly.

I sighed, deeply and looked him square in the eyes.

"We thought we saw Rudi waving for help as we came back, thought she'd gotten on top of the Rover somehow." I shook my head slowly. "Three or four of the fucks were using her torso like a hand-puppet."

"Jesus!" Cal breathed. "I hope she got out alright."

A shaft of anxiety pierced the lead-weight of my stomach, the first sensation I'd felt since the world greyed out over the horrifying sight. "It's not an image I'll be able to forget any time soon." I replied hoarsely.

More co-operative players were heading over to the vehicles.

"Hey!" I called, sudden anger drowning my unease. "Keep back until we've checked under the trucks, or do you *want* to get bitten off at the ankles?"

Cal watched me thoughtfully and his next question held no fear, but was simply matter-of-fact.

"Is there any chance the horde's heading for us?"

"I don't know," I admitted. "We put them behind us as fast as we could. The turning to the co-op is a couple of miles from the checkpoint. They should just wander right past it."

"Look," he spoke slowly. "I know it's mid-shift but you and your friends haven't signed on with us officially so, if you want to log out for a bit no-one's going to hold it against you."

I considered it for a moment.

"I'm going to go check on my friends," I stated. "I'll decide then."

As I stalked toward the farmhouse, Ned hurried out and practically dragged me to one side.

"Christ Ned, what the hell are you up to?" I demanded.

"It's Jay," she hissed. "He asked me to grab you as soon as you got back, he was *very* insistent."

I wrestled my arm away from the other player's grasp. "Alright, alright. Where is he?"

"Upstairs, waiting with Indi. Come on." Ned's voice was hushed as she hustled me inside.

I stepped into the upstairs room we'd all 'slept' in just a few hours before.

"So?" I demanded. "What's going on?"

Jay, Indi and Ned shared worried glances.

My anger flared at their unwillingness to answer me and I thumped the wall with a fist. "God damnit," I growled. "Look, I was just on a pretty hard raid and we lost a couple of characters, so spit it out!"

Jay grimaced and nodded.

"Okay, so, you remember I told you about the life-line programme I was working on?"

"To hold a connection to the central server? Yeah, what about it?" I wasn't in any mood for a long-winded technical lecture.

He avoided my eyes. "I think someone's noticed it," he admitted sheepishly.

"Oh for fuck's sake!" I snapped. "How? Who?"

"That's the bit you're not going to like," Indi chimed in.

"Well somebody fucking tell me."

"I asked Cal about the whole Leadership trait thing and if we could test it," Jay began.

"And?" I was grinding my teeth by this point.

"Well, they have a practice area, like a little enclosure they use for just the purpose, and we went to give it a test."

"Get to the point."

"Well, for a start you were right. I wasn't 'capped' by my Squeamish trait when Cal let a mob in, but that's when things got weird."

I narrowed my eyes suspiciously. "Weird how?"

"Well, at first it just looked at me," he stated hesitantly. "Cal didn't see, he was holding the door on the Z-shed, but the thing honestly just looked at me then it pointed and said 'hacker', and it attacked me."

"Hacker?" I asked incredulously. "Did Cal hear it?"

"If he did, he didn't say anything, I managed to fight it off, just, but there are two things I noticed that have me worried."

"Go on."

167

"Okay, when the Z came at me I would swear it ran. I mean, the practice ring isn't huge, but I'm telling you it ran, and the second thing is that, the main reason Cal didn't see this is because the two other Z's in the shed went for the door too. It was all Cal could do to hold it closed."

Worried was a bit of an understatement, what Jay was describing was a switch up from 'Romero's' to 'Rage' zombies. "Are you sure? It couldn't just have been a coincidence, maybe a glitch?"

"I can't say for sure," Jay erred and it wasn't at all like him to be non-committal, "but I think we should get out of here, soon as possible."

I raised a weary hand to my forehead. "Alright, we've been in-game for hours, let's secure the room and log out. Meet on messenger in an hour to discuss our next steps?"

The other nodded. So, after locking the door, and giving Ned my online contact details, I logged out.

I let the VR rig rise from my head, the sprung mechanism lifting it away. A nagging pain was building in my head so I rubbed my temples. I looked at the time: 9pm.

I needed some tea, something to eat and some painkillers for my head.

I slogged down the stairs and into the kitchen. Light from the living room drew me over to see Mum asleep on the sofa. With a sigh, I roused her to a semblance of semi-consciousness and guided her upstairs until she fell, snoring, into bed. Back downstairs the TV was on, volume down, subtitles blinking at the bottom of the screen. Stories of rising civil unrest, racially and politically motivated attacks, inter-community violence. I stood and watched it as the kettle boiled, my blood boiling alongside it as another privilege-steeped MP was wheeled out to give their overblown opinion on matters they knew nothing about.

The screen on Mum's computer was dark, but the power light pulsed gently. Taking my coffee, I tapped the touchpad, simply intending to turn the laptop off, but a strange idea stopped me. What had Mum working so late? Could it be the same case she'd been working on before? The lock-screen waited patiently for the password. Big deal, I'd known my mother's password since I was fourteen.

The screen lit up with windows. A quick look through showed dozens of cases, not just in the UK but all over the world. At the back of the queue of windows was a letter from the World Health Organisation. I was shocked. If the WHO was involved, and so soon after the DHSC, they must be really concerned.

A brief look told me all I needed. All the sufferers or victims had been found at home, near their computers. Some had clearly been using VR rigs, but I was willing to bet they all had. I emailed myself the names and locations, turned the machine off and hurried upstairs.

It didn't take long with the details to social-media stalk the victims. The feeds were full of 'thoughts and prayers', but that wasn't what I was looking for. I wanted to know if any of these gamers had streams, and just *what* they were streaming.

Lex? My messenger window jumped up on my screen, had it been an hour already?

Ned, good to see you found me, I typed back. Jay and Indi couldn't be far behind.

So, what do *you* think is going on?

I looked up from the pages I was scrolling through.

I honestly hope I'm wrong, I typed. *I'm just doing a little research of my own. Hopefully I'll come up with something shortly.*

I'd worked down my list until I reached a page that came up with a site-link. The mouse pointer hovered for a second before I clicked.

For a moment the window whited out, a hiccup in the bandwidth, and then it filled. There were thumbnails for videos, a header for the title text and side-bar menu and, in the top-left corner, an avatar in an action pose.

I stared. I stared long and hard as messages from Jay and Indi flashed up in the bottom of my screen but I ignored them. My fingers tapped out my next message slowly.

I think the game is killing people
No Way!
You're kidding, right?
What the fuck?

My friends' messages came thick and fast, but I was sure. The screen-cap image stood there, flipping me off in hi-def, clad in nothing more than high-top combat boots, white briefs, and a welder's mask.

Lex, how do you know? Jay's message brought me back to the conversation.

I thought about how to say it, then decided to go with the truth.

My mum's a neurologist. There was a case referred to her. I got a look at the files tonight and there are more cases. The DoH and WHO are concerned. I lifted some details and tracked down one of the victims' streaming pages. Here, take a look. I copy/pasted the link and waited.

That's privileged information, Lex, you could get in a world of trouble for this.

I know, I typed. *But if I'm right there are who knows how many players in danger right now.*

I don't get it. Ned messaged finally. I guessed Indi and Jay were as overwhelmed as I had been.

We saw this player, Ned, outside the supermarket, before you showed up. His avatar was the same as the one on his page, the boots, underpants and welder's helmet. I guess it's his trademark.

It was true, from a brief look at his page and the avatar displayed in the corner, this streamer tailored his avatars the same way every time.

I think I've seen some of his videos. He was new to the scene, trying to carve out a following by doing stupid stunts in games. The last video was uploaded the day before we saw him. Jay messaged.

I guess we should take a look, see if it really was him.

I skipped most of the content, the player bragging and making bad jokes, generally rambling. The graphics from the stream were much poorer than in-game, whether he was screen-capping or filming from within his helmet I couldn't tell, but there was no denying that he was playing *Rendered Flesh*. I had to stop toward the end, wind back just to make sure. There was the chainsaw and the promise to try it out in the next video, but there were no more videos.

So, after we saw his avatar die? Indi asked.

We talked about the trauma of being eaten alive, especially with the feedback we experience in-game. I'm not a doctor, but I'd say the trauma was too much. He's catatonic, unresponsive, and his organ functions are failing.

So, if you can't exit before they really tear into you…? That from Ned.

Real world death, eventually, I supplied.

That can't be right, it's not possible. Jay's cursor blinked. *Even if it was the dev's couldn't be allowing it to happen.*

Maybe Jay was right, maybe I was being paranoid, jumping to conclusions, but I had the proof, finally here at my fingertips.

All I know right now is that these people, these victims are dying, slowly in hospital beds in different countries and the only link between them is Rendered Flesh.

So that's it. I guess we stop playing then? Indi asked. *Hit the boards and warn everyone?*

If they believe us, Ned cautioned.

There's something else, Jay typed. *I took a quick peek at the code when we logged out, just looking for basic stuff to get my bearings, but there's something wrong with the game world clock. It's going backwards.*

Backwards? I typed.

And not just backwards. It's actually counting down. I don't know why. I'd have to go back in, establish a better connection to the central server to look more closely.

So, what do we do?

I still say we hit the forums.

Even though you know what they're like Indi? I replied. *We'd be down voted as frauds, worse, people who *did* believe us might start playing the damn game to see if it was true. No, we have to get players out of the game from inside or find a way to shut it down.*

Should we contact the police? Maybe tell your mother?

I doubt the cops would take us seriously, and my mother *might* try to stop me playing.

You mean you're not? Indi messaged. *You're the one saying the game is killing people.*

But why? Something must've come through in the beta, they've got to have tested the trauma feedback. At this point, the game is the only thing we've got to go on.

Still, why go back in? What can you do?

Somebody has to do something, even if it's just to try and pull people out, so I'm going back in. I stabbed the keyboard with my fingers. *But I'm not expecting any of you to come with me.*

The cursor blinked back at me for a few moments.

I don't know that I really believe this, Jay typed, *I don't know if there's a real risk, but I really want to learn all I can about this proprietary software. Maybe I can pull something that'll tell us what's going on too,* Jay replied.

We owe it to Cal and his clan to at least try to warn them, Ned typed.

Indi's message took a little longer to come through, a subtle but significant pause.

I guess I'll have to come along, just to make sure you don't get yourselves killed for real. When *are* we going back in?

No point in going back now, Cal might listen to us but I doubt any of the other shifts would take our word for it. Besides, I'm fried. I'm struggling to think straight as it is.

So we go back to meet Cal's shift, 2:00pm GMT.

I checked my clock, it was nearer eleven than ten, and, despite the urgency of my discovery, it didn't seem real. The faces were all pictures on a screen, the details simply text on a page. My vision hazed for a moment before I shook my head to clear it.

Right, I'll see you all later then.

Chapter 21

"People don't want to hear the truth because they don't want their illusions destroyed."
– Friedrich Nietzsche

> Auto Lvl 3 bonus applied:
> Vehicle durability increased by 16%, handling
> improved by 7%

Screams and gunfire assaulted my ears, a miasma of decay, blood and smoke filled my nostrils, and I could feel the struggle and press of bodies at my back as I wrestled against the clinging, biting dead. The farmhouse was properly ablaze now, the windows shattered by the heat. It was good that we hadn't tried to hide, wait the attack out. With a groan of metal and cracking of timber, another section of the outer wall fell. A chaotic melee roiled around me. I had my gun out, I hadn't had time to switch to my blade and, true enough, without the firearms skill I felt my hands were bound together at the wrists. Whenever I made to raise the pistol, my gun hand dragged the other with it. A zombie lurched forward, grabbing my shoulders as I tried to fend it away. I tried to angle the weapon, fighting the programming even as I wrestled the zombie, but the combination of code and the snarling, snapping corpse in my face prevented me from getting the barrel to point anywhere useful. Over the corpse's shoulder I spotted a couple of zombies headed my way.

Held as I was, my forearm jammed under the zombie's chin, my gun hand pressed into its soft, pustulent stomach, there was little I could do. The cadaver thrust forward to snap at me and I let it, swinging us both, trying in desperation to slip the zombie's grip. The Z held tight, its ragged nails raking at my skin. Another shove from the zombie, and I could feel the heat from the blazing farmhouse on my back. I'd barely realised we'd been pushed that far back from the gate. As it lunged again, I took what hold I could on its fetid clothing and stepped back, hauling harder to throw it off balance and pitching it into the burning house.

Free of the thing, I raised my pistol to the incoming threat when a burst of automatic fire took both zombies down from the side. Even as the chatter of the gun faded, more screaming cut through the chaotic scene. A player's avatar beyond the zombies was caught by friendly fire. Too many zombies, too many players, no organisation. The chaos and carnage threatened to consume us, we had to get out.

I'd woken in the late morning, gone downstairs to an empty house to eat and checked my messages. I had a PM from Ned. She still hadn't heard anything from her previous clanmates and wanted to know if they were on the list I'd taken from mum's case notes. She supplied their tags, the names she knew and approximate locations.

I'd searched for an hour or more. Social media, chat boards for the games they played, but hadn't been able to find a concrete link. I didn't really want to say unless I was sure. I mean, if I told her they were lying in hospital beds, vital functions slowly fading away, and then one of them popped up alive, would that be better than the idea that they'd ghosted her for surviving? Or the creeping dread that they just hadn't been found yet? In the end I replied that I'd try to get another look at Mum's files so that I could be certain. Maybe the truth was that I didn't want to be certain.

We logged in, just as planned. I scanned the room and checked my status bars.

STM	

HLT	

STR	

"Everyone ready?" I asked the room in general.

Jay rubbed absently at his wrist. "As we can be," he supplied.

"I don't know how we're going to convince them," Indi grumbled. "It still seems crazy to me,"

Ned's reply was solemn. "We just have to do our best,"

Maybe that was why I didn't look out the window of the farmhouse in-game; I was caught up with a selfish moral dichotomy of what to tell Ned, when I really should have been paying attention. We were outside before I picked up on the tension in-camp. The food tent was untended, the lookouts were fully stationed, and over by the barn where the bulk of the players left their dormant avatars, more players were emerging with weapons in hand.

I glanced at my companions; we were all armed so, at a crouching run we headed for the gate. From the top of one of the ramshackle watchtowers Cal spotted us and held up a hand, finger to his lips. He scrambled down to the ground and beckoned us forward. I gestured for the others to stay and slid silently forward. This close to the wall, I could hear the wheezing susurration of zombies outside the walls, the little noises as a ring or a hand bumped the corrugated steel.

I kept my voice down to a harsh whisper. "What's going on?"

"The herd you encountered yesterday, it must have managed to trace the salvage party back somehow. We're trying not to set them off, but it doesn't look good," he whispered in reply.

My heartbeat started to pick up and my wrist started a gentle pulse of its own. "You've got to log out, all of you. Right now," I hissed urgently.

"Why?" he asked, confused. "If we keep our heads down they might just drift on by. We've called on the whole co-op just in case, there's still a dozen or so dormant but all the leaders are here. If it goes bad, we'll give it our best shot or die trying."

I flinched at the phrase. "You don't know how right you are. Listen Cal, people are dying IRL because of this game."

He stared at me, scepticism and surprise at war on his avatar's face.

"Really!" I urged anxiously.

His expression squirmed as he tried to rationalise what I was saying, it was that or he was deciding if I was nuts or not. "I mean, I guess that light blast as you log in might trigger epilepsy?" he shrugged.

I eyed him steadily. "It's not that, Cal, we don't have time for me to explain but trust me. If this goes south you don't want any of your people in-game when it does."

He frowned down at me, and reached a conclusion, the grey eyes of his avatar hardened.

"Oh I see, you're after the prize money and you're trying to scare us off," he nodded slowly, sadly. "I thought better of you, Lex. Once the horde passes, you take your group and leave." He turned his back on me.

"Cal!" I reached out and grabbed his arm.

He turned, his speed belying his avatar's age, and punched me. Just a little rabbit-punch to my jaw, but enough to sit me hard on my arse in the dirt.

"Lex!" I heard Jay cry, his voice a whip-crack in the quiet. Turning I looked to see him dash forward. In the same moment, all the other little noises, the 'tinks' and 'thuds', the wheezy breathing from beyond the wall, stopped.

We froze. I turned my head slowly toward the gate.

The horde screamed. All of a sudden the quiet exploded as the zombies hammered on the tin barricades and the gate bulged.

"Cal!" I heard a watcher from the tower shout before gunfire erupted all around us.

I scrambled to my feet and dashed back to my crew.

"Back in the farmhouse!" I ordered.

Indi planted his feet. "Have you seen *Night of the Living Dead? Non, merci.*"

"But we moved all our gear inside!" I insisted.

Ned shook her head, "If we go back in there we're as good as dead!"

As if to reinforce the point, there was a loud crash from beyond the farmhouse and more frantic shouting.

There was a sharp, metallic 'pop' as the chain on the gate snapped, and Indi stepped past me, squaring his broad shoulders.

An engine revved, drawing more howls from the horde and a car lurched forward then sputtered. Whether or not they had planned to block the gate with a vehicle when the horde got riled, someone had fucked up and flooded it, rolling to a stop only halfway across and zombies swarmed the stricken vehicle. Another truck, an old and battered utility vehicle that probably came with the farm, lurched out of the vehicle shed and, tyres spinning in the mud, churned its way toward the gate and the zombies crowding through. I don't know if the driver meant to add to the barricade or lost their nerve and tried to ram an escape route, but, as the thick knot of Z's came around the gate, the Ute ploughed into them. The truck smashed the zombies crowding the car and pitched upward, piling over those coming through the gate as it slid sideways, slewing across a shifting carpet of zombies to smash into the opposite side of the gateway. The wall shuddered along its entire length, even the watchtower swayed. The Ute's engine roared as the driver stomped on the gas. The back end, hung up on a pile of squirming zombies, fountained lumps of flesh and gouts of black blood. I didn't see the zombies get in, but the driver started screaming and the engine rose to a howl and stayed there.

My voice quavering and my nerve faltering I demanded. "What do we do?"

Indi turned to me, a feral smile on his lips. "We fight!" my friend ordered.

"Why?" Jay demanded, eyes wide in fear.

"Because that's what they're going to do," Indi replied grimly.

He was right. Cal's crew were going to fight the horde, ignorant of the risk. We couldn't just leave them.

A screaming, burning figure staggered out of the farmhouse and I raised my pistol to shoot, my gun hand dragging the other behind it with inexorable gravity until I held the pistol in a teacup grip that I'd never intended.

Ned grabbed for my gun, panicked. "Don't, it might be a player!"

"I know!" I rasped and pulled the trigger.

The first shot went wide so I gritted my teeth and fired again, dropping the blazing figure face first into the mud.

"How do you know you didn't just kill that person?"

I rounded on Ned, eyes reddened by smoke and tears, lips pulled back in a mad rictus grimace. "I don't," I rasped.

I'd decided, there and then, that I wasn't wasting bullets on the zombies. It stood to reason that an instant death would likely just lead a player back to the login screen; lots of characters must die in this game, only a few IRL, so it must be the tortuous deaths that were killing those unfortunate souls. Right or wrong I'd made the choice, each of my bullets was saved as a get-out for players who couldn't get themselves out. It was all I had to cling to at that moment.

"Indi, we have to go!" I screamed amidst the erratic gunfire and howling zombies.

With a groan and a mighty crash, the metal wall by the damaged gate caved under the weight of putrid bodies pressing against it. It collapsed inward, bringing down the watchtower with it. More screams erupted and

I flinched, hands covering my head as a line of stray bullets stitched the ground nearby.

"Where's Cal?" Indi demanded.

A zombie coming toward me caught sight of Jay, and its unsteady gait became a ragged run as it veered toward him. I swung my hook as it completely ignored me, catching it across the eyes as it passed. It flopped limply to the ground, its brain matter oozing out of its new sun-roof skull.

I swept the bloodied steel toward the barn where our erstwhile host was organising a ragged defence of the inert avatars.

The farmyard was a tangle of players and mobs struggling, fighting, dying. The smoke from the farmhouse was giving us some cover, but whenever a Z spotted Jay, they would make a beeline for him and others would turn to join them.

Indi took off toward the barn. "Get them out of here!" he ordered over his shoulder.

"What the fuck, Indi?" I screamed after him but he didn't stop.

Whatever progress had been made with Cal hadn't prepared Jay for this chaos. "We need to get to the shed, get our truck," he gabbled frantically.

With a quick nod, Ned led Jay and I through the chaos, my hands shaking and my wrist pulsing gently. As we reached the big open doors I stumbled. Looking down, I saw a hand around my ankle reaching from under a couple of true-dead zombies and, gazing up at me, Carrie's wide-eyed, waxen and tear-streaked face.

"Log me out, please!" their voice emerged, a ragged thing, hoarse with pain.

I shook my head in confusion. Carrie's health bar, low to the point of failing was falling agonizingly slowly, just a small chunk at a time; as the zombies ate, I realised in horror.

"Kill me!" Carrie insisted but my brain rebelled. Why couldn't they log out? What was wrong, couldn't I just get them out of here, bring them with us?

I hauled the first zombie's body off them and recoiled in shock and revulsion at the wet meat and metallic blood reek that washed over me. The player's stomach was a mess of torn, glistening flesh and bulging, shivering entrails. The second Z wasn't dead as I'd first thought; it was just intent on eating. Even as I watched, it jerked its head to worry at a stubborn mouthful, and Carrie sobbed through teeth gritted so hard I'm sure they cracked with the pressure. I struck down with my hook, a cry of revolted anguish escaping my own throat as I dragged the second zed away. Carrie screamed, ribbons of gut still caught in the thing's splintered teeth pulling out of their stomach, so I dropped the corpse.

Beyond the ruin of their body, I could now see the bloody stump that ended Carrie's right arm at the elbow, the menu arm. My mind raced, trying to think of ways to save them, but my gun hand was more pragmatic.

I put my pistol to Carrie's head and squeezed the trigger. At least the mercy-killing didn't require two hands, my brain supplied coldly. The tin wall behind was suddenly dark, dripping scarlet. I turned away, hand to my mouth, trying not to be sick. My wrist throbbed alarmingly. The stench of cordite from the pistol helped, just a little. The echoes of the shot ringing in my ears.

> Psychological Trauma Imminent, seek assistance

As I straightened up, Jay and Ned stared at me in wide-eyed horror.

"Get inside!" I half barked, half sobbed. "Get in the truck and wait for me!"

I hauled the squealing door closed behind them and pressed my back against it. I felt as though cold fingers had wrapped over my collar bone, piercing my flesh and pulling down on my ribcage. The rising panic and horror threatened to drag me down as surely as any rotting zombie.

I sniffed, a damp sucking sniff, and wiped away the worst of the tears, snot and spit from my anguished face with my bloodied hands. I couldn't stop, couldn't lie down and die, so I took off again, running for the closest of the big army rigs we'd recovered the previous day. If I could get it over to the barn, then maybe Cal could evacuate some of his people. Maybe then Indi would agree to leave. I slammed my hand on the corrugated steel. Screaming with choked rage, I hammered the door with my palms, heedless of signalling any nearby zombies. The pulse in my wrist eased. Whether the devs reasoned catharsis or primal scream therapy an appropriate treatment, I managed to pull the meter down a bar by almost sheer will.

Three steps from the garage, the propane tank that fed the farmhouse went up. Smoke, flame and the concussion wave nearly knocked me from my feet and left my ears ringing. As I flinched under the hail of debris, I realised it was too late. Zombies were flooding the yard through the breaks, and the remaining walls were collapsing under the strain. A zed lunged at me. I stepped away and to the side, bringing the brush hook down on its head and letting the weight of the stinking body free the blade as it fell.

> **Combat Lvl 3 achieved, bonus will be applied after rest period**

I pulled back to the garage, hauling the door wide and jumped into the familiar silver Ute.

"I thought you were going after Indi?" Jay exclaimed from the back seat.

I turned over the engine, revving it aggressively. "So did I!" I snapped, Jay shrank back, cowed by my fury.

"Will this thing survive?" Ned quavered. "Will it make it through all the geeks?"

"I don't know, but I'm not risking it!" I declared and turned to face back over my seat.

I'd noticed in my trips out and back that the garage shed, built of corrugated steel like the other farm buildings, had been used as part of the perimeter wall. I threw the Ute into reverse and hammered back, crashing through the thin sheet steel with an echoing 'bang', like ringing a massive dinner-gong. We lurched out into the sparse trees and dappled sunlight that fronted the farmyard. Quickly I switched into forward gear and, tyres spinning, swung the truck toward the exit road, jouncing over the uneven forest floor.

Slewing to a stop under the trees I yelled, "Ned, try to lure some of them off!"

Ned gave a determined nod, opening her door to step out into the billowing smoke when the front passenger door wrenched open and someone, bloodied and soot smeared, jumped into the seat beside me reeking of smoke and shit.

"Hey, asshole!" I heard Jay shout, but I was so shocked by the sudden arrival I'd forgotten what I was doing.

The filthy figure shoved a gun in my face. "What are you waiting for? Drive!" it demanded. Its head snapped back and forth taking in the clumps of zombies all around but the gun never wavered. They yelled, "drive!" again. Snapping out of my shock and surprise, I did.

As Ned dropped back into her seat, we raced away from the farm, speeding through the little village and emerging onto the dual carriageway.

"Keep going," my new 'passenger' growled, and finally the kaleidoscope fragments I recognised slotted together in my shock-addled brain.

"Kay?"

"What?" he snapped.

Fuck.

Chapter 22

I gripped the wheel hard to stop my hands from shaking. Ned and Jay slumped despondently in the back seat. Indi's absence weighed on the group in silence. For his part, Kay stayed scooched hard against the passenger door, pistol in his lap, mumbling to himself and twitching occasionally.

"Pull over here," he blurted suddenly.

I might have been in shock, but I wasn't about to be ordered around by 'Killer-dot-exe'. "Why?"

"I need to make sure you're not bitten!" he snapped and started tugging at my clothes and snatching at my arms.

Ned reached forward, maybe to restrain Kay. "Hey, don't fuck with the driver, dude!" but the agitated gamer turned in his seat, bringing his gun up again.

"Back off!"

"Put that down!" Jay raised his arms defensively. "Haven't you seen *Pulp Fiction?* Jesus?"

"Think I'll shoot you by accident? Keep running your mouth and I'll shoot you on principle!" Kay snapped before turning to face front.

"Fuck!" he raged, hammering on the dashboard to punctuate his exclamations. "Fuck, fuck, fuck! All my gear, my rifle, the meds, the food, all gone!"

"Quit whining, you goddamn man-baby," Jay sneered.

"Hey, fuck you. I'm still not past the point of shooting you to make a damn point!"

The argument rang hollow in my ears, the voices and words meaningless, diffused as if through water while I stared at the durability bar that floated just above the centre of the steering wheel. Thanks to my maintenance, the bar had been full when I turned the key. With everything that had happened since, it had dropped a good fifteen or so percent. I wasn't sure how well I could maintain it without the co-op's tools and, for some reason, the idea of simply bouncing from vehicle to vehicle made me slightly nauseous.

I brought us to a slow stop, laced my arms over the top of the wheel and laid my forehead against them.

I didn't shout, didn't cry, just quietly said the words.

"Stop it."

They subsided to silence, the buzz of their bickering quietening.

My voice sounded tired even to me as I spoke. "I need to check the truck, so put the gun down, stay quiet and try not to kill each other." And then I stepped out. I left my passengers to sit like naughty children as I walked around, looking for any significant damage that might cause us problems later. I didn't recall hitting anything, or anybody, but the smears of black blood on the silver paintwork told a different story. Aside from some dents and deep gouges to the paintwork, our exit through the wall didn't seem to have cost us badly. Stopping only to glance under the chassis for unwanted hangers-on, I finished my circuit and climbed back in.

"Should we go back?" I asked.

"Fuck that," Kay grunted. "I should never have signed on with Cal and those other pricks. My kill-count could be into the thousands by now if I hadn't hung around there."

"Not that I was asking you, but thanks for the input." I managed to squeeze out a little sarcasm as I looked in the rear-view at Ned and Jay.

"Hey screw you! I'll blow all your heads off and go out on my own with the food *and* your truck!" Kay snapped.

I turned my head slowly and glared coldly at him.

"Go on then."

"Or I would if I could afford the ammo," he grumbled lamely, turning away.

Jay shook his head. "I don't know that we can go back. Did you see how they reacted to me? I shouldn't even have logged back in."

I wanted to say something reassuring but the numbness was receding and I didn't trust my voice not to crack.

"They were in danger anyway. We'd do them no favours by going back and dying now," said Ned, a sentiment I silently thanked her for.

A deep feeling of guilt crawled into my stomach doing turns like a drowned cat on a necrotic pillow. Doubt and 'what if' gnawed at my guts like rats.

183

"The fuck are you talking about?" Kay decided to butt back in. "Sounds like you want to claim responsibility? The game saw a gathering of players and an algorithm decided to hit us and the noobs couldn't handle it, simple as, end of."

I gripped the steering wheel, fingers flexing angrily. "For God's sake Kay, will you stow your 'Alpha-Gamer' bullshit? You have no idea what's going on here!" I snapped suddenly. "This game is killing people, IRL killing people, and someone's got to stop it!"

Kay shook his head. "You're crazy, games don't kill people, people kill people."

"Then you've got three choices," I stated grimly. "One, kill us like you say, because we're not getting out of this truck. Two, grab your shit and get the hell out of the truck and our way, or three, sack-up, shut-up and come with us. You never know, you might get those thousands of kills you're jonesing for, and if it all goes to hell, you can run away while zombies eat us."

His eyes hardened. He was probably butt-hurt from me calling his bluff, but I wasn't about to pander to his ego.

"Fine" he blurted suddenly. "So, what's the plan?"

"We should head for the base," Ned pointed out. "We were headed there anyway. If Indi's alive he should be heading that way too."

"It might even be secure!" Jay chimed in with an optimism I attributed more to desperation than sense. But optimism was a trap we couldn't afford to fall into right now. "We shouldn't get our hopes up," I cautioned. "Maybe we ought to find a secure location, get Jay out of sight, then run a little recon first."

My hands were shaking and I realised I was in shock. My stress meter was still throbbing away steadily. I hadn't noticed it while I argued with Kay, buoyed up by anger, but now I pulled the battered cigarette packet from my pocket, slipped a coffin-nail between my lips and thumbed the jet-lighter to life. I puffed the cigarette angrily. Adrenaline might help me meet Kay's bravado like-for-like, but much as I wanted to act like a strong leader, I was reluctant to make a call, and indecision could get us killed right now.

"Just drive!" Kay insisted and, with no real reason not to, I got us rolling again.

We drove in silence for a good twenty minutes. A few discarded cars littered our side of the road, but soon the opposite carriageway became nose to nose with abandoned vehicles. Clusters of them nothing more than blackened, smoking shells on the tarmac.

According to the map we'd seen, there was a city farther down the road, so this, I reasoned to myself, was the evacuation. In places, zeds watched us as we rolled by, waiting patiently for the impetus to follow us to kick their atrophied muscles into motion. That map was still in the glove compartment of our truck, but I'd be damned if I was going to let Kay see it yet. I worked from memory as far as I could, and just as I was starting to get hazy, there was a sign to show me the way.

I rolled on to the verge and stopped, just to be sure.

Stepping out, I looked up at a billboard attached to the side of a big warehouse looking building. It rose above the fences and scrub at the side of the road. Over the generic-looking advertising someone had scrawled in bright blue spray:

"The biggest risk in life is not taking one."
– Rebecca Solnit

I hoped, come the apocalypse, that I'd have the presence of mind to tag uplifting quotes on random walls like that.

Kay scoffed. "That's fucking stupid, killing people is much riskier."

I almost felt that his ignorance was killing me by inches. "It means 'risks' *George*!" I drew out the name venomously. "The biggest risk in life is not taking risks!" I snapped impatiently.

"How did you…" he gawped impotently for a moment, the expression comical on his grizzled face.

"It's nihilism, genius. More than that, it's a clue. It means we're on the right track."

I took us off the road, following a sign intended for military traffic, and into the sprawling, rambling suburbs of the town. Clouds had covered the sky and the sun was setting. The scene was a washed-out grey: lifeless and dead.

I was reminded, as I let the Ute crawl forward over curbs and through crashed cars, how different this British-styled town was to the American suburbs I'd seen in films. Those sets were all wide streets, low houses and long sight-lines. This suburb was closed in and tight packed, circa 1970's architecture with steep drives and pebble-dashed walls. Where the houses weren't terraced, the gaps between them were narrow and strangely dark. Unlike the village we'd left behind, the signs of violence were clear here. Soot stains from fires, smashed vehicles, blood and bodies. Not all the signs indicated the zombies as the clear offenders either. Subtle details here and there hinted at human-on-human violence. My mind boggled at the kind of person who could use a disaster as an excuse for creating more harm, more fear and more loss in the world, but, as I knew from simply watching the news, all some people needed was an opportunity.

I watched warily for any signs of movement. If we got caught out here, our chances of escape were slim. I didn't want to turn a corner into a patiently waiting horde any more than I wanted to cross paths with some adrenaline-fuelled player armed with military grade weaponry. Even as the thought crossed my mind, the chatter of automatic gunfire echoed over the cold, quiet buildings.

"Not close," Jay mumbled. All my passengers had their eyes glued to their windows watching for trouble.

Another thought struck me and I started to watch the road with more purpose than just scanning for threats. After a hundred metres or so, I spotted what I was after and stopped the truck.

"I just need to grab something," I informed my crew and eased my door open.

Another staccato sound of gunfire carried in the rising breeze, and I felt my skin prickle with gooseflesh. What I wanted was just ahead. The broken window of a small car-accessories shop yawned like a mouth full of broken teeth. The power was out here and the interior was shadowed, but I wasn't too worried; what I wanted was scattered on the pavement in front of the window. Spray cans, all colours.

I squatted, picking a couple of vivid neon shades from among the shards of glass and stood, shifting my weight as I did so and knocking a can spinning with my foot. The can rattled away and I froze.

From within the darkened shop came the rasp of dry throats and small sounds of motion.

I scrambled back to the truck as shadows took form in the dark window, and clawed, grasping hands reached through what was left of the fractured, tempered glass.

"I hope that was worth it!" Kay scolded coldly as I put us in gear and, resisting the urge to floor it, let the engine growl low as we prowled steadily away. Looking in the mirror, I saw the zombies trip on the three-brick high wall of the shop facing. Some stumbled through but others fell, flailing limbs entangling still more.

"If it leads Indi back to us, it was worth it." I grunted.

"I don't get it," Kay mused. "When you talk about Indi you say 'him' but then he must be about twelve because he's got a voice like a…"

"Don't even finish that thought," I snapped coldly. "He's a he, I'm a they, and you're an asshole so you get no say in the matter anyway."

Kay thought for a moment, then came that leering grin like he thought he'd cottoned on to a particularly dirty joke.

I grimaced, tasting bile in my throat. "Just shake the fucking can," I ordered and swung around a corner, breaking line of sight, and pulled to a stop.

Taking the paint, I hopped out again and hurried to the corner we'd just left. On the wall I sprayed a large, neon pink arrow pointing the way we were travelling.

It wasn't going to be enough. The walls around us were screaming with graffiti. 'Help', 'Dead Inside', 'Still Alive!' Everywhere walls and doors and windows were tagged with anguish. Bloody handprints beside dripping neon letters begging for help from the army, from God, from me. The spray painted words announced the end, the beginning, the futility of resisting, the importance of struggling on.

Among all that, how did I get Indi's attention?

In the end I highlighted the arrow's point then sprayed a circle on the trailing end, tagged a cross on the bottom, and added a smaller, struck-through arrow. Finally I sprayed Indi's name above the whole thing. Indi would get it, I was sure.

Back in the car, Kay was sulking.

"We need somewhere to hole up." The reminder was probably unnecessary but I said it anyway.

Pointing over my shoulder Ned said, "what about over there?"

The cavernous mouth of a multi-story car park yawned. Hung from the height restriction barrier was a white bed sheet. On the soiled material someone had sprayed the word "Safe" and an arrow pointing up.

Kay grimaced. "I don't like it,"

"Well, tell me when you find something you *do* like, *George!*" I replied snidely.

He raised the pistol again but, this time, Ned surged forward from the backseat. One hand wrapped over the gun, twisting the wrist away while her other arm looped under Kay's elbow, forcing it up and pulling inward, bending the joint unnaturally. Kay let out a pained squawk, his fingers flexing, allowing Ned to rip the gun from his grasp and sit back hard in her seat.

Now released, Kay rubbed at his elbow. The whole thing had taken a split second.

"That, was risky," I stated slowly, Kay was staring daggers at Ned via the rear-view.

"You'd rather I let the shithead keep the gun?" Ned challenged.

"You know what, no. Thanks Ned." I smiled. "Is this going to be a problem, Kay?" I asked, using his tag. He didn't need aggravating further.

"No ma'am," He replied sullenly.

"Good," I replied, too relieved to bother correcting him, and steered our truck toward the parking structure.

The inside was grey and grimy. What cars there were either sat forgotten in the bays, or skewed where they'd been hit by others making panicked exits. I drove us, slowly and quietly, up the levels, noting how the stairwells had been blocked by carefully positioned cars. When we got to the penultimate floor, the 'Up' ramp was blocked, again by a barricade of carefully positioned vehicles. I set the handbrake and switched off the engine, slipping the keys into the driver side door cubby. If we needed to leave in a hurry I wanted the keys in the truck.

Slowly I opened the door, stepping out into the gloomy interior.

Beyond the barrier I could see the stairwell door, unblocked on this level.

I watched as my companions emerged from the truck.

I could hear the distant moans of geeks carried to my ears on the wind, but there was no sign of anything here.

We hopped over the car barrier. Scuffs on a bonnet showed where others had done the same. With my brush-hook in hand I went to the stairwell door, looking through the narrow, safety-glass window. The stairs down had been blocked. Shopping trolleys, rubbish bags, all manner of debris had been carelessly tossed into an impromptu barricade.

I pushed the door open and looked up. All seemed clear.

One behind the other we slowly ascended to the topmost level, stacking up at the door like in a hundred tactical sims.

I gave a nod, pulled the door wide and Kay moved swiftly through, followed by Ned and Jay with me close behind.

Ahead of us, a camper and car with a caravan sat on the tarmac, a tarpaulin canopy strung between them flapped forlornly in the breeze.

"Pair off, sweep and clear." I motioned Jay to come behind me and we approached the caravan while Ned and George went to the camper.

Blade in hand, I let Jay take hold of the door and counted three on my fingers. The door opened and I swept in, ready to fight, but there was nothing. No zombies, no bodies, not even signs of a struggle.

I checked the toilet and closet, then stepped out, shrugging.

"Clear!" I called across to Ned as she stepped out of the camper.

"Same," she called back.

It looked like whoever had set up this camp had gone, maybe for supplies and simply never come back. The thought sent a shudder down my spine.

Speaking of spines, it looked like Kay had found his.

He strode up, clearly angry again.

"You three have some fucking explaining to do," he announced.

"Jeez, *George*," it was petty I knew, but I drew out the name again, watching his eyes flash with anger. "I thought we cleared this up already," I sighed.

"Yeah, yeah, yeah, the game's killing people, we've got to stick together, blah blah blah." He squared his shoulders and set his jaw. "But what happened back at the farm, the more I think about it the more I think those fucking zeds weren't behaving like any I've seen so far. What the hell was going on?"

Dammit, I shouldn't have riled him more than he already was. "We don't know for sure," I replied, trying to calm his obvious agitation.

"You seem to know everything else, what the hell happened back there?"

I tried to think of some way to soothe the bridling '*Alpha gamer*', but before I could offer anything Jay spoke.

"It's my fault, I was tampering with the code."

"You're a *hacker*?" Kay snarled. "Bullshit, if there were any exploits in RF I'd know about them."

"Not that kind of hack, goddamn Hanzo main," Jay spat back.

Kay's eyes narrowed then, with a snarl, he lunged for Jay.

Chapter 23

Kay's rangy avatar, auburn hair shot through with grey, tensed. The goatee framing his lips curled in a snarl, as he launched himself at Jay.

Small and spare as he was, Jay was a seasoned gamer. He ducked aside, but he obviously didn't have combat stats like Kay, who managed to snag his shirt before he could get away. As the bigger avatar drew back his fist, I leapt forward throwing both my arms around his cocked one. Kay grunted as he tried to swing. The force tugged me forward but I managed to stop him from striking.

"Stop it!" I insisted, but with a savage yank Kay dragged me off-balance, driving his elbow back into my stomach. The wind went out of me and I stumbled, gasping for breath as I fell to the ground. My palms stung as I instinctively thrust them out to catch myself. I might be able to fight a couple of slow zombies, but a living opponent was another matter entirely.

Distracted as he was, Kay didn't see Ned come in, already launching a heel-kick at his sternum.

With a "whuff" of expelled breath, Kay fell back, dropping Jay who had been flailing ineffectively at his arm, and hit the ground.

Unlike my graceless collapse, Kay rolled with the blow and came to his feet panting, eyes locked on Ned. I scrambled to my feet and assumed a boxer's stance, Jay hanging in my peripheral vision.

Ned came on again, throwing jabs. Kay ducked and side stepped. He managed to toss her into Jay. I rushed him from behind, prepared to do my best, but he anticipated my move and I walked straight into his incoming fist. It wasn't a heavy blow, but lights, sharp and bright, exploded across my vision, and pain spread through my teeth and lips as I tasted the tang of blood and fell heavily on my arse.

Ned attacked again as I fell. With Kay swinging for her, she stepped in, took his outstretched arm over her shoulder and, with a twist, hip-tossed the angry gamer.

He landed heavily but rolled again, coming up in a low crouch. For a moment I saw his hand stray to the holster where his gun had been.

Suddenly he straightened up, grunting.

"Fuck this," he swore and stormed off toward the caravan.

Dusting my hands carefully together, I got back to my feet and checked my stats.

HLT		

The fourth bar was flashing but solidified as I watched it. As far as I remembered, I'd been on four bars since we left the farm. Kay hadn't actually taken any bars off me. It raised a question in my head about whether PvP was actually possible, but then I remembered Carrie and shuddered.

Ned helped Jay up.

"Thank you. I'm sorry I'm so goddamned useless," he grumbled apologetically.

Ned smiled kindly. "Don't worry about it, but we ought to figure out how we're going to deal with him. George is a bully. He's uncertain of my stat rank right now, he might try to take me out to get at you."

I was brushing grit from my hands and clothes as I added. "He knows he can't take all three of us, not if we can see him coming. If he does try to push it he'll try to get us alone."

"Yeah, I've come across his type before online." Jay sucked his teeth in distaste. "We might have to deal with him first."

"But not right now," I shook my head wearily. "Let's make sure we're secure and then we can log out," I instructed. "We need to make sure Indi's okay."

With a clatter of hurriedly tossed cupboards and the squeal of rusty hinges, George burst out of the caravan. He strode to a couple of camp chairs set around a gas cooker and slumped down heavily. Picking up the kettle off the stove he gave it a shake. A hollow sloshing signalled it as nearly empty.

Taking a deep breath I walked over, setting my feet and planted my hands on my hips.

"What are you doing?"

Stretching, George put his hands behind his head.

"Leaving you to it. I'm not part of your mob and you can't tell me what to do."

"This is for all of us, not just us here but everyone in-game," I insisted. "This game is killing people George, and we want to find out why."

He shook his head mockingly. "Look, I'm sure you believe that, but if it's all the same to you, I'll be making my own way from here."

I stood for a while, then turned and stalked back to Ned and Jay.

Jay didn't sound surprised as he said. "He's not helping, huh?"

"No," I confirmed angrily.

"What's to stop us," Ned suggested, "waiting for him to log out and then pitching him off the roof?"

I smirked but shook my head. "As much as I like that idea, we're not doing it."

"What's to stop *him* doing the same to us, or fucking off with all of our supplies?" Jay muttered thoughtfully.

"Right now he's unarmed and sulking. It'll take him some time to work up the nerve. In the meanwhile," I stretched, sore and tired. "All we can do is lock the camper. If Kay decides to leave with our supplies? At this point, I'd call it a fair trade," I groaned wearily. I was exhausted, strung-out and in desperate need of respite.

"So, are we out?" Jay asked.

"Yeah," I sighed, "there's not much we can do here and Indi may be trying to reach us IRL."

We traipsed back to the camper and sat around the table. I took a last look at the down-at-heel decor before turning my wrist, swiping to the main menu and tapping the 'Exit' command.

The screen dimmed, fading to black before...

"There may be more beautiful times, but this one is ours."
— Jean-Paul Sartre

Combat Lvl 3 bonus applied
Dmg increased by 16%, stamina drain reduced by 7%

I started and jerked my eyes open.

I had a definite sense of passed time; the sky was darker and I felt somehow more alert.

I looked across at the avatars of Jay and Ned, sitting up, blinking in much the same slightly disoriented way.

"What the hell was that?" Jay asked, anxiety plain in his voice.

"I didn't log out," Ned stated bluntly. "What about you?"

Jay shook his head emphatically, looking more and more worried as he turned imploring eyes on me.

Words failed to form as the implications of our situation started to spin around my mind so I just shook my head numbly.

"Well that's fucking brilliant," Ned spat grimly.

"They've locked us in," Jay breathed, his voice equal parts horror and awe. "I don't know how, but they have."

My wrist started to pulse.

Jay started to breathe rapidly, a frantic panting. "Oh Jesus, oh Jesus!" he repeated.

"Calm down," I held out a hand to take his, "you're hyperventilating."

I sounded calmer than I felt. A wave of anxiety also threatened to carry me away, and Jay's panic was feeding my own, that was the last thing any of us needed.

He pulled his hand away. "Am I? I hadn't realized" he shot back caustically. "It's not bad enough we voluntarily came back into a game that kills people, now we can't log out!?"

"We have to figure this out," Ned said slowly, thoughtfully.

"Right, right." Jay raised hands to his temples, elbows on the table. "First we need more information. I think it's fair to say that this 'lock-in' is in response to my hack."

"Are you *still* doing that?" I demanded.

"Of course I am," Jay waved the question off like an annoying fly. "But what about George?" he ventured suddenly.

"What about him?" I demanded.

Jay replied evenly. "We should establish whether he's affected too." It didn't follow that he couldn't look at a zombie without dry-heaving but faced with this new virtual nightmare he was apparently unfazed. It seemed that Squeamish had its own limits.

Jay was looking at me hopefully.

"Well, shit," I replied. The idea of voluntarily engaging with George was only slightly preferably to French-kissing a zombie but, given our new situation it had to be done.

Standing up reluctantly I fixed them both with a hard stare. "Stay here," I ordered firmly, "give me a few minutes to process this and sound him out. I don't want him trying to use it against us."

George had stated that he would settle in the caravan, so it was just the three of us in the camper. My wrist pulsed steadily with residual stress, and I snatched up a bottle that had been conveniently left behind, slipping off the cap as I stopped on the step of the camper and slugged back something cheap and nasty.

I tried to distract myself from my growing horror at our predicament by considering the impact of the game's tacit message of alcoholism as a coping mechanism in a survival situation, and its place against Maslow's hierarchy of needs, before I decided I was being fucking pedantic and stepping out from under the faded awning of the mobile home to gaze up at the clouds. The camp seemed all the more desolate under a darkening sepia-stained sky.

I stood for a moment to think. How was I going to play this with George, what if he already knew? If he'd tried to log out and discovered he was trapped he might get violent but, considering that an amount of time *had* passed and he hadn't murdered us while we were dormant, he likely didn't know. That led to the question of just what he'd been doing in the interim and, desperate for a distraction as I was, there were some avenues of thought I wasn't prepared to venture down.

A few spots of rain dropped on my cheek and I let out a sigh. As I lowered my head I caught an impression of movement from the caravan. With a frown I hurried to the door of the camper. Even as I went to pull it open George emerged, rucksack on his shoulder and hammer in hand. His eyes widened when he saw me.

"Where are you going, George?" I asked evenly.

He seemed to relax, shrugged, and then bolted for the stairwell.

I rushed after him.

As I burst through the door behind him I called out. "Don't do this!" but he ignored me.

Leaping down the stairs, George pushed off the wall and then down the next level and out onto the concourse where we'd left our truck, with the keys still in it.

I shouldered through the door as he was sliding over the barricade of cars. As I leapt over he was pulling open the truck door.

I grabbed for the sill of the door, wrenching it open only to be met by Kay's boot as he kicked me away. I fell, rolling on the hard asphalt, coming to a rest on my hands, the sting on gravel in my palms.

He hesitated just long enough to smile smugly before he pulled the door shut, the locks clicking closed automatically.

"George!" I hissed from the ground. I might be angry but I wasn't going to risk attracting a horde. "Get out of the car!" I demanded and slapped the window. He just gave me a sickly leer and then the engine growled to life. I hopped back as the big wheels started to turn and stood, impotently, as he backed up, turned and rolled away through the dim concrete structure.

"Mother fucker!" I spat as he stole our wheels and our food.

My spray can rattled as it rolled on the tarmac. It must have fallen out as George was stealing our car. I resisted the urge to kick it away and picked it up as the stairwell door squealed behind me. I span, raising the spray can on instinct.

Ned backed up, hands raised. "Whoa, calm down."

"Sorry," I mumbled, lowering the can before plodding, dejectedly back up the stairs. Jay opened his mouth as I passed, as if to say something, got a look at my expression and closed it again, stepping back out of my way.

Jay had been right, but there wasn't going to be much in the way of victory in his 'I told you so'. I also didn't feel nearly as good about the trade-off as I'd professed I would.

Back at our bleak little camp, I ripped through the caravan for more supplies, angry at George and myself. I managed to put together three new bags with two bottles of water each, maybe three tins and a chocolate bar apiece and some scavenged torches. We only had one incomplete medkit, however. I also found some binoculars. It occurred to me to point them in the direction of the base, see what I could see, when I remembered.

The map and the key card were in the fucking truck.

I sank down in one of the cheap folding camp chairs and put my head in my hands. I didn't cry, not quite, but it took me a moment to collect myself. I'd started to feel strong, capable even, but after the farm, after this? I was shaken.

I managed to gather myself together enough to use the last of the spray on a banner that had been draped over the side of the car park. Someone, maybe the programmers, maybe a player, had daubed *'Help here'* in blue letters three feet high. Using the can I added *'Indi'* in the vibrant neon pink and tossed the banner back to hanging over the side.

I stared out over the drab cityscape for a moment, seeing squat buildings and billboards, roads and abandoned cars. The occasional shape of a shambler moved unsteadily through the streets. With a sharp cry of frustration, I threw the empty can as far as I could.

Dejectedly, I wandered back to the camp chair, sinking into its flimsy embrace. My wrist pulsed gently.

STR					

After a moment, I pulled the cigarettes out of my pocket and lit up, sucking the foul-tasting smoke down and listening to the maudlin sighs of the wind. I didn't have a clue what to do. I had a very rough idea of where we were and where we were going, but without the map I couldn't be sure, and without the key card the chances of us even getting into a military facility dwindled to nothing, and now? Now we couldn't even leave the game.

I sat there in a simulated world I couldn't escape, under a simulated sky heavy with simulated rain clouds, knowing real people were going to die real deaths because of my carelessness. With that thought, the face of Indi's avatar drifted into my mind. I didn't know if he was alive or dead, but it was telling that his avatar was how I pictured him now…With an effort, I swapped the face for Indi's real-world features, but they were fuzzy and unfocussed in comparison.

A screech of tyres and a crash sounded from a distance away.

So, George had crashed, terrific. I glanced in the direction I thought the sound had come from.

No point in running that way. Even if I found the crash, it'd be swarming with zombies when I got there, and without backup there was probably nothing I could do. Better to wait for the Z's to eat George and pick up the pieces afterward.

Bastard deserves it, I thought cynically as I blew lazy smoke and watched the dark-bellied clouds roll by.

The next thing I knew, there was a hand on my shoulder and I started in the chair.

My head was fuzzy and I didn't know why. I had to blink several times to clear my hazy vision.

"What's going on?" I mumbled, my mouth was dry and I had the urge to yawn and stretch.

"I think you were asleep." Jay came to sit in a chair beside me. "I figured it was best if we left you alone for a bit."

"What time is it?" I asked, the sky above was considerably darker. Stars were emerging. I hadn't been in-game during the night cycle yet.

"About eight, in-game time," Jay offered.

"Any sign of Indi?"

He shook his head sadly.

I rubbed my temples. I'd been asleep for about an hour. My skin crawled at the possibility of falling asleep in a game where a flesh eating zombie might creep up on me at any time.

"George took off with the truck," I admitted reluctantly.

Jay nodded. "I know, I saw."

"I think he crashed it a ways out," I said, "if we can track it, we can recover the map and stuff."

"No need," Jay smiled. "I've got the map, and the key card if that's what you were worried about?" He pulled both from an inner pocket of his jacket.

Relief and disbelief flooded me, whipping away the blanket of depressed lethargy that had fallen over me. "What, why?" I babbled animatedly.

"I like to keep important plot items in my inventory," he said.

I leapt up and threw my arms around him.

"Jay, you're awesome," I sighed into his shoulder with only the barest hint of a hysterical giggle.

Chapter 24

We waited another hour, the three of us taking turns to watch the roads. Despite my joy at the revelation that Jay had kept the most significant items for our escape, the weight of our situation now pressed down on us. I managed to make the full twenty minutes of my watch before sheer nervous energy had overcome me.

"We've got to do something," I declared firmly.

"And what do you suggest we do?" Ned asked. "We're not exactly in a fit state to make a run on the base. Even if it's deserted and intact, we're low on supplies and our vehicle is gone, just getting there's a massive risk."

"Well, we could do something about that," I said and, after a moment's thought added, "or we could try to get the word out about what's going on?"

"How would we even do that?" Ned replied, incredulous.

I considered it briefly, "Jay's phone, he could hack a message out?" I suggested.

"The phone's part of the programme, Lex, I doubt it would work." He sighed but something he said caught my attention.

"Part of the programme," I mused thoughtfully before snapping my fingers sharply. "I've got it!"

Jay stared at me, waving his hands for me to continue.

"The cameras," I explained. "You remember the website, the 'cinematic' it played on the screen? George told me it was real-time gameplay, streaming from within the game itself."

"How does that help us?" Jay asked. "We have no idea if we're being streamed."

"Because," I smiled smugly, for once I knew more about a game than Jay, "the filming points are fixed, I've seen one. It looked like a Go-Pro mounted on a stick. We just have to find another one."

"To *you* it looked like a Go-Pro," Jay held up a cautionary hand, "but I'm guessing that's just a familiar brand digital camera to you. For us it might look like something else, I doubt the devs are indulging in a little product-placement, y'know?"

"The point is that it was incongruous," I explained, getting more and more excited. "It was a digi-cam stuck to a pole on the side of the road and, since our experience of security cameras proved those to be actual in-game mechanics, I think we can assume that it's an aspect that will be repeated. Like, they built the world and the mechanics and then tagged this on as a last detail or an afterthought. It's not the first time a studio shoe-horned something in that didn't quite gel."

Jay nodded. "Okay, so how do we find one?"

I looked out over the dark city and its patchy street lighting.

"We go look," I said simply.

Jay grimaced, his unwillingness evident. "That's a huge risk,"

"But it's all we've got," I replied earnestly.

Ned came to her feet, I could see the same need to act in her expression. "How will we know if someone sees us? It's not like we can stand in the road screaming into a camera for hours on end," she observed.

"Then we take it," I countered firmly. "We bring it back and we live-stream what's happening to us until someone figures out a way to help us."

"And how will we know if anyone sees our little webcast?" Ned insisted.

I turned to Ned, fully aware of the weakness in my plan. "We won't," I said simply.

We decided on balance that it was safest if we all went. While going at night was a risk we could at the very least use the darkness against the zombie's poor eyesight and, trapped in the game, time was against us.

Leaving our rucksacks we only had our personal inventories. I had our partial medkit on my hip (apparently the hip-slots could switch between utility and weapon slots), my cigarettes for dealing with stress (luckily the packet wasn't a one shot item but I *was* down to my last few cancer-sticks), a bottle of water and my hook blade. Jay and Ned filled out their slots as best they could, Ned at least had Kay's gun but we were woefully low on helpful supplies.

Looking out over the layout of the streets we picked a direction away from Kay's ill-fated expedition and the inevitable attention it had drawn that way. We resolved to head straight out for a couple of hundred metres and then zigzag through the streets on our return. Straight out, sweep back. We discussed checking houses but, since the two cameras' we were aware of had both been outside, we figured we'd hang our hopes on that being a common factor.

With plans laid as best we could, we headed down the stairs and then into the parking bays, winding our way down the shadowy concrete edifice of the multi-storey and out to the street.

The overhead lamps stuttered, pools of shadow interspersed the few working lights. Beyond the point where we'd driven in, the road was a tangle of abandoned and crashed cars, a possible hive of hidden z's just waiting for a trigger to rise up, rend and feast. Even though George had basically rung the dinner bell, we couldn't assume that we were safe. With agonizing care, I climbed onto the bonnet of the nearest car. The panelled metal creaked and popped softly under my weight and, when I flinched at even that little noise, the metal popped more.

I stood, surveying the tangled metal field that the road had become for signs of movement.

"Come on." I held out a hand to pull Jay up as Ned climbed confidently up the next car over.

We walked slowly, the creak of flexing metal marking our passing, down the road. I'd heard a biker call a car a 'steel coffin' once. If that was the case we were passing over a graveyard. After maybe a hundred yards, the tangled sprawl of cars started to thin out. We would either have to start jumping from car to car, increasing the noise we made, let alone running the risk of a still-active car alarm, or drop to ground level. I shivered at the memory of the child zombie hiding under the car at the checkpoint.

"Do we get down?" Ned asked quietly.

Jay nodded. "But we get to the pavement, quick as we can. Watch where you step."

'Don't step where you can't see' that was another of our rules. Too many characters in the movies got bit in the leg or arm by zombies lying out of sight under counters or cars. I was thankful I'd managed to replace the canvas sneakers but, beyond the leather work boots I now wore I hadn't found anything to protect my lower legs. I'd always thought I would be able to loot something, in the event of a zompocalypse. I'd day-dream about 'effective zombie armour' but, like so many things in this nightmare simulation, those plans had been savaged, chewed up and consumed.

I crouched at the edge, looking into the shadowed gap between cars. I remembered times as a child when I would scamper across my room and leap into bed, or stand on the bed and jump during the night to avoid getting grabbed by the boogieman. As I hung on the edge of the car bonnet I was that frightened kid again, and the short hop loomed like a yawning precipice.

'Get it together,' I chastised myself, took a breath and hopped down, stepping quickly away from the car at a hurried pace that belied my outward appearance of calm.

We scurried to the pavement and, as desolate as the days had been, devoid of the sounds of life I was so accustomed to in real life, the night was a whole new board-game (one of Jay's phrases, I didn't know if it was sports euphemisms or Americanisms that annoyed him specifically, but he'd coined this one and it had stuck with us).

From above the irregular illumination caused by the damaged and defunct streetlights hadn't looked like too much of a problem but, at street level, the patchy illumination rendered shadows deeper. The distances between islands of light stretched farther, and our hurried steps as we hopped between those islands sounded crisply, much louder than the quiet groans of the bonnet panels, on the concrete slabs of the pavement. When you walk along in the crowd you learn to tune out the constant noise of the remorseless march of progress. Here we couldn't help but mark that our own 'progress' was taking us farther and farther from relative safety.

Alleyways and open doors yawned on either side, pitch black and silent. The phrase 'doorways to hell' played across my thoughts, but the truth was colder still. Hell was supposedly a place of fiery torment, full of noise and activity, the darkness here was more like a void, portals to oblivion. One wrong step might see us dragged inside and, after a few screams and wet sounds; it would be still and silent, as if we had never been at all.

I shivered again and focused on the pavement and putting one foot in front of another.

The road led, after a couple hundred metres, to a roundabout, flanked by old, Edwardian buildings. It didn't matter that our sightlines were so restricted, we weren't worried about snipers and, given the lack of traffic we could walk in the now clear road. Crossing quickly to the island, Jay scanned around.

I hurried to his side. "Which way?" I asked quietly.

"Right," he chose, apparently arbitrarily.

"Are you sure?"

He nodded, some of his real-life surety returning to his expression. "I've got a good feeling about right."

"Right?"

"Right."

"Alright." I nodded and he grinned. Ned just stared at us open mouthed.

"You two are mad," She grumbled finally.

We followed the road as it snaked first left, then right. We passed a car showroom, vehicles shunted aside, broad windows smashed and the facia scorched by a car that had obviously crashed and burned some time ago. Whether a setting piece or player action I couldn't tell, and didn't want to dwell on.

An intersection led off north, back toward the multi-storey and, possibly, in the direction of George's crash. I gestured to it, but Jay shook his head, motioning forward with a wink and a tap on the side of his nose.

We came to a high wall with barbed wire atop it and a sturdy iron gate, wide enough for vehicles, further ahead. A sign on the wall which I only noticed in the dark when I was standing beneath it, declared a Royal Mail depot.

We hugged the wall until Ned, moving ahead of us, froze.

I stopped immediately and Jay bumped me gently. I shot him a tight-lipped look and he shrugged apologetically. I turned back to Ned who had a hand cupped to her ear. I listened myself, the silence of the night oppressive until, on the edge of my hearing I caught a quiet, breathy moan. Of course, 'quiet' didn't necessarily mean 'distant'. The three of us traded wary glances and edged toward the gate. Ned leaned out, snatching a look into the yard and snapped back, pressed against the wall, rigid.

I laid a hand gently on her shoulder and she turned wide eyes to me before I eased her back and took her place. Moving slowly, I leaned to the corner of the brickwork and peered into the darkness of the yard.

I saw a couple of fixed body commercial trucks rising from among a horde of tightly packed Z's. Trying my luck I stayed silent and still, watching the throng and, whatever else George had done, he'd certainly helped us out here. The horde had its back to us, all of them. I leaned back and turned to my companions. Turning my wrist I brought up my skills and indicated 'Stealth' before pointing across the gateway. I pointed deliberately to myself, then Ned, then Jay who shook his head vigorously, but I scowled at him and he nodded reluctantly.

I took a deep but silent breath and, holding it, stepped out into full view and my wrist began to throb like a second heartbeat.

The zombies stayed; obviously drawn by the sound of George's crash they had no stimulus to turn around unless I offered it to them. Stepping slowly and deliberately, I placed one foot after the other as beads of cold sweat formed on my brow. It can't have taken nearly as long as it seemed to me, but I crossed the gap and took a place by the far wall, releasing my breath in silent relief. A glance at my stress meter showed the first bar pulsing gently but not filling, yet.

I beckoned Ned and she scurried, low and fast, across the gap, flowing past me like liquid and coming to a stop on my far side. We waited, not a sound from the zombies, so I gestured to Jay to make his way across.

Looking like nothing less than a cartoon villain, Jay took step after hesitant step with exaggerated care. I leaned back out to watch the horde as, with pantomime actions, he made to close the distance. It might have been funny but for the very real threat of death.

Careful steps brought Jay closer, his footsteps almost in rhythm to the pulse of my wrist until his foot fell on a piece of loose grit. The stone on stone made an agonising grinding noise that, in a normal place, on a normal day would have passed without notice. I glanced at Jay, he'd frozen and we shared a horrified look before I turned back to gauge the horde's reaction.

At the very back, closest to us a zombie started a slow, shuffling turn toward the noise. My heart hammered in my chest as it twisted its body and head in Jay's direction. In the soft orange of the yard lights I saw the glint of what I thought, absurdly, were glasses still perched on the bridge of the zombie's nose. As the details resolved in the dimness, I gestured urgently to Jay to keep moving. The metallic glimmer was actually some kind of circular saw blade, embedded in the zombie's skull in such a manner that it must have completely destroyed the thing's eyes.

As Jay scurried across the remainder of the gap, the blind zombie turned back to gaze sightlessly at the backs of its fellows. I risked a glance at my stats:

STR				
	███			

Briefly I considered doing something about the meter but no, there would be more stress by the time this excursion was finished, and we didn't have the resources to waste on a single bar.

We hurried on in silence, as the road wove another shallow s-bend. Up ahead I could see what looked like artillery guns set with tow-hooks together, barrels pointed out into the night, but there were no sandbags, no munitions crates and no dead soldiers.

"What's that?" I murmured aloud.

Jay stepped up beside me, only a slight tremor in his voice as he ventured. "Some kind of memorial?"

"Check it out?" Ned asked, her head on a swivel, trying to watch all directions at once.

I nodded. "Yeah."

Moving closer, I started to make out details of the further surroundings. In the dark it was almost like horizon spawn in a regular game. The road beyond the memorial was wide, and across from the guns was a bus station. A rank of buses pointed toward us, the plastic windows and ad boards of the covered shelters separating us from the silent vehicles. It was hard to see into the depot. The darkness, dirt and graffiti on the shelters reduced visibility to almost nothing, but I watched the depot intently. Mass transit hubs, like hospitals and shopping centres, were a stock spawn for zombies.

Both Ned and Jay must have shared my thoughts, because we all watched the depot shelters as we approached the memorial. Sparing a momentary glance I thought I spotted a stick with a small box perched atop it placed between the guns, and I stepped quickly forward. My impression was correct, as I closed the distance I could see one of the camera sticks and my pace quickened further over the last five or so strides to our objective.

I noticed idly that the camera wasn't pointed toward the silent darkness of the bus depot but almost ninety degrees to our left. I ignored the observation as I quickly looked over the camera. It looked almost like a selfie-stick shoved into a convenient flower bed at the base of the monument. I took a firm grasp of the shaft and, just as I was about to tug it free of the ground, Ned laid a hand on my shoulder and I heard Jay whimper.

I turned my head, following the direction the camera and Ned's shaking hand pointed.

"Trains in," She whispered breathily.

The train station, the station I hadn't even noted in my hurry to get the camera, lurked in the darkness, squatting next to the bus depot. Even as I watched the station lights flickered and the scene unfolded before me.

There was a train at the platform. There may have been more, but the platform and the station office heaved with zombies.

"Fucking rush hour," I whispered, cold claws of horror digging into my chest.

The light flickered again and, through the automatic doors of the station, I saw a zombie, a ragged and wasted youth in a shredded hoodie start to mouth and hammer at the glass. The muted screams didn't reach us as any more than a dull howl, but once the other zombies lent their weight to the barrier it would not take long to fall. More of them turned to howl and hammered on the doors even as I thought it.

The spell of shocked inaction that had been cast over us broke when, with a sharp 'crack' the first pane of the doors spider-webbed.

"Run!" I hissed and yanked the camera pole from the dirt, turning to flee as I did.

I checked over my shoulder to see my friends keeping pace through the darkened streets.

The snap of breaking safety glass sounded like a rifle shot as we ran directly north, away from the station. There was no question of retracing our steps; the moans of the postal depot zombies drifted through the streets from the east. They'd be drawn to the station first.

We took the first left we found, trying to reconnect with the road that ran along the front of the multi-story. A crossroads ahead was blocked by a jack-knifed and overturned artic' so we turned north again, running parallel to the road we wanted.

"We're headed toward where George crashed," I panted. "We can't stay on this road."

Even though we'd only been running a couple of minutes, Jay was already wheezing.

"Stop," he begged, breathlessly. "Stop!"

I wished I had one of the vile energy drinks for Jay, but we'd left our gear in the truck. All I had was a bottle of water in my pocket, but I pulled it out and handed it to Jay.

He popped it and glugged down the contents. With a little effort, and thanks to my First Aid skill, I could see his bottomed out stamina bar come back up to a lousy twelve-and-a-half percent. Dammit, water was supposed to be good for you!

A howl rose behind us. The station doors must have finally given way.

Ned beckoned from the side-street shadows, holding open half of a glass double-door. "In here!"

I hustled Jay through and we stepped off the street and into darkness. The click of a torch heralded a beam of light from Ned's outstretched hand.

Catching us staring at her she shrugged. "Lex is the medic, Jay's the tech guy, I'm the scout. I keep a torch on me at all times. Come on!" and she hurried into the dark.

A few hurried steps in, Jay leapt for Ned, catching her wrist in both hands.

"What are you doing, man?" she hissed, but he guided the torch up and panned it left and right.

Shop fronts, names I recognised, passed under the beam.

"Oh God. We're in a mall!" Jay spoke through gritted teeth.

"Calm down Jay, that's just another trope." I laid a hand on his shoulder.

"But we've no idea how many z's are in here," He insisted.

"Then it's a fucking good thing we're not staying," Ned growled, taking Jay by the lapel, dragging him on, as I hurried to keep pace.

We dashed through the 'mall', really nothing more than a small enclosed shopping precinct. Pale faces and grasping hands, trapped behind glass doors flashed by in the beam of the torch until, after a left and a right turn, we saw the intermittent strobe of streetlights through more glass doors ahead.

We emerged onto the street just south of the multi-storey and retraced the path, climbing over the cars, toward the entrance. I could feel the relief radiating off Jay, and even Ned seemed to have perked up, but as we neared the cavernous mouth of the car park I slowed.

"Wait here," I called softly and took a few running steps up toward the connecting road we'd left not so long before.

"What is it?" Jay hissed urgently.

"Headlights," I replied. "Someone's coming this way."

Chapter 25

From the top level of the car park, the three of us watched over the buildings. The vehicle lights seemed to move, then pause, then move again. The engine noise grew steadily louder until headlights came around the corner and blazed up the side of the multi-story.

On instinct we all ducked.

"Could that be...?" Jay whispered.

"Maybe, let's not take a chance though," I replied, hating myself for quashing hope with pragmatism.

Ned nodded toward the road just as the lights disappeared. "They're moving."

I looked over the edge. Maybe they'd simply turned the lights off and continued on their way. I could hear the engine, it sounded different, but I couldn't see the vehicle. Then a horizontal strip of light illuminated the buildings across from us.

I pushed away from the wall, pulling my pistol and checking the load. Seven bullets remained in the magazine. "They're in the car park, coming up."

"What's the plan?" Ned demanded.

"We could bottleneck them as they come out of the stairwell," I suggested.

Ned shook her head. "We should take cover behind the cars downstairs. See who they are, leave ourselves the stairs as an avenue of retreat."

Jay nodded in agreement. "Identify, assess and then we can withdraw up the stairwell if we're outgunned."

Ned nodded and we took off down the stairs, and had our backs to the barrier of cars just as headlights lit up the level.

"Are we being paranoid?" I asked, taking rapid breaths as my adrenaline started to spike.

"No," Jay grimaced. "Just prudent."

Although we each had a pistol, I had no idea how much ammunition we had between us. If the interlopers were hostile, well-armed and supplied, we were screwed.

The grumbling diesel engine rattled to silence. The car was a Land Rover, which was about all I could make out in the gloom. I couldn't even make out the occupants. Laying out my hand flat, palm down, I gestured for us to stay out of sight.

One of the rear doors creaked open and someone was pushed from the back seat. I heard the landing rather than saw it, and it sounded rough.

"You say they're here?" a voice I didn't recognise asked.

The reply sounded despondent, and pained. "They're here," It was George, I realised with a start.

Another door creaked then. "You better not be lying, *mon ami.*"

I bolted upright into the glare of headlights.

"Indi?" I piped, my voice much higher that I intended.

"Don't shoot, don't shoot!" I heard Indi's voice, and it took me a split second to realize he was talking to his companions.

"Lex?" He called, his accented voice unmistakeable. "*Merde!* Don't jump out on people, you almost got shot!"

I jumped over the cars and Indi rushed forward and swept me up in a bear hug.

"I was worried about you," I wheezed under the pressure. "Did you log out?"

"I've been in this entire time." Indi released me and held me at arms' length. "We were trapped in the barn, only just made it out ourselves. I'm glad you weren't there, Lex, it was a fucking slaughter. If people weren't going to believe the game was killing people before, they will now."

"Cal?" I asked hesitantly.

Indi looked me in the eye and shook his head sadly.

My voice faltered when I asked, "was it clean?"

"*Non.*" Indi's voice was rough, eyes hard and distant.

"Oh god," I breathed, "you mean?"

My friend shook me gently. "Better not to think about it now. Come, meet our new party members. This is *Akay, Roper* and *Frakt*. He, he, her," Indi clarified.

"It's A.K.A. Like 'also known as'," AKA clarified tersely.

Roper held out a hand. "My full handle is *Tightrope Walker*, 'Roper' is easier." His Afrikaans accent, rich and deep, sounded really strange coming from the compact, femme avatar.

Unsure that I'd heard right I asked. "'Fragged'?"

"*Frakt*, with a 'K'," she corrected. "It's a play on *Cataphract*, the medieval warriors." The player's voice was quiet but level, her gaze steady. "I toyed with *Valkyrie* for a while," she continued, the words tripping slightly in an anxious rush to be spoken, "but sometimes it's just inviting trouble to advertise as femme online, am I right?"

Her avatar was tall, with powerful, tattooed arms and colourful but worn-looking dreadlocks. Frakt put me in mind of an alt-metal Viking.

I beckoned my friends to stand.

"I'm Lex, this is Ned and Jay."

Ned, her voice dripping acid asked, "where did you find George?"

Suddenly reminding of his sulking presence I hauled off and punched the dickhead right in the face. His head snapped back and he dropped to his knees. I rubbed my hands and glanced around. The most anyone had raised at my attack was their eyebrows. Frakt smirked as I rubbed my shocked knuckles.

"You mean Kay?" Roper asked slowly, standing over the groaning figure.

Ned gave a mean little smile. "His *real* name's George."

"*Aikona!*" Roper grinned and shook his head.

"This arsehole nearly ran into us, yeah? Tanked his truck into a streetlight and woke every rotten scumbag for a mile around." The player called AKA had the distinctive east London accent my dad would call 'Wideboy'. His avatar's features and complexion reminded me of Mr Nadkarni's youngest son, a young man only slightly older than I was. I briefly wondered how my neighbour's recovery was going, and then felt a flare of anger at the thugs who'd attacked him. AKA moved with a barely constrained energy. Even standing still, he twitched and fidgeted.

"Are you okay?" I asked.

"Yeah? No," his version of 'no' emerging a drawn-out 'nah'. He never touched us." AKA waved me off.

"That's good," I replied. "You just seem nervous, is all."

"Oh really?" he bridled, "I bet you think I'm slurring me words too, you think I'm drunk?" The player was drawing himself up for a confrontation but subsided quickly. At most I'd assumed a slight lisp maybe.

He waved dismissively, relaxing. "It's just me CP, yeah? Trust me, it's worse out in the world."

I just nodded as Indi asked. "So what's the situation here?"

"Not good," I replied. "We took a little walk and now, thanks some to George and some to us, the streets are crawling. It'll take some time to settle down."

"Urgh! *C'est comme ça.*" Indi shrugged. "Nothing to be done for it right now. Besides, George needs some medical attention."

"Why would I help *George?*" I sneered.

Indi smiled coldly. "Because I told him he could help us raise your medicine skill voluntarily, or *non.*"

I considered that for a moment. "That's cruel, I like it," I chuckled. "But, speaking of, we've only got one part-built medkit. Did you manage to bring anything?"

Indi nodded. "We've got some. I hate to waste it on 'Killer-dot-exe' here, but if it boosts your level I can stomach it."

"Let's get him upstairs," I slipped one of George's arms over my shoulders. "By the way, have any of you tried logging out?"

Indi shrugged. "I think George was trying before we dragged him out of the car, but he must have been too shaken up."

At that moment Roper came up alongside us.

"Indi has been telling us some worrying things, is the game *really* killing people?"

I flinched. "It gets worse," I admitted. "We'll tell you everything upstairs."

> **First Aid Lvl 3 achieved, bonus will be applied**
> **after rest period.**

Later, with George secured in the back of the car, the rest of us sat around the gas stove between camper and caravan. We'd managed to rustle up water and teabags and everyone held a steaming mug.

Jay had finished sharing what we knew and what we suspected. "I know it's a lot to take in," he said slowly.

"You're telling us." Frakt held the mug close, inhaling the smell. The three new members of our group sat in thoughtful silence for a good while.

"So, none of you can log out?" Roper asked slowly.

I traded glances with Jay and Ned then shook my head. "And from what Indi was saying, it might have spread to George," I ventured quietly.

"Why would it do that?"

"I don't know," I said simply. "Maybe proximity, maybe time spent in company. You'd have to ask the devs."

"In response to trying to access their code?" Roper's voice was urgent, like he was digging for something, but for now I couldn't say what.

"After we became suspicious that the game could kill, I wanted to know how. The first step was to understand how they achieved total immersion," Jay explained.

I cast my eyes around the group. "Maybe not now but soon, you might want to try logging out yourselves."

I let that sink in for a while, before trying to break the tension.

"Just as an aside," I went on quietly. "Back at the beginning, we learned that the game world is quite malleable. Indi sees text in French, Jay in Swedish; only the plot relevant stuff appears the same to any two players, so... and I know this is out of left field, but what I guess I'm asking is, what tea does everyone have?"

That brought them all out of their silent reverie, stunned by my question.

Finally Roper broke the silence. "Rooibos."

"Really?" I asked. "I've got English Breakfast."

"No, Yorkshire." AK (we'd shortened the gamer tag to AK) chimed in. "It's the only tea worth having, yeah?"

Indi grunted and smiled. "Huh, I have coffee."

I shot him a wry look. "I know, I made it. You're just lucky we found some of those instant packets, heathen," I teased.

"Assam," Frakt offered softly.

"Camomile," Jay supplied.

Ned stared around at us for a moment.

"You're all nuts," she sighed and stood. "If you lot," she gestured to our new arrivals, "take the caravan, the rest of us," her gesture encompassed our original quartet, "can take the camper." She took a couple of steps away from the circle before she stopped, turning back to us with a sigh.

"Earl Grey," she admitted with a rueful wink, swaggering away to the RV.

Jay rose to his feet with a groan. "We should all turn in," he commented. "We've been through a lot today and there's more to come. If you can still logout, we won't blame any of you if you don't log in with us tomorrow."

I watched the others leave, making no move myself. There was little point; if our experience with the lock-in proved anything it was that, whether the new players managed to log out or not, there would be a period of inactivity while their new skills and buffs were applied. We wouldn't know anything until they 'woke-up'.

Finally, it was just me and Indi sat in the darkness. The air was warm and close, like it was building up to a storm.

"You're not turning in?" Indi asked.

"Not right away," I reached down beside me and pulled out the digicam. "I've got to do something with this, try to get the word out, and I doubt I'd sleep anyway."

We sat for another moment.

"You want to talk about today?" Indi asked.

"Only in so much as I thought I'd lost you. I'm glad you're okay," I replied. "You?"

"Not so much. It was pretty horrifying. I really don't want to think about it. I had to swallow half a bottle of rum to get my stress bar down."

I chewed my lip thoughtfully then pulled myself up.

"Okay then." I hurried over to the car which sported an open top-box and rummaged in the gloom for something I'd seen earlier.

Indi twisted in his camp chair to watch me. "What are you doing?"

"Taking your mind off it," I grunted as I pulled out a couple of sleeping bags and blankets. I carried them away from the camp, off to one side of the multi-storey's roof and tossed them down on the tarmac.

"No really, what are you doing?" Indi demanded, a little more forcefully.

The clouds parted briefly and the moon shone down on me as I pulled my top off.

The close night air pricked my skin with soft static.

"You don't want this?" I teased, gesturing to my avatar's skin.

Indi stepped up to me, hands on the material of my constricting sports bra.

213

> Notice, you are initiating sexual activity. Both
> players must be consenting.
> Continue Yes/No?

His voice was husky as he replied "I do, I really do," and he dragged the garment over my head.

A warm rain began to fall.

I raised on tiptoe, arching my spine, pressing my chest to his and whispered into Indi's ear, "I always wanted to do it under the summer rain," as my lips brushed his earlobe.

Under the shining virtual moon, amid the horrors of a make-believe world, where death was an all-too-real possibility, we once again gave in to our passions. Our slick bodies writhed in the downpour, the moonlight glistening on our wet skin, the heat of our efforts keeping us warm.

Where our first experience of sex had been tentative and somewhat clumsy, this time we had a better idea of each other's expectations. Indi's strong hands grasped at my skin and tangled in my hair. His mouth trailed over my neck and shoulders, hungry to consume my flesh. For a moment I thought Indi *was* going to bite into me, tear at me, savage my soft body, and in those heady moments, swimming in the haze of our shared arousal I longed for it. I brought my own mouth to his neck, the tight pull of my hair exciting as I bit him, tasting his skin in my mouth, encouraging him to reciprocate.

My friend's motions became urgent, desperate and demanding but I continued to tease. Drawing out the anticipation and eventual, mutual surrender to both Indi's needs and my own, both of us coming to a willing, joyous climax.

We panted, moaned and even laughed under that simulated sky. Eventually we sagged onto the sodden blankets and asphalt, spent from our efforts.

With his head pressed to my chest, I could feel Indi trembling.

The horrors of the past hours having finally caught up to my friend, I did all I could in that moment.

I held him as he cried.

Not long after we were finished, we dressed and I led Indi back to the camper. He accessed his menu and tapped the 'Exit' command. His avatar fell dormant but, like with the others, I wouldn't know if he got out until the 'Appropriate Rest Period' had passed.

How I'd started to hate that phrase.

I wandered back to the circle of camp chairs, the camera in my hand. Sitting down I examined the thing. Just a small plastic box, maybe two inches on each side, with a lens on the front. The only sign it was even active was a tiny green LED just offset from the lens.

This was it. This was our lifeline.

I turned the camera, aimed it as best I could and, running a dirty hand over my tired eyes, I looked out across the darkened city, choosing my words.

"If you're watching this, I beg you, record it, stream it, share it everywhere. Use whatever platform you have but please, above all, listen."

I waited, daring to hope people were keying up software, apps or just getting their phone-cameras out.

"My name is Lex, my gamertag is *LeZion,* and I want to tell you about the game *Rendered Flesh.* If you're seeing this firsthand, you've found it and are thinking about playing it."

I stared hard at the lens.

"Don't," I said firmly.

"The game kills people. Me and my friends *JoaKingKong* and *1ndéfin1* found this out, and now we're stuck in here with *NegKD-twenty-ten.* They won't let us log out, we don't know how they're stopping us, but we need help, please."

I sat thoughtfully for a moment.

"Most of you will think this is a gag. You'll think that we're trolls or jokers, but we're not. We're trapped, scared, and desperate to get back to our families and friends. I'm going to hook this camera on my gear, stream for as long as they let me and maybe, maybe one of you out there will call the authorities and get us out. Oh," I glanced side-long at the camera. "And for any of you thinking of sending 'thoughts and prayers' our way?" I held the gaze of whoever might be on the other side of the screen.

"Fuck off and do something *actually* useful."

Chapter 26

"You ache with it all; and the more mysterious it is, the more you ache."
— Dostoevsky

> First Aid Lvl 3 bonus applied
> HP restoration increased by 17%

Sleeping in-game was a strange experience. I had no recollection of dreaming, but had a vague impression of horrific images. It was like the login screen, the game trying to imprint nightmarish memories of the chaos when the zombies rose and pulled down the walls of civilisation. I didn't feel refreshed or eager, just a creeping feeling of dread underpinning my waking thoughts. But, having lived with depression, it was a feeling I was familiar with. The thought reminded me that I had no idea how long I'd been without my meds. I was probably headed for a hell of a crash if we managed to get out of here.

I awoke in Indi's arms, looking up to find him watching me, a slight frown on his broad face.

I didn't want to ruin the moment but I had to know.

"Did you, log out?" I asked softly, Jay and Ned were starting to stir but Indi just took a breath, I felt myself rise on his chest, before he looked away and let out a deep sigh.

I didn't push it, I had my answer.

The previous night's rain still pattered against the RV's roof, and the sky was heavy and grey as I looked out of the windows. Jay and Indi sat across from me as Ned handed out snack bars to top up our health meters, while I told them what I'd said, with the camera on the table between us.

"Sounds fair to me," Jay nodded. "Whatever's going on, we have to stop it any way we can."

Indi's shoulders were so broad he had an arm slung across the back of the chair behind Jay, he raised a bushy eyebrow. "What do you mean?" he questioned.

Jay leaned forward, eyes intent upon his clasped hands. "I spent some time last night messing with the smartphone, and I managed to access my tether programme."

"Jesus," Ned thumped a fist down on the table, startling Jay and me. "I thought you'd have switched that off?" she snapped at Jay accusingly.

"They've already locked us in, wouldn't do us any good," Jay argued, retreating into the thin foam cushioning of the camper seats.

Ned leaned further forward, teeth bared. "They might let us out!"

Jay's eyes narrowed, became hard and now he leaned forward. "How often have you forgiven a hacker or griefer?" he asked, low and even.

Ned gaped for a moment before subsiding reluctantly. "Point," she acknowledged.

"So, anyway. I learned some stuff," Jay continued stiffly.

Indi seemed vaguely amused by the whole confrontation. "Like what?" he asked gruffly, tipping his head back and putting a hand over his eyes.

"I got a bunch of data from the tether. The interface system is something else. I mean, looking at the code it's like nothing I've seen, but it amounts to light patterns and waveforms that would probably mean more to your mother than me, Lex."

"Shame we can't ask her," I said. "Okay, what else?"

Now he leaned into his subject, eager to divulge his findings. "From what I can decipher, the 'graphics' we see are actually light patterns. I'm guessing the whole subliminal signal, full-immersion shtick was no joke, but there are layers in the programming. I can't say what half of them are for, but I have an uneasy feeling some of them aren't part of the game."

"Why would you think that?" Ned asked, still visibly upset but grimly curious.

"There's a file-name attached to the immersion programmes, Satori-twenty-three," Jay spoke the words ominously.

We sat, caught in a moment's silence. "Well? What does it mean?" I prompted.

Jay steepled his fingers, fully settling into his 'lecture mode'. "It's a Japanese Buddhist word meaning 'awakening'. It's also a creature from their folklore said to be able to read minds, but in this instance, I think it refers to a cold-war project related to mind control."

217

I wasn't sure where this rabbit hole was going but, like Alice, we were in it now and had to follow where it led. "Like MK-Ultra, or the Russian Sleep Experiment?" I asked, Jay followed some conspiracy theories out of academic interest, but I wouldn't have labelled him a believer.

He huffed an annoyed breath. "The Sleep Experiment is an urban legend, it's a fucking Creepypasta," Jay hated it when false report was taken as fact.

"As far as I can remember, Satori-twenty-three was a Japanese military programme using sensory stimuli to evoke a desired response from a subject."

"What kind of stimuli, what kind of response?" Indi grunted, thick arms folded over his broad chest.

"You name it, they tried it," Jay replied. "Scent markers, subliminal audio suggestion, touch pattern triggers. They tried to make soldiers more resilient to pain or exhaustion, tried to pre-programme deep-cover agents and assassins. It was the Cold War; everyone was at it, not just the Americans and Russians. The UK gave Royal Marines LSD in the name of creating 'super-soldiers' for Christ's sake."

My tongue flicked over dry lips. I had only a vague idea of how long we'd been trapped but we must be getting dehydrated. Why hadn't mum or dad unplugged me? I wondered briefly, but the way we lived, the different timetables, shifts and routines... They might not have noticed, or worse, assumed I was coming and going from the game as I normally would. The danger of having understanding, gamer parents.

"Did any of it work?" I asked.

"Supposedly they had some success with photo-reactive suggestions, flashing lights to induce euphoria or hallucinations for the purposes of interrogation, but sections of the test group suffered seizures, so they canned it."

"Photosensitive Epilepsy wasn't identified until nineteen eighty-one," I offered. "They must have thought it was a side-effect of their process." My friends stared at me. "Mum's a neurologist," I reminded them.

"Whatever they thought, the records I've dug up read like MK-Ultra fanfic."

"What's it doing to us?" Indi asked after a thoughtful moment.

"I couldn't say," Jay admitted. "I don't have the expertise. I'm not feeling any strange impulses, or having any sudden, unexplained bouts of murderous rage. How about you?"

Indi grinned. "No more than usual."

"What about your countdown?" Ned asked.

"There's a few days left. I've run an algorithm to predict the endpoint, and it's troubling." He paused.

"Well? Don't hold us in fucking suspense," Ned snapped.

When Jay replied, every aspect of him was screaming 'serious'. "Unless this is just some local or national level plot, the event that impacts the largest slew of the population is the new Wi-Fi network coming online,"

"I mean…" I paused thoughtfully. "That would definitely affect all the RF players, but not everyone plays RF, so what's going on?"

"Damned if I know," Jay admitted. "It might not even be connected."

"Hang on," Ned chimed in, "how many players *are there* on RF?"

Jay started slowly, dragging the details from his memory. "The main site had a counter," he began, his voice picking up pace as he became more certain. "When we downloaded the game, that counter was climbing upward toward the three mil' mark."

"Jesus," I breathed to myself, sitting back in my chair.

"That's not much by game standards admittedly, there are fifty-five million players on Call of Duty. But if there *is* something sinister going on, that's a massive number of casualties and/or fatalities," Jay concluded.

I leaned forward, eager to ask and intent on Jay's reply. "But then, why would the game be allowed to kill players before the due date?"

"Again, I couldn't tell you," Jay admitted. "Maybe it's just some sick publicity gimmick."

I frowned. "Maybe we'll find out more at the base?" I suggested.

Jay, Indi and Ned traded sceptical looks.

"What, you have something better to do? You want to sit here and wait it out?" I snarled accusingly. "We're dying in our chairs in the real world. Our best hope of getting out is learning what's gonna happen, and to do that we have to keep going."

Jay finally met my gaze albeit timidly. "Well, trapped survivors of natural disasters have survived days beyond accepted limits without food or water, by the very virtue of not knowing how much time had passed," Jay ventured.

"So, you're suggesting that because we don't know what day it is outside, we might not die for a while longer?" I scoffed.

Ned chuckled. "Fuck that."

"Lex makes a good point," Indi replied, evenly.

Jay mused, hesitant but thoughtful. "We'll have to keep an eye on the Z's if I'm going to keep running the tether."

"You're damn right you're running the tether," I spoke eagerly, rising to prop myself on the table. "We need all the information we can get! There are over three million players, fathers, brothers, mums and sisters, siblings and parents in *Rendered Flesh,* and no-one to save them but us."

Ned blew out a breath, raised her hands placatingly. "Alright, settle down Captain melodrama." She grinned wryly.

A knock on the RV door preceded the appearance of Frakt, Roper and AK.

"So, what we doing?" AK greeted us matter-of-factly, the new arrivals squeezing themselves into the seats and cramped RV kitchen.

"First things first," Jay began. "Did you three manage to log out okay?"

The three shared vague nods and shrugs.

Roper answered. "Yeah, no problems our end."

"Well, let's hope it stays that way," Jay nodded cautiously.

"How long were you out?" I demanded.

"About four hours," AK supplied. "Tried to get a message to Indi but no reply so we decided to come back in."

So, if the game emulated a standard eight-hour sleep period, each hour in-game was like half an hour outside, although it felt as if time was passing normally to me.

Jay picked up the thread again. "So, our original plan was to look for the cure to the zombie infection. The base was just the next step. Of course, the whole idea of 'winning' is a moot point now. What we're looking for now is any clues in the game world that might tell us what the designers are planning IRL."

"We've been following clues. The load screen you see when you log in displays quotes from nihilist philosophers, so anything that relates to or references nihilism could be a clue," I added.

"Alright," Roper rumbled thoughtfully. "So we're breaking into an army base, what do we need to do?"

Jay spread his hands on the camper's flimsy table. "Well, we don't have to worry about the personnel. If this was GTA, things would be a whole lot harder. The soldiers might be zombies now but we still have to worry about physical securities, locks, alarms, that kind of thing. We should probably put together a tool kit, bolt cutters, power drill and the like, just in case. We should also address our provisions. If we get trapped and have to wait-out a pack of deadheads, we'll need food. Besides that, there's just the question of what weapons we have and what we can do to improve that situation."

Our weapon situation ranked at somewhere around 'underwhelming'. "We've got short blades and guns, but not more than a handful of bullets between us, we've got what we managed to save from the farm," I supplied.

"We didn't do much better," Indi grunted. "But, there's a corner shop I spotted on the way in, we can get food there, and it has a tool place next door. If I take Roper, AK and Frakt, we can split into pairs and hit them both at the same time."

Jay nodded, but he was still fleshing-out the overall plan. "Once we're properly supplied and ready to make our run on the base, we should do a drive-by. We can either draw the geeks off the gate or, if there's too many, find a quiet spot and cut through the fence."

"If we get a second car, we'll have more mobility," AK observed thoughtfully. "Then, if one gets stuck we have a spare."

"Ned and I will check the cars on the lower levels for keys," I volunteered.

"It needs to be able to carry seven," Jay pointed out. "They both do."

"What about Kay?" Ned asked, confused.

Indi growled, "I vote we leave him."

Jay tried to brush over the subject. "He's secure, not a priority." He sounded dismissive.

Ned held up a hand. "But we tied his hands behind his back and locked him in a car, so he *is* our responsibility, and," of all people she looked at me imploringly, "he can't log out if he gets into trouble."

I tried, tried to be cold and even cruel. In the dark hours of the night I'd secretly wished painful death on any number of trolls, griefers or agents of the establishment. Here it was, the power of life and death, I sighed. "He might be a shithead, but I don't want him on my conscience if he gets his dumb ass eaten," I conceded grudgingly.

"I don't know," Frakt spoke up, her contributions were rare enough we all listened. "I know people who'd pay good money to watch a grown man get his ass eaten. Dumb or not."

We all exchanged wide-eyed glances sharing a chuckle, except Roper, who frowned in momentary confusion causing us all to laugh harder.

"Alright, let's get to it," Jay stated as the moment's levity passed. "We'll cut Kay loose when we leave."

The resource runs didn't take long. By the time Ned and I located a suitable people carrier with keys (and driver) still inside and got it back up to the top, Indi's crew was already rumbling back up in the Land Rover.

As they disembarked I called over, "How's it look out there?"

"It's quiet," Indi smirked and shot me a wink. "Too quiet."

As if we didn't have enough on our plate, now Indi was baiting the universe. "You had to, didn't you?" I called back in mock exasperation. "You had to test the trope and jinx us."

We headed upstairs and took stock as a group.

Glancing over the haul Jay grimaced. "No radios?" he asked.

Indi shook his head sullenly.

Twitching his eyebrows toward Indi, Jay indicated another item, "you couldn't find any bigger, huh?" He gestured ruefully at the huge pair of bolt-cutters Indi had slung over his shoulder.

"Eh," Indi shrugged. "Two birds, one stone, I can cut bolts or crack skulls as desired."

"Heavy, unwieldy. Nearly as bad as the chainsaw," Jay insisted before taking a calming breath, "Which reminds me," he announced. "What is our situation fighting skill-wise?"

Indi pointed as he spoke. "AK has combat two, Roper and I are sitting pretty on combat three, Frakt is at four."

"Really?" I raised my eyebrows as Indi went on. Frakt smiled proudly.

"Roper has firearms at two, AK at three."

Ned grinned at AK "Sniper huh?" AK simply winked by way of reply.

"How are we doing?" Indi gestured to our group.

"Three," I volunteered. "Four," Ned added her voice.

Jay made a face. "I still haven't unlocked it," he finally admitted.

Indi shrugged. "So what? It's not like we can punch our way through security doors, just means we'll have to watch your back."

Jay smiled sheepishly. "Thanks."

The three of us shared a moment of camaraderie before Indi's eyes glittered with mischief, "bags not baby-sitting!"

"Alright," Jay sighed theatrically, rolling his eyes. "Let's pack up and roll out."

We each loaded up and made ready. Despite the scavenger run, we still only had two medkits between the seven of us. Our weaponry was an odd mix of bats, both baseball and cricket, and tools, with Indi's bolt-cutters being both stand out strangest and most fearsome. None of us were eager to use the guns we had, the noise would draw the whole town down on us. The car park was fine as a stop-off, when we hadn't drawn any real attention, but we weren't planning to use it for a fall-back point with a horde on our asses. If push came to shove, we could maybe reach the neighbouring roofs but it would be very risky.

"So," Jay announced as we headed down the stairs, his voice echoing slightly off the concrete walls. "AK and Roper take the Landie, the rest of us follow in the wagon. We'll park up a few hundred yards from the gate, one flash of our headlights and you blow past and draw any lurkers away. If it looks too risky we'll flash twice and then follow you to look for a quiet spot in the fence to cut through, okay?"

"I wish we had some radios," AK grumbled.

"We'll look for some in the base," Jay reassured him.

"Shouldn't I drive the decoy?" I suggested.

Jay shook his head. "Chances are we won't be able to see that far into the compound. We might need your skills to get us out if it gets too hairy."

AK raised an eyebrow. "You're not the only one with drive, Lex."

"Oh yeah," I challenged, squaring my shoulders theatrically, like a gunslinger at high noon. "What's your level wide-boy?"

"Well, I got it. That's what matters, eh?" he replied hesitantly.

I gave a smirk of my own and shot finger guns back at him. "Level two, loser. Maybe if you spent less time on Fifa, 'eh'?" I shot back in my best mockney accent, teasing playfully.

For his inspired reply he offered a rueful grin as he flipped me off.

"I'd estimate it will take you twenty minutes to drive a circuit and get back to us." Jay cut in, shaking his head in mock exasperation. "Once you've lured the Z's away we'll head into the compound. Come straight on in once you've done your circuit. Look for the admin building, we'll be there."

The map led us out of the town, up a short, twisting hill road. Soon, we looked down a long, straight and wide road that stretched into the middle distance. Lined with trees, occasionally intersected by other roads and traffic lights, the road was flanked by rows of two-storey, semi-detached military houses. The houses and their fenced-in gardens sat behind tall chain-link fences topped with razor wire and hung with signs about security, military police and guard dogs. Beyond that, I saw a large yard, three hanger-like structures to one side, and a couple of drab green vehicles, all behind more razor-wire topped fences. Occasional wisps of black smoke rose between us and the horizon.

I slowed at the lip of the hill and Ned rolled back the sunroof and stood in the passenger seat, staring ahead with our precious binoculars.

Jay leaned forward, trying to get a better view from the backseat. "What does it look like?" he asked.

"The road's a bit of a mess, and I can see a couple of clumps of geeks. Wait a minute." She leaned forward slightly like she was straining to see further. "I can see the gatehouse: it looks wrecked but clear."

Patting me on the shoulder Jay said, "give them the signal."

I flashed the headlights twice. It was around noon in-game, so I couldn't be sure Roper had seen the signal until, with a throaty roar, the Land Rover leapt forward and sped off down the road.

I watched it weave through the scattering of abandoned vehicles, mounting the grass verge at one point. As it reached a point roughly two-hundred yards ahead of us, I heard the strained wailing of the vehicle's horn as they passed what we'd identified as the eastern gate.

"And now, we wait." Jay settled into his seat while Ned scanned both in front and behind.

I might have been uncomfortable with the limited visibility to either side of us, but the fences stretched unbroken, and the few small gates they *did* have sported padlocks. Still, I kept my hands on the wheel and glanced frequently in the rear-view, as if a herd might appear behind us like magic instead of having to shamble slowly up the hill.

Frakt was humming. I couldn't identify the tune, but it was somehow soothing and I managed to ease a little of the tension out of my shoulders.

Jay tapped the back of my chair. "Let's go." I shifted into gear and rolled us forward.

More details became apparent as we neared the gate. Vehicles and buildings were riddled with small arms fire, and scorch marks and blast marks indicated heavier ordinance. Some of the buildings behind the fence still smouldered and I saw a tank, its turret sitting at an odd angle, pouring black smoke from its topmost hatch. It wasn't immediately clear to me how zombies overpowered a modern battle tank but, I thought wryly, *'more things in heaven and earth, Horatio...'*

Chapter 27

The gatehouse wasn't just wrecked, it was gone.

I could see as we approached that the gates had been hardened. Sandbag emplacements with machine guns sat on either side, withered and decayed corpses littering the ground. A wide, black rubber mark left the road, deep tyre marks gouged the grass beyond the pavement, angling for the base entrance. The chain-link mechanical gate that ought to have imposed itself between new arrivals and the gatehouse was gone. Whatever had blitzed though had ripped it away and snagged the fence for good measure. A section of the thick diamond-weave wire protruded, stretched and deformed like the ragged end of a frayed, metal sweater. Whatever was left of the gatehouse and barrier arm was smashed, scattered on the tarmac alongside more spent brass casings than I could even hope to count. Beyond the gate, a barracks block had been gouged, and pieces of brick rubble lay strewn in the road, alongside the smashed and pulped remains of any zombies unlucky enough to have been in the way.

"What happened here?" I mused aloud.

"If I had to guess, I'd say someone took a run at it with a JCB," Ned murmured from the back. "Maybe going for the armoury? I mean, you don't have to worry about guards or anything, so why be subtle?"

"It's a sure-fire stash of weapons," Indi explained. "If we'd thought of it, we might have brought our own digger."

"It might present us with an opportunity," Jay said. "I doubt anyone could have emptied the base armoury in one hit unless they were ridiculously organised. There's a good chance they left a lot of ordnance behind."

"That's if the soldiers' bots didn't strip it bare while the zompocalypse was actually going down," Ned countered.

"Still," Jay wasn't going to give up the point, "it's a good place to start, rather than combing the entire base for leftovers."

"What about the guns we just passed on the gate?" Indi twisted in his seat to point.

Jay's voice came from behind me. "Too big, too bulky, too much ammunition to carry. Doomguy might not have to worry about weight, but we've only got so many inventory slots *n'est-ce pas*."

I started to see occasional zombies standing idle down the side roads of the base.

"Jay, get down," I instructed, and he scooted as low as he could manage.

"Should we split up?" Frakt asked from the back.

"Maybe," Jay replied thoughtfully. "If you're willing Ned, you could hunker down until Roper and AK come by and flag them down. Then the three of you can go see what's left of the armoury. If you think your Stealth skill is up to it and if you're prepared to do it?"

"I don't know," I cautioned. "There are more zombies here than I'd banked on."

Sure enough, as we progressed I was seeing more of the dead standing alone or in clusters. The noise of our car was drawing them slowly toward us.

"I can decide for myself Lex," Ned countered.

In the mirror I could see her scanning about, eyes intense. "We do it now or not at all, it could get worse from here."

"Or it could not." Indi turned in his seat. "Don't split the party man. That's the rule, remember?"

Jay's voice held an edge. "And it's hard enough to keep to it when it *is* just a game, in here we don't get the luxury, we do what we have to."

"Okay, stop," Ned ordered. "If I'm going to do it, better to do it now before there are more of them."

Reluctantly, I pressed the brake and Ned scrambled out of the car, knife in hand, and hurried off towards the nearest building. As she reached the door, a shambler lurched out. Ned danced aside and stabbed the thing in the temple, weaving past the toppling body and into the shadows of the interior.

The door slammed shut and I rolled us on, following signs for the administration offices. Beyond the higher barracks blocks, the building arrangement was more spread out. We passed a mess and a gymnasium, and some office looking structures before I finally spotted the admin building.

The base's central offices lurked ahead of us, a squat, three storey central hall with steps leading up to dark glass double-doors, and wings stretching to either side of a cul-de-sac road with a decoratively-planted central reservation.

For a moment I had the impression of a zombie, its mouth yawning wide, reaching its arms toward a bowl of salad.

I stopped the car at the foot of the stairs and stepped out into the weak sunlight. I could hear the wheezing of zombies, but it was at a distance. I looked around, and, seeing no present threats, nodded to my cohorts.

Hurrying up the steps Jay reminded us, "Our fan-club will be here soon, we should get inside." As if we could forget.

Indi followed close behind him as Frakt and I watched our surroundings for trouble.

Glancing over my shoulder, I saw Indi and Jay share a worried look before Jay swiped our stolen ID card through the reader.

The light on the little box blinked and a low chime sounded quietly. Indi hefted the big blue bolt cutters and pushed at the door.

It opened.

"*Quelle surprise!*" Indi muttered as Frakt and I swept up the stairs and into the admin foyer.

"It stands to reason," Jay said. "If the back-up generator was working in a local supermarket, then a government military installation ought to have power."

The foyer had two double doors leading off of it, a lift and a front desk with the door for access behind. A couple of floor standing plants had been knocked over, and the smell of damp earth hung in the air.

"Where do we go from here?" I asked.

Jay glanced toward the admin desk. "Just a minute." He hurried over, laying his hands on the chest-high counter setup, preparing to vault over. Indi dropped a big hand on his shoulder, startling him but holding him back.

"Wait, wait, wait, *mon ami.* Never step where you can't see, zombie survival one-oh-one, remember?"

Relaxing Jay stepped away from the desk, a sheepish look on his face.

"Sorry, I got excited. I finally get a chance to be useful, y'know?"

Indi offered him a rueful half-smile and, standing on tip-toe, leaned to look over the desk.

A ravaged, lipless face swung toward him. With an uncharacteristic yelp, Indi reeled back, swinging the bolt-cutters into the lunging corpse's head.

The zombie's skull snapped to the side and collapsed messily as three feet of cast iron cutters smashed into its cheekbone. It was another gag I'd seen in games and movies, another illusion dispelled. The explosion of red gore I was expecting would have been much preferable to the ripped and pulpy balloon of flesh and brains I was faced with.

Jay started to gulp like he was going to be sick as Indi, swearing at the corpse, set down the weapon and grabbed the fatigue tunic, hauling the slack body over to our side.

"I'll just chuck this outside."

"Wait!" Jay called, mid-gag. "Ident card."

Indi patted down the corpse and held up another plastic badge, very much like the one we already possessed.

Jay wiped a hand across his mouth, "What's the name?"

"Lambert," Indi read, his accent smoothing the 'T' so it came out 'Lamberrr'.

Jay shook his head. "Not a nihilist to my knowledge."

"Keep it anyway?" Indi asked gruffly.

"You are such a packrat," I teased, "let me see."

I scanned the name. 'Lambert,' just as Indi had said.

"Reads the same for me," I stated.

Jay blinked, leaning toward us, interested. "Keep it for now. We'll check any ranking officers we find. I doubt the card we have will get us all the way. Remember, nihilist philosophers," Jay reminded us, seemingly having gotten himself together.

Frakt frowned, confused.

"It's a breadcrumb trail to the 'goal'," I explained to her. "Even if you don't recognise the name as a philosopher from the school of nihilism, if it reads the same for two players, it's important."

"Better tell the others when they get back," the rangy fighter observed, a slight hesitation in her softly-spoken statement brought on my own thoughtful pause. Was it possible the player behind this Viking-esque avatar was shy or had social anxieties?

"You're right, we should." I nodded. I was rewarded with a slight smile as Indi boosted Jay over the desk.

He dropped down to the floor, scanning around for threats before dragging up the fallen office chair and sitting in front of the computer.

In the still space of the foyer, the slight whine of an electronic device, the hum of the fans and the click-clack of Jay's fingers over the keys seemed inordinately loud. While Jay searched and muttered softly to himself I stepped away to look out the door.

I was starting to worry about Ned, Roper and AK. Although I had no reason to believe they were in trouble, the drift of zombies into the admin building's courtyard was increasing the risks to them when they *did* arrive.

"Got it!" Jay announced triumphantly.

I snapped toward him, hissing across the room, "keep it down!"

"Sorry," he replied churlishly. "But I think I found something."

"So, share?" Indi urged him.

He waved us over. "Come here and read this."

Indi glanced over to me and, with a sigh, I stepped away from the glass door and let myself be boosted over the desk. On the screen, Jay had brought up what looked like a personnel list, but nothing on the screen screamed 'clue' to me.

I shrugged. "And?"

Jay side-eyed me for a second. "I started by looking for our friend Captain Pisarev, I thought if he had an office here there might be some information on his terminal, but he's not on the list of base personnel."

"That sounds more like a dead-end to me," I muttered.

He pointed at the screen. "It is, but look at the name of the base commander."

"Brigadier R. Solnit?" I read, frowning.

Jay sighed. "Am I the only one who's been doing the research?" he beseeched the ceiling. "Solnit, Rebecca Solnit? The American writer who essentially quantified the behaviour and coined the term 'mansplaining'?"

"Is she a nihilist, or a feminist?" I asked.

"Really?" Jay chuckled. "You can be both y'know. Anyway, I don't mean to tell you your business. You're the social activist; I'm just the cishet white dude."

I shrugged. It seemed the most loquacious explanation I had to hand.

"She's much more than that, but yes, she forays into nihilism," he confirmed.

I leaned down, examining the screen again, "I mean, that's still the prize trail, have you tried digging deeper?"

He nodded. "I did, this station doesn't have the capacity to reach the game code as far as I can tell. I'm hoping a higher priority station will be able to reach the console."

"And the brigadier has an office?"

"West wing, top floor," he confirmed.

I glanced at the lit panel beside the lift.

"Stairs?" I asked.

"Stairs," Jay confirmed.

'Don't step where you can't see' was the rule. You couldn't see anywhere outside of a lift you were in. A lift might be a nice convenience in everyday life, but in the zompocalypse it was a one-way ticket to chowtown. Imagine, riding up to your floor in safety and comfort, only for the doors to open on an engulfing wave of animate, rotting flesh and ravenous teeth. None of us were in any hurry to offer the dead a packed lunch.

Indicating what I thought were the westernmost doors I asked, "that way?"

"Yup, check the window, then I'll buzz you though," Jay offered.

I vaulted the counter, conscious of the noise we were making and aware that I probably couldn't have done it if I didn't have Athletic. What more *could* I have done if I'd managed to level that skill I wondered as I approached the double doors. The windows were small, barely the size of a sheet of paper. The foyer was well lit, mostly by the game's ambient light, but beyond the door it was dark. It took me a moment at the window to register the red emergency lighting casting the corridors in sanguine shadows.

Indi joined me at the door.

"Not much room if we have to fight," I observed, "maybe leave the bolt-cutters. I don't feel like getting my head caved in."

Indi jostled me gently in rebuke. "Much as I hate to admit it," he said softly, "Jay was right, they're a shit weapon. Glad I brought this." He hefted a short crowbar.

"It's a classic," I noted and gestured to Jay to open the door.

"Wait," Frakt's soft voice nonetheless pulled us up short. "Should someone stay here to let the others through? I'm happy to do it." She raised the point in her now familiar, well considered and understated way.

I glanced across at my friends. "That's a good point, they don't have an access card and we can't bank on them picking one up on the way."

"We shouldn't split up any more than we have already," Indi objected.

Jay fixed him with a stony look. "Like I said, luxuries, the quicker we can get the information and get out the better."

I noted the new shift in the dynamic, having proven to us (and maybe to himself) that he was still useful, Jay wasn't so ready to bow unquestioningly before Indi anymore.

I glanced toward the front door, willing the others to come speeding up, but no grumbling diesel engine sounded beyond the glass doors, just the low, constant moaning of the dead from their slowly building numbers in the courtyard.

Both Jay and Indi seemed to be looking to me to cast the deciding vote.

For a moment I reflected that it didn't matter who considered themselves 'the leader', our situation was dictating our course and we had two choices, move or die. "If we don't go now, we might not be able to get out," I told them.

"Alright," Jay nodded, beckoning Frakt over. Her tall avatar vaulted easily over the counter, conversely offering Jay a boost to return to our side.

With Jay, Indi and myself at the door and Frakt ready at the computer, we swiped. A buzzer sounded and I quickly handed Captain Pisarev's card back to Frakt as Indi eased the door open and stepped through. Jay followed and I brought up the rear.

I glanced worriedly back at Frakt, who smiled bravely. We had our rule about 'not splitting the party'. It was half trope, half joke, but there was too much at stake. So, as much as I hated it, I let the door close behind me. In reality, the choice wasn't really ours to make.

The corridor was murky; none of the other doors had windows.

Despite the gloom I could see scattered papers, an overturned water dispenser, fire extinguisher and, in the red light, smeared black handprints at intervals on the walls.

A white light flicked on and I watched Jay raise the Smartphone he'd co-opted at the supermarket, holding it in torch function over Indi's shoulder.

"I don't know how long this will last," he murmured softly.

We crept along the corridor.

The first door we came to, Jay signalled a stop and leaned to listen against the wood. Apparently hearing nothing, he tried the handle, then eased the door open to peer within. Daylight flooded through, illuminating a slice of the corridor. Jay hissed and withdrew.

"Zeds?" I whispered.

He nodded.

Indi hefted his crowbar. "Sweep and clear?"

"No," Jay shook his head. "We should get upstairs quickly and quietly."

We hurried on, checking only for a sign that would indicate a stairwell. Finally, Jay's light picked out a green and white sign.

The door beside it had a slit window from top to bottom, but the space beyond was darker than the red-lit corridor we were in.

Indi edged forward. Even from where I was I could see the back of a head and military uniform through the glass.

He turned suddenly and put his back to the door "*Merde!*" he hissed.

Jay killed the light before we alerted the zombie to our presence.

I kept my voice hushed as I asked, "what do we do? The door's 'push only'."

"Then we push," Indi growled.

"But we can't see past the Z," I argued, "we don't know if there are any more of them."

Glancing over his shoulder Indi shifted his weight. "I'll open the door, hopefully I'll pin our friend there against the wall. We deal with anything else we find, and then him." He seemed set in his plan.

"I don't like it," I murmured reluctantly. 'Don't step where you can't see' and we couldn't see past the zombie. But I didn't exactly have anything better to offer, and we didn't have a whole lot of options.

Jay shrugged. "It's all we have."

"Okay," I held up my hands in surrender. "Let's get it done."

We stacked up, Indi at the door, then me, then Jay, ready to shine the phone's torch up the stairs.

Indi held up three fingers, curling each one in a silent countdown before shouldering the door hard. The zombie thumped against the wall, caught by the door, the sound loud enough to worry me, but I stepped in behind Indi and looked up the stairs. A couple of zeds loitered on the first landing of the switch-back stairs, turning slowly at the noise.

All of a sudden, craning its neck behind the door, the trapped zombie gave a wheezing cry.

"Oh shit," Jay breathed, locking eyes with the corpse through the door's glass panel. The door, despite Indi's bulk, lurched.

"What the fuck?" Indi swore and pressed hard, banging the door and zombie against the wall, but struggling to keep it there.

Momentarily distracted, I turned back to the stair zombies. Despite the glare of the phone's light, whether they saw past it or used some other sense, however they perceived Jay's presence, they did. The zeds whirled around like dancers, crouching and leapt from the landing. The first cannoned into me, knocking me into Indi, who stumbled. The flailing limbs knocked Jay back through the door, the phone flying from his hand, casting us in red-hued shadows, before the second deadhead piled into us. The force took the four of us, me, Jay and my two dead dance partners out into the corridor, struggling in the dark.

Chapter 28

I raised my hands defensively on instinct as the corpse leapt on me. I could feel the rough stubble of the zombie's jaw, the soft, pulpy flesh of its lips and the ragged edges of the teeth in its yawning mouth. In a panic, I whipped my hand from the zed's face as the teeth came gnashing together and we rolled into the corridor.

Somehow I'd managed to hold on to my brush-hook, but I couldn't use the long blade while I was trapped under the flailing zombie. We hit the floor together, the impact winding me, jarring my bones. The hands grasped at me, dragging over my body and clawing at my face, raking as I flinched away from the pain. Its weight pressed down on me, its fingers seeking, probing into my mouth, making me want to gag.

Something kicked me in the side and a further weight landed on top of me. The second zombie tripped and landed on us but even as I fought with the first, the weight on me started to lessen and I realised the second Z was rising to go after Jay.

I shoved my forearm under the chin of the zombie on top of me and reached out, my grasping hand snagging the trouser leg of the second zed where it bulged out of the military boots. The zombie tried to leap for Jay, jerking my arm and dragging both me and the flailing rotter atop me along the floor as it fell and scrambled, frantically crawling towards its prey.

I heard the door to the stairs slam, and then a muffled ring of something hitting the stairs and swearing in French.

"Jay, run!" I yelled as grubby nails raked my cheek.

I struggled and twisted, wrapping my outstretched fist in trouser material and trying desperately to hang on to one zombie while writhing to get out from beneath another. The spitting, snarling zombies jostled and dragged me, but I realised, my stress bar was a manageable sensation. Maybe I was getting used to this at some level.

235

But, then again, the carcass that held me down wasn't trying to eat *me,* I realised in a sudden flash. At least, not exclusively. Fast and strong though it was, it was trying to break away and get to Jay as much as it was trying to bite me. In the tumult of our three-way struggle, the zombie on top of me couldn't find purchase to get itself up to chase Jay *and* concentrate on taking a bite out of me. Its boots scuffed and raked my shins, its hips pressed and bucked in perverse parody against my groin and its hands either grasped and pulled or splayed and pushed in turn. It would snap its teeth at me and then look, almost longingly down the corridor toward Jay. Aside from straining to break my grip, the other was paying me no attention at all.

None of this helped me, trapped as I was between the feverishly struggling corpses.

Suddenly the strain on my outstretched arm lessened. My hand flexed in my surprise and I glimpsed Jay bearing the rasping zed to the ground, stabbing downward with his knife in a frenzy all his own. The zombie on top of me twisted as the pair rolled past us. With a hand free I pushed upward, took my weapon and swung, hacking desperately at the zombie's head.

I felt it spasm as old blood gushed, but I let it roll sideways as I killed it.

I rolled to my feet to see the stairway door open and Indi come bursting out, and we both turned to check on Jay. He rose unsteadily to his feet, panting and shaking as he turned to us.

"One," he sighed raggedly.

We shared smiles, but our triumph was short-lived as the doors around us erupted with the frantic hammering of dead fists.

"But, they can't even see me!" Jay cried despondently as Indi grabbed a fistful of his shirt, dragging him through the door and up the stairs.

I stooped to grab the phone, it's torchlight a thin line on the floor, and followed, the three of us leaping up the stairs two at a time.

At the top, the thin window revealed another zombie, thrashing and gnashing at the glass. It couldn't have seen us, couldn't really have heard us, but still, somehow it knew we were coming.

I looked to Indi and he nodded grimly.

Taking the Lambert swipe card, I ran it through the lock and opened the door inward, staying behind it.

The zombie's efforts to breach the door caused it to lurch forward, off balance, so Indi used its momentum to heave it up and over the railing. It twisted in the air and came down across the handrails. A sickening, wet snapping sound signalled its back breaking, and it lay on the stairs, glaring and reaching for us, its entire lower half twisted to an unnatural angle.

Three stories up, I'd hoped we'd be free, but the doors still rattled as bodies thumped against them. Here even the emergency lighting was patchy. The walls and ceiling, where the light of the torch passed over them, were pockmarked with bullet holes, and the glass of light bulbs crunched underfoot.

Head swinging left and right Indi demanded. "Which way?"

"Right!" Jay urged and the three of us hurried along the darkened corridor, stepping over bodies in the gloom.

We came to a halt at a set of double doors. From the grisly remains on the floor, they had once been guarded, probably the source of the damage and death on this level. I swiped the card and waited for the lock to click. Instead, the card reader flashed a red light and buzzed harshly at us.

"Shit," I swore, "we need a new card."

"One of the guards ought to have one. If we backtrack we can find the bodies."

I nudged a larger glob of viscera with my boot.

"If there's that much left," I muttered.

We took tentative steps, sweeping the torch from side to side. The few bodies we stopped to check seemed devoid of any paperwork or clearance. It seemed the game was directing us toward the guards. There was a thick trail of dried blood on the carpet, lumpy with discarded shreds of meat and offal. The thumping from the doors persisted, lending urgency to our search. I wished fervently that Ned and the others would get to us soon.

The sweep of the torch illuminated hunched backs in the dark.

The five or six zombies crouched, dressed in camouflage and huddled close together, clearly intent on whatever, or whoever, they were eating. In the light a limp, pale hand raised above the scene. The hand, minus a couple of digits, flopped loosely from side to side like a school kid trying to ask the teacher a question. The zombies' focus in their grisly meal could be the only reason they hadn't attacked us already, but I couldn't fathom why whatever drew zombies to Jay hadn't affected them.

It was Indi who had a flash of inspiration.

Turning to us, eyes suddenly white in the phone's light he grinned and asked, "Boss battle?"

"Climax event," Jay clarified, he was trying to joke but there was a tremor in his voice.

"I don't like it," I whispered harshly. Something was nagging at me. The situation was too straightforward, too 'easy' for my liking.

"Only one way forward," Indi shrugged, raising his gun and firing. One of the zombies, its head tilted back to gulp down a hunk of flesh, jerked as a plume of rank grey brain matter sprayed out from its skull.

In the confined space, the gunshot struck like a physical blow. My ears rang and my vision swam. I took a staggering step sideways, shaking my head.

In the wavering light from Jay's torch, the pack of huddled zombies turned, eyes and teeth showing dirty white as they snarled.

My vision flickered, like a glitch or a snag in an old ciné reel. The banging ceased and the zombies froze, all except one. The zombie soldier's features relaxed as it stood slowly. In the light, I could just make out the ragged tears in its clothes, the rents in the exposed flesh that glistened darkly against its sallow skin.

It stepped forward, like a figure from a half remembered dream and then, it spoke.

"I see," it declared in an electronically distorted voice. "You're the hacker."

Still recovering from the effects of the gunshot in the confined space, all I could do was gawp at this new twist.

"Are you...?" Jay gasped, a hand to one side of his head. "Are you one of the devs?"

The 'zombie' smiled and inclined its head.

"It's interesting to me that your intrusion doesn't appear to be an attempt to 'beat' the game, not yet in any case," it said smoothly.

Jay steadied himself but his words were unsure, hesitant. "I just, I wanted to look around your handiwork, the programming, the interface? It's sublime work, really."

The zombie-dev smiled again at the compliment.

"But it's killing people," Jay finished coldly.

The smile froze and zombie-dev watched us for a moment.

"Unfortunate," it spoke slowly, "but necessary."

238

I'd been almost sure the devs knew, but I'd so wanted to believe that they didn't. "You knew?" I snarled.

Zombie-dev nodded sadly, "It's a side effect. The feedback required for the conditioning necessitates a level of stimulus that can be, unfortunately, fatal under particular circumstances."

"Conditioning? For what?" I demanded.

The zombie-dev shook its head with a sly grin. "I can't tell you that. Suffice to say you will discover in time."

Jay interrupted us. "When the countdown finishes? Not a lot of time left on that, is there?"

The dev blinked, surprised. "It seems your intrusion has pierced deeper than expected," it muttered.

"We can stop you," I stated, flatly. "Whatever it is, we can kill you here and now and stop it."

The zombie-dev laughed, the ravaged tissue of the mob's neck quivering with the motion.

"That's assuming I'm working alone. Assuming what's going to happen hasn't already been set in motion? And assuming you *can* take me down. Even if I don't have a God-mod running, you've clearly seen what it takes to inflict the mental trauma required to kill someone IRL. Do you think you have what it takes, player?"

I bridled impotently. I couldn't see myself ripping even this arrogant ass limb from limb. I doubted I could pare the flesh from their body, rip the organs from their still-living avatar as they howled and screamed if it meant saving a hundred lives, a thousand. To kill this dev I wouldn't have to simply become a murderer, I'd have to be a monster.

"Anyway," the zombie waved dismissively. "Your goals might be," it made air-quotes, "'Noble', and your hack largely benign, but I'm afraid I'm going to have to leave you to the 'Swarm' protocol. Or hadn't you noticed how the zombies change around your friend here?"

"We noticed," Indi stepped forward threateningly. "We just don't care."

"Well, on that note I'll leave you. Do have fun, gamers," the dev sneered.

"Wait!" I challenged. "What is this about, what are you hoping to achieve?"

The dev tilted the zombie avatar's head quizzically.

"We're going to change the world. I hope you live to see it. By the way," the zombie held up a desiccating hand. "I'm afraid I can't let any of you, or your friends leave to spread the word, so I've disabled the exit commands to your comrades over at the armoury too. Fun fact," the dev grinned, "the motor signals your brain sends to your real bodies are highly diminished while you're in-game. Without the exit prompt, you can't actually remove your VR gear and you can't call for help." With that, the zombie-dev's shoulders slumped, its head tipping forward to its chest.

Again, there was the sensation of a graphics glitch, and the zombies started to rasp, the doors thudding with the pounding of undead fists once more.

"Mother-fucker," Indi growled.

The zombies lurched to their feet. In the torchlight I saw the glint of steel.

The pack leapt forward swinging their blades. "They've got knives!" I shouted in warning.

I danced back from the wicked steel and brought my brush hook down, severing an arm at the elbow. I heard Indi grunt as he dipped low and hoisted a zombie up-and-over on his hulking shoulder.

Zombies didn't fight like living opponents, even in games; they don't worry about injury, they don't fear a bared blade, not like I feared theirs. They pressed in even as I hacked at them while I was forced to dodge and give ground.

One got in close and we wrestled, me trying to avoid its knife and get a shot at its head, it trying to shoulder past or through me to get to Jay.

I could hear swearing, a stream of hysterical babbling as I imagined Jay was trying to finish the zombie Indi had thrown over his shoulder.

I brought my weapon down on the zombie's head, the blow glancing off the skull biting into the shoulder, lodging in the bone. The zed made an ungainly thrust, trying to stab at me, and even as I twisted, the blade left a searing line in my flank.

I hissed in pain and let the brush hook go. I got a hand around the zombie's wrist and one around the back of its skull. Twisting the joint, I wrenched the arm upward and forced the knife back on the Z. Gradually, eye to cataract eye, fighting for every inch and gagging at the stink of its rotten 'breath', I forced the zombie's own knife into its eye. It fought me the whole time, to bite and tear, right until I hit the spot that switched it off. The slow blade might penetrate, but it's fucking gross. Swallowing down my gorge I yanked my hook from the corpse's shoulder as it fell.

Another zed lunged for me and I tucked and rolled, taking it in the shins and it flew over me. I surged to my feet, turning, and swung the hook across the back of the zombie's neck. Putting my boot to its back I wrenched the blade free and hacked again. The head lolled, meat parted but the spine held. Another savage blow parted bone and sinew, and the head thumped wetly on the floor followed closely by the rest of the zombie's corpse.

I stood there panting and felt a needle-like pain in my wrist. A glance told me the problem.

STM	███			

STR	████		

The second STM bar was flashing and failing. Luckily Jay and Indi had dealt with the remaining three rage-zombies.

> **Combat Lvl 4 achieved, bonus will be applied after rest period**

I was about to give a rueful chuckle, thinking I was doing fine without, when a sound froze me to the spot.

The hammering on the doors was joined by the splintering of wood.

I shared a panicked look with my friends, and we hurried back to the site of the pack's grisly meal. Jay held the torch, Indi ready to fend off any mobs while I knelt at the ruined remains of one of the door guards.

The torso and upper thighs were basically gone. Jagged, broken ribs hung, attached only by strips of sinew. I gagged at the smell and sensation of wet flesh under my hands. I stretched across the corpse, reaching over for the tattered remains of the shirt, trying to check the breast pocket for the key card. I tried not to look at the face, the remaining humanity, but a twitching movement drew my eyes as the lolling head rolled toward me and the eyes opened.

I froze in abject horror as the ruined lips parted. The jaws, their cheeks bloodied, yawned wide and the zombie, with what was left of its neck and chest muscles, snapped its head forward toward my outstretched arm.

I couldn't move, I was frozen, I couldn't avoid the bite, couldn't stop it. My wrist throbbed like a nail had been driven through it as my stress bar spiked and I felt pressure. Someone screamed, but it wasn't me.

The jaws clamped down on a hand, fingers wrapped protectively around my bicep.

With nightmarish slowness I watched the teeth worry at the fingers, bright blood pumping, feeling the pressure in my own flesh. I turned my head, following the skinny arm back up to the anguished face of Jay's avatar. Finally, I cried out myself, ripping my arm from the zombie's mouth. The teeth clamped shut, crushing the delicate bones in my friend's hand and Jay pulled back, clutching his wrist and holding the bleeding stumps of his severed and mangled fingers right in front of my panicked eyes.

In a sudden rage, I turned to the zombie, grabbing a handful of hair and slamming the head back into the wall. I dragged it forward and slammed it back again.

"Drop it!" I snarled, like the zombie was a misbehaving dog. In that moment it became imperative that I reclaimed Jay's severed fingers, that I make the zombie drop them. I slammed its head back again and again, each blow sounding wetter, each impact spongier, until the mouth lolled and the torn remains of my friend's fingers flopped grotesquely out of the mouth.

I scrabbled to gather up the mangled pieces and turned, on my knees, to proffer the bloodied handful to Jay as he stood, cradled in Indi's thick arms.

"It's alright," I gasped, a desperate smile on my face so wide it hurt, "I got them."

Indi glared down at me, eyes full of anger and horror.

"What did you do?" he rasped.

Psychological Trauma Imminent, seek assistance

Chapter 29

Jay mewled through clenched teeth as Indi grasped his wrist, examining the shredded stumps before turning the injured hand over to check his stats.

I sat, rocking on my haunches until my friend's hulking avatar reached out to drag my own wrist closer, scattering the pitiful handful of mashed finger meat as they did so.

"Hey!" I protested weakly but Indi just grunted in disgust. Taking off his pack, he rummaged inside, producing water and a bottle of pills before my unfocussed eyes.

Shoving both into my unresisting hands Indi commanded brusquely. "Take them!"

I swallowed the pills without making any conscious decision to do so.

As the throbbing in my wrist subsided, rational thought returned. Jay cradled his hand, pale and unsteady. The sound of splintering wood assailed my ears.

"Oh shit," I babbled, frantic. "What can I do?"

Hoisting Jay up by the shoulder Indi snapped at me, "Get the fucking security card! We have to get secure and deal with this."

I fumbled through the remains of the guards until the *Loot?* Option flashed up, finally coming up with the bloodied card.

I hurried ahead as Indi, growling in frustration, helped Jay down the corridor.

Fists punched through the doors, reaching blindly for us. I swiped the card and the light flashed red. Swallowing a curse, I wiped the dirty plastic on my hoodie and tried again. The lock clicked, and I hauled the doors wide just as Indi, grunting and looking pale under the dim emergency lights, carried Jay through. The doors swung closed and I moved from door to door, reading the name plates until, finally I found the one that read 'Brigadier Solnit'.

I waved to Indi, swiped the card and pushed the door.

Even the washed-out daylight proved dazzling after the corridor's gloom. I scanned the room quickly, identified an indistinct shape and launched myself at it. The zombie rasped as I shoved it against the wall, then took a step back and finished it off, the tip of my hook burying itself deep in the zombie's skull. Old blood spattered my face. I tasted it on my tongue and spat in disgust.

My vision cleared as I moved to the inner door, leading to the NPC brigadier's office proper, and peered through the glass. A body lay slumped, unmoving, in the chair behind the desk. I opened the door quietly and crept inside. Holding my hook high, I whistled sharply.

The corpse stayed just that, a corpse. It seemed the devs had tried to give the brigadier an air of quiet dignity in death. She lay slumped over the desk, gun near to hand, her head positioned with the simple dark, entry wound marring the temple uppermost. The suicide might have seemed tranquil but for the blood-matted hair, bone and brain fragments splashed on the cracked window and wall.

Aside from the desk and its computer with a chair for the brigadier and a facing chair for visitors, the room had a bookshelf, filing cabinet and couch.

Indi set Jay down and I pulled out the medkit and bound his hand.

"What the hell happened?" Indi winced as I worked.

"I froze," I stated bluntly, "my stress bar topped out and I froze." I pulled a bottle of liquor from my bag and handed it to Jay who took a long pull. "What were those pills by the way?" I asked.

"Antidepressants, found them on the road." Indi shrugged and winced again.

I stopped for a moment, trying to recall when last I'd taken mine IRL. Not that there was anything I could do about it.

"What's up with you?" Jay, sweating and shaking from the pain but lucid again, spoke to Indi. "It's not like you to be squeamish."

Indi ignored the question. "How's he doing?" he asked.

"The hand is bound, stress meter is falling." I assured him. "He'll be okay,"

"Good," Indi grunted and sagged.

I gasped as I finally saw what he'd been hiding as we fled through the corridor; the hilt of a combat knife protruding from his side. I hurried to help him gently to the floor and pulled his wrist to me.

HLT						

The bar was flashing urgently.

"Shit!" I swore and rummaged in Jay's discarded pack for the partial medkit. I wasn't sure what I could do, but I wasn't about to let Indi die on me, not after I'd failed Jay so completely. It was probably the influence of my skill, but I felt a cold detachment as I did what I could with Indi's seeping wound. I packed around the knife with gauze and taped it in place. The flashing bar slowed to pulsing and a message flashed up on my HUD.

Stabilised, seek additional treatment

"Did you catch that?" Indi grunted.

"Yes," I replied, my teeth gritted in frustration. "But I'm out of supplies, I'll have to go see what I can find."

"Check the doors, make sure the others can get through." Jay's voice was still a little shaky, but I noted it was coming from the chair behind the desk. Ruined hand or no, Jay was firing up the Brigadier's desktop.

I thought about chastising him but reconsidered. It was what we were here for, and we were on a timetable.

"Try not to fuck up again," Indi commented dourly and I felt a pang in my chest as I pushed through to the outer office. I knew Indi was upset, disappointed in me for getting Jay hurt, but I was sure much of it was down to the stress mechanic. If it had been down to me, I would have moved; I was pretty sure Jay had meant to pull me away, not shove his hand in a zombie's mouth, but with the stress bar peaking, any action the player was allowed was uncoordinated, somehow random. Indi hadn't had to deal with it. His build made him almost immune, and so my friend was making assumptions that the whole incident was *my fault* and I resented him for it. But more than that, it hurt, and I was glad to put a little distance between us.

In the corridor I paused with my back to the wall and looked down at my shaking hands, turning them over. I stared at the child's shin pads I wore on my wrists and tore them off in disgust. A lot of use they'd proved to be then. With a guilty sigh I bent to retrieve them. My side burned where the zombie had cut me and I winced, but I still had a full three bars of health. I could look at the wound later. Turning my attention back to the corridor, I glanced left and right, intent on looking for a kitchen or somewhere there might be a first aid kit. In the real world I would be calling an ambulance. There was little chance of being able to do much for a severe penetrating wound with a simple first aid kit from an office, whether that office was military or not, but in-game the assigned skills counted for more.

First I hurried back to the security door, shouts and the sound of fighting came from beyond.

I checked the glass and saw Ned scrabbling with a key card as Roper, AK, and Frakt fought zombies behind her.

Looking up from the reader, Ned smiled in relief as I swiped my card and pushed the doors open. Ned reached back for a couple of large, heavy looking bags and slipped through with a shout, signalling our newest clan-mates who almost fell through the open doors.

We let the weight of the zed's push the doors closed as the four of them stood panting in the gloomy hallway.

"You could've cut that closer y'know," Ned grinned. "Would've been a lot more dramatic about twenty seconds from now."

I forced a smile I wasn't feeling.

"Indi and Jay are hurt," I told her. "I need more medical supplies."

Ned winced. Under the emergency lighting her dark skin made her almost invisible, but the whites of her eyes and teeth showed bright.

"Can't help you there, we ran into a few problems of our own," she admitted. I took a better look at the team and saw the new stained bandages they were sporting.

"I'll keep looking," I sighed. "Indi and Jay are in the last office down the hall."

"We should do something to strengthen these doors," Frakt suggested.

I nodded thoughtfully. "I'll leave that to you. We should also look around for another way out, pair up. Two of you reinforce the door, two of you look for an alternate escape route. I've got to help Indi," I stated flatly and left them to it.

Unable to find a kitchen, I went from room to room, quietly opening doors to check for geeks and then sweeping for medical supplies. Unlike the school, all those logins ago, the military offices were devoid of wall-mounted aid packs. Trying to come up with a solution, I stood gazing out of the window. I was at the rear of the wing, looking toward the back of the camp, and, I realized as my eyes focussed in the light, the base medical facility.

I considered it for a moment. It was a long walk to be sure but maybe, just maybe...

No. I was about to discount the idea entirely as too big of a risk when, in a break in the buildings between the offices and the facility I spotted an overturned vehicle. It was big and blocky and green, like all the military vehicles I'd seen, but emblazoned on the upturned side, was a bright red cross.

I scoped out the ground below and decided, although the med bay was too far, the ambulance was just close enough to risk it.

Back in the corridor I approached the fire-exit, then stopped and glanced over my shoulder toward the far end where my friends were. I was about to break the 'Never go alone' rule again, and this time they wouldn't even know where I was. But I had to do it, had to redeem myself, regain Indi's confidence in me.

The door announced that it was alarmed 'in case of emergency' and I hesitated. A fire alarm going off at this point would be a major hassle for us. For a moment I stood and examined the door until a small box popped up in my vision.

Stealth option: Disable alarm? Y/N

'Hell yes,' I murmured to myself.

A slight highlight led me to a wire, protruding slightly from the pneumatic hinge. With a defiant smile I cut it with my knife. I eased the door open and slipped through, careful to leave it ever-so-slightly ajar for my return. Hurrying down the fire escape stairs, I flinched at every ringing footfall on the galvanised steel, and gave an audible sigh of relief when I finally hit the grass. I loped in the direction of the ambulance, favouring speed over stealth. The zombies were definitely more numerous than when we'd arrived. I guessed our actions and maybe the 'swarm protocol' had something to do with that. Who knew how many spots in the outer fence were compromised, letting the Z's trickle in? The sooner we were gone the better.

Reaching the back doors of the ambulance, I gave silent thanks. The doors had been popped and supplies littered the ground. I ripped off my pack and quickly gathered what I could, sweeping the closest undamaged supplies into my bag. Out of the corner of my eye I spotted what looked like an intact kit, just beyond the crashed vehicle. It seemed odd, with all the debris scattered out of the back doors behind the ambulance, that this one pack would fall parallel with the rear axle. Still, in my hurry, I scampered around to snatch up the medkit.

Over the low moans of the dead I heard a sound, a sharp rapping like knuckle on glass. I looked up, straight into the eyes of George. He grinned maliciously and I looked desperately for a gun, but he wasn't holding one. I quickly gathered more details. The window, the building, it was the guardhouse. But if George wasn't going to shoot me, what was he...?

He gave a sneering grin and I saw his shoulder flex with effort.

The sound of klaxons filled the air, wailing horrifically loudly in the near silence.

The base alarm, he'd triggered the base alarm.

I scrambled to my feet, shouldering my brimming pack. George waved at me patronizingly then vanished into the guardhouse's darkened interior.

My side burned as I ran full tilt for the fire escape, leaping the stairs two at a time, dragging myself with my arms and gasping at the pain the whole time. As I wrenched the fire door open, hands reached out and grabbed me, hauling me inside. The door slammed and I was thrust up against the wall. I panicked until I saw who it was, and the panic was washed away as a wave of confusion flooded over me.

"What are you doing?" Frakt demanded, hand full of my hoodie.

Roper pressed in beside her, snapping, "are you trying to get us all killed?"

Between them they had me pressed up against the wall. In their questions, accusations and anger all I could see were gnashing teeth.

A quiet voice cut through my confusion. "How could you?" AK's eyes pierced me, hurt and anger plainly illustrated by the gun he had pointed at my head.

"I didn't, it wasn't," I stammered. "I went out for medical supplies for Indi!"

Another rough shove. "So setting off the sirens was just for fun?" Roper growled.

The three of them dragged me, struggling and protesting, to the office.

"I get it," AK sneered to the others, "they rope us in with that bullshit story about the game killing peeps, then lure us into this ambush. They lock themselves away while we get shredded!"

"No, that makes no sense!" I protested desperately. "It was George!"

AK let out a barked laugh, a brittle and cynical sound. "Don't give me that," he snapped, "how'd he follow us? How'd he even know we were here?"

"He listened," I guessed, frantic. "He played possum in the back of the car to listen in?"

They thought on that for a moment.

"He *is* just that flavour of arsehole," Roper said.

Eventually AK agreed. "I wouldn't put it past him."

"Dick," Frakt said, succinct as ever.

I let out a relieved sighed as they released me.

"Okay," Roper said, "but we've still got to go fix it, and for that we need a plan."

AK let go of my arm and grinned ruefully, "maybe one that involves kicking George's teeth in, am I right?"

"You're not wrong," I nodded and took a deep, relieved breath, "the bastard."

Chapter 30

Indi pushed himself up on his elbows as we walked in. "What the fuck is going on?" he demanded from the couch.

AK spoke for me as I threw the bag down and went to work on his wound. "George, fucker found his life-long calling as a griefer. He triggered the base alarm."

Jay, waxen-faced behind the desktop computer, asked. "Why?"

Frakt grimaced, "too chicken-shit to come and kill us himself."

"He must figure that a horde will do the job just as well," Roper suggested. "We should leave."

"We can't," Jay muttered. "Not yet," he added, noting that he'd caught the room's attention.

"Why?" I asked as I knelt on the floor. "You found something?"

He nodded, one hand tapping shakily at the keyboard, "Yes, but I need time."

"We can barricade," Roper suggested. "Jam all the ground floor stairwells with office furniture, call up the lifts and jam the doors."

"I'll clear the floor," Frakt volunteered. Thinking back she had seemed remarkably fresh compared to the others when they arrived. Combat four must have some real bonuses.

AK raised a good question. "Then how do we get out?"

"The fire escape?" I suggested. "If we don't go near it, don't draw it to the zed's attention, they'll walk right past it."

"That doesn't help if the building's surrounded." AK's tone of voice suggested this should be obvious to all of us.

"Without a clear stimulus the zombies will gather, but they won't focus," Ned mused thoughtfully. "So we provide a focus somewhere else."

"Won't work, while with the sirens going." I snarled, not bothering to keep my frustration with George from my voice. "Nothing we do will draw them away from this racket, and they'll keep coming until the whole area reaches capacity." Having stripped the temporary dressing from around the knife in Indi's flank, I was preparing to elongate the wound on either side. I had to, or the serrated back of the blade would rip the flesh as I pulled it out. I jabbed a syringe of anaesthetic into the site, and handed Indi a plastic wrapped bandage. "Bite on this," I told him.

"Then we have to switch off the alarms," Ned spoke slowly, "sooner, rather than later. Luckily the armoury wasn't totally stripped."

Indi jerked, tensing as I took a scalpel and cut on either side of the combat knife while Ned went on.

"That's what took us so long. The duffels have sixteen slots apiece, we were working out the best way to max inventory on them."

"Yeah," AK chimed in. "Loose ammo was, like, fifty rounds. Boxed was better, five boxes of twenty, but the best way was mags. Five mags of thirty rounds each, one-hundred and twenty rounds per slot. We had to hand load some mags ourselves just to max out what we could fit in. Didn't work for shells, but we brought some anyway." He sniffed dismissively, his sniper bias against shotguns pretty clear.

"Anyway," Ned cut in impatiently, "we have guns and ammo, so I'll go shut off the alarm."

"Wait for me, I'll come with you," I told her, my hands shaking as I fixed a clamp on the bottom edge of the enlarged wound and let the weight of the scissor-like instrument pull the skin down. I began easing the knife out, careful not to cause further damage. I briefly wondered why my stress bar wasn't rising, but then I realised the First Aid skill was insulating me from the anxiety of treating my friend.

"I can't wait for you." I could hear that Ned was moving to the door but I daren't look away from the delicate operation before me.

I heard a metallic rustle. "Don't worry, I've got your back," AK said brightly. The sounds that followed I knew all too well from the movies. The sounds of a magazine sliding into the receiver and then the 'snap-clack' of an assault rifle bolt.

I spared a split-second glance over my shoulder just in time to see Roper grasp AK's arm.

"Don't do anything crazy, dumbass," he said softly.

AK replied with a strained grin. "As if I would, dickhead."

Roper stepped back, all business. "All right, you get the sirens, we'll block the stairwells." He indicated to himself and Frakt. "We'll isolate this building as best we can, but we'll leave the lobby lift in place, come back that way.

"Once I get Indi back on his feet, we'll help," I needed to do more than stitch up my friends.

"But," Jay repeated, "no-one goes near the back fire escape, if we don't draw them there, it's our best avenue of escape."

"Where are we going?" Ned asked, and I supplied directions to the guard house. I had Indi pressing a pad to the wound, but I was still trying to mop away blood and thread a needle with my teeth at the same time.

"Be careful," I cautioned from the corner of my mouth. "George might be holed up in the security office."

"I bloody hope so," Ned murmured, teeth bared.

Once the others had gone, it was just me, Jay and the grimacing Indi.

"When are we going to tell them they can't log out?" I asked. I couldn't hide my concern, because of us, three more innocent players were trapped in the game. Four if you counted George, but I doubted he fell into the 'innocent' bracket.

"As soon as we find a convenient moment, when our lives aren't in imminent danger. Knowing won't change their immediate situation," Jay replied.

Desperate for the distraction as I prepared to push a needle into Indi's flesh I asked Jay, "What have you found?"

"Okay," Jay was tapping rhythmically at the keys, "whoever did this is good, really good. Most of this in-game system is purely cosmetic, but in replicating a series of directories in a network, it has shared properties that I can adapt and implement with a little help from my tether programme."

"And what are you doing?" I wanted to hear it, but I also needed him to keep speaking.

"The bread-crumb trail we've been following is now telling me that there's a World Health Organisation lab that was conducting tests at the time of the zombie outbreak. The military was transporting infected subjects that way, so it's the best-case location for a working cure sample."

That confused me. "But we're not looking for a cure anymore."

"True, it's also about the same distance from us as from Stockholm to Örenbro."

"Which is?" I prompted.

"Two hundred miles, give or take."

"London to Manchester, right," I grimaced. "So how does that help us?"

He leaned close to the screen, his voice distracted as he concentrated on something, "I figure that, if the game world network becomes more detailed as we get closer to the goal, then it runs closer to the framework programming, the servers and, maybe, to the admins' own machines."

"Doesn't that all exist in the same space while the game's running?" I queried.

"Simply put, no," Jay sighed. "This isn't like a page in a book that can be read all at once, Lex, it's more like a library. We don't even want the books, we're after the librarian's computer. Rather than us navigate all the way to the lab, I'm going to establish a connection from here to there for remote access."

I snapped the thread and Indi let out a string of velvet-smooth expletives as I doused his side in medicinal alcohol, and started taping a dressing over the wound.

Health restored +30% for skill level

Another message followed that one:

First Aid Lvl 04 achieved, bonus will be applied after rest period

And another:

You have unlocked the Medicine skill select now and it will be added after a rest period. Yes/No

"New skill," I announced. "Medicine, shall I take it?"

"Couldn't hurt," Indi muttered.

Checking the rest of my menu I pointed out, "It's my last slot."

HLT				

Jay shrugged. "As long as we don't need you to suddenly learn how to defuse a bomb, this is probably more useful in terms of skill balancing."

Steeling myself I doused the wound in my own flank with alcohol, hissing through my teeth as it burned.

I selected the skill, taping a pad of gauze in place on my wound, ripping the tape with my teeth. I checked my bar again.

HLT	

'Take that, fucking '*fifty percent appropriate to skill level,*' I sneered at the game.

I glanced across at Jay. "How's the hand?" I ventured hesitantly.

"Still a bit stiff," he muttered absently. "What do you think? It hurts like hell," he followed up testily, not lifting his eyes from the computer.

"That's a good point," Indi stood and pulled his torn shirt down, a brief pained sound escaping his lips. "What do we do about you, Jay?"

He looked up at that, confused. "What about me?"

"You've been bitten, shouldn't we shoot you, or amputate or something?"

Jay regarded the bigger avatar coolly. "You ever notice how often MCs in games get bitten but never turn? Not without it being part of the narrative anyway."

"We don't know that being bitten is the infection vector anyway," I suggested.

Indi wasn't letting it drop. "But it's the most basic canon."

"In that case, if it's canon you want," Jay stated hotly, "I've got at least twenty-four hours, maybe longer, by genre standards. You two get out there and help get us locked down." He said in a way that announced 'conversation over'.

I shook my head. "I'm worried about Ned and AK," I admitted. "I'm going to follow them."

"Are you sure?" Jay asked. In the quiet following his question we all heard the muffled 'crack!' of gunshots.

"Yeah," I nodded, my guts squirming with barely suppressed anxiety.

As I turned to go, Indi stepped in front of me, a shotgun in one hand and box of shells in the other.

He grinned and thrust the gun at me. "Standard Benelli M-Four, easy to use, hard to miss." His words were clipped and precise. "Seven in the tube, one in the chamber. Six round speedload attached to the offside rail." He opened the box and held it toward me. I worked the slide as I'd

254

seen in the movies and started to slip the bulky ammunition into the loading port.

"These are slugs, not shot," Indi told me. "Hell of a kick, but even if it's not a kill shot they ought to knock a Z off its feet."

I loaded seven, pumped the action and slipped in a final round, then added six to the loops on the stock and pocketed a handful more, my inventory combining ten shells into a single item stack. Indi held out a couple of pistol magazines. My friend frowned at me a moment, then pulled the cigarette/lighter combination from my pocket.

"You don't have the inventory slots," he sucked his teeth, clearly unhappy.

He shoved the magazines in my cargo's thigh pocket. Again, the inventory stacked one over the other. Ejecting my near empty magazine from my pistol, he slipped a fresh one in.

"One in the chamber?" he asked and I nodded.

"Thirty-seven pistol rounds total," he commented apparently satisfied. "Turn," Indi ordered. As I complied he pulled my hook blade from my belt for a brief inspection before replacing it, and then the same with my knife from my hip.

"Your blade's at about a third durability, so be prepared to pull the knife, that's only down about a fifth. I could maybe give the hook some DP's back, but it would take time."

I considered asking for a replacement, but I was comfortable with the billhook, it was a familiar weight in my hand.

The sounds of gunfire rang out again.

"No," I shook my head. "If George has Ned and AK pinned I need to get going."

Indi looked like he was going to argue but he said softly. "Look after yourself,"

"Look after Jay," I replied with a grin.

He gave a rueful chuckle, "God Dammit."

I paused. "What?"

He smiled a broad, genuine smile. "Guess I ended up baby-sitting anyway."

"I resent the implication!" Jay called from the computer.

I paused. There were so many things I wanted to say. I wanted to tell them both how much I loved them, my 'found family' as Indi would say, how their friendship was one of the most treasured things in my life and how, having fallen into this hellish nightmare, there was no-one in the world I'd rather have at my side.

But my throat closed, the words wouldn't come and, with little more than a nod I hurried out into the corridor. I rushed past Roper and Frakt who were navigating a desk toward the stairwell and hurried down to the first floor. Below me, at ground level, office furniture had been tumbled into the space behind the door, jamming it shut. I picked a door, careful to choose the front of the building, the fire escape being at the back. Slinging my shotgun, I pulled my knife and eased my way into the office. One zombie, facing toward the window. I slipped up behind it and, one hand reaching around to its forehead, I slid my blade into the base of its skull with no more noise than the faint grinding of steel on bone. I let the body sink to the floor and glanced around. Office, cubicles, otherwise empty. I moved to the window and looked out.

Scanning around, I could see zombies approaching through the buildings. The forecourt of the admin block must have been host to a couple hundred by now, and more were shuffling determinedly toward us. I took a snorting breath and blew it out hard, readying myself for what came next.

I eased the window open, sliding it back on its runners as far as it would go, then climbed over the sill, pushing away from the wall as I dropped to the ground.

I landed, bending my knees and rolled, coming up with the shotgun in both hands. I used its dark length to fend off a Z who lunged for me. Shoving the thing back, I jabbed at its head savagely with the butt. I wasn't here to fight, so as it staggered, I ran. I hugged the wall, moving toward the east wing, away from our fire escape exit. It was the long route to the security wing, but I couldn't risk compromising our exfil strategy.

As I ran, the sirens wailing overhead still sounded their clarion, carrion call and I wondered what was happening with Ned and AK. I ducked and dodged, swinging wide around the corner of the building and any hidden zombies there. I took a broad, straight road that ran along behind the admin block, headed for the guardhouse. Ahead I could see the ambulance I'd raided what seemed like hours ago surrounded by a couple of dozen zombies.

The Z's around the back door were frantic and some kind of struggle was taking place. Swapping to my pistol I sighted, still advancing on the scene, and started snapping off shots. My aim wasn't the best. The game's enforced tea-cup grip made me support my wrist for stability, and the percentage change held true as I dropped six geeks with eight bullets before the pack turned on me. I wished I'd had time to learn the fire-arms skill back at the farm. Then I'd have been shooting one-handed, and without the twenty-five percent fail chance, because I was a good shot, damnit. My FPS experience had seen to that, but I didn't have time to dwell on it. With pressure on the door lessened, AK kicked it open, scurried out of the stricken vehicle and hurried to my side.

Hauling me to one side he urged, "Come on!"

"What happened?" I demanded.

He took me out of line of sight of the guardhouse.

"George," he panted. "I guess, on the roof, with a rifle. He pinned us down behind the ambulance. I got him to get his head down while Ned rushed the door. When I pulled back to reload I was surrounded."

"If Ned's inside, why haven't the sirens stopped?" I demanded.

"I don't know," AK hefted his rifle. "Guess we better go check."

We dashed across the tarmac, cutting past the ambulance well out of reach of the pack of zeds. No gunfire sounded at our passage, so I swept right up to the door, shouldering the shotgun. AK reached for the handle and I gave him a quick nod, signalling him to open it.

The room was square with a low table, some seats and a front desk topped with a glass partition, probably bullet-proof. From upstairs came the sounds of feet stamping.

We headed for the one door, leading deeper into the building. Someone had jammed it open with a severed leg.

"Get in there and kill the alarms," I barked as we passed the door to the desk.

I took two steps before hearing a thump as AK put his shoulder to the door.

"It needs a card," he announced.

In my moment of distraction, a zed lurched around the corner ahead. I flinched back then sighted down the barrel, leaned in and opened my mouth a little before, 'Boom!'

The shotgun roared and bucked in my grip as the zombie's head erupted. My ears filled with that high-pitched whine of noise overload, but I wasn't nearly as disoriented as before.

Even as the corpse fell, I rushed forward and snagged the security pass from the clip hanging on its belt.

"Here!" I called, tossing the card back to AK as I rushed deeper, looking for the stairs.

Spotting the stairwell I shouldered through, using the hours we'd spent on knock-off Tom Clancy tactical sims to my advantage. I rushed the stairwell door, checking the corners, looking only where the barrel was pointed, and clattered up the stairs. I stopped at the first floor landing and listened at the door. I could hear the sounds of a fight, heavily muffled, but I could also see shambling bodies. Taking the opportunity, I fumbled a shell from my pocket. Ejecting the one spent shell, with that ever-so-satisfying and familiar metallic 'clunk' sound every action-movie and game fan knows so well, I slipped the shell in and shot the pump forward, 'clack'. I nodded to myself, satisfied, and barged through the door.

Chapter 31

I moved behind the zombies, almost pressing the barrel to the back of their heads as I fired, executing the first two shamblers one after another in sprays of malodorous, cloying gore. There must have been six in the corridor. The remaining four turned on me as the shotgun bucked for the second time, the ringing in my ears drowning the sound of the blast, but the kick in my shoulder real enough.

Number three reached out toward me and the slug tore through the hand, middle finger disappearing and the remaining digits fanning sickeningly as the face collapsed around the tumbling projectile. Four took the heavy slug in the mouth, and although the rotter behind was showered with stinking blood and peppered with fragments of teeth, the thing kept coming. I adjusted my aim as it reached for me, filthy fingers raking my cheek and conveniently pressing its forehead against the muzzle as I coldly racked another shell and squeezed the trigger.

The toppling body dropped into the arms of zombie number five who hugged it reflexively as I stepped forward, chambered another shell and added another geek to my kill count. The last tripped on the fallen bodies of its companions, sprawling full length at my feet and I finished it point blank. I hurried to the door they'd been clustered around and shouldered my way inside.

My ears were ringing, but I still heard the muffled report of a pistol. The door glass beside me shattered and a shard cut a searing line across my cheek. I flinched aside then brought the shotgun back to my shoulder.

Silhouetted against the sunlight streaming in the windows, George held Ned across her upper chest with one arm; the other held a pistol to her temple.

He was shouting something but it took a moment for the ringing to recede so I could hear.

"Drop it, drop it or I drop her!" he shouted.

As my eyes adjusted I could see the swelling and bleeding on both of their faces. They'd obviously had a knock-down, drag out fight, but George had managed to come out on top. He probably cheated, I thought as I flexed my finger on the trigger. I could read both Ned and George's health bars in my display, the wrecked room attested to the violence of their brawl, the damage they'd inflicted on each other. Ned in particular was down to two bars, her eyes glowering fiercely through the bruises and abrasions on her face.

"You log her out, I log you out," I growled.

He grinned manically. "How do you know that's it?" he shook Ned savagely, she struggled to break free but he had the greater leverage.

"You really believe that this game kills people? How do you know you're not killing us both?"

I kept my gun up. "Why?" I demanded. "Why couldn't you just push off and leave us be?"

"Are you kidding me?" he sneered. "You fucked up my game! I was made, I was security chief in a good-sized clan, free to come and go as I pleased. I could requisition whatever gear I wanted and schedule and co-ordinate raids as I liked, when I liked, against who I liked. I was just about to really get my PvP game going, and then you fucktards showed up and now I can't even log out!"

I stared daggers at him through narrowed eyes. "Don't do that," I growled threateningly.

"Do what?" he pushed the barrel of his gun hard against Ned's head, making her flinch.

"First, don't blame us for how the game played out. Even if it was 'just a game', PvP was only ever going to get your waste-of-space, 'alpha-gamer' ass ganked anyway, and second," I spat the words. "Don't go using bull-shit ableist slurs around me."

He smiled mockingly. "You know what?"

"What?" I slowed my breathing, sighting for a clean headshot, but still part of me wouldn't let me take it. Despite my bravado, I was unwilling to end his life, turgid as it was.

The sirens ceased their wailing.

"Fuck. You," he enunciated in the sudden quiet.

Taking her opportunity, Ned jabbed backward over her shoulder with a thumb. George recoiled as it connected with his already swollen eye. Ned tried to break away but George grabbed two handfuls of her jacket, hauling her back as I stepped forward, shotgun raised and a threat on my lips.

Stepping back, he dragged Ned around, as she stumbled he hooked his gun hand behind her neck lending him more force as he tossed her through the window. The glass shattered and I just caught sight of Ned's puzzled expression as she dropped out of sight.

My wrist pulsed and I gritted my teeth to take the shot, but George was moving on me. He grabbed the barrel and pushed it up, the hammer dropped and the shotgun roared but George was already driving his fist into my wounded side. I gasped and reeled as pain stabbed at me. Using my instinctive recoil he dragged the shotgun partially from my grip. We wrestled back and forth for the gun, turning around and around the room.

He tried to hit me again but I flinched away. Taking one hand from the gun I grabbed his face, hooking clawed fingers around his ear and driving a thumb into his eye. He bellowed in pain and reeled away but I stayed on him, furious and desperate he grabbed my wrist, backpedalling to the window and pitching backward, dragging me with him.

Shards of glass stabbed my hip, my world upended drunkenly as I flipped over the window sill.

The landing wasn't nearly as hard as I expected, thanks to all the zombies.

Between the siren and the gunfire, the density of geeks on the base and around the guardhouse in particular was rising, dozens flooding in every second. I rode George out of the window and right down on top of a thick knot of them.

Zombies stumbled and fell beneath us. I rolled away, falling to the tarmac with my wrist throbbing, the shotgun scattering from my grip as I went.

I ducked behind a zed as George snarled and came to his feet, raising his pistol. I shoved the Z toward George. It gripped the barrel of the gun and reached past it, flailing fingers in George's face.

The rage in his eyes was nearly truly incandescent but, nonetheless, he calmly kicked out, coldly snapping the geek's knee and lowered the barrel of his gun to its head. I ducked and looped through the pack as the pistol 'cracked', tearing away from grabbing hands, staying in motion. I heard the 'click-clack' of the shotgun, it roared and a zed dropped beside me, another 'click-clack' and then the impotent, hollow 'thunk' of a trigger pulled on an empty chamber, followed by a stream of swearing as I snuck through the rank crowd.

I spotted Ned, groaning and rolling on the floor. Pallid-skinned hands reached down, but the press was too much for the zed's that *could* see her to get down to her.

I was cold all through, the fall and dead-eyed, slavering mob driving me to panic. My wrist pulsed as I fought the desire to curl into a foetal ball. Hunkering down, I strove to weave my way through the forest of legs to get to her. I was just reaching out to pull her free of the mob, when strong hands clapped heavily on my shoulders and dragged me away. I came upright, stumbling past George as he flung me into the thick of the pack. I watched him pushing zombies away, forcing a ring in the snapping, biting crowd.

I staggered to my feet, tearing free of the reaching hands around me and drawing my pistol with shaking hands.

Psychological Trauma imminent, seek assistance

The sensation of my stress bar was nearly a constant thing, pulsing through my forearm and hand as George took quick steps toward me. Rage and hate filled his eyes as he disdainfully backhanded my weapon away from my slack fingers, sending it tumbling through the air into the herd. He wrapped a strong hand around my throat and punched me in the gut, doubling me over before shoving me back toward the zombies. Once again, he took a turn around the 'ring' shoving zeds back, keeping the space open. I tried to right myself, but a cadaver had its fingers tangled in my hair. Choked sobs coming from my throat and my eyes watering, I ripped free, leaving a fistful of hair in a zombie's clawing fingers. Gasping, near sobbing, I turned back to my opponent. My entire arm was burning, the pulsing reached the back of my skull like the steady rhythm of a hammer. He came for me again, fists raised. I couldn't fight him, my skill was no match for his, so I ducked, the motion desperate, ragged and uncoordinated. He frowned and came at me again, snapping off a smooth jab. Again I ducked, trusting in my Athletics skill to keep me out of his reach. This time he snarled and his swings became wilder. One whistled past me and I took his wrist and lashed my fist across his face, a sound, mewling and fearful slipped from my lips as I scurried away. In my haste I overstepped, a fallen zombie snagged my trouser leg, I jerked and looked up into the furious grimace of George. In the midst of this hell-forged fight club, the thrumming sensation of my stress bar peaked like the snapping of a guitar string.

> **Psychological Trauma Randomised Effect Result Applied:**
> **Acute Emotional Detachment**

The words flashed in front of my hazed and panicked eyes, and the agony in my hand turned to a numbing cold sensation, while my thoughts came into crystal clarity. George meant to kill me; I had to kill him first.

This time when he came savagely toward me, I dropped and kicked out at his ankle. He stumbled into the ring of zombies and I stood, leaping onto his back, holding him as they clawed and tore and bit. I held him there for a moment, a small part of my brain screaming in horror that I was allowing a man to be eaten alive, and another part of me, coldly and dispassionately arguing that he fucking deserved it.

With a yell that was more a scream he thrashed free, blood flowing from bites and scratches. He flung himself at me again, fuelled by rage and pain, and again I managed to sideslip him and shove him away, only to get behind and hold him in the ravenous crowd. He tore himself free, both from me and the zombie, his cries more sobs, but his rage unabated.

He came at me unsteadily, so I swept his legs and he stumbled, turning as he fell. He snatched at zombies to steady himself from his headlong fall, but only succeeded in dragging them down on top of him. I watched him screaming as they bit into him, feeling nothing.

"It didn't have to be like this," I told him coldly.

He screamed hysterically, "Fuck you!"

"No," I shot back, placing my boot on the back of a fallen zombie's head. "Fuck *you* George." And, with a slight effort, I drove the zombie's head down into his crotch.

His screams became frenzied, high-pitched howls as he pulled his arms, trailing ribbons of sinew, from the devouring mouths of the zombies. Sobbing, he scrabbled at his wrist with shaking hands. The zombie at his waist savaged and worried at the tender flesh, blood soaking the ground as I turned my eyes away from the scene. I didn't know if he could log out, and I didn't care.

I turned to look for an avenue of escape. Ned's body ought to occupy enough of them for me to slip away, my brain was telling me.

Suddenly my mind raced as the hollow feeling fell away and emotion came back like a tidal wave. I dropped low, fear clutching at my heart, and scrambled between the legs of the tightly packed zombies. I knew I had to get to Ned, but it was only an academic knowledge. I knew I had to save her, but moment to moment it was becoming a fight on the knife edge of leaving her to save myself and an effort of will against the urge to curl up in a ball and scream. Frantically I shoved and scrabbled, happening across my discarded shotgun on the way to the place where she had fallen. My fingers felt huge and unfamiliar as I grasped for the gun, just catching the strap by luck more than judgement, the press of bodies and grasping hands of the herd above me lending frantic strength to my progress. Ned was the goal, the anchor between psychosis and surrender. Movement was key, if I stopped I was dead.

I could just about make out Ned's imploring eyes as I reached for her outflung hand.

"It's going to be okay!" I insisted and heaved.

I felt movement and pulled harder until, with a sickening, wet tearing sound, the arm pulled away from Ned's body.

Crowded in, huddled amidst the legs of the herd, I nevertheless fell back clutching the severed limb.

I sat back heavily, shock, anguish and revulsion rising up in my chest as my eyes locked on Ned's tear-streaked face. Unthinkingly I hugged her arm to my body as, with the motion of the pack swarming around her, more mind-numbingly grisly details became evident. That second stretched, drawn out like molten glass into an unending eternity of horror until, with an effort I couldn't begin to appreciate, Ned mouthed in silent torment, 'help me.'

The pit of my stomach dropped away as I fumbled. I had the shotgun, empty with little room to reload it, my pistol was gone. All I had was Ned's severed arm.

I held the cooling limb, turning it over desperately, and the menu screen sprang into being, flashing desperate warnings that, in the moment, I couldn't process. I swiped wretchedly at the screen, only one word fixed in my head as shambling feet kicked at me, their undead owners striving to reach down, to violate my virtual flesh just as their comrades were doing to Ned with every split-second that passed. I rolled onto my stomach, shielding the screen and stabbed at the command 'Exit'.

Nothing happened.

She screamed aloud. In horror I dropped her severed limb as she convulsed, in some kind of racking fit. I dragged my knife, my last resort weapon from its sheath and crawled forward frantically on my elbows. A word sprang to the front of my mind and I babbled it quietly as I dragged myself toward Ned.

'Mercy.'

I reached out, cupping her cheek in my hand, our eyes locked together as I brought my knife around, outside her view. I had to fight the urge to close my eyes, to look away, I had to be there with her as I plunged the sharp tip into her temple. Ned sagged, her mouth hanging slack and her eyes now staring dully into mine but her shoulders and head still jerked and lolled as the pack of zombies continued to feast.

Now the tears came, mewling sobs of horror and terror ripping themselves like horror movie parasites from my throat. I crawled, clawing my way away from the scene, buffeted by the forest of boots, shoes and trainers. I tried not to hear the sounds of tearing, gulping flesh as the Z's ate my friend.

I pulled myself free of the herd, like a tormented soul ripping itself from hell's own claw, and staggered away from the moaning throng, my gun hanging loose in one hand, Ned's arm still clutched in the other. I stumbled as mindlessly as the zombies before I fell, rolling to sit on the asphalt. Fingers fumbling with adrenaline and trauma-induced mania, I slotted shells into the Benelli. With an unstable chuckle, I pumped the action and fired on the herd with no rational thought beyond sharing the pain that overwhelmed me. A zombie staggered and fell. I don't know if it got up, most likely it was crushed under the herd as they turned on me. I scrambled backward on my ass and, with another manic sob, fired again.

Pump, fire, pump, fire, chuckle, sob, chuckle, sob. With every roar of the muzzle and buck of the stock against my midriff, the swirling dragging pit in my stomach subsided; my emotions roiled just a little less until actual thoughts crept past the wall of mindless agony and grief that filled my brain.

I pulled myself to my feet, backing away from the oncoming horde, slipping more shells in and firing, taking some care to aim, until my pockets were empty. I threw the spent, smoking shotgun at the zombies and cast around. Spotting my pistol on the tarmac, I snatched it up and sighted down, firing, emptying the magazine in a blink. I changed mag, worked the slide and emptied another and the last of my ammunition into the throng, trying to lend the power of the grief that was tearing at my guts to each and every shot.

The pistol clicked empty and I flung that at the approaching pack too, drawing my brush hook from my belt.

"Come on!" I howled, my voice stricken and strained. "Come on, you assholes!"

Before they could reach me, hands turned me and I looked into the terrified eyes of AK.

"You alright, you in there, yeah?" He twitched from side to side like he couldn't decide if I was about to take *his* head off.

I blubbed incoherently and rubbed a hand at my sodden face, my eyes and nose streaming, spit flecking my chin as my mind drowned in grief, anguish, horror and fury.

"Jesus H. Mother of Christ," he muttered, taking a firm hold of my wrist. "Come on!" he urged and dragged me, unheeding and unresisting, away from the scene of horror and carnage. Taking me step by step away from an event that would, regardless, haunt my dreams and waking moments for the rest of my days, no matter how many or how few they might be.

Skirting the edge of the admin building, AK swore softly.

"Foyer's completely blocked," he muttered. "Come on. We'll have to go up the fire escape."

I let him guide me, dodging Z's who inevitably followed our slow progress, around to the metal staircase that was meant to be our salvation.

As we climbed the stairs, a chorus of dull moans followed us, and all I could think was that the metal staircase, our 'road to salvation' was now merely the lid of our tomb.

Chapter 32

"Why'd you come up the backstairs? That wasn't the plan!" Hands guided me down onto the sofa.

"We didn't have a chuffing choice! It was either that or dive down a zombie's throat, you get it?"

Someone took my hands and I felt the cold smooth surface of glass, the shifting weight of fluid.

"Where's Ned?"

The words seemed to come from far away as the neck of a bottle found its way to my lips. "She's binned mate, nothing we could do."

"Here Lex, drink." My wrist felt like it was broken, but even that pain was distant.

"Are you sure, if she's still out there..."

"She's binned, get me? Bee, Aye, En, En, Ee, Dee. Binned. Ouzo? Where did you get that shit?"

"Jesus fuck, Ned... it was in the Brigadier's bottom drawer. And George?"

"Last I saw there was a geek chewing on his family jewels, courtesy of Lex, and that's less than the bastard deserved to my mind."

This conversation was going on rapidly over my head as I sat on the couch in the office. At some point, as aniseed flavoured alcohol stripped my sense of taste, I realised I was shaking.

Indi appeared, hunched down in front of me, "Lex, Lex?"

I stared, glassy-eyed, through him.

"Hm?" was all I could manage.

I heard Roper asking gently, "Did Ned get to log out?"

I twitched my head in a vague gesture and looked up, Indi and Jay shared wide-eyed looks.

"Did she get out?" Roper insisted again.

Eventually, Indi answered, "She couldn't."

267

"How do you know? You weren't there," Roper countered, confused.

"Lex, Ned and I were locked in by the devs a little while ago," Jay started shakily, "and now you three are too."

All movement in the room stopped, everyone shocked into silence.

"We're what?" Roper asked slowly.

"None of us can quit the game," Indi mumbled.

AK just shook his head. "No, between this and the alarm I'm starting to think you guys are in a guild with George. You're fucking trappers, this is some twisted PvP fantasy you lot worked up. 'Can't log out'? What kinda bullshit is that?" he hefted his gun and Roper and Frakt followed suit.

Roper was nodding in agreement, "the way this situation goes from bad to worse is too convenient. It's some kind of ploy, if you even *are* players and not bots leading us down some twisted quest-arc."

Finally, my stress meter dropped enough for me to realise what was happening.

"No, no! Come on, you've got to believe us," I insisted, thinking feverishly of a way to prove our innocence.

AK reached for his wrist. "I'm going to log out now," he growled.

"Don't," Jay said softly. "If you trigger the exit command you'll drop into a rest state while your levels and stats are applied. You'll be incapped; helpless."

"Bollocks!" AK spat, "that's bollocks!"

I scrambled around the disjointed mess of my thoughts then... the breadcrumbs, I realised. The trail that led to the game had been on social progressive websites. The only assholes in the game were the ones we dragged in with us. I just had to hope that Roper, AK and Frakt were all part of the target demographic. I clung to that idea as I started fast-talking. "I voted for Corbyn, I support workers' rights and the NHS, I'm pro-Palestine but condemn the violence employed by Hamas, and I question my stance every single day," I gabbled, desperately. "I'm for increased corporation tax and greater accountability for MP's. I stand for trans rights, reproductive rights and social care, I hashtag Black Lives Matter. Please, listen," I begged from the couch.

They hesitated, clearly still sceptical so I dove on.

"I'm for legalizing cannabis and more resources to help addicts without stigma or judgment, I'm supportive of sex workers, I try to use my friends' correct pronouns and beat myself up whenever I get it wrong, even in private! Please, believe us," I gabbled.

Frakt's weapon wavered, then relaxed.

The viking-avatar glared down at me, her mouth a tight line and eyes hard for a moment.

"I believe them," she said finally.

"Given the way Lex's pissing their pants and about to cry? Yeah, I believe it," AK admitted finally.

"We'd never have killed you," Roper's voice was earnest but there was a hint of uncertainty colouring his words. "Even if you were NPCs. We'd lock you in here then leave before the horde arrives." He traded looks with Frakt. "We're not *those* GTA players who kill the hooker," he stated disdainfully.

Kneeling beside me Indi took my hands, "Are you okay?" he asked me softly.

AK looked abashed, "your stress bar went crazy. It was pulsing so hard I could feel it, and for a good long time. I'm sorry we put you through that, just now."

As Indi settled back on his heels I nodded, then finally managed to speak again. "I did what I could for Ned, but it wasn't quick."

The players in the room traded silent glances.

"Where does that leave us?" Roper asked tersely.

Frakt shrugged, "We're surrounded."

"What are we going to do?" Roper growled. "Jay, how close are you?"

"I'm getting there," Jay replied from the desk, his one hand steadily tapping over the keys. "But I think they might be on to me."

"I want to go home."

"What do you mean, 'on to you?'" AK shot back.

"I mean that this is probably about to get a whole lot worse," Jay stated matter-of-factly.

"I want to go home."

"Well," AK picked up his gun, sliding the bolt back to check the chambered round. "I guess it's time to party then, isn't it?"

"*I want to go home!*"

The voice that had been barely a whisper cut through the conversation like a cracked whip, sharp and insistent, and mine. Everyone stopped to look at me.

I sat, staring at my hands, the harshness of my voice a shock, even to me.

"Lex," Jay spoke hesitantly. "You know you can't? Right?"

I nodded, woozy from the drink and the trauma. "I've got to do something," I sobbed. "I want… I want to say goodbye to my parents, just in case."

The room went silent and still. No-one moved, or spoke or even breathed for a moment.

"Have you still got the camera?" Jay said slowly.

I hadn't checked it since I'd secured it to my belt. It would have been a miracle to still have it after my fight with George.

My hands were still shaking some until Indi took them in his and set them on my lap. Then he reached to my waist and, cupping it like something very precious, he unclipped it, holding the camera up to me.

"We're as secure as we're getting," Indi observed thoughtfully. "Now might be our last chance, should things go bad."

Again silence descended for an uncomfortable moment.

Eventually Jay cleared his throat. "Who's going first?"

"Why not you?" Indi asked.

"Bah! *Det är ingen ko på isen,*" he announced waving us away. "Don't worry, I have arrangements in place already."

Indi regarded him coolly. "Oh yeah?"

Jay grinned ruefully. "I'd have upset some very wealthy, very unscrupulous people IRL, if they knew who I was. I have messages and a video Will pre-prepared."

"Alright," Indi nodded. "I'll go."

He held the camera up, pointed toward his face.

"*Maman, Papa,*" I struggled some with the French but mostly followed the message. "*You always accepted me for who I am, you never judged me or rejected me, and I will always be grateful for that.*" He paused. "*But, if these are the last words of mine you ever hear, know that you've got to be more accepting, more understanding. The people you hate, the people the government tells you to hate? Most of them are very much like me, trying to get by in a world that increasingly judges them by what they are instead of who they are.*"

I watched his shoulders shudder and, in that moment, the hulking avatar was gone and my friend sat there, vulnerable and afraid as he went on, his voice quavering with emotion.

"In a world that, as much as it accuses people of sectarianism, actively encourages it through messages of division and hate. Don't be part of it. Spread your arms wide. I love you. Goodbye."

Indi blinked up at me, a smile on his lips and the beginnings of tears in his eyes. I took the camera, feeling my own budding tears, but his open expression of love had eased my tension, my trauma, just a little. Just enough.

"Hey mum, hey dad," I spoke softly into the lens. "I don't know if you can see this, I don't know if you ever will." I sucked in a shuddering breath. "I just want you to know that I love you and that, that I saw something bad happening and thought I could do something to stop it. Just like you taught me," I laughed and sniffed, wiping unshed tears from my eyes. "I'll tell you all about it when I get out, but for now, look after each other, and look out for our neighbours, especially Mr Nadkarni, okay? Goodbye."

I handed the camera on to Roper and lurched to my feet. I'd spent what little resilience I had left on the message and I couldn't sit by listening to more. I heaved myself through the door and weaved down the corridor to a little office kitchen, tucked into a small alcove room and shrouded in shadows. I slumped to the floor, arms around my knees, hugging myself in a ball and sobbing wet, racking sobs until everything finally went black.

"Destroy or be destroyed, there is no middle way. Let us then be the destroyers."
– Mikhail Bakunin

It wasn't long after that I opened my eyes to someone shaking my shoulder gently and a notice.

Insufficient rest for Combat/Medicine skill bonuses to be applied
Bonuses will be applied after a rest period
Trauma debuff applied, seek assistance

I swiped it away. My face was wet but my thoughts were clearer, less muddled. I glanced up into Indi's concerned expression and smiled weakly. I wiped my face on my sleeve and sniffed noisily.

"Are you okay?" Indi asked cautiously.

271

"Let's see shall we?" I tried for 'jaunty' but it probably came out as 'manic'. I held up my wrist all the same. I had no idea what the 'debuff' might entail, so checking my stats seemed the best way to find out. It didn't make sense for it to have hurt my HP, so it must apply to my mental fortitude in some way. I certainly couldn't tell from my meters, though they'd looked healthier:

STM	███████████		
HLT	███████████		
STR	███████████		

"I didn't know if I'd be able to wake you," Indi said softly, "but I didn't want to panic the others."

He sat next to me on the floor, my avatar cradled against his huge side, concern radiating from his expression. I gave him another weak smile from just a couple of inches away.

I might not have been at my best, but Indi was still down some bars; we all were and with limited supplies. There's always an argument for the party healer to look after themselves as a priority, but I couldn't, not here and not now. I'd just have to be careful. Indi helped me to my feet and we returned to the office.

"So, what have you got, Jay?" I asked, determined to seem confident.

He sucked at his teeth and shrugged, "More questions than answers."

"Tell us," I insisted.

"There's definitely something bigger going on here, due to happen out there," he pointed upward in a gesture I took to mean the real world rather than the game.

"There's lots of medical stuff, psychology and neuroscience that I don't understand. Waveforms and signal strengths too, which I'm guessing ties into the new Wi-Fi activation."

"Have you got anything about the conditioning?" I pressed.

He winced. "You won't like it."

I glared at him.

"I managed to tie it to repeated uses of the phrase 'Survival Mechanism'."

"As in?" I asked, confused. "Come on Jay, stop babying me, I'm fine now."

"As in," he sighed, "'After twelve hours of play the subjects should have developed the required 'Survival Mechanism'." He was reading directly from the screen.

"But that means–" Indi didn't finish the sentence and shuffled on the couch.

"Whatever or whoever the admins are attacking–" Jay began.

"–It's not the players," I finished, and it felt like someone had shoved a glacier into my stomach; a feeling of monumental weight, cold and nausea.

"Are we sure this isn't just another aspect of the game?" Roper asked uncertainly. "Like an *Existenz* or *Inception* style thing?"

"I don't know," Jay admitted, holding up his hands, one whole, one swathed in bandages. "The pieces I'm putting together and the manifesto I'm skim-reading along with them seem to suggest a plan akin to the biblical flood, but with zombies."

AK pinched the bridge of his nose wearily, "That sounds like a bloody meme."

"I can only hope that it is," Jay replied. "Listen to this. 'The 'developed' world that we know (for the term 'civilized' cannot accurately be applied to such a cutthroat, mercenary, and ceaselessly predatory social hierarchy) cannot be rectified. The ultimate holders of global wealth and influence have no interest in surrendering their grasp. Indeed, they have no interest in the ongoing survival of the species or the planet, only in enjoying the benefits, illegal, amoral or perverse, that their influence grants them. As such, the order that is must be unmade in its entirety, wiped away and rebuilt from scratch, the current incarnation being used as a cautionary tale by the survivors.'"

"Survivors?" I blurted.

Jay motioned around the room. "The players," he said simply.

"Let me get this straight," AK raised his head, goggle-eyed. "*Rendered Flesh* is, what? Some kind of inoculation against whatever they're going to use to *cleanse the bloody planet?*"

"Think about it," Jay spoke evenly. "The nihilist dogma, the apocalypse theme, the breadcrumb trail spread over left-wing and social activist sites. The admins are cherry-picking, indoctrinating and training the people who will inherit the earth, if this scheme is to be believed."

Indi shook his head vigorously, "They can't get everybody."

There's some stuff about 'remote indigenous populations' and 'strategic isolation of transmitters in some places'. Like I say, it's all closeted with medical stuff I don't get, but it ties into the Wi-Fi and zombies. That's all I have so far."

"Are they wrong?"

I glanced at Frakt. Her tentative question hung in the air as the others shared worried looks or turned away guiltily. An uncomfortable silence stretched out between us all. While Frakt herself had sounded so uncertain, I couldn't deny, at least to myself, that my first thought had been 'No'.

I heard an abrupt burst of typing from Jay, and I glanced around as he frowned at his screen and then leaned back in his chair, eyes wide and fearful.

I stood and hurried around the desk. "What?" I demanded, but it was there on the screen, clear to see.

Uh, uh, uh! You didn't say the magic word!

The text appeared in an old-style MS-Dos style window, then began to replicate itself over and over until the window filled the screen and the text started to scroll, faster and faster until it was just a flickering of static against the black.

Outside, hundreds upon hundreds of dry, ruined throats gave rise to a nightmarish ululation, a cry of outrage and hunger.

"They're onto us," I shouted across the room.

Frakt and Roper dived into the gun bags on the floor, separating arms and the appropriate magazines and ammunition. There were even grenades and (I murmured a silent thanks to the loot gods) radios.

"Roper, AK, left side!" Indi barked. "Frakt, Lex, with me on the right. Jay? Take a radio and watch the stairwell for intrusions."

Jay blanched a little but stood.

As he rounded the desk, Indi lifted a holster belt and secured it around Jay's waist. Then he took a pistol, loaded it and worked the slide before slipping it into the holster and picked up a grenade, holding it in front of Jay's face.

"Last resort." Indi's words were clipped and clear.

Jay nodded, but Indi held him there for a moment. *"Après la pluie, le beau temps mon ami,"* he said softly and Jay swallowed, but seemed more confident as he headed into the corridor.

Roper and AK hefted their arms and one of the bags, and hurried away. Frakt gave us a nod and followed. Indi turned to me.

"What's the plan?" I asked unsteadily.

He handed me a compact British bull-pup rifle.

I held up my hands, "I can't use this!" I protested.

"You're *Educated*, remember?" He winked, "just watch me!"

Indi turned back to the duffle on the floor. After a few moments of metallic noises he stood, hefting a much larger gun with an ammo-box hung on the side. I could see the brass flanks of rounds partially obscured by the dull grey of belt linkages.

"When did you get Firearms?" I blurted, surprised.

He let out a short bark of mirthless laughter, "Oh, so you're the only one who can get a new skill?" He racked the action, the solid sound of the bolt snapping forward underscoring the cold, hard gleam in his eyes.

"Aim for the head and make every shot count if you can. Let's go."

Frakt was waiting for us in the office that spanned the right hand side of the building, looking down on the cul-de-sac road layout with its sculpted topiary decoration. The greenery was mostly obscured now, jutting out here and there from among the shoulder-to-shoulder press of the zombie horde.

The tattooed and dreadlocked Viking held her rifle to her shoulder but released the pistol grip and held up a finger, signalling for our attention, and pointed out into the courtyard.

In direct contrast to the blood-chilling cry that had prompted us to action, the horde, stretching away from the building and off into the camp, now stood in silence.

There was maybe a twenty foot gap between the front of the building and the first rank of zombies. Into that gap a zombie stepped forward, its movements co-ordinated, sure and purposeful.

"I know you can hear me!" the zombie-dev called to us. "Your little in-game hack is impressive I'll admit, but besides a few archived files we built the game around, there's really nothing you can influence in there."

The dev offered each sentence as a smug little nugget, a helpful little observation for us poor mere players.

"We had hoped to dissuade your little data-breach earlier but, since you have persisted, we feel that our only recourse is a disproportionate response."

The smug-nuggets were now dipped in patronizing sauce and I clenched my teeth angrily at the dev's superior tone as they gestured to the horde behind them.

"Get your grubby little fingers out of our code or I'll set this lot on you at expert difficulty!"

I looked across at Indi. Jay had left the computer, but I didn't know if he'd stopped whatever search algorithm he'd been running.

The dev turned to return the zombie avatar to the horde but stopped and called back over their shoulder. "Just an FYI, in case you have been less than honest with your new guildmates–," at that point, I was sure the dev was running a mod so all of us could hear the next sentence, "–we've disabled your 'Exit' commands. If you decide to test us, you won't be able to log out." They gave an exaggerated shrug and continued their walk back into the crowd. "You have thirty seconds!"

I chewed my lip anxiously. Not content with holding a zombie horde over our heads this guy *actually* thought we wouldn't tell AK, Frakt and Roper about the lock-in and was trying to use that against us. Add that to only giving us thirty seconds to make a life or death decision? This dev really knew how to make friends and influence people. Asshole.

Chapter 33

The radio squawked, "Did everybody catch that?" Frakt's comment sounded crisp over the radio.

"I'll pull the plug on the search," came Jay's reply.

"Just you hang on." AK's London accent crackled over the radio. "Fuck this dude."

I blinked in surprise.

"I agree," Roper's voice came deep and smooth despite the slight static. "Who's this douchebag to think he can strong-arm us?"

Indi grinned at me and raised the radio to his lips.

"*Mais oui*, we are not noobs to be cowed by some arrogant prick."

"If their plan is legit, if they want to bring on the zompocalypse?" Frakt spoke evenly. "We need to find a way to stop it. Keep digging."

"Alright," I sucked in a breath and blew it out hard. "Let's do this."

Indi shot me a wink. "I never did like deadlines," he announced and strode forward, smashing the window with the butt of the machine gun. The glass shattered and one zombie in particular looked up in surprise.

"*Allez, raclure de bidet! Ta gueule!*" Indi roared and fired.

The thunderous chatter and strobing flash of the weapon lit up the window as the screaming rounds chewed the zombie dev's avatar into so much chunky soup.

"Whatever happened to 'make every bullet count', huh?" I called over, rummaging for a handful of magazines as I took up my own firing position.

Relenting into short, controlled bursts Indi called back, "Asshole had it coming!"

In fact, Indi's impulse control issues seemed to work in our favour. The zombies held position as we hosed them for a good few seconds before reacting. I'd have guessed the dev was caught by surprise, or maybe the transition from Z to Z took a little time, but we gunned down a good few of the geeks before the horde howled in challenge and charged. No Romero's this time, a screaming wave of full-on rage zombies stormed the ground floor. Forget 'Expert' the difficulty level had visibly shifted from 'Hurt me Plenty' to 'Nightmare'. I heard the windows smash as zombies hurled themselves bodily into the building.

I took a deep breath, trusted to my Educated skill and raised my rifle. I pulled the trigger and the rifle bucked, spitting fire and lead. I watched through the sight as a zombie fell.

Boom! Headshot! The words echoed in my head as, with a grim smile, I sighted and shot and sighted and shot, thirty rounds down in a worryingly short time to little apparent effect on the horde's numbers. Beside me, Indi had flipped out the tripod legs and settled them on the window sill. His shoulders weaved from side-to-side as he scythed down the massed ranks of the dead.

"Jay!" Indi called into the radio. "The first sign of them breaching the stairwell door, you grenade those fucks, *vous m'entendez?*"

"*Jag hör dig,* I got you!" Jay called back.

I remembered, between the muzzle flashes, the roar of rounds and the stink of cordite, watching a film. A big Hollywood blockbuster where, rather than the shambling corpses of films before, the scrambling rage zombies flowed over each other like ants, heaping and surging like a flood. I remembered thinking how cool the effect was and how, if zombies were real, with their lack of pain or fear response and their singular drive to consume, they might move like that. Watching the screaming, gnashing and scrabbling horde below I realised it wasn't cool, not at all. It was terrifying.

Where a zombie failed to clear the sill or got hung up on the smashed glass, another clambered over it. Where the scrambling zombies got stuck there, another would try. Even as I watched, the zeds pressed against the now blocked windows and started to heap, the ones beneath no-doubt being remorselessly crushed under the weight and stomping feet of their fellows.

"Indi!" I called across, pointing down.

My friend glanced, nodded and reached into the bag beside him, tossing a small object to me. I caught it and paused for just a second. It took me a second to recognise what I was seeing. I fumbled as I realised that what Indi had casually tossed to me was an anti-personnel explosive, dropping the thing. Like so many others I was still used to the old 'pineapple' style grenades, which Jay reliably told me were American Mk2's, circa World War Two. The ball in my hand had the familiar pin and trigger but, other than that, was round like a tennis ball. A box flashed briefly before my eyes:

L109A1 Fragmentation Grenade

I flinched, but of course grenades don't go off just because you drop them. Cursing myself for behaving like a clueless civvie, I snatched it up as it bounced. I didn't even wonder if I needed an 'Explosives' skill but I needn't have worried in any case, apparently the devs had accounted for mass media exposure. I hooked my gun in the crook of my arm, hooked a finger through the ring and, with a firm tug (the very idea of trying to use my teeth like in the movies brought nauseating visions of wrenching those self-same teeth out), pulled the pin. I didn't even chance a throw, I just let the thing drop over the window ledge and into the growing stack of zombies beneath us.

"Grenade!" I bellowed and ducked behind the sill. Indi and Frakt followed suit just as the thing detonated somewhere in the pile below with a dull, wet 'crump'.

Blood, bone and other things flew upward, spattering the side of the building, and the scent of charred meat and effluence assailed our senses.

Wiping zombie juice from his face, Indi snarled, "Shout, then throw!"

"Sorry!" I called back, loading another magazine into my rifle's receiver.

Two more detonations shook the building from the other side as Roper and AK deployed their own munitions as Frakt, Indi and I went back to grinding more xp. That's how I had to think of it; without the detachment of screen and keyboard I was again in the middle of a visceral nightmare of sound and fury.

The shots that killed were a mercy, not for the target but for me. A brief splash of gore and the zombie fell back into the pack or was buoyed aloft in the press, but not all of my shots were that clean. I left more than a few zed's without their jaws, scraped the flesh from their skulls or popped their eye sockets without actually killing them. One or two even stumbled on, gaping holes in their skulls marking where the bullet had ploughed through the grey matter but not destroyed the lower motor-cortex.

279

Soldiers and gamers alike will tell you that a lot can happen in just a few short minutes, whether it's a firefight in the Middle East or a raid boss in a dungeon on Azeroth. The fallout from either one can last a lifetime. And here we were, caught halfway between both.

The zombies continued to surge and pile as I emptied more and more magazines. Indi fed another belt into his gun, a swift and practiced procedure, and started to blaze away again, roaring in challenge over the thunder of the weapon. Frakt was point shooting like a machine, her movements smooth, sure and precise. The thunder of grenades punctuated the fight but, regardless of the explosions shaking the building, the zombies stacked up to the second flood. Try as they might to break in, they had no momentum, no leverage under the heap, they simply foundered against the glass, gradually rising ever higher.

We dropped more grenades, the growing heaps of zombie bodies shuddering with each detonation as the explosives were consumed by the mass. The blasts tossed bodies and body parts into the air, the heaps sloughing off the ruined remains as new meat scrambled upward into the mouths of our guns.

Another blast made the whole structure quiver.

Indi eased up. "That came from inside, time to go," and off he went. I emptied my last mag. Dropping the assault rifle I snatched another Benelli and a box of shells from the desk beside me with Frakt hot on my heels, slinging the bag over her shoulder.

We met AK and Roper in the corridor.

"Where's Jay?" I demanded.

He came hustling up from the office. "Here, here," he panted, winding wires around the Smartphone, shoving it into his pocket.

"Come on," Indi commanded, heading down the corridor. "We'll swing over to the other side, maybe there's a way out over there."

"If there isn't," Frakt held her bag out, flashing a coil of rope, "we make one."

We hurried through the building, bursting through the doors to the lobby mezzanine, the sound of smashing windows echoing behind and the dry throaty cries of zombies coming up from below, and into the east wing offices.

The doors on either side of the corridor rattled as we passed.

The corridor on this side ended at a big window. I hurried forward, threw the catches and slid it open. The zombies on the ground were less numerous than on the other side, and they weren't climbing the building.

Frakt slipped the rope from the bag, looking up at us she nodded, uncoiling the length.

"Can we all climb down three stories?" I asked, concerned for Jay mostly.

"We won't have to," Frakt shook her head, taking one end of the rope and tying a loop. "You step in this, we lower you down. We toss the other end and whoever's on the ground helps."

I looked out at the zombies, still unaware of us but champing at the air, prowling on the fringes of the horde that was engulfing the building. "Pretty risky for the people on the ground," I replied.

"Don't worry," AK assured us enthusiastically, "it'll be fine."

I'd become accustomed to AK's enervated nature and sometimes gung-ho approach, but there was something else in his voice now. I glanced over as he raised a small item in his hand, which wasn't shaking at all now. There was a pin which he pulled, eyes intently focussed, hungry with anticipation, but it wasn't a grenade. AK flipped a big red safety cover up and his thumb hovered beside a shiny switch.

My mind blanked. I watched dumbly as he exerted the pressure on the trigger of the radio detonator.

In a reflexive flash I yelled "Grenade!" and threw myself to the floor. The others glanced around, hunkering down in confusion.

I don't know when AK had rigged the west side of the building, or what was going through his mind when he did. Maybe he'd been saddled with the Demolitions skill and been desperate to give it a try. And in whatever was left of the armoury there must have been explosives, primers and fuses, a goldmine for any player with the skill to use them. Now, suddenly, everything was noise and dust and a storm of sensation.

The blast wave tore through the building, smashing windows and tearing plasterboard. It flung the doors to the mezzanine off their hinges, surging down the corridor and pummelling those of us who had hunkered down.

I opened my eyes once the storm had subsided. The surviving lights flickered, a few intact, most of the tube fittings hanging from the ceiling. More still had disintegrated. The fast approaching twilight cast the corridor in gloom, and the smoke and dust filling the air, making me cough, didn't help visibility much. My chest felt like I'd been beaten, my eyes were full of grit; my wrist was pulsing and my head was spinning. I couldn't hear anything but that single, piercing tone, like an old TV test signal. I spared a bleary eyed glance for my wrist and saw my HP bar flash and fade from four to three before stabilising.

The building trembled and I looked around. Frakt was prostrate on the floor. Indi and Jay had clung to each other during the manufactured maelstrom, and AK was glancing from side-to-side, a look of confusion and panic in his wide eyes.

I realised then that I couldn't see Roper.

I hauled myself painfully upright and lurched to the window.

Down below, through the fog of debris, I spotted him. A good thirty feet clear of the building he lay sprawled in an ungainly heap on the ground. Zombies flapped brokenly around his avatar, but Roper himself didn't move.

AK appeared next to me, guilt and desperation written across his features. He tried to give me the rope to hold, though I couldn't hear his shouted instructions. I held up my hands, shook my head vigorously and tried to communicate that I couldn't hold his weight alone. Then I hefted my shotgun and gestured to the rope and over the side.

I saw the muscles tense in his jaw as he thought briefly, then looped the rope around his waist and sat back on the floor, bracing his legs against the wall. He gave me a nod.

Slinging the Benelli over my shoulder I took up the rope, eased myself over the shards of glass left in the frame and half abseiled, half dropped to the ground. I landed heavily but rolled to my feet in a gymnastic move I could never have managed IRL, and sprinted to where I'd seen Roper. The cloud of smoke and debris was thicker down low and, as I arrived at his prone body I kicked a zombie, dragging what was left of its torso with a lone arm, away from him. I crouched low, gun in my shoulder, turning slowly and watching for anything to come out of the cloying, claustrophobic haze.

I focussed briefly; his HP bar was low but stable.

A shadowy movement caught my eye and I tracked it, unwilling to pull the trigger until I'd identified either friend or foe. A zombie staggered out of the haze, almost on top of me before I saw its jagged teeth and sunken eyes. I pulled the trigger and the gun bucked, the shot a mere echo to my still ringing ears. I had to hope that the zombies had been similarly affected by the pressure wave. If they were deaf too, their decayed and fragile eardrums punctured by the blast, we might have a chance.

Another shadow ran across my vision but not near enough to see clearly. I turned a slow, continuous circle trying to watch every direction at once. A zombie barrelled into me from behind, knocking me down and going sprawling over me. I managed to snatch the strap of the gun, getting to my knees as the zed came back to its feet and turned on me. I nailed it right between the eyes, the solid slug ammunition dragging the flesh of the snarling face back through the hole it punched in the skull.

I'd lost my orientation. I didn't know which direction the admin building was in and, as the dust and smoke gathered and billowed, I realised that I couldn't randomly fire for fear of hitting my friends as they came down to ground level. I gritted my teeth, holding my gun defensively across my chest and waited, still watching the twisting clouds.

A shadow came toward me and I steeled myself, but then AK dropped to his knees beside me and reached tentatively toward Roper, stopping his hands inches away.

I took his distraught face by the chin and turned his eyes toward me, thrust the shotgun into his hands and made a circular motion in the air. As he took up to watch, I turned my attention to Roper. I checked for a pulse, weak but there, then moved my cheek to his lips and felt a whisper of breath against my skin. I sat back, passing my hands lightly over his limbs and torso, feeling for differences, abnormalities and malformations, letting my Medicine skill take over. His shoulder was dislocated, one leg broken and, as I applied gentle pressure to his chest he writhed, his eyes flying open. Broken ribs, at a guess. Some sound was coming back, the crackle of flames and crunch of falling debris all around us. Indi, Jay and Frakt arrived together. Taking in the scene, Indi motioned to Jay and me to carry Roper while he, AK and Frakt watched out for us.

AK had a hand to his mouth, looking down wide-eyed and shaken, keeping his distance from the fallen Roper and standing at the edge of the fog. I doubt he'd had any idea that the blast was going to be that strong; maybe his gamer head had overruled his sense briefly. I didn't know and I didn't care. Frakt was glaring daggers at AK, and I knew a reckoning would follow. Except, as my eyes passed over AK again, the strap of the bag over his shoulder went taut, and he was yanked back into the smoke.

I shouted a wordless protest and scrambled that way, but a blast of wind momentarily cleared the fog. AK was gone; all I could see was an approaching wall of the living, ravenous dead.

Chapter 34

We ran, with the sounds of AK's screams echoing through the all-engulfing fog, rising to a hysterical crescendo around us, taunting and accusing all at once. I spared a glance toward Roper and his bar appeared for me, flashing, slowly but steady. Indi shouldered his machine gun and rattled off the rest of the belt at head height, a desperate cry of pain and fury dragging itself from his throat.

We hustled through the thick fog, zombies rushing through at random, barging into us, tripping and falling in front of us.

With AK gone, Jay struggled under Roper's half-conscious weight while Indi, Frakt and I ran interference.

We spent hellish minutes in the shrouded purgatorial aftermath of the explosion. Adrenaline surged through my veins and my pulse thudded in my head, squeezing my brain, and in my wrist where my stress bar pulsed. My thoughts had narrowed to point, shoot, and move. I took a hit and went down, rolling to my feet to execute the zombie that had knocked me over. I thumbed more rounds into the shotgun, clipping a passing zed with the butt in a spray of teeth and black blood.

Frakt spat a curse, slinging her rifle, smoothly unlimbering a couple of long-handled hammers from her belt.

We stumbled onward finally, blessedly breaking free of the clinging and choking dust.

A zed came barrelling toward us and Indi swung the machine gun like a bludgeon, the empty ammunition box flying away, such was the impact. The zombie went down, straight on its back and Indi battered it again, both hands on the barrel. The body twisted and bent as my friend pounded the zombie's head.

I grabbed his arm and screamed "Run!" into his uncomprehending eyes.

I took point. The zeds could see us now. They weren't blinded by dust or deafened by the pressure wave. These remorseless monsters came straight at us at full tilt. We were only lucky we were far enough from the admin building that they'd thinned out some. Point, click, point, click, fire and move on, target to target, rinse and repeat.

I pulled the trigger to a dull metallic 'clink' and fumbled in my pocket. Empty.

Frakt stepped past me, a whirlwind of precise, measured strokes, hammers blurring and zombies dropping with each strike.

I pulled my hooked blade, desperately lopping off a hand that grasped for me and dragging the zed past me, tripping it as it went.

"Move!" Frakt urged and led us through a loose knot of the dead toward a big, glass-fronted gymnasium.

Reaching the door, Frakt tugged it open, diving inside. I took the handle, holding it for Jay (Roper seemed to be trying to help Jay at least a little now) and slipped in as Indi, closely followed by a snarling, snapping throng, came behind me.

Grabbing the inside handle, Indi hauled on it even as filthy, clammy arms forced their way inside. Teeth gritted, Indi braced and heaved.

We had one bag left. I had no idea how much ammo was in it, but that wasn't my current concern. I grabbed it from Frakt, stripped the shoulder strap from its spring-clips and went to the door, winding the nylon webbing strap through and around the big handles while dirty, torn and bloody fingers reached for me, clawing my skin even as I pulled the knot tight.

"Come on!" I yelled, but as Indi eased up on the door, the webbing slipped a fraction of an inch. The big avatar lunged for the door again, arms straining and bulging under the red flannel shirt.

"It won't hold, *mon ami*. It helps, but one of us has to stay."

"I'll stay!" I blurted. "I've got more stamina, I'm faster than you, I'll catch you up."

Indi gave a chuckle that turned into a grunt as the zombies tugged at the door.

"*Non*, I'll stay. Speed doesn't make a difference if you can't hold the door. I'm stronger, take the others and go!"

"I can't leave you Indi, I won't!" I near begged.

"Don't worry," his grin was forced, strained. "Heroic last stands aren't my style, I'm a winner." He winked at me.

I gave a choked laugh that was almost a sob and turned to lead the others away. Then, my mind in turmoil, I turned back, wrapping my arms around Indi for a deep, hard kiss.

Stepping back, I hurried to the others, wiping my eyes as I went. Frakt looked up from the floor where she was hunkered, reloading our weapons.

"Let's go," I commanded firmly.

Jay's voice was uneven and panicky as he asked, "Where's Indi?"

I hesitated. "He'll catch us up," I replied hollowly.

Both Jay and Frakt spared hollow eyed glances toward the rattling door, before Frakt nodded with grim finality and handed me my shotgun.

Helping Jay to hoist Roper back to his feet, we moved deeper into the gym, the corridors here wide and glossy. I led the way through a dark changing room, stopping at doors and corners to peer carefully through the gloom, and into a deserted weights area. Machines and mats stood silent sentinel to our passage, backlit by a wall of windows and the orange glow of streetlights in the oncoming dark. Gyms, my mind supplied in the distorted shadows, are superficial temples to an arbitrary and exclusionary standard of acceptable beauty. For just an easy monthly payment, you too can starve and abuse yourself until you conform to an idealised body shape at the cost of your self-confidence, sense of worth and social life.

The fire exit loomed. I'd seen the lurching shadows outside, but they were relatively few now compared to our headlong rush from the bombed-out admin building. I burst through the doors leading the way. A hardback, drab green Land Rover ambulance, the side emblazoned with a white circle and red cross, sat a little way away across the concrete. I stopped. Turning to Jay, I grabbed Roper by the lapels and thrust him into Frakt's arms.

"Go," I ordered harshly.

Frakt stared at me, confused. "What?"

I gritted my teeth, forcing the words out between them. "Get away, get out. If you get far enough away from us, you might be able to log out. Go on!"

"And what if we can't?" Frakt argued.

"Just get somewhere safe," I snapped, "barricade and wait. Roper can't handle much more in his condition, but he'll be alright in the ambulance, I'll call you if the situation changes, but until then you need to get away from us!"

The gymnasium echoed with a hollow sound, a hundred throats calling out in primal, animal hunger. Shadowy figures started lapping through the shadows on either side of the huge square edifice.

Frakt just stared at me in sullen defiance so I shoved her away.

"Go!" I shouted, waving toward the ambulance.

Again the silent, defiant stare.

I racked the shotgun, the hollow 'chu-chunk' sounding against the backdrop of moans and wails as I pointed the gun at Frakt.

"Go. Now," I hissed.

Dragging Roper with her, Frakt backed away and went to the vehicle. Once inside she fixed me with a look. Hurt, confusion, anger and gratitude flashed across her features as she flipped the ignition and pulled away.

"Well, that's great," Jay waved at the departing vehicle. "So now what do we do?"

I stood in the open air, looking up at the dark sky and listened to the sounds of the horde. I didn't know. Run, hide, fight? Everything seemed too hard, too pointless in the face of the mountain of putrescent flesh that was tumbling down upon us.

A hundred yards away the ambulance horn started to blare. It sounded again and again getting farther and farther away.

The zombies roared in reply. Frakt, I smiled up at the night sky; goddamn you.

"We run," I declared and took off at a sprint.

The gym car park conveniently linked to the road, but the gates had been drawn, probably shutting automatically during the initial emergency. We followed the fence at a crouch, skirting the pools of light cast by the streetlamps just beyond the perimeter fence.

We hugged whatever cover we could, trying to stay quiet and hidden. Approaching a road crossing, I heard the clatter of a can skipping across the tarmac. I looked back to see Jay flinch and stepped forward, right into the fetid embrace of a lurking zombie. The corpse gave me a rictus grin before I reflexively pulled the trigger of the shotgun trapped between us. The grin disappeared in a blinding flash. The hands spasmed, releasing me and I staggered backward, dropping the weapon as I clutched at my ears.

Jay grabbed my shoulder, guiding my disoriented steps as we ran from the gunshot's dinner bell chime.

Zombies started to appear, running at us from shadows and behind buildings. We pulled our pistols and started picking off any that came too close as we went, but the trickle became a tide, then became a flood.

A truck had hit the fence ahead of us, the chain link flattened and struts bent over. A few mangled zeds lay snagged in the razor wire, and I urged Jay through the gap, stepping quickly over the grabbing hands.

The road stretched away on either side, pools of orange light and darkness, distant figures massing together and approaching from either side.

"What the fuck are we going to do?" Jay demanded.

I rounded on him in the middle of the street, taking him roughly by his avatar's narrow shoulders.

"You got all that stuff right, the manifesto, the plans, do you have it?"

He gave me a confused look.

He held up the phone. "Yes, it's all here."

"Can you get it out?" I asked urgently.

He stared at me. "Maybe, I'll need time but, yes?"

I grabbed his shirt and dragged him across the wide road to the grass verge and fence beyond. I dragged him along as we ran toward the thickening crowd of zombies ahead, and, just before we reached them, the gatehouse to this section of the camp.

I couldn't stop, if I stopped I'd think. Think about Ned, AK, about Indi, about them being dead and it being my fault. So I ran, dragging Jay behind me, focussed on getting a warning out to the world.

This gate hadn't closed. The only control for the flow into the camp on this side was the gatehouse drop-down barrier, so we slipped under the flimsy bar and into the camp's residential sector. Houses lined the roads, laid out like any other suburban residential development, just situated behind high fences and razor wire.

The horde pressed against the fence, which started to roll back and forth with a metallic rustle, the chain link like breakers at the tip of a tide of flesh. I ran from house to house, looking for an open door, but they were all locked. Jay's pistol sounded then clicked empty. I dashed back to the road, snapping off shots at the nearest scrambling corpses as they headed toward Jay with singular determination.

"What are we doing?" he pleaded.

"I need to get you somewhere safe to upload the data," I growled, snapping off another shot. The slide locked and I cursed vigorously.

With a metallic groan, the chain link collapsed.

"Shit!" I swore vehemently and dragged Jay further into the residential streets, tugging my trusty hook blade from my belt. I spotted something under a streetlamp. An open-backed truck with a cage in the bed like the road cleaners used. Four zombies stood between us and it. With barely a moment's pause I rushed them, swinging hard. The first went down before it even registered our approach. Number two turned and the blade bit into its cheek, sliding between the teeth. It didn't sever the head entirely, but bit deep enough to hit the brainstem, and the corpse fell to the floor. Number three lunged at me, but I stepped back and brought my weapon down hard.

The blade split the skull but broke with a sharp 'pink', the spine breaking off into a short spike of metal. Before I really had time to realise what had happened, number four barrelled into me and got the shank in the eye, the motion more reflex than choice.

I could hear the wheezing of the horde closing in as I hurried Jay into the cage.

Glancing over my shoulder I could see the zombies encircling us. "Get that data out!" I ordered. I needed a weapon.

The bed of the truck wasn't the usual black bags of rubbish and broken, fly-tipped furniture and bedding. The truckback was strewn with branches, logs and leaves, cuttings from hedges, the refuse of horticultural maintenance.

A lumpy metal shape near the back caught my eye and I grimaced. *Fucking perfect*, I thought sarcastically. I hauled the lumpen thing from the tangle of branches, tugging the wire door closed behind me and locking Jay inside as I leapt back down to the road.

"How does it work?" I yelled to Jay of the unfamiliar tool in my hands.

Jay lunged at the wire mesh, fingers grasping. "Trigger on the handle, squeeze it, button under your thumb, push and lock."

I followed the instructions quickly. The zombies had formed a circle; they didn't seem in a hurry to tear us apart, which meant they were being controlled. Zombie-dev was nearby.

"Set the choke, the lever there!" Jay waved frantically. "Now, stand in the trigger guard, push down with your lead hand and pull the chord!"

I yanked on the plastic grip, the motor roaring to life.

"Now reset the choke and squeeze the trigger!"

I did so, lifting the chainsaw to my best approximation of 'enguard' and revved it to a shrill scream.

"I hope you like your tropes thick-cut, you sonuvabitch!" I yelled.

The throbbing engine in my hands overlaid the throbbing in my wrist as zombies broke from the crowd and rushed me, first one, then another, then two. I heaved the screaming blade in an arc like the vlogger had done what seemed like so long ago in my memory. The head flew from the first zombie in a spray of dead, reeking blood, even as the heavy weight tugged at my arms. I kept my momentum and turned, taking the chainsaw low, and lopped the next one off at the knees, just below its shorts. It carried forward on its own momentum, head hitting the back of the truck with a ringing 'clang'.

The next was wearing a spaghetti-strap crop-top; I wanted to avoid clothing as much as I could. I punched forward with the flat, heavy bottom of the engine block. As the zombie reeled I swung down with the blade, right into the crook of the neck, forcing the zombie to its knees as I angled in, running the ripping teeth along the collar bone into the neck proper, pushing down while the motor sputtered and grumbled, blood spraying, the blade skidding on bone and tearing through meat and viscera.

I was howling, the sheer horror of dismembering human figures with a chainsaw tearing at my brain, and my blood rising with the timbre and scream of the saw's engine. It felt like there were two of me, the one recoiling from the horror show and the one with their hands on the grips, finger on the trigger, revelling in the thrill of fighting and winning.

In the mist of flying blood I didn't even see the next one approach. As the head of the crop top zombie flopped wetly to the floor, the next ran straight at me and onto the lowered blade. The chainsaw bucked, teeth ripping and binding in the clothing, dragging upward. I fought the convulsions of the machine and, as the trailing threads snapped the engine roared and the teeth bit into the belly, dragging coils of ripped intestines out of the clawing, snapping zombie. Blood and meat were cooking as they spattered the howling engine, the reek filling my nostrils as I fought down the urge to gag.

Regardless of the ragged hole in its gut, the zed grasped my shoulders and leant in, biting down on my shoulder.

Pressure, pain, teeth on bone as the zombie shook, worrying at my flesh. A pulse from my wrist shot through my panicked thoughts as I screamed and shoved at the thing, spurred on by a wave of adrenaline. I ripped the whining blade of the chainsaw back out of the corpse, raising it high and swinging it down right between the zombie's eyes. The zombie staggered under the blow, the steel teeth merely chipped away splinters of the hard bone of the skull, finding no real purchase as the zed buckled, but stripping the delicate flesh of the scalp. The blade slipped until it fell onto the shoulder, biting again and ripping savagely into the flesh. With a protesting shudder, it bit and chewed until the arm dropped away. Rather than the numbing fear, the pulsing of the stress meter thudded like a second, hammering pulse. I was angry, I was raging and I was enjoying it, for the first time in my life; blood-soaked, hurt and so close to death, I was truly alive. I pulled back and tried again, swiping at the neck, but the teeth snagged the shoulder of the zombie's suit jacket. They ripped and tore down into the body and bone, finally snagging in the mix of shredded meat and clothing.

The bloody rags that clad the zombie snarled up into the gears, and the engine grumbled and rattled to a halt, my feral joy turned to frustration as my weapon betrayed me.

"Motherfucker!" I shouted. In desperation I yanked the zombie around, using the weight of the chainsaw to off-balance the cadaver, and swept its leg. It fell and I raised my booted foot and stomped down. The white of the exposed cheek bone, the side of the face ruined by the saw, crunched under my heel as I stomped down again and again, howling and panting and spitting.

I turned, chest heaving, with a feral snarl on my lips to meet the next zombie.

Chapter 35

It came at me, followed by another, and another. I slipped the first, guiding it into the trailer of the truck with a solid 'clang', but the next caught me and bore me to the ground. Teeth sank into my flesh and I screamed again. I reached for my wrist menu but more hands grabbed my arms, spreading them wide. The pulse of my stress meter rose up to overwhelm me, no longer the driving engine of my rage but an unstoppable juggernaut rolling over my reason and will. I thrashed and screamed, mindless terror drowning my thoughts at the prospect of being eaten alive. Teeth pressed against the skin of my stomach… and stopped.

I lay there, shivering. My body drenched in cold sweat, my limbs quivering from effort and my mind numb with horror in the sudden stillness.

A slow clap started and I glanced up to see a figure shouldering its way to the front. Haggard, torn and bloated with decay, hair matted and patchy, the zombie came forward, grinning.

A modulated voice insinuated itself into the scene. "Let's deal with this, shall we?"

At a gesture, the locomotive rhythm in my wrist eased off, and the zombies released my limbs and stood meekly back. I scrambled to my feet, shivering and shoving the slower zombies away, the ebbing panic still charging my movements. The zombie I slammed against the truck trailer rose, probably to step away, but I kicked it, kicked its head against the metal and the skull cracked under the impact.

I turned on the zombie dev with a snarl, reaching toward them to rip and tear but, with another slight wave I was frozen too.

"Well done, well done," it declared mockingly. "So, this is the 'tolerant left' we targeted, huh?"

I snarled reflexively, surprised to find my voice still working. "Happy to disappoint you."

Spit foam flecked my lips as I leaned into my words, "The tolerant left is dead. We're the chain-ourselves-to-the-railings, burn-down-your-facto-ries, storm the Bastille left who are thoroughly fucking done with this shit! This is the nineteen-twelve coal strikes left, the 'Emily Davidson punch-ing a copper and marching on Parliament' left, the Marsha Johnson Stonewall left, and we have never, ever been tolerant of oppressors!" I raged.

The zombie avatar smiled through ripped lips and spread its hands wide, "That's what we're here to find out, Lex."

I gawped and the smile widened, the flesh tearing ever so slightly. "Yes, we know who you are, we've traced you IP and checked you out. We've seen your social media, checked out your Likes, your Follows, even read your blog and now we really want to know." The zombie left a pregnant pause.

"Know what?" I asked cagily.

Another smug smile.

"Just how *hard* left you are. When this started I'd have said you were as revolutionary as Martha Stewart but at least *she's* been to prison. But I watched you. *We* watched you. You're not just following the piper. Not just another puppet clicking and liking, sharing and supporting, signing the petitions that *they* want you to."

With the emphasis the Dev loaded on 'they', they could only mean the establishment.

"But we need to know if you're really the radical you think you are Lex. Prove to us, once and for all, that you're not just another pawn. Are you really a warrior for change, or are you ultimately just another con-sumerist zombie, no better than these poor shambling fucks right here." A wave of an arm encompassed the still and silent horde around me.

I struggled to follow the meaning in the words, shock and blood-loss making me fuzzy, "What're you saying?"

"I'm saying," the Dev raised their arms and turned a graceful circle, "congratulations! You won!"

"But we weren't even playing your game, we were trying to stop you!" I insisted.

Zombie Dev shrugged. "You still played. You formed an effective co-op group, learned to survive. Worked with others in the face of prejudice and mistrust and drew others to your cause under threat of *actual* death. You suffered a full on psychotic break before you killed a player who gave you nothing but grief, Lex! Just think what you could accomplish without that negativity looming around every corner?"

I paused, overwhelmed. "We're, we're going to stop you, we're going to save the world." I stuttered.

I was getting cold; my blood was running out of the bites and onto the pavement.

The zombie smiled at me, "I've taken control of your avatar's motor functions, you couldn't stop me if you tried but, more importantly," it gave a slight shrug of its shoulders, "why would you?"

That stopped me in my mental tracks. "What?"

"Your group have accessed our files, no-doubt you've read some of our mandate. In case the specifics have escaped you, we've isolated a way to not only trigger the most savage impulses in the human brain, but also to insulate a sample population against the effect. You might be doing your best not to play their game but us? We're upending the whole fucking board and replacing the mods with people who are empathic, inclusive and tolerant. Now you know what we're doing I ask you, why stop us?"

"You're going to trigger an honest-to-God zompocalypse; you're going to massacre billions!" I protested.

"And?" the dev shrugged. "Since time immemorial, the privileged wealthy have murdered and massacred in the name of money and control. The Middle-East, Vietnam, the World Wars, the American Civil War, Imperialist western expansionism and colonialism. Even back beyond the Crusades, the ideology of money and oppression has been the instigator for those in power, and the so-called 'duty' borne by those beneath them. Hundreds of billions, trillions of lives expunged to gain land, resources, influence or," they sneered through torn and ragged lips, "wealth."

"But there are people, good people who will suffer and die!" I argued.

The dev rounded on me angrily, ticking off points on their torn fingers, "They *are* dying,"

"Look around you! A child dies of hunger every ten seconds, somewhere in the world. A hundred-and-thirty women a year are murdered by their spouses or families for not 'fitting the mould'. We have Nazis, actual Nazis. We have concentration and death camps for trans, gay and ethnic populations in this so-called developed, civilised world. If the political extremism and oppression wasn't bad enough, we have corporate fascism, mega corporations who could make things better, stripping and raping the most important ecological sections of the planet, the places that ensure

295

our continued survival. When a third-world government threatens their profits in defence of the environment they rally. They employ mercenaries to topple that government and wrest control of natural resources away from the country's control, installing corrupt and greedy puppets in their place. During the Covid-19 crisis, the South American drug cartels did more to protect the people's health than their Governments did."

"But…" I tried to interject, but the dev hadn't finished.

"A handful of white men control the wealth of the world, wealth which is based upon a construct that they promote tirelessly. It's a theology little different from the various faiths and theisms, the institutions that those who have nothing are forced to cling to for comfort. But, in their case, with no overriding moral compass, no 'good' or 'evil', no 'paradise' or 'purgatory', only 'risk and reward'. Those 'wealthy' individuals could provide comfort and care to the world, but instead they sleep upon their hoarded wealth like dragons, their greed running as deep as the black strands of their hereditary influence."

I just stared. At the edges of my vision I saw something, like a mirage slowly taking shape but the dev was still talking. "A little melodramatic, I know. But this is what we are fighting, it's not simply an ideology but society itself, a system of being that has been nurtured and cultivated since the time of the Romans. It's an ideology of predation and parasitism that holds a mocking mirror up to nature. The corporations, hulking, bloated societal parasites that they are, are tended to by us, even as they feed themselves from our revenue streams, and all we can do is crawl over them, tiny and helpless. We cannot repair it, we cannot heal it. The cancer runs too deep and has held for too long. The only option is euthanasia. We have to start over, learning from the lessons of the present. A nuclear option would ruin the planet and, as you've seen"—they jabbed an emphatic finger at me—"the 'hearts and minds' campaign only results in 'thoughts and prayers' and more toxicity and conflict."

"You're going to destroy the world." I breathed the words, I needed to keep them talking, the haze in my vision was resolving, a HUD of some kind creeping into my peripheral vision.

"Now *you're* being melodramatic," the zombie smiled. "With or without the human race, the planet itself, 'the world' as you say, will spin on. No, we're going to change the human experience, the world 'as you know it'. But in order to do that, we have to tear down what has gone before."

"And the game? This training ground?" I tried to gesture around, I could feel the tension of the thwarted movement, but still couldn't move.

"Albert Camus said *'Fiction is the lie through which we tell the truth.'* This is our truth; this is where you learn *your* truth. Do you really hold to those values you profess are so important? We've watched, we've tracked you, Lex. You're winners, each of you. You've displayed courage, ingenuity, willingness to sacrifice and, you above all Lex, empathy. Out of three-million plus players you stuck to your ideals and now you get your prize."

Caught off-guard I blurted, "My prize? I thought the prize was a sham?"

"The money was a lie, yes." The Dev nodded, "You get the real prize, you get to find out, once and for all, will you die for your principles? Or, more importantly, will you kill for them?"

The throng gave a shuffle and, out of the horde, Indi limped, escorted by a pack of twitching zombies.

My friend was favouring one leg, cradling his arm and covered in minor wounds, but otherwise whole. For a moment I forgot the overlay, the relief at seeing Indi alive consuming me before a deep suspicion grasped me.

"What's this?" I asked.

"It's a choice," the dev said softly. Reaching behind their back they produced a gun. "Two options."

"Number one." They held up a finger. "Stop Jay over there from trying to broadcast our intent to the world, which isn't going to stop us by the way, and shoot your friends…"

I made a choked noise of protest.

"Now, hear me out." The Dev held up a filthy hand, "This isn't about averting our apocalypse, you can't do that, you never could. This is about you, about who you're going to be in the world that comes after."

"It's a sick joke is what it is." I spat, struggling impotently.

"Maybe it is but, if you shoot them, you at least spare them the agony of being torn apart and you'll be saving them in another way too."

The dev smiled broadly, a little too broadly, the flesh at the corners of its mouth tearing ever so slightly as it took a deep, wet breath.

"Every day we allow the world to spin on as it is, and everyday millions struggle and die just because society labels them as 'other'. They continue to fight the adamantium edifice of the way things are and the death toll rises. Injustices continue to pile one upon the next upon the next and your friends are a tragic part of that mindless conveyor belt. So save them, save them from being chewed up Lex, literally and virtually, get them out of the grind. Or—" they held up another finger.

"Number two. Refuse, do nothing. Prove to me, them and yourself that you're just another gutless, fence-sitting conservative with no real moral fire in your chest. Either way, in a few minutes the rich and influential and corrupt will fall upon each other in an orgy of self-serving bloodletting of their own making. Those who are satisfied with their place in the status quo will learn the price of their complicity and their privilege. The slate of human indecency, corruption and parasitism will be wiped clean for the struggle to a better, more inclusive and cooperative tomorrow. You can be out there, in the new world or you can die in here, a slave to the old one."

"What kind of prize is that?" I spat, my anger rising, driving back the cloudy haze of shock, "I shoot Indi and Jay, and you let me live. I refuse and we all die."

"Horribly." The Dev nodded and fixed me with an intense gaze. "If you're willing to spare them this gruesome fate we'll know that the players in here are ready, ready to survive the brief horror of the transition, ready to put themselves on the line to build what must be built afterwards, so. How devoted are you to the established ways of the old world? The status quo, the corporate overlords, the patriarchy?" they enunciated patronisingly.

"What about my parents, what about the people who never got to play the game?"

"What about the people who grew up south of the border? Who fled wars and drug lords only to be forced into camps and into cages? Who were born gay in a country that doesn't approve and will kidnap, punish and kill those it deems 'deviant'? We can't save them all Lex, we've tried and we've failed but, we can stop it. We just have to have the strength of our convictions."

Tears welled in my eyes. "My parents," I repeated weakly.

"Now you're just being selfish." The tone wasn't demeaning or combative. The dev seemed truly saddened. "How many have lost parents, siblings, children to the wars, the conflicts, not just between nations and religions, but between ethnicities, ideologies and economic divides? How many children starve while their parents wait on Universal Credit? What about the tower-block fires that destroyed lives so just a few could pocket the difference of the price of cladding? The smoking cancer cover-up and all the other lives that were laid down or stolen to pay for some billionaire's newest yacht? Well this is the price of change Lex, this is the price of actual, monumental change, and it's not pieces of paper, it's not numbers on a screen or even shiny rocks. It's the price we need to pay, us. Not the planet, not the marginalised and indigenous people the coverage of capitalism doesn't encompass but us, the privileged and 'civilised'."

He'd settled into his speech now, pacing and gesturing expansively.

"No, no my friend. We are the truly 'woke'. Money, authority, morality, it's all a construct, built to restrain us, and corrupt us, and oppress us. The only power they have over us is that which we give them. Do you truly believe that the paper and tin money, the ticks and checks of your bank account amount to anything of actual worth? They're pebbles, shiny pebbles that mark the days, hours and minutes of your life that you've sold to the man so you can live in his world. They are ultimately worthless when measured beside what you *could* achieve in that time."

"And what could I achieve?" I mumbled.

"Spend time with a loved one, help a friend in need, create art for yourself and for others. Crush your enemies and see them driven before you, that is what is best in life, now..."

My hand came up of its own accord, palm flat.

"Here," the Dev slapped the gun into my waiting palm, "let's make a down-payment,"

My fingers closed around the grip, my hand came up straight and aimed, unwaveringly, at Indi.

"No!" I screamed. The Zombie Dev quirked its head at me questioningly.

"Why?" I stammered. "What gives you the right to decide who lives and who dies?" I choked out.

"We didn't," it shrugged. "We just asked who was paying attention. You decided to live, you decided to fight and to strive and to help. You proved our point for us, Lex."

I couldn't take my eyes off the gun in my hands, the dull shine of it reflecting the lamplight. The silhouette of the sight and the barrel as it pointed at Indi but the focus brought the strange HUD back into my peripheral view.

"But why the countdown? You can't start if it's not turned on!" I babbled desperately.

The Dev scoffed, a mirthless chuckle. "The infrastructure is all in place. The system is live right now, it's just not open to the public. It's only a matter of wave modulation after all, and the count was more of a guide anyway. A day or two either way makes little difference."

Jay's voice, low and fearful, came from behind me. "Lex…" he stammered my name.

"Still, you're stalling," the Dev announced and I felt the tension in my hand.

The gun fired before I could give voice to a protest, the tremor running up my arm.

The bullet took Indi in the chest, ripping through the big bear-like avatar, rocking him on his feet.

A puzzled look spread across his avatar's face and he crumpled, falling boneless to the floor.

I gasped in shock, mind numb as fresh tears pricked at my eyes.

"So, how about you do the next one yourself, eh?" The dev smirked.

"Go to hell," I stuttered through gritted teeth as I stood there, bleeding and aching in body and soul. If looks could kill the venom in my eyes would have dissolved the dev but again, at the fringes of my vision I could make out more details, code and command lines, a menu of some kind. It had taken me long enough to see it but, give the politically active a soapbox, an audience, and they will talk, at length.

"Ah, here's your defiance huh? A new dawn for *LeZion?* A victory for capitalism, commercialism, the military industrial complex and, eventually, fascism I suppose." Zombie-dev paced a step away and came back, anger in the modulated voice again. "I had high hopes for you Lex, I thought you would see but I guess you're just now figuring out that you really are just another zombie."

All emotion drained from them as they spoke next.

"We live by their rules, Lex. We protest by *their* rules, we keep saying we'll tear it down." The zombie chuckled dryly, a moment of dark mirth before that stony expression returned.

"But. We. Don't." It sneered. "We live and fight and die, by their rules. It's time for new rules."

I glanced at Indi, I thought I saw a weak movement and my vision swam. For a moment I thought I glimpsed my parents in the horde, unmolested, alive, just as I knew them to be now, outside the game.

The dev caught my eye, their veiny, milky eyes holding my gaze.

"Why me?" I asked, my voice hoarse. "Why are you doing this to me?"

"If not you, then who?" Pacing back and forth the energy of the dev's motions echoed the excitement in their words, "Maybe it's because you're here, because you won." Tears ran down my cheeks as the Dev paced, explaining with unnerving serenity. "Maybe it's the *absolute power corrupts absolutely* motif, maybe I'm just fucking with you." The Dev chortled before holding up a finger, expression schooled, calm and unreadable. "Or, maybe this is a golden opportunity for you. A chance to sweep away all the crap, all of society's expectations and find out who you are."

The zombie avatar stopped pacing and faced me, squaring its shoulders.

"But really? It's not just about you, Lex. It's about *us* right here and right now!" It jabbed fingers at the pavement, animated to the point of mania. "We stand on the precipice. It's about time I got to know who I really am too. I've been fighting the system for a long time, y'know?"

"There's a... a quote, um," I stammered, still trying to inspect the shimmering shapes in my peripheral vision. They disappeared like mist when I tried to focus on them. "Fighting the monsters, staring into the abyss..."

"Battle not with monsters lest you become a monster, and if you gaze into the abyss the abyss gazes into you," the Dev chuckled knowingly. "Nietzsche; you believe we have been corrupted by that which we oppose."

I could almost hear my parents' voices in my head. I might have expected them to urge me one way or the other but in my mind, their voices raised against the government, the patriarchy and its institutions, the injustices of the world? Although they sounded righteous, and angry, they also sounded... tired.

"Well? Haven't you? What you're doing is monstrous."

My arm swung smoothly, my body twisting of its own accord to point at Jay.

"Sorry," the dev spread open hands. "No easy outs. No distractions, shoot your friend or be torn apart by zombies. I don't want to threaten you, but you have to make this choice. You either take the shot or you'll be locked in here. You'll be eaten alive in both worlds, as if the world that is isn't chewing you up a piece at a time already. Now, if I return your control, will you shoot Jay? And don't think you can shoot me. I'll just hop to another avatar and you'll all be savaged to death by the horde while I spawn in again."

The gun was heavy in my hands; my parents' weary voices ran around in my head. I had no more arguments, no more ploys. It came down to a trigger, and a choice.

"Make me," I growled.

The Dev sighed. "Alright, that's how you want it."

There was a moment of silence and the Dev frowned.

With a cold smile I sighted, turning to line up the front sight on the Dev's forehead as its eyes widened in shock.

"How?" It demanded.

Through all the Dev's mockery, all it's posturing and grandstanding I'd been busy navigating menus and code, regaining my agency to act.

"You're in here with us," I sneered. "Not typing at some keyboard, your command prompts are just another skill-set and I've got *Educated.*"

The zombie-dev raised their hands blustering, "You can't kill me," as I coolly pointed the gun.

"Maybe not, but maybe I can hurt you," I snarled, taking a breath in through my nose and squeezing the trigger.

It was a gamble, that they'd assume their omnipotence in the game world was total, that they'd not disable their own pain feedback out of sheer hubris but then, they hadn't figured on someone using the *Educated* skill to steal their own control mechanics. I guess people are people, whoever they are. The bullet blew through a kneecap, dropping the screaming avatar to the floor.

Jay gasped from the cage, "How?"

"They control the game through a skill package, Educated lets me emulate skill packages," I explained hurriedly, "I didn't have time to figure out much but I reactivated your permissions, get out!" I snapped.

The zombie horde shook themselves like dogs as the Dev's hold over them slipped.

"Can't you stop them?" Jay demanded, whether he meant the zombies or the Dev's buddies I didn't know, but the answer was the same in both cases.

"No, no time. Get out!" I repeated and hurried toward Indi.

"Lex!" Jay grasped the side of the cage, fingers in the thick mesh. I turned and we locked eyes. "You get yourself out too, you hear me?"

I nodded and went for Indi.

HLT	███				

The last bar flashed urgently as the horde pressed forward. I grabbed the big avatar and dragged it back. Indi was sweating and shivering.

"Don't worry." I grasped their arm and opened their menu. "I'm getting you out."

A big hand clasped over mine. "Wait." Indi grunted painfully before taking my chin and drawing me into a kiss.

It was brief and chaste, warm and real and over far too quickly.

"Might not get the chance again," Indi smiled and then grimaced in pain.

I tapped the 'Exit' command and the avatar sagged.

I scrambled out from under the dead weight, zombies closing in around me.

With a cry of rage Zombie Dev piled into me, taking us both to the floor and into the waiting press of the horde.

"Why?" they slammed me against the tarmac, "I had such hopes for you, *we* had such hopes for you!" The Dev snarled slamming me down again.

"You needed to build a better monster, to live to see your new world," I grunted as we struggled, "Congrats, you got me."

I felt teeth in my legs, a flash of white-hot sensation and I snarled in pain and defiance. The Dev let out a yelp that turned into a scream as the horde ripped into them, trying to get to me. I couldn't make their avatar 'human', but I could make it appear 'not zombie'.

My guts twisted, my heart was heavy, leaden in my chest and my limbs where alight with pain. From the depths of my memory a phrase crept into my mind, blowing a calming balm across the fire of my scattered and panicked thoughts.

'*The passion for destruction is also a creative passion.*'

The choices we made in a moment, the press of a button, a word spoken in anger, the pull of a trigger. They change us; change our worlds and the worlds of those closest to us. I changed my world.

I pressed the barrel of the pistol under the Dev's chin.

"Tell me your name and I'll spare you!" I demanded.

"Why?" the dev sobbed, unable to order their thoughts through the pain, unable to log out.

I grimaced at the weakness, "So I can kill you."

I wouldn't, couldn't let another person go out like this, not like George, not like Ned, not like AK.

Eyes red and face streaked with tears the Dev lifted their chin defiantly and told me.

I pulled the trigger.

The zombie avatar jerked and slumped, its spasming limbs pushed my arm out and a zombie grabbed it and started to worry at my flesh. Agony flooded my body as teeth tore and my flesh was rent. I couldn't get to my menu but I still had one way out.

"I am not a zombie." I gasped as I pressed the barrel of the gun under my chin and pulled the trigger.

Game Over

I logged out, ripping my VR rig from my head and letting my handhelds hang from their straps. I felt an itch, about a quarter inch behind my ear and an inch into my skull that wouldn't go away as my fingers blazed over the keyboard. From outside my window came a scream and the sound of a car crashing.

Indi, Jay? I messaged desperately. I left the screen to toss clothes into a rucksack which I dragged out from under my bed.

You shot me. The text was waiting for me when I next looked.

I'm sorry, but we have to think about next moves. I heard noises from downstairs, thumps and crashes followed by honest to goodness growling.

I don't think there *are* any next moves. Jay typed. *This is it.*

I glanced out the window. Two people wrestled in the street. Even as I watched, one grasped the other's wrist, turning, taking the arm under their own and wrestling the wrist up to their mouth, biting at the flesh and bathing in the spray of blood that issued forth.

My hand went to my mouth in horror. Part of me had hoped it *was* a gag, a layer of gameplay within the game, but it was real, all too real.

A crash and a cry from downstairs brought me around. I couldn't do anything for my parents, the thought tore at my insides but it was far too late for that, but maybe.

How do I get to you? I typed feverishly.

You can't, Jay typed. After a moment the video call icon flashed and I clicked it. Jay and Indi appeared on my screen in conference.

"I don't know how long this will work so I'll be quick," Jay spoke rapidly, his accent thick with emotion. He ran a hand through his short dark hair.

"It's real, it's trending. Don't treat this like a game; don't assume you know it all. Be careful, observe, learn and act. In that order."

"We can get there, we can get to you," I insisted.

Jay jumped and I heard a pounding at his door coming faintly across the microphone.

He smiled sadly, "It's too late, they're here."

"Jay, run. Just run!" Indi urged.

"I would, but—" he pulled back from the camera, showing us more of his shoulders, body, arms and his wheelchair. "They were going to install the accessibility ramp next week." He smiled bitterly. I reeled back in shock.

"Barricade," Indi cried. "Lock down and call for help, wait there and I'll come for you."

Jay looked to the door as the pounding grew louder. "I can't ask you to do that." Reaching down out of shot he lifted an honest to goodness baseball bat.

"Look after yourselves, look after each other," he sighed sadly, and his screen cut out.

"What do we do?" I demanded.

Indi's voice was thick and choked with emotion, "There's nothing we *can* do, not anymore!"

"I... I'm sorry," I stammered.

He shrugged diffidently, "We wanted to change the world, I guess, for better or worse, we get our wish." He sniffed and wiped his eyes on his sleeve, delicate features red-rimmed from burgeoning tears. "For what it's worth, I really liked it in there, being with you," he finished timidly and killed the connection. Something cracked in my chest, like my sternum had been split in half.

There was another message in my inbox, a single line of text.

I'm out. Thank you, Lex.

It was from Ned and it was a couple of hours old already.

Before I could do anything else, the connection failed, the computer blanked and the power light died. Everything died. I flicked the light switch but the power was out.

Everything dies.

Numbness crawling over me I picked up my old college bag and identified the things I would need. I looked toward the bedroom door, beyond it the stairs and, down them, my parents, or whatever they were now.

Our semi was Victorian; the drain pipes cast iron, sturdy enough for me to climb. Throwing open the window, I emerged into the bright sun of a brave new world.

Epilogue

The old world didn't die well. It was noisy, messy and undignified, a bad day in human history but turned up to the Nth degree. The people succumbed just as they were supposed to. The power grid took a beating but, here and there, pockets stayed alight for a time. Some places even had cell service for a couple of days into the apocalypse. We, the survivors, shared blogs and vlogs, survival tips and such until the system finally crashed. Some formed groups, collectives, to wait out the end of the world as it had been.

The ones who 'died', 'the afflicted' I called them, it took some of them differently too. The ones who just freaked out, started tearing into anything around them, they didn't last long, a couple of days at the most. If they didn't succumb to the injuries they suffered during their frenzied attacks on anything around them, they were pulled down when they attacked the packs. The packs worked and hunted together. They had a loose structure but all humanity was gone. They attacked and gorged on anything living, people, animals, even the other Afflicted.

We didn't have to worry about 'turning', people didn't turn. If you were bitten you ran, you fought or you died. Most died early on, but no-one turned. The itching stopped when the networks collapsed. I'd held out hope that the Afflicted might recover, but whatever had been done left lasting, irreparable damage.

I ran from my home, my family and everything I'd known. For a couple of days I ran straight to the bottom of a bottle, barricaded into a convenience store. Eventually I headed to the coast, running and hiding when I could, fighting when I had to.

Standing on the cliffs at Dover gave me pause. I had plans to cross, to find Indi, so we could band together, survive and to wait it out, but as I looked out across the grey gulf of the Channel, as I thought over the weeks it had taken me to get that far, I realised I couldn't. Not that I couldn't cross the water, or couldn't search the continent to find him. I could do those things, maybe. But I had something else I had to do first.

I steeled myself then, hardening something inside that never ought to have been hardened and turned to a new purpose.

The apocalypse lasted weeks at most, although time gets a little muddled when you spend days at a time hiding in darkness, holding in your sobs so as not to be eaten alive. Once the survivors got organised, got walls up, the Afflicted, who would gorge themselves to bursting (literal, messy bursting) on cattle, soon found that most animals were too wily for them to catch. Humans without tools or intellect are poor predators.

From the coast, the White Cliffs, I headed north, travelling from place to place. I saw nightmares and horrors on that road, but also people being people, helpful, supportive and brave. It took me a year, walking and talking, into the following winter, to find what I was looking for.

The village had windmills on the surrounding hills. They'd rigged a connection, done some clever engineering and gotten the lights on. In the months since the last Afflicted had starved, certain things had lost their value; guns and bullets mostly, but I had a number of bottles of antibiotics left to trade and a hard day's work would always buy bed and board. I washed up, ate with my hosts and thanked them before going up to the guest room. With the door closed, I dropped the false smile, took my gun from my bag, opened the window and climbed out into the night.

The trail of clues had led me here; phonebooks, public and hospital records. I'd pieced it together laboriously over months of running and hiding, and then simply moving from place to place, scavenging what I could, working for the rest.

I moved through the quiet streets, the stains and marks of the days when the world changed, the blood of the dead and graffiti of the hopeless, washed away by rain and people with brushes and soap. A light was on in the town hall and I opened the door quietly and went inside.

Most of the side rooms were dim but, farther into the little village hall, one room had been set aside for planning. Which fields to use, what to plant, how to rotate; important things for the village's survival. Less so for the person pulling a late one within.

Inside, a woman, late twenties, early thirties maybe, leant over a table of maps and factsheets, tally charts and stock sheets. I closed the door with a click.

"I'll turn the lights off when I leave, I promise," she said, straightening and turning to me. She gasped when she saw the barrel of a gun pointing, unwaveringly at her.

"Jasmine Rowden," I said my voice hollow, "AKA Evermore."

Her eyes widened a moment.

"I thought so. Makes sense you'd be in charge. If the *Rendered Flesh* devs didn't have well thought out zompocalypse plans, what hope was there for the rest of us?"

"Who are you?" she asked cautiously.

"Tell me your name," my voice held no emotion, "so I can kill you." She gasped. "Lex?"

"Give me the other names," I demanded.

"Why?" she stammered. "We won; we're building a better world."

I repeated coldly, "The names."

"They're all over the world, coordinating the rebuilding; you can't get to them all."

I thumbed the hammer back. Needless theatrics but I was making a point.

"We have the plan, we're connected, we're the best chance," she babbled.

I rushed her, snarling, pushing her against the table, the legs squeaking across the floor as it shifted under our weight. She flinched and cried out as the metal of the barrel bit into the skin of her forehead.

In that moment I must have resembled one of the Afflicted, mindless, savage and hell bent on her destruction.

She talked. She gave me names and locations that I later committed to memory even as her bladder evacuated into her heavy cloth work trousers.

"Why?" she asked, panting and crying as I let her fall to the floor.

"It's about freedom, more or less," I said simply. "You wanted freedom from the oppressive structure of the world as it was. Well now you have the freedom to face the consequences of your actions."

"What are you hoping to achieve?" She cried quietly, "What is there to gain?"

"Nothing," I replied flatly.

She grimaced, regaining a little composure, "Revenge, that's it?"

I smiled coldly. "The sentiment has been shared many times, by many people, but I think Solnit put it best. 'There is no-one as dangerous as he or she who has nothing to lose.' I might have said 'those' or 'they', it's more inclusive, less binary, but I'm sure that's what she meant. Oh well." I shrugged and I shot Jasmine, the Zombie Dev, in the head.

I could have said 'Admin privileges revoked' or something similar. Maybe I would next time. For now, I heard distant voices responding to the gunshot. It was time to leave.

I didn't bother reasoning whether it was revenge or righteous vengeance, because it was all that I had left.

I wouldn't let the people who ended the old world take the reins of the new one. It wasn't right. The blood that bathed my hands was as much theirs too. There was no way in hell, I thought as I sloped off into the night, that I was going to let the nihilists inherit the earth.

The End

David Cartwright was born in 1981 and raised in a Golden Age of Saturday morning cartoons. From that time and forever after he has been an avid watcher and reader of Fantasy and Horror, encompassing the likes of The Hammer Horror catalogue and *Friday the 13th*, to *The Walking Dead*, *Train to Busan*, and the works of Stephen King and James Herbert.

David has been a Jack of many trades, but, so far, a master of none. Previous jobs in manufacturing have given way to writing full-time whilst his academic background includes studying in Media and Counselling. His credits to date encompass work in both literature and RPG.

He lives in Hampshire, England with his family, his cat, and his growing collection of flannel shirts.

Level Up publishing specialises in LitRPG and GameLit books. If you have enjoyed *Rendered Flesh* you might be interested in our other titles, which can be found at www.levelup.pub/books

To join our mailing list for news about forthcoming books and opportunities to be an ARC reader, just fill in the form on that page.

You can also find us on:
Facebook @LUPublishing
Twitter @LevelUpPub
WhatsApp chat.whatsapp.com/LFqK3cuDDJkINzJsZpZ78U

Lightning Source UK Ltd.
Milton Keynes UK
UKHW010106060921
390023UK00001B/40